THE PLAN

THE

THE PLAN

Stephen J. Cannell

WILLIAM MORROW AND COMPANY, INC.

NEW YORK

Can
c 1

Copyright © 1995 by Stephen J. Cannell

It is the policy of William Morrow and Company, Inc., and its imprints and affiliates, recognizing the importance of preserving what has been written, to print the books we publish on acid-free paper, and we exert our best efforts to that end.

Library of Congress Cataloging-in-Publication Data
Cannell, Stephen J.
    The plan / Stephen J. Cannell.—1st ed.
      p.   cm.
    ISBN 0-688-14046-7
    1. Presidents—United States—Election—
Fiction.   2. Organized crime—United States—
Fiction.   3. Mafia—United States—Fiction.
I. Title.
PS3553.A4995P56   1995
813'.54—dc20   94-35145
                        CIP

Printed in the United States of America

First Edition

1 2 3 4 5 6 7 8 9 10

BOOK DESIGN BY DEBORAH KERNER

**To Marcia
who sees me through
and to
Derek, Naja, N'Gai,
and Garrett who all left too soon**

ACKNOWLEDGMENTS

I WANT TO THANK A FEW PEOPLE WHO WERE INSTRUMENTAL IN the conceptualization, shaping, and eventual publication of this book. Without them, I'd never have reached the finish line.

RANDY PRIOR gave me the first germ of the idea, encouraged me to start, and then acted tirelessly as my researcher.

GRACE CURCIO, my assistant for almost twenty years, who alerted me to my mistakes and pushed me when my confidence lagged and got the first draft down the way I wanted it.

CHRISTINE TREPCZYK, who was there for me through every draft, Saturdays and Sundays included, working tirelessly translating my typed gibberish onto the computer.

PATRICK CADDELL, who let me peek into his brilliant mind, helped me see the complexities of politics, and gave me insights into the political process I never would have known.

WAYNE S. WILLIAMS, my greatest cheerleader, who believed in this book in the darkest hours, who beat down doors and cashed tickets to get it into the right hands, and worked tirelessly to help me edit.

Acknowledgments

JOE SWERLING, JR., who proofed each draft, encouraged me, and never stopped helping.

MORT JANKLOW and ERIC SIMONOFF, my agents, who gave it the push and held my hand when the book was in the market and the phone hadn't rung yet.

PAUL BRESNICK, my editor at Morrow, who was an enthusiastic and a wonderful critic, helping me tighten and improve.

PAUL LEVINE and RICHARD CHRISTIAN MATHESON, fellow authors who held flashlights while I stumbled along.

THE PLAN

P R O L O G U E

THANKSGIVING WEEKEND
SADDLEBACK, NEW JERSEY
1974

"**DAMN NEAR NAILED TINA LAST SUMMER. DRY HUMPED THE SHIT**
out of her. I would a' got in but her dad came home," Mickey
bragged. "I'm telling you, Ryan, I was two inches from the goal line."
Mickey's black eyes and round cheeks were shining like polished fruit.
He ran a chubby hand through his oily curls and grinned at his prep
school roommate.

They were sitting in Mickey's upstairs bedroom under a huge
brown plastic B-25 that hung from the ceiling by a thread. Two fif-
teen-year-olds on a hormonal bombing run, engines roaring, diving
out of boyhood, bomb racks full, searching for targets of opportunity.

It was Thanksgiving vacation, and Mickey Alo had invited Ryan
Bolt to his parents' huge house in Saddleback, New Jersey, for the
weekend. Ryan who lived in California, would otherwise have been
stuck at boarding school. The boys were at opposite ends of the physical scale. While Mickey was short, dark, and round, Ryan was tall,
blond, and angular. He was handsome in a way that most teenagers
could only dream of. But Mickey was the leader. What he lacked
in looks he more than made up for with charisma and energy. He
was always at full throttle, balls to the wall on everything . . . a

1

chubby adolescent kamikaze leading a charmed life.

"So what do I do, stand around and take pictures while you and Tina do it?" Ryan asked.

"Fuck no. Her sister Gina, she's a year older, tits out to here. My mom and dad are picking up guests at Levit Field. They're gonna be gone for at least three hours. We steal the Olds and zip over there, take the girls out to Frazier Lake, peel them and feel them."

"We're gonna take your dad's car? We don't have licenses. What if we get stopped?"

"We can't ride over there on bikes like fucking Beaver Cleaver and hope to get laid. Come on, I'll call her."

"You got rubbers?" Ryan was trying to act as if he knew what he was doing.

"You pull out before you come. Ain't you ever done this before?"

Mickey jumped off the bed and moved to the hall phone. Ryan trailed along, scared of the adventure yet drawn to it. If anybody could get them both laid, it was Mickey. Mickey could make stuff happen.

He was on the phone now, talking to the girl he had almost scored with last summer. "Hey, Tina . . . it's me. Yeah, I'm home. For only four days. I was thinking I'd drive over and we could get together."

He was so confident, talking with no hesitation.

"Listen, is your sister home too?"

While Tina was talking, Ryan held his breath and crossed his fingers.

"Great, 'cause I brought my roommate with me. He's a surfer from California. Blond guy, good enough looking to be on *American Bandstand*."

There was a pause.

Mickey cupped the receiver and turned to Ryan. "Can you be seventeen? Gina won't go out with a fifteen-year-old."

"Shit, seventeen. She's not gonna believe that."

"Lie to her, man. That's the secret with women. Tell 'em what they want to hear." He was back on the phone without waiting for an answer. "He's almost eighteen. Are your parents around?" He listened to her, while Ryan bit his fingernails. "Well, look, just tell the maid you're gonna go to the store. I'll pick you up in a few minutes."

He hung up and grinned at Ryan. "Let's get outta here."

They ran down the stairs into the marble entry hall with its statues of Roman figures on Doric columns, white marble muscles flexed and shining. They moved out into the porte cochere. A light snow had fallen that morning, and patches of it still remained. Mickey's seven-year-old sister was throwing snowballs at the garden wall.

Ryan thought Lucinda was the prettiest little girl he'd ever seen, with her olive skin and perfect features. She looked at him with the most remarkable green eyes, almost the color of emeralds.

"Listen, Lu . . . Ryan and I are gonna take off for a while. Don't tell Mom and Dad."

"It's Marta's day off, and I'm not supposed to stay home alone," she said softly.

"Come on, Lu, me an' Ryan got an important errand to run . . ."

"You're not supposed to take the car," she said, reading the mischief in his eyes.

"If you tell Dad, I'm tellin' him you're giving kitchen scraps to Rex. And you know how Dad feels about feedin' bird dogs from the table."

She nodded but said nothing.

"You go inside and lock the door," he commanded as she moved toward the house.

Mickey backed the red and white Olds two-door out of the garage and floored it, spewing gravel like bird shot.

Gina and Tina were stamping their feet to stay warm when Mickey pulled up. Tina got into the front seat with Mickey, Gina in the back with Ryan. Tina leaned over and kissed Mickey, who grabbed her around the neck and pulled her close.

"Come over here you," he said playfully.

"Mickey," she protested as he drew her roughly to him.

"Ryan, meet Gina and Tina," Mickey said.

Tina and Gina were more than Ryan had even dreamed of. Both had dark hair and dark eyes. They were well fed but not fat, with large breasts.

Gina was sixteen, and Ryan thought she looked hot to trot. "Where in California are you from, Ryan?" Gina asked.

"Santa Monica." Ryan's adrenal glands were wide open, jolting

3

his senses, hardening his erection. He put his arm around Gina's shoulder and pulled her closer. She laid her head on Ryan's shoulder, without even being coaxed.

I'm gonna get laid, Ryan thought.

They parked out at the lake. Neither of the girls had worn bras, and within minutes all were locked in deep embraces. In the front seat, Mickey and Tina were rolling savagely on the leather. In the back, Ryan fumbled awkwardly with the buttons on Gina's shirt.

"Let me," she whispered, quickly shrugging off her blouse. Stripped to the waist, she pulled him to her . . . In the dim glow from the dome light he could see her nipples were erect.

Ryan had never encountered a girl like this one. He'd just met her and she was half-naked, dry humping like a bunny. They rolled on the back seat, fighting for better embraces. The windows dripped with steam. He reached down for her panties, but she grabbed his hand.

"Not yet," she whispered.

They pushed their hips at one another, and then he felt himself ejaculate. His erection went down like summer wheat. "I love you," he said to the girl he had just met and prayed that his hard-on would come back. Ryan had fumbled on the one. In the front seat, Mickey streaked into the end zone, the score was celebrated as Tina let out a squeal.

They got home two hours later. Lucinda was watching television, and they sneaked upstairs without disturbing her.

An hour later, Penny and Joseph Alo arrived from the airport with Paul Arquette and Meyer Lansky. Penny checked on the boys, who were lying on the twin beds in Mickey's room reliving their adventure. "Lucinda was supposed to be in bed at eight-thirty," Penny said.

"Sorry, Mom. Forgot."

She gave him a disapproving frown. Penny Alo was tall with a long neck and marble-white skin and the same dazzling green eyes as Lucinda. The same lustrous black hair. She reminded Ryan of a model in the soap ads.

"Your father's having a meeting in the den. Don't bother him. Nice to have you with us, Ryan. You boys get to bed soon."

*   *   *

Downstairs, a fire crackled as Mickey's father, Joseph, crossed to the bar and poured some port out of a cut crystal decanter, filling three of the long-stemmed wineglasses. Joseph, like Mickey, was physically unimpressive. At fifty-one, he was dark-skinned, short, and wide around the middle. Like his fifteen-year-old son, however, he radiated power. He crossed to Paul Arquette, handing him a glass.

"That's a nice port. I get it sent over from Oporto," he said, handing the glass to the tall, aristocratic governor of Nevada.

Paul Arquette wore a perfectly fitted gray suit. His sandy brown hair and box-of-Chiclets smile was a recruiting poster for his state. Now forty-five, he had been a behind-the-scenes friend to the Alo casino interests in Las Vegas for years.

He took the glass of port from the Sicilian and watched as Joseph Alo crossed to Meyer Lansky, seated in a large wing chair near the fire, breathing heavily.

Meyer was in his early seventies and had withered physically since Paul had seen him last. His hands shook, but the laser-sharp eyes were windows to his shrewdness. "Ain't supposed t' drink," Meyer said. "Fucking doctor has me eatin' Gerber's. My colon X ray looks like nine miles a' dirt road." The mob financial genius took the glass of port from Joseph anyway.

"When did Wallace say he'll get here?" Joseph asked.

"Nine-thirty. He's a punctual nitpicker, the fuck. He'll be here," Meyer said.

They talked about Meyer's lawsuit against the State of Israel. Lansky had been trying to move to Israel with his wife to live out his days until his cancer took him. But the Israeli Supreme Court invoked a constitutional clause denying immigration to Jews with criminal histories. "What'd I ever do to them?" Meyer lamented. "My own people quitting on me like that."

Then Penny let C. Wallace Litman into the den.

Litman was as short as Joseph Alo, but with a Prussian general's bearing. He was trim in all departments from his tailored suit to his diminutive frame. A Wall Street wizard, he had already been on the cover of *Fortune* magazine, and he was only forty years old.

"This is Meyer's meeting," Joseph said, "but before we start, I want to invite all of you to a duck hunt I've arranged tomorrow. I bought

Mickey a new hunting dog for his birthday. A trainer has been coming here for two months, and we're going to try him out in the morning. Meyer, I know you have to get back to Miami, but I hope Paul and Wallace will stay."

Paul didn't want to go duck hunting, but he was trapped; Joseph had arranged for him to take a casino jet back to Las Vegas. He nodded and smiled.

C. Wallace Litman stood his ground. "I'll have to take a rain check, Joe. We're in the in the middle of a stock acquisition. Gotta drive back tonight."

Joseph nodded without expression. "Meyer, you have the floor."

Meyer started to speak in a nasal voice. "I don't have to tell you what's been going on since Hoover died," he said. "We had that butt-slamming fairy in a box. He hadda look the other way or I'd a released them pictures a him in that motel in Detroit. But Hoover's gone and things have changed. We got nothin' but trouble in Washington. The off-track betting, the drug business, numbers, vice, everything is getting hit by these new bastards. We got the head of the FBI running unchecked and shitballs like this renegade fed in Vegas, this Solomon Kazorowski, trying to bust everybody. Now the Congress goes and passes this RICO Act."

They all knew about RICO, the Racketeer Influenced and Corrupt Organizations Act; it said that any prior knowledge of a crime made you as guilty as if you had committed the crime yourself. All the feds had to do on a RICO prosecution was get just one member of the outfit to admit that he had discussed a crime with his don and the boss was automatically culpable. In La Cosa Nostra, you couldn't commit a crime on outfit turf without notifying the boss and giving him a "taste," so all of the top guys were now at risk. The feds were also setting up a witness protection program to encourage informants. It was a depressing law to contemplate.

"We gotta find a way to shut this fucking thing down," Meyer wheezed.

"How we gonna do that? It's a federal law," the Nevada governor said.

"Joseph and I been talking and we got a way maybe works, but you gotta be involved."

C. Wallace Litman straightened his shoulders. He had been a silent financial puppet of Meyer Lansky's since the sixties. Wallace had been Theodora Lansky's investment adviser in Chicago. Meyer had spotted him working on his wife's account and saw that Wallace was shrewd and ambitious. He'd recruited him ten years ago. Litman was to set up a holding company called Litstar Industries. Meyer would funnel offshore mob money into blind accounts that C. Wallace could draw on to buy legitimate businesses. The businesses were technically owned by Litstar, but the real owners were Meyer Lansky and Joseph Alo. The three men rarely met and nobody suspected that C. Wallace Litman was a shill and a laundry for organized crime. He had risen rapidly on the wings of illegal financing.

"It's not smart for us to be involved too closely in anything," Paul said.

"Our plan is simple, but it's going to take some time. We have decided that you are going to be the President of the United States," Meyer said without preamble.

Wallace could see a change in Governor Arquette's demeanor. He seemed to glow with the prospect.

"How we gonna do that?" Paul asked softly.

"The world has changed," Meyer said as he picked up his glass of wine. "Radio made it small, TV made it smaller. Politics is changing. Nixon was smarter, better qualified than Kennedy to be the President, but Kennedy with them Boston manners and that fucking hair. He looks like a movie star, so the schmucks elect him. Nixon always looked like he should be selling dirty magazines. TV killed Nixon. TV is the future. You control TV, you control what people see, what people say, and what they think."

"Wallace and I have already begun to liquidate the real estate we own and started looking around for electronic media properties to buy," Joseph continued. "Once we own a television network, we're gonna use it to put Paul in the White House."

". . . And once you're there," Meyer said softly, "you're gonna fire these new fucks in the FBI and over at Justice. You're gonna appoint a new attorney general, new head of the FBI. You pick guys like Hoover who will look the other way. And then, when you get Supreme Court openings, you're gonna start packing the bench with judges who don't like RICO. We're gonna either overturn this thing or neutralize it with friendly cops." Meyer tried to set the wine glass down on the table but misjudged, and it tipped over.

All of them watched the drops of port as they spattered on the beige carpet, leaving a stain that looked like blood.

The pale morning sunlight woke Paul Arquette early. He was still flush with ambition and the thought of being President. He showered and, before he went down for breakfast, heard Joseph's limousine leave to take Meyer Lansky to the airport.

The dining room was huge, with a forty-foot-long marble table and high-backed chairs that Joseph had imported from Italy. Mickey Alo was already in the room with his prep school roommate. Paul couldn't take his eyes off the remarkably handsome boy. Penny sat at the foot of the table.

"Ready to murder a few ducks?" Joseph said as he swept into the room a few minutes later. Paul had always thought duck hunting was one of mankind's least noble adventures.

"Did you get enough to eat?" Penny asked.

"Up to here." Paul motioned as he smiled broadly.

It had always amazed him that Joseph had managed to hook a woman like Penny. What could she possibly see in the Sicilian gangster? She came from a wealthy family. She was cultured and refined. She was like a pearl in a pan of gravel, and Paul thought she didn't belong married to Joseph. But maybe she found his power seductive. He wondered what she would be like in bed.

The men walked into the den, where the twelve-gauge bird slayers were in slots behind the glass of a built-in oak wall cabinet.

Paul chose an English Purdy over-and-under, with an initialed stock and solid-gold butt plate.

"That thing was custom-made," Joseph bragged. "Cost more than a hundred grand, so don't drop it in the mud, Paul."

Joseph lifted out a Beretta with a five-load magazine and engraved barrel.

They slogged along, their valuable shotguns broken open to expose the breeches. Mickey Alo had an English handmade Purdy, the stock cut short for his pudgy arms. Ryan Bolt walked beside him, unarmed.

The dog Rex was still a puppy and in high spirits. He was snapping at the air and, barking with mischief, charging right and left, eyes happy, tongue lolling. Joseph Alo yelled at him and he cocked his head, a "Whatsamatta guys?" look on his friendly face.

He was a Chesapeake, and beautiful—a rich, chocolate color with soft brown eyes.

"Fucking dog," Joseph cursed under his breath. "Gonna scare the ducks off. Get back here, Rex."

The dog wagged his tail and trotted back.

"Dog's supposed to be trained. Hired a guy in Jersey City to come down here every day for three months."

Rex looked up, puzzled. They tramped on through the damp yellow grass, sprinkled with the red and gold paint chips of autumn.

Paul moved across the marshy land, his borrowed rubber boots making slurpy sounds.

Then two ducks broke in front of them, flapping hard, rising at desperate angles, their long necks stretching. Joseph snapped shut his breech and started firing. One of the ducks went down, fluttering and spiraling. It hit with a rustle a hundred yards away. The other was still airborne. Paul had it in his sights, but he couldn't bear to shoot it and pulled off, aiming to the right just as the pudgy clown prince fired. . . . Two hundred thousand dollars' worth of English Purdys thundered in unison. Mickey got the second bird.

"Fetch, Rex," Joseph commanded, and the dog headed off in the wrong direction.

"Back, Rex!" Joseph yelled as the confused dog turned and trotted back.

Joseph tried again. "Fetch, Rex."

The dog looked up at him, perplexed.

"Fetch, damn it!" Joseph was turning red with anger. He kicked the dog in the hind end and it squealed and took off, ran fifteen or twenty feet, then turned and looked back, his brown eyes puzzled.

"Fetch," Joseph screamed, nearly out of control.

Rex bolted into the high grass. They could hear him crashing around, breaking reeds, barking.

"Your dog is worthless, Mickey," Joseph said, trying to contain his anger.

9

"Pretty disappointing." Mickey's black eyes were dancing.

And then Rex came back, the duck hanging from his mouth. He dropped the bird proudly at Joseph's feet. Joseph picked it up. A deadly shadow crossed his face.

"Chewed the fucking duck. Broke all the bones! How we gonna eat this?" he yelled at the dog.

Rex stood there, panting happily. Joseph went wild with anger. He tried to kick the dog again, but Rex was too fast. He dodged Joseph's boot, and Joseph went down in muddy water.

Rex backed up, spread his front legs, and barked at the mobster, who was sitting on the ground, his clothing filling with brackish water. Rex kept backing up and barking.

Then, smoldering with hatred, Joseph yanked the Beretta up, aimed it at Rex, pulled back the hammer, and fired.

Rex flew backward, his shoulders and head instantly turned to red mist . . . obliterated by the buckshot. He landed on his side in the yellow grass, his feet reflexively running, going nowhere.

Paul Arquette felt like throwing up. He looked at Ryan, who had his hand to his mouth in absolute shock. Then Paul noticed that Mickey was smiling. The only two people who understood Rex's death were Joseph and his fifteen-year-old son. For some reason, Mickey thought it was funny.

They walked numbly back to the house, where Lucinda was waiting.

"Where's Rex?" she asked. Nobody answered. "Daddy, where is he?"

"Rex didn't make it," Mickey said. "He accidentally got shot."

She was halfway up the stairs before they could hear her wailing in grief.

THE WALL STREET JOURNAL
February 5, 1981

C. Wallace Litman, controlling stockholder in Litstar Industries, a holding company he established in the mid-sixties,
announced today that he had acquired nearly ten percent of
United Broadcasting Company. The TV network has been
riding high in the ratings and is scheduled to broadcast the
Summer Olympics in 1984. C. Wallace Litman said that
Litstar has no plans to launch a full-scale takeover of the
network.

DAILY VARIETY
September 10, 1992

An overlong Emmycast produced few surprises last night. The
Mechanic swept up most of the dramatic Emmys as expected,
winning in the Best Actor and Actress categories along with
Best Drama. Series creator and executive producer Ryan Bolt
accepted for the show, saying that he was overcome with gratitude. The Mechanic, which depicts the adventures of a simple,
blue-collar garage mechanic, has been heralded as a breakthrough in dramatic television, touching on humanity and the
depth of the human spirit. . . .

LAS VEGAS SUN
November 8, 1986

HEAD OF VEGAS

ORGANIZED

CRIME UNIT QUITS

Solomon Kazorowski put in his papers for an early retirement Monday. Kazorowski, who had headed the Las Vegas Organized Crime Strike Force, was a legend in this city. He ran his elite group of crime busters from a deserted dress shop on Calvary Street and was noted for his tenacious pursuit of casino mob connections, specifically targeting alleged Jersey mobster Joseph Alo. Kazorowski, known in Las Vegas circles for his flamboyant Hawaiian shirts and reckless enthusiasm, was recently embarrassed by a bill at the Flamingo. He had allowed the casino to comp him for over five hundred dollars' worth of champagne and food. The resulting furor led to his resignation.

THE NEW YORK TIMES
March 9, 1982

A RICO prosecution of Anthony Colombo of New York was announced Friday by members of the U.S. Attorney's office in New York. The alleged gang boss was indicted on counts of murder, attempted murder, extortion, narcotics trafficking, postal theft, mail and wire fraud. The defendants included three sons of the late family boss Joseph Colombo. Twenty-two of the family's more active associates were included in the indictment. Sources close to the prosecution speculate that several of those indicted have made deals with the government to testify against Tony Colombo and his top lieutenants.

THE NEW YORK TIMES

January 10, 1996

Veteran network TV news reporter Cole Harris was discharged from his post as correspondent for the UBC news division in New York. The dismissal was apparently over Cole's refusal to drop a story on organized crime in American politics. The exposé dealt with the underworld's attempts to influence politicians, with emphasis on Atlantic City's political ties to hotel gambling and the Mafia. The documentary was scheduled to air on Sunday, January 9, and according to inside sources was pulled at the last minute. Steve Israel, head of UBC's news division, said that the documentary entitled "Mob Voices" had been inconclusive and that UBC had elected not to air it for legal reasons.

MIAMI HERALD

Saturday, January 22, 1983

Meyer Lansky is dead at 80. His departure is cause for an odd sadness, not for Lansky, a gangster who had a long run and died in bed. But for the rest of us, because now it will be impossible to discover the full history of the United States in this century. The man who was born Maier Suchowljansky was crucial to that history, and he has gone without breaking the code of silence.

It was Meyer, they said, who nailed J. Edgar Hoover. The way the story goes, Hoover was a homosexual operating in the deepest of closets. Meyer found that closet, had photographs made, and used those photographs as a grant of immunity.

His name is part of our history and our legend. But when the obits ran the other day, there was a sense that the true story was now gone forever.

THE SPORTING CLUB

JANUARY 3, 1996

MICKEY ALO TIPPED THE SEAT BACK BUT DIDN'T SLEEP. HE looked out the window of the Lear-55 at the blue-green reef fifteen thousand feet below. His father's pilot, Milo Duleo, had just announced that they were about to make their descent into Grand Bahama island. Mickey rubbed the stubble on his chin and wondered what the hell Paul Arquette was trying to pull. The call had been screwy. Paul's voice screeched at him through fifteen hundred miles of Atlantic Bell cable.

"I can't tell you on the phone . . . but it's important. You can land at the deserted military field at Sand Dollar Beach. You won't have to clear customs or immigration. Nobody will ever know you're down here."

In the two rear seats of the plane, New York Tony Demarco and Little Pussy Bono were snoring contentedly. New York Tony had been Mickey's bodyguard since he was at Harvard back in the late seventies; now he was his capo, or right hand. Tony was short and muscular with a head as big as a truck tire and a complexion like lunar lava. Little Pussy Bono had gotten his name and reputation as a cat burglar in New York, but now he handled special assignments for the Alo family. He had been working mostly for Mickey, now that Joseph Alo was sick. Little Pussy was slender and hawk-faced. Like most cat burglars, God had designed him for air-conditioning vents and small openings.

The pressure in the rich gray and burl-wood cabin changed as New York Tony and Little Pussy sat up and rubbed their eyes.

Two minutes later, the plane touched down at the end of the apron and taxied to a stop. Mickey turned to face the two men in the seats behind him. "I don't know what's going on. Get a map of this fucking place and line up a car, don't rent it, steal something, and stay handy. In case I need you, I want you ready to move. No phone calls, no contact with anyone, no record we were ever here." Mickey didn't quite know why, but he sensed impending disaster.

"Right," New York Tony said, stretching out his stumpy legs.

When Milo got the jet door open, Mickey was hit by a wall of heat and humidity. A blue English Ford was parked under a shade tree. It pulled out onto the field, stopping near the door. Mickey looked down at the car. A handsome young man got out. He was dressed in tennis shorts and a teal-blue polo shirt. "Mr. Alo, welcome to the Bahamas." The young man smiled.

"Who the fuck are you?" Mickey said, disdain crawling up in his throat.

"Warren Sacks. I'm Senator Arquette's media consultant."

Mickey turned back to Tony and Little Pussy in the cabin. "This is fucked. What happened to all the secrecy? We go to all this trouble to stay off the immigration sheet and Paul sends some dipshit to drive me." Mickey didn't wait for them to answer. He moved down the steps carrying his sport coat and got into the blue Ford. Warren put it in gear and pulled off the tarmac.

"The air conditioner doesn't get much better than that, I'm afraid," Warren said pleasantly.

"Where's Paul?"

"The senator's at the club. We're having media planning sessions. He said I should drop you at his bungalow." And then Warren flashed

Mickey a dazzling smile that seemed to say, "Don't worry, I'm in on the secret."

The Sporting Club had originally been a haven for blue-water fishermen, but it now mostly catered to conventions and vacationers. The clubhouse was a large stone building with a tile roof that faced the water. Palm trees and red hibiscus vibrated in a strong, offshore breeze. There was a picturesque wooden wharf where three 30-foot sport-fishing boats with outriggers for trolling were tied. Warren drove the car past the clubhouse and down a shell road lined by dense mango plants. He pulled to a stop in front of a secluded bungalow.

"The afternoon conference should be breaking up soon. I'm sorry there's no cooler place to wait, but the senator said you'd understand."

"I'll see you," Mickey said, dismissing the man whom he had taken an unreasonable dislike to.

Warren put the Ford in gear and zipped off, gunning the engine unnecessarily.

The bungalow had a wood plaque on the door announcing it as the FLAMINGO SUITE. The front door was locked, so Mickey walked around to the back, where there was a louvered glass door next to an outdoor shower. Also locked. A window air conditioner had been cut into the wall, and it growled ominously. He cursed under his breath, then kicked a louver out with his foot, breaking a glass pane by the handle. He reached through the shards and opened the door.

The Flamingo Suite was small and neat. He looked around the living room, which was decorated with flamingo-pink wicker furniture, then moved into the bedroom and looked at the king-size bed, covered by a red and white floral bedspread.

Mickey began a thorough search of the room.

He found some Polaroid pictures in Paul's shaving kit in the bottom dresser drawer. Six shots of Warren and Paul and a young girl who couldn't have been older than sixteen. They were disgustingly pornographic but didn't surprise him. They confirmed what he already suspected . . . Paul Arquette was a big mistake.

When Paul entered the Flamingo Suite twenty minutes later, he found Mickey stretched out on the pink sofa, his stockinged feet up on the armrest. Paul was in white tennis shorts and a Sporting Club T-shirt. At sixty-seven, he was still handsome and fit. The tropical sun had turned him a rich, deep shade of brown. Paul smiled at the little fat man. At five-four, his head and toes barely reached both ends of the couch.

"You got down here fast."

"You call, I come, Senator." Mickey sat up and slipped his feet back into tasseled loafers.

Paul thought Mickey hadn't gotten any better looking over the two decades he'd known him. He was still round and oily . . . a medicine ball in pants.

Mickey got to his feet as Paul moved to the minibar. "Something cold?"

"Why don't you tell me what's on your mind, then I'll be outta here before somebody else sees me."

"Else?" Paul sounded alarmed.

"Yeah, you sent some guy to pick me up. Nobody is supposed to know you have connections with our family. You're only six weeks from the Iowa presidential primary."

"Oh, you mean Warren . . ." he said, the frown evaporating. "Warren knows everything. We can trust Warren."

"We can?" Mickey asked, his voice rough as hemp.

"Yes, we can. And don't use that tone with me, Mickey, 'cause I'm not gonna take it from you or your father." Paul had grown accustomed to having things his own way. He'd had limited contact with the Alos over the years. He wasn't used to being challenged. He had forgotten the duck hunt twenty years before and Mickey's strange smile when Rex was murdered.

"What's going on? You said you had something important," Mickey said.

"Yes, I do . . . very important. I think it answers all our questions." He paused, then plunged on. "I have been contacted by Harlan Ellis at the Democratic National Committee. As a matter of fact, I spent two days with him down here. He left two DNC pollsters behind. We've been going over strategies for the past two days. They've done some tracking polls and some demographic projections, and I'm scoring huge in the West and Midwest. I should get fifty percent in Iowa."

"Yeah ... I know. That's 'cause we've had you on UBC-TV's national news every night for a month. I hope you didn't bring me down here to tell me that."

"The Democratic National Committee wants *me* to be their candidate. They want to throw all the party resources behind me." His voice couldn't contain his excitement.

"Then we all want the same thing. Tell 'em to get off the field and we'll make it happen."

"But if the DNC is pushing me and financing me, I don't think it's necessary for you and your father to stay involved."

"You're kidding me, no?"

"Mickey, it doesn't change anything. You know there's a big risk using offshore laundered cash to run my campaign. What if somebody finds out?"

"You mean like maybe Warren?"

"The DNC has a huge campaign war chest. They have a preexisting staff ... media consultants, polling experts, issue experts, advertising and media buyers, stature strategists ... the whole setup. Plus, they can put pressure on other candidates to get out of the race."

"Forget it."

"I'm not going to forget it. I'm gonna take it."

"Uncle Pauly." Mickey used his boyhood form of address sarcastically. "Lemme get this straight. ... My dad and Meyer buy a TV network and use it to get you a national profile; use it to get you a U.S. Senate seat; get you on the Ways and Means Committee and make you a political front-runner, and then, when these fucks at DNC decide to poach on our deal, you think you can invite me down here, keep me waiting in this pink wet dream, and then kick a board up my ass?"

"That isn't what I'm doing."

"I'm gonna do you a huge favor, Paul. ... I'm gonna tell my father that you felt lonely and missed me and that's why you asked me down here. Then you're gonna tell these assholes at the DNC to get the fuck outta our way, and if anything like this ever comes up again, I'm gonna personally empty a dustpan full a' glass into your head."

Paul and Mickey were a few feet apart, but Paul could feel an almost ungodly warmth coming off the little man, as if he were standing in front of an electric heater.

Paul took a step back, then held his ground. "You're threatening me?"

"Fucking-A. Glad you recognize it."

"I will not be threatened. I'm a U.S. senator. You can't possibly think I'll put up with a threat from you or anybody else. The DNC picks one candidate every four years. It virtually guarantees me the Democratic nomination. And I've already said yes."

"Do you really know what you're doing, Paul?" Mickey asked, his voice even and cold.

"That's why I called you down. I don't want to have any further involvement with your family or your money. It's too dangerous. Now I have to get back to a political strategy-planning session."

Mickey picked up his sport jacket, with the Polaroid photos in the pocket, and folded it over his arm. "You're making a mistake."

"I don't think so, Mickey. Everybody agrees, taking this offer is the right thing to do."

"When everybody agrees on something, Pauly, you can always bet it's wrong." Mickey didn't say good-bye as he closed the door of the Flamingo Suite behind him. Warren Sacks was waiting in the blue Ford. Mickey got in and sat next to the media consultant. They headed back to the deserted airfield.

"Nice place," Mickey said, smiling at Warren. "Boy that suite of Paul's is nifty. Are they all that good?"

"Pretty much the same. Mine's the Seafoam Suite, all done in green, really restful."

"If I get back down here, I'll ask for it. Is it on the beach?"

"Just one road down from Paul's, right on the sand," Warren said, helping to seal his own awful fate.

After they took off, Mickey sat in the back of the Lear-55 in a chair facing Little Pussy and New York Tony. "Tony, go up and tell Milo t' put this call on the scrambler."

Mickey waited for the three tinny-sounding beeps that indicated the voice scrambler was on, then dialed. In a few minutes, he had his father on the phone in New Jersey.

"Yes," Joseph said to his only son, who was now circling at ten thousand feet over the Great Bahama Bank. Joseph Alo's voice sounded hollow through the scrambler. His emphysema was getting worse. Fluid in his lungs gargled when he spoke.

"We're on the scrambler, Pop. I wouldn't call you from the air, but we got a problem."

"Gimme."

"Pauly's had a brain fart. The DNC offered him the nomination. He's going to take it. . . . Wants us to go away."

"Change his mind," the old man said softly.

"It's blown, Pop. He's already said yes. Beyond that, he's risking security. He basically told me to take a hike."

"Whatta you suggesting?" the old man wheezed.

"I wanna send him over. I got Tony and Little Pussy here with me. We can make it look right."

"I ain't gonna be here much longer, Mickey, maybe a couple a' months, a year at the most. After I'm gone, this is your business. You know what's at stake. You know how hard we worked, how difficult it will be to replace Paul. You make the decision, you're gonna have to live with the result."

"I'll be home tomorrow." Mickey hung up and looked at Tony.

"Tell Milo to hang around out here for an hour till dark, then we go back and land without lights."

THE FIFTY-MINUTE HOUR

FIVE THOUSAND MILES AND THREE TIME ZONES AWAY, RYAN
Bolt was fighting an anxiety attack.

"You've got to talk about Matthew eventually," Dr. Driekurs was
saying.

Ryan was sitting in her beige-on-beige office, focusing intently on
his Air Jordans, trying to keep from jumping up out of the reclining
chair.

"He's been dead a year and you've barely said anything about it,"
Dr. Ellen Driekurs continued.

The neon red and green shoe colors strobed momentarily. He felt
dizzy.

"Okay, let's talk about something else, then." She brought him
back.

"Like what?" He looked at his gold Rolex. . . . Shit, twenty-five
more minutes. He was having his weekly fifty-minute hour. He knew

lie was wasting his time and money but he had to do something, because his life this last year had been a psychotic nightmare. It had started with Matt dying . . . And then Linda filing for divorce, and then the dreams that had scared him, keeping him up nights. And on top of that was all the career shit dragging him down, making him wonder if he really had it or had just bowled a few lucky frames.

"Let's talk about what happened at NBC. You said they asked you to leave?"

She had a stumpy build and kept her mid-brown hair pulled back tightly in a bun. She was beige, like her office . . . As if lack of color was what would soothe all the manic Hollywood head cases that paraded through, plunking their Gianni Versace asses on her beige sofa, unpacking emotional luggage, putting a good face on career hijackings and drive-by divorces.

"Does it seem funny to you that I stopped dreaming two weeks ago?" He lied, trying to get off the fiasco at NBC. He hadn't been asked to leave. . . . They'd had security remove him from the screening room when he'd threatened Marty Lanier's life, promising to beat the shit out of the quivering head of drama development while three of Marty's loyal Jedi made no move to save him.

"You dream, Ryan. Everybody dreams. You're just not remembering your dreams."

"Why is that?"

His right eye began to twitch, a nervous tic that had been coming and going for almost a week now.

"Are you asking me why people dream or why you aren't remembering your dreams?"

"I guess why people dream . . ." Filling up more of the hour with bullshit, hoping he could skate through, the Brian Boitano of session therapy.

"Mental images are produced by the subconscious during sleep. Your dreams are the day's residue being reprocessed by the mind. Dreams offer us a look at the subconscious."

"I see." But he didn't. He hadn't told her about the terrible nightmares. Twisted and frightening dreams. Always he was in the water, always a dark shadow chased him. Sometimes he would be swimming, trying to get away, and then, suddenly, he would become the monster. Last night he'd been after Matt . . . chasing his dead son, mouth open, trying to devour him while the boy screamed. His own screams woke him up, drenched with sweat.

If it weren't for him, Matt would still be alive.

"I know you think this is all wrapped up with Matthew's dying"— his eyelid doing a machine-gun chatter—"but I've done my grieving. I've dealt with his death." A triple-Lutz lie.

"You don't dream. You don't think about Matthew or your divorce. You're afraid to leave your house. You have your secretary drive you. You're being asked to leave the few appointments your agent can set up. Ryan, I think you'd better start taking our work more seriously. You can spend your money here, dodging me, trying not to deal with what's bothering you, but it's not going to lead you to any solutions."

He glanced at his watch . . . ten minutes more. Some things he couldn't share. He couldn't talk about Matt.

He felt so goddamned guilty.

"That mess at NBC . . . I can clean that up. After all, I'm the guy who gave them *The Mechanic* and *Dangerous Company*. Those two shows made the network hundreds of millions." But that was four years ago, and back then he'd have found a way to get Marty Lanier laughing at his own ideas, instead of calling him a cocksucker and threatening his life in front of the assembled network Jedi. Marty's ideas were creative arsenic. Thoughts delivered from the hip with no real reasons, just "interesting notions" he called them—this from a man who probably got erections playing Nintendo.

"I want you to think about why we can't discuss Matthew," she was saying. "I want you to work on a reason."

"Okay." He looked at his watch: eight more minutes. "Look, Ellen, I don't want to cut this short, but Elizabeth is picking me up and she has to get back to the studio by three. So I better leave now."

"If that's what you want."

He made it out the door, his eyelid doing the fandango.

He got in the elevator.

Too small. It felt like a coffin, out of control, cableless, falling down the side of the steel and glass building, about to bury itself and Ryan in the oil shale deep below Century City.

He walked into the sunshine. The fifty-minute hour was over. He just hoped Elizabeth wasn't late and he could make it home without cracking up.

THE FISHING PARTY

"**MAN, THIS THING SMELLS LIKE SOMEBODY HURLED IN IT,**" LITtle Pussy said, wrinkling his nose in the backseat of the ten-year-old rusted-out Chevy wagon they had stolen in town. It was eight P.M. and they were heading back to the Sporting Club. New York Tony was driving with the headlights out.

Mickey, in the passenger seat, was trying to spot the shell road that led to the beach. "There it is," he said, pointing to the opening in the shrub line.

The wagon groaned and shook as it made the turn. Tony shut off the engine and coasted to a stop near Paul Arquette's bungalow. They sat for a minute, listening to the hot engine tick in the dark.

"Okay, Puss, we're going fishing, so we need one of those cabin cruisers tied out on the wharf. Make sure nobody's on the dock, then get aboard and see about getting it started. Don't turn it on till me an' Tony get aboard."

"Right." Little Pussy got out of the car and moved down to the beach. He waited for his eyes to adjust to the dark. Once he could see that nobody was on the wharf, he crossed the strip of white sand and climbed up on the dock, his lace-up leather shoes making clacking sounds on the freshly painted wood.

Mickey and New York Tony put on gloves and got out of the car. The Flamingo Suite was locked and empty. Mickey moved around to the back where he had broken the glass and saw that it had already been fixed. "Shit," he said in mild disgust. This time he removed the pane without breaking it, opened the door, and fitted the glass back into the slot. He let Tony in the front door.

"Okay, this Warren guy is in something called the Seafoam Suite. It's the next one down. Pick him up and bring him here. And keep him quiet."

"Right." Tony moved silently out the back door and disappeared down the beach.

Warren and Paul were having dinner in the big dining room with the two pollsters from the DNC. They were scheduled to go back to Washington tomorrow. People at other tables stole glances at the famous senator. They talked about the Iowa caucus and how Paul should get there early and start working the state in late January. Paul's wife, Avon, called him long-distance from Washington. He took the call on the head waiter's phone. By nine o'clock, Paul and Warren said good night to the pollsters, and they all headed back to their respective suites.

When Paul put his key in the door, he was yawning. He moved carelessly into the room, turned to lock up, and felt the cold touch of a gun on his temple.

"Whaaah!" he yelled in fright.

"Hands behind you, Paul. Don't fuck with me or I'll blow your nuts off."

"I . . . You . . ." Paul sputtered.

Paul put his hands behind him, and Mickey wrapped them quickly with some silver electrician's tape Milo had given him. Then he spun Paul around and pushed him against the door.

"You can't do this to me. I'm a U.S. senator."

"You're puppy shit, Pauly. You shouldn't a' forgot who you were dealing with."

A few minutes later, the back door opened and Warren Sacks was pushed into the room with a pillowcase over his head. Tony pulled the case off once they were inside, and Warren stared at them, his eyes bulging with terror. He had a pair of his own tennis socks taped into his mouth.

"Tony, get a couple a' pair of swim trunks outta the dresser . . . an' some socks for Pauly."

"Just what the fuck do you think . . . ?" Paul didn't get any further because Mickey hit him in the solar plexus. When Paul's mouth flew open to exhale, Tony shoved the socks into the opening, then Mickey pulled him upright and pushed his head back against the wall.

"How do you guys feel about fishing? I know it's late, but what the hell. . . . Wanna see if anything's running out there?"

Warren and Paul looked at Mickey through wild eyes.

They stepped out of the pink Flamingo Suite, closed and locked the door, and headed toward the cabin cruisers.

Little Pussy was in an Egg Harbor with a flying bridge. He stuck his head out of the cabin. "Over here," Puss whispered, and they loaded Paul and Warren aboard. On the stern of the boat, printed in corny circus letters, it said REEL FANTASY. They pushed Paul and Warren down into the padded fighting chairs.

"Any live bait aboard, Puss?"

"In that tank," Little Pussy answered.

The bait tank in the stern was full of medium-size sea bass swimming lazily in the brackish water.

"Is everybody ready for a Reel Fantasy?" Mickey asked. "Puss, let's get outta here."

Little Pussy had found the keys hanging on a hook inside the starboard hatch. He started the engines while New York Tony cast off the lines, and the thirty-foot fishing boat moved slowly out to sea, its running lights off. Within moments, the *Reel Fantasy* was out of view of land.

They cut the engines somewhere over the Great Bahama Bank, and

Mickey grabbed the small hand fishnet, scooped several of the bait fish out of the tank, and started to chop them into little pieces. When he was finished, he scraped the fish and innards into a drain bucket. All the while, he talked to a terrified Paul Arquette.

"What I don't get, Paul, and maybe you can explain it to me, is what the fuck you think was going on all those years . . . ? This was never anything but a straight business deal. How'd you get so far off the fucking road?"

Paul tried to grunt an answer muffled through his sock-stuffed mouth. Mickey ignored him and turned to Tony. "Turn on that spotlight and throw this chum in the water."

Tony flipped on the night fishing lights. Fifty feet down in the ocean's green water, they could see colored fish swimming on the reef. Then Tony threw the bucket of chopped fish, blood, and guts into the water.

"Puss, move the boat around while Tony spreads it out." Paul's eyes were bulging and he started to choke. Mickey reached over and pulled the spit-wet socks out of both men's mouths.

"Look, Mickey, I'm sorry. I didn't think it through. You're right. I'll tell the DNC no. We'll put it back the way it was." Arquette was frantic.

"Yeah, but Paul, that still leaves me with a problem. Once a guy rats me out, I can't ever trust him again. What if we get you in the White House and I ask you to do me a favor and you tell me to fuck off, like this afternoon? What'm I gonna do to you once you're the President? . . . See the problem?"

Paul swallowed, sweat formed on his forehead.

"You don't get a second chance," Mickey continued. "This was a one-chance kinda deal. Now we gotta get you changed." He picked up the trunks and flipped them at Warren and Paul. The trunks hit their legs and fell to the deck. "Untie 'em, Tony."

"Why do we need trunks?" Paul whimpered.

" 'Cause I said so, okay?"

"I'm not gonna do it," Paul said.

Tony jerked Paul up onto his feet and hit him lightly in the stomach. "Okay, okay," Paul gasped, and Tony untaped his wrists so Paul could unzip his pants and get into the swimming trunks.

Warren was pleading in a singsong voice. Mickey couldn't even tell what he was saying.

"Shut the fuck up," New York Tony yelled at Warren.

In a few minutes, both were wearing swim trunks.

"Bring me some ropes," Mickey ordered. Little Pussy scrambled to find them. Mickey looped rope under Paul's armpits and knotted it under his breastbone, stuffing towels underneath so there would be no rope burn.

Then Mickey shoved Paul hard in the chest and Senator Arquette jackknifed off the transom of the boat into the bloody water. Mickey looped the end of the line over the stern cleat. New York Tony fastened another towel-padded rope around Warren, threw him overboard, and cleated him off on the port side.

Paul was yelling. "Let us in! . . . Why are you doing this to me?"

"Let's drag 'em around a little," Mickey said. Pussy hit the throttle and started to pull Paul and Warren through the bloody chum.

"Stop!" Warren screamed. "This blood will draw sharks!"

"Now you're on my wave length," Mickey said to himself as he scooped out more fish and chopped them up. "Come on, boys. . . . Dinner's on," Mickey said to the empty sea.

They didn't see the first dorsal fin for almost twenty minutes, but once it came, several more were there within seconds. Tiger sharks with strangely beautiful yellow markings on their backs.

At first, the sharks made slow passes while Warren and Paul screamed in terror. The sharks brushed up against them, not quite sure what they were, making tighter and tighter circles. Then a nine-foot monster turned and came hard at Warren. It hit him in the kidneys, ripping and tearing with its razor teeth. Warren screamed in pain as the tiger shark arched its back and slashed its tail, tearing a huge piece of Warren loose.

Blood spilled into the water.

"For the love of God! For the love of God!" Paul screamed, seconds before a shark slammed into him. The shark rolled on its back and threw its head, tearing half of Paul's shoulder away. The sea boiled red with the feeding frenzy as dorsal fins and teeth flashed in the floodlit water.

"We got the right bait on now," Mickey said.

Unexpectedly, Little Pussy vomited, spewing up half a bag of M&M's and two peanut brittle bars he'd eaten on the plane.

The sharks were feeding with abandon, ripping and tearing. Within seconds, half of Warren Sacks was gone. Paul was missing one leg along with his right arm and shoulder to the chest.

"I don't wanna lose 'em completely. Let's get outta here," Mickey said.

Puss, with peanut-chocolate vomit still on his shirt, hit the throttle, and they roared away from the sharks. The lifeless torsos were skipping and turning at the end of the ropes, doing a macabre dance in the churning wake.

They cut the bodies loose twenty yards from shore and watched until they washed up on the beach.

They hosed down the boat, retied it to the wharf, and returned to the airfield.

"Everything work out?" Milo asked.

"Went fishing but we lost our bait," Mickey said.

Minutes later, they were headed back to New Jersey.

Everything had taken less than an hour.

SHADOWS

RYAN STOOD OUTSIDE THE CENTURY CITY HIGH-RISE, SHAKING.
He had just spent fifty minutes in therapy and he was a wreck.

Ten minutes later, Elizabeth finally pulled up in her Karmann Ghia with the top down and beeped her horn. He moved quickly across the sun-cooked sidewalk and got into the car.

Elizabeth had been his secretary for almost ten years. She was a good worker with a sense of humor, in her mid-forties. She must have been a striking-looking woman once but took no pains with herself now, tying her long brown hair back with yarn, wearing sack dresses without style. She was divorced with no children. Lately things between them had changed—a shift in power more than friendship. She sensed his weakness and had been taking advantage of it. He was no longer in charge.

She made a turn on Pico and headed up on the 405 freeway.

"Elizabeth, I can't take the freeway. I told you. Go through Culver City, will ya?"

"This is nuts, Ryan. People use the freeway every day. My mother's coming over for dinner. I have a gazillion things to do. If I go on surface streets, I'm never gonna get home."

She stayed on the 405 to Santa Monica as he held the armrest and battled a panic attack. He didn't know why the freeways had started scaring him. For the last two months, he had been incapable of driving his own car. The minute he got into his Mercedes and turned on the engine, he was filled with such bone-numbing fear that he couldn't get out fast enough.

Just a year ago, he'd been in control not only of his life but most of his relationships. He'd won Writers Guild awards and two Emmys. He'd been lionized by the press.

Then Matt died and everything went wrong.

They were scooting off the end of the Santa Monica Freeway and heading up the Coast Highway. As a kid, he had surfed this whole coast in the summer, cruising the black ribbon in his VW convertible.

In college he'd been an all-conference wide receiver at Stanford University. He'd been too small for the pros, but football and his blond surfer good looks made him a king on campus. He'd won the school lit contest in his senior year. Against his father's advice, he began writing TV scripts on spec instead of taking an entry-level job flipping Happy Burgers at one of his father's Happy Boy restaurants.

Two years later he sold his first script and moved into a small office at Universal Studios. Nobody could churn out work faster or better, and he'd gotten a big reputation. He'd made enough to marry Linda, his college sweetheart. She was as beautiful and blond as he was handsome and popular, and it took them a long time to find out that they weren't in love with each other as much as they were in love with the image they could create together. It was cool being half of somebody else's fantasy. But the envy of others failed to sustain them. And after Matt died, the lights went out for Ryan.

They roared out of Santa Monica. Elizabeth hadn't asked about the fiasco at NBC. She had to know. Probably one of the secretaries over there had called with the news and it was already spreading like wildfire, scorching his reputation, driving lies and half-truths ahead of it like fleeing animals. In show business, failures clung like wet clothing.

"You didn't ask about the screening," he finally said, to take his mind off a red pickup that was beside them. A big, burly six-pack, with heavy tattoos ringing his biceps like African jewelry, was crowding the passenger door of the Ghia.

"I heard you threatened to beat the shit out of Marty Lanier and called him a Jew faggot."

"I never called him a Jew faggot." His stomach did a slow porpoise roll.

"Well, that's what they say. It's all over the lot."

"You gotta call people, say it's not true."

"I already tried, but these things have a life of their own, Ryan."

Thirty minutes later, Elizabeth pulled the Ghia up in front of his condo north of Malibu. It was a Spanish complex with arched doors and red-tiled walks. He got out, and she started to back out of the drive, in a hurry to get home.

Ryan's condo was on Broad Beach, amid heavy sand dunes. Inside, the apartment was more to Linda's taste than his—lots of French floral prints on overstuffed chairs. Linda had taken the big house in Bel Air and he was out here. He preferred the beach. He couldn't bear the upstairs hall of the Bel Air house, with all those pictures of the three of them before Matt drowned. The faces stared at him from behind antique lacquer frames. What had they been thinking . . . smiling at the base of a ski lift . . . or on the back of the *Linda*, his fifty-foot sailboat named after his ex-wife? The pictures seemed to be of three strangers. So he'd left the house with its framed reminders and moved to the beach.

He saw his message light was on. He hit the playback.

His own voice, tired and lifeless: "Hi, this is Ryan. After the tone, leave your message."

Beep.

"Ryan, this is Jerry. What the fuck went wrong at NBC? I got six calls already. Call me. I can't deal with this shit."

His agent. Great! There were no other messages. It was as if he'd already been thrown off the Hollywood bus.

Why was this *happening*? Ryan looked out at the ocean . . . at the white foam, skipping playfully ahead of the green water. Then he picked up the channel changer and absently turned the TV on.

". . . not a matter of employment or even deficit reductions," the man on television was saying. "This is hardheaded economics . . . not the pabulum President Cotton tried to make us swallow." Cotton, plagued by ill health, had decided not to seek a second term.

It was Senator Paul Arquette on a taped weekly news show. The United States senator from Nevada had been getting more airtime lately than any other presidential hopeful. He had not announced yet, but he was obviously about to. Ryan remembered him from twenty years before, when he'd been just fifteen and had visited Mickey Alo at Thanksgiving. He hadn't been in touch with Mickey since Matt died. Then he remembered Mickey's dog Rex, running ahead of them, snapping at the air. And he remembered Rex lying on the grass. Headless. Dead.

Ryan turned off the set and went out on the porch to watch the sun go down, painting the Pacific with greens and reds. And then, for a brief moment in his mind's eye, he saw a seven-year-old red-headed boy. He was on a swing, pumping his legs to make it go higher. He didn't remember ever seeing him before, but somehow the memory of the boy was familiar. Then, almost before he could focus on him, the image was gone, leaving him with a feeling of dread he couldn't comprehend. Ryan had no idea who the boy was. He sat in the reclining chair and put his head back.

He fell asleep, and again his dreams were dark and deadly. He was swimming with Matt. There was a black shadow in the water next to him, and as always, it terrified him. It was after Matt, but Matt was laughing. As the shadow beast swam past, Matt climbed on, riding its back. And then the giant blackness swerved and came at Ryan. . . . A beast he couldn't make out or identify but which seemed to contain all the evil in his imagination. His dead son was laughing. "Here we come, Daddy." For a second he glimpsed the huge monster's eye, rich with red and green markings—a paisley eye—then the shadow was ripping into him, eating his flesh. Matt was still laughing. "Does it hurt, Daddy?" And Ryan woke up. For almost a minute he didn't know where he was, then realized he was on his deck.

Shaking, he went into the house and lay down on his sofa.

Ryan was bone-tired but too afraid to close his eyes.

CANDIDATE

MICKEY AND HIS FATHER WERE IN JOSEPH'S ROOM WATCHING A news report about the return of Paul's mutilated body to McCarran Field in Las Vegas. The UBC anchor, Brenton Spencer, told America that Bahamian police surmised that the senator and his media consultant Warren Sacks had gone swimming late at night and been savagely attacked by sharks.

Paul's wife, Avon, met the plane, dressed in a dark suit. She was crying as Paul's casket was unloaded from a military cargo plane, and Brenton Spencer droned on about the late senator's political accomplishments.

Mickey watched, without feeling. He had not told his father about the inflammatory Polaroid pictures he'd found in the Flamingo Suite because it served no purpose now. The pictures showed Paul and Warren and a pretty sixteen-year-old Bahamian girl, locked in a bisexual daisy chain of anal bliss. Mickey had cut them up and flushed them down the toilet. They were of no use to him now and only defined the depth of his father's mistake in judgment about Paul. As the funeral procession left the airfield, Mickey switched off the TV and moved back to his father.

"I think you're right," Joseph wheezed. "This Rhode Island governor Haze Richards looks good, but this whole thing happens now or not at all. We got no time."

"Okay, but it's not like with Paul," Mickey said. "We knew Paul since he was governor. Haze Richards is a stranger. We need somebody who's got the candidate's ear and can control him. Somebody who can godfather this whole thing. I've been checking it out, and I found a guy who could help. He's real tight with Governor Richards—all the way back to grade school—helped him win the Rhode Island Governor's mansion. If we pick Haze Richards to be our candidate, this guy could rope him for us."

"What's his name?"

"Albert James Teagarden," Mickey said. "They call him A.J."

"What kinda leverage you got on Teagarden?" Joseph asked, then exploded into a coughing spasm, cursing as he barked out stale air and phlegm, spitting it into a wastebasket. Mickey turned on the oxygen tank, but Joseph waved it away, his eyes hard and yellow as dry corn.

"I talked to our people in Rhode Island. They wanted to get a handle on Haze Richards before he was elected governor 'cause of all our racetrack action up there. Teagarden was running the governor's campaign. Our people threw a party in a hotel room in Providence. There was pussy and booze, and then in comes some guy with this suitcase and he turns it upside down and spills out two hundred and fifty large all over the bed. It still had racetrack wrapping bands on it. They told Teagarden it was to buy campaign TV ads and to take what he needs. This fuck, A.J., is stuffing his pockets like some kid at a Halloween party. They also got a video of him with one of the girls. We got the prick by the balls."

Haze Richards had made his way to the top of their short list. Paul's old campaign manager, Malcolm Rasher, had found him. Ken Venable and Guy Vandergot, the two pollsters they had hired for

Paul, had confirmed the choice at a meeting they had with Mickey the day Paul's body was found.

They'd been in the back booth of one of his father's Mr. A's steak houses in Atlantic City. The dinner crowd was just streaming in from Resorts International next door. They were wedged into a booth in the back, hidden by a partition from most of the crowd. The din was growing as the tables filled. Ken Venable was dissecting the Democratic field along with a turf 'n' surf special, gesturing with a serrated knife blade, pointing the tip at Mickey. Guy Vandergot, fat and sloth-like, was eating with his head down, grunting in agreement as Ken rambled on.

"Thing you gotta understand here, Mickey, is the Democrats are factionalized, always have been. They can't agree on shit. You got liberals in the North and conservatives in the South. You got New Age intellectuals in the West, labor guys in the Midwest, along with farmers and subsidy protectionists. It's a patchwork of ideologies, and Malcolm thinks this gives us a chance . . . and I agree with him."

"How so?" Mickey said.

" 'Cause in a four- or five-horse race where nobody is winning, there's a chance with financing to jump in and grab the thing early. . . . While the rest of these guys are fighting over little pieces of the pie, we sweep in and grab the whole deal."

Ken looked over at Guy Vandergot before continuing.

"Okay, here's the Democratic field now that Paul's gone. All these guys have announced, and in a week or so, all of 'em are gonna be in Iowa cornfields, sitting on Jap tractors, talking about farm subsidies like they actually give a shit. . . . So we gotta get in this now if we're gonna," Ken said, still pointing with his knife. "Your front-runner is gonna be Leo Skatina, the second-term U.S. senator from New York. He's got name identification, good local organizations, and the media likes him. He's the early poll leader. He's been real vocal about women's issues. I think the Democratic National Committee is getting set to endorse him. The DNC probably thinks he has the strength to win against Vice President Pudge Anderson, who we all know is gonna be the Republican candidate. Then you got the Democratic senator from Florida, Peter Dehaviland. Environmentalist, that's his beachhead issue—offshore drilling, air pollution, nuclear waste. He also has a strong stand against unrestricted immigration. . . . He's gonna fade unless he gets really lucky in Iowa and New Hampshire. Malcom agrees."

"Go on." Mickey took out a notepad and began making notes.

"Okay . . . Eric Gulliford, nickname Gilligan 'cause he kinda looks like Bob Denver. He's an old-time Democrat. Hubert Humphrey in a fishing hat. U.S. congressman from Ohio. He's for all the traditional Democratic Party stuff: labor, welfare, jobs for everyone, government spending. Tax the shit out of everybody. He's strong with the old party hacks. Could only be trouble if, for some reason, the party shifts off Skatina. And then the last announced candidate is Benjamin Savage. He's a New Age liberal from California, a three-term U.S. senator and he's got all the hot-button Melrose Avenue issues western liberals love—recast the workplace to fit society, tough sex harassment laws, animal rights, gay rights, women's rights, health care for everyone, legalized drugs . . ."

Mickey winced slightly, but they didn't see it.

Ken set down his knife pointer and leaned back. "That's the field," he concluded. "These guys couldn't agree on due north if they were each holding a compass. Malcolm thinks we should try and lump them all as insiders and run against the whole lot like they were one candidate. Tar them with the same brush. That means we should try and find a candidate that has never held a national office, somebody who's never bounced a check on the congressional bank or cast a midnight vote for a pay raise. Rhode Island governor Haze Richards is our choice. He has no legislative record to attack that would mean anything to anybody. He's photogenic. Show him the picture."

Van opened his briefcase and slid out a glossy print. Mickey was looking at a very handsome man in his mid-fifties who could have been in a Ralph Lauren ad—close-cropped gray hair, square jaw, blue eyes.

"He's a second-term governor, and all we need is to find a guy who can steer him for us so he does what we say."

The choice of that person, Mickey knew, was critical. It was a problem that had led to the meeting in Joseph's bedroom two days later, and now it seemed to be a man named A. J. Teagarden.

Mickey looked at his father, who was losing energy . . . His eyes were still fierce and bright, but his head was sagging on his weak neck and his cough was appalling.

"Mickey, you go up there tomorrow, let's see if we can get to this governor you found."

SOLOMON KAZOROWSKI

THE CLUB WAS ONE STEP BELOW A VEGAS CARPET JOINT. THE
slots were ringing and croupiers were keeping up a steady drone, making the place seem more interesting than it was.

Toozday Rohmer had started as a tall, seventeen-year-old blond dancer at the Stardust, but she'd had a fling with a pit boss who'd gotten her initiated into drugs and then into the sisterhood of the towel. It was just a short cab ride from high-roller hooking to fifty-dollar grudge fucks in seedy hotel rooms. While Solomon Kazorowski was still running the Organized Crime Bureau Strike Force in Vegas, he had trained her as an informant inside the hotel. She'd never been able to give Kaz the big bust he'd wanted but they'd become friends over the years. At Christmas he always gave her a magnum of Dom Pérignon. "Real class," she'd tell him.

There was something tragic about the Tooz, and Kaz couldn't bring himself to lean on her hard.

She had been born poor in one of those farm states that begin with a vowel. She soon became a victim of her own great legs, jutting breasts, and lack of curiosity. At age forty, she was still flatbacking and watching cartoons on days off.

She and Kaz had gotten drunk together one night, ten years ago. In what seemed like an obligatory salute to their sexuality, they had made listless love on the sofa in Kaz's apartment while his marmalade cat, J. Edgar, looked on.

It had been a mistake, so they'd never done it again and had agreed to be just friends . . . and they still were, even though Kaz had been dumped out of the FBI nine years ago for too actively pursuing Alo family ties to Governor Arquette and the casinos.

The way it had happened was almost impossible for him to believe. He had taken his mother to the Flamingo Hotel for dinner and the head waiter sent over a bottle of complimentary champagne and some caviar to commemorate the occasion. Kaz, who had never accepted a dime from organized crime, somehow had a lapse of reason and accepted the bottle and the tin of caviar. Maybe because it made him look good to his mother and he was showing off, letting her see what an important guy he was. Whatever caused the lapse, the underworld had hung the five-hundred-dollar tab around his neck like a dead fish. The Las Vegas press danced on his forehead. They ran a six-part story and sank his career in that magnum of champagne. All his life, Kaz had wanted was to be a fed—to stand tall in a company of men fighting for justice. He knew it was corny but he believed in the mission. The Alo family had orchestrated the end of his career, had convinced Governor Paul Arquette to put the heat on with his superiors. He'd been forced to go "stress-related" and put his papers in early to save half his pension. His life had been stripped from him. After all these years, Kaz still harbored a seething resentment. Even though he was benched by the "Fyc," his heart still pumped Bureau-blue. He was still looking for an opening, and was still dangerous.

"Fucking stage manager is always trying to cop a feel and this guy looks like he was bred in a mayonnaise jar," Tooz was saying. "I swear this place is a dump, the costumes don't fit. My G is climbing up my ass and I gotta wear Clorinda's extra shoes. She's two sizes smaller." Tooz was looking at Kaz, filling time with her bitching, thinking he looked old. He still wore the horrible Hawaiian shirts, but he'd gained weight and looked ten years older than his fifty-four years. Liver spots dotted his beefy hands. Getting busted out of the Frisbees had really taken a toll.

"Well, Tooz, whatta you gonna do?"

"Yeah," she nodded sourly. "You doing okay? I heard the Licensing Board turned you down again."

Kaz had been trying to get a private detective's license so he could get some of the growing divorce work that was hitting the town. Plus there were half a dozen runaways a month that had good repos on them. Most of them were teenage strawberries on the strip. Because of the enemies he'd made while he was busting mobsters in the casino counting rooms, they blocked him four times.

"Gonna have to get a job selling used cars pretty soon," he said.

"Listen, reason I called is I got something sorta strange the other day."

"What's that?"

"Well, there's a girl I dance with, Cindy Medina. Her sister works in the Coroner's Office and there's a rumor down there that when they did the autopsy blood screen on Senator Arquette, it showed he was H.I.V. positive."

Kaz looked at her, his mind going back ten years. He always suspected Arquette was a shill for the Alos. He had gone in and swept the governor's suite in the Sands after he'd checked out, hoping to find something. He hadn't gotten anything to confirm his suspicions, but he had found a man's bikini wadded up and stuffed in the Jacuzzi drain. It had a hotel gift shop label. He'd gone down there and found out it had been put on Paul Arquette's bill by somebody he didn't know named Warren Sacks. Warren turned out to be Paul's media consultant. Warren and Paul had died together last week in the Bahamas. Kaz had his suspicion that something was going on between Warren and Paul, but nobody had anything to prove Paul was bisexual so they'd let it drop. Maybe, just for the hell of it, he ought to see what he could find out. God knows, he had plenty of time and he still had one or two friends in the Coroner's Office.

"Thanks, Tooz. You're a doll and you're prettier every day." He thought she looked tired and whorey.

"And you're aging like vintage Dom Pérignon," she lied, wishing he would lose weight and get a haircut.

They leaned over and kissed. They could smell the sweat and Scotch on each other. When he left, they both felt sadder than when he had arrived.

It had taken Kaz four calls from the pay phone in the lobby to finally track down the medical examiner, Chuck Amato. Chuck was on the golf course and he finally answered his cell phone.

"It's Kaz."

"Jeez, Kaz, I'm playing golf. I'll call ya back."

"Question. You handled 'the cut' on Senator Arquette when they sent the body home two days ago. . . . Right?"

"I ain't got time, Kazy. I'm hanging up a foursome behind us."

"Was Paul Arquette HIV positive?" He dropped it without preamble, listening for a gasp of confirmation. What he got was silence.

"Where'd you get that?"

"It's on the street."

"Look, he was our ex-governor and our senior senator. Let him R.I.P."

"R.I.P.? What's that stand for, rot in purgatory? The guy was shacked up with hoods all his life."

"I gotta go."

"I've gotta take this evasive answer to mean yes."

"Don't do this to me, Kaz. Besides, what difference does it make? He's dead."

"I have a piece nobody else has. Believe me, it makes a difference."

"Go fuck yourself. I'm gonna get beaned with a golf ball I don't get outta here." And he was gone.

Kaz knew he'd hit pay dirt. Ten years ago, he'd hung an illegal wire on Paul's house. Kaz was the only one who knew that. Back then, Paul Arquette had occasionally been sleeping with Penny Alo. He'd been saving that info to use at just the right moment on Joseph. But before he could use it, he'd been canned.

Solomon Kazorowski got into his old, gray Chevy Nova and drove slowly back to the Lazy Daze Hotel. It was a flophouse and cost him ten dollars a night. He climbed the stairs to his second-floor apartment and stuck his key in the door and opened it. There was a note from what was loosely called the Management. He was a week behind on his rent. The note was a warning shot. He didn't know how he was going to pay it unless he sold the Chevy. He wadded up the note and dropped down on the bed. The springs creaked with age but Kaz was smiling.

How can I get these fuckers with this? he thought. And his new roommate, a black and white tabby named Jo, jumped up on the bed and looked at him.

"I wonder if Pauly gave it to Penny? That would be something worth knowing," he said aloud. "I wonder if Joseph found out and had Pauly killed?" The black and white cat sat on the bed, licked his paws, and purred. "What if that shark attack was bullshit?" The unanswered questions tumbled in his mind like criminal laundry.

CHAPTER 7

SEARCH FOR INTREPID FARMS

DAWN BROKE LIKE A CHEAP WINE COOLER SPREADING AN UGLY red stain on the gray ocean. A sadistic construction crew was working a jackhammer in Ryan's head. His stomach was on an E ticket ride. By eight o'clock when he had started to feel like he might live till noon, his agent called. Jerry Upshaw was raging.

"Look Ryan, I don't know what you expect from me, but I can't represent a guy who's calling the head of Drama Development a Jew faggot and threatening to knock his teeth out. Jeez, what the fuck is that?" Jerry had been Ryan's agent since his hit television show *The Mechanic.*

"Jerry, this is really pissing me off. I never called him a Jew faggot. I just said it was his fault the picture turned out bad."

"The bottom line is I can't represent you any longer."

"Jerry, look . . ."

"Hey, no looks, bunky. I've got other people I have to try and sell to Marty Lanier. If I keep you on my list, it's like I'm saying I don't care that you threatened his life and called him a Jew faggot. It's like I'm in tacit agreement. End of story. I'll send your other material back to you. Good luck, Ryan." And the line went dead.

End of story, Ryan thought.

He looked out at the beach. A man on horseback was coming toward him, riding the horse carefully in the dry sand. It reminded him of the day that Matt had died. Ryan and Linda had been up in Santa Barbara having a weekend together while Matt had been sent off to stay with friends in northern California. It had been Ryan's idea. He'd insisted on it.

He'd sent Matt away to die.

He and Linda had driven up to the Biltmore in Santa Barbara for the weekend.

Linda wanted to take a walk on the beach and they had ended up almost a mile down the strand sitting on the sand, looking at the water. A man on a beautiful Appaloosa had ridden up the beach. Linda was on her feet, talking to him.

"He's beautiful," she said, rubbing his shiny coat. "Where'd you get him?"

"Intrepid Farms," the man said. "They raise the best Appies on the Coast."

Linda ran her hand down his flanks and withers, looking in the horse's eyes, smiling and cooing at him, giving him affection.

It was two o'clock and they hadn't eaten so they walked back up the beach to a restaurant on the pier that overlooked Santa Barbara Bay. They sat out on the sundeck and ordered beer and sandwiches. Then Linda started to obsess about the horse.

"I really want a horse like that. Did you see him? He was gorgeous." Linda was becoming nervous.

"Yeah, really great," Ryan said, seeing tension around her eyes, stripping beauty from her.

"Intrepid Farms. I'm gonna call." She bolted and Ryan, startled, followed. Linda was already talking on the wall phone in the bar.

"Operator. . . . It's got to be there . . . Intrepid, I-N-T-R-E-P-I-D."

Finally, she slammed down the receiver. There were tears in her eyes.

And then she was grabbing the phone book, tearing at the Yellow Pages under "Breeding Farms." Nothing.

"It's gotta be there. It's gotta be there!" Her frenzy was building and it was scary.

He finally got her back to the sundeck and they sat looking out over the sparkling bay. She drank her beer but silent tears were coming down her face.

"Ryan, we've got to find it." She was begging. He'd never seen her like that and he'd known her for fifteen years.

He paid the bill quickly and they left the deck.

"It's got to be someplace nearby," she said without logic, almost running to the car.

Ryan drove his red Mustang down random streets looking for a sign. They asked at half a dozen gas stations. It was a silly exercise, but he didn't know what else to do. She was wild with anxiety.

"Intrepid Farms," she said over and over to herself, her desperation growing. Ryan looked at his watch. It was three-fifteen. And then, suddenly, Linda got very still. She sat looking at her hands in her lap.

"We can go home now," she said, her voice limp.

"We can keep looking."

"No, it's okay."

The phone was ringing when they arrived at the Bel Air house.

"Is this Matthew Bolt's father?" a woman's voice asked.

"Yes," he said. "What is it?"

"This is the Montecito Hospital. Hold on for Dr. Marples."

And then he was on. A voice Ryan didn't know.

"You have a son, Matthew Bolt?"

"What's going on? What's happening?"

"I'm sorry, sir, but your son was swimming in the surf and he got swept out to sea. . . . By the time the lifeguards got to him, he'd been under for almost five minutes. We tried to revive him. He died at three-fifteen this afternoon. I'm very sorry."

Ryan let the receiver fall and looked at Linda.

"Is he dead?" she asked softly.

Ryan could only nod. She sank to the floor and put her head on her knees. He stood there, unable to get his mind to accept it, unable to see his life without his son.

That had been the end of Ryan and Linda. What little cord was binding them had been severed by Matt's death. But one thought never left him. She knew Matt was going to die and she knew when he was dead. At three-fifteen she had stopped struggling against it.

What let her know he was dying while Ryan had no inkling?

Why had he been left out of the cosmic conversation?

It was as if he didn't deserve to know.

WONK

ALBERT JAMES TEAGARDEN WAS STILL A BACHELOR AT FIFTY-
five. His belly was beginning to hang over his trousers. He had a
permanent stage-three dandruff storm that fell on his dark suits
like Idaho snow. His personal habits were sometimes gross, and he
was often seen wearing flecks of his breakfast in a bushy beard that
was turning gray. It was also rumored that he was hung like a fire
hose. All of this acted as camouflage for the laser weapon that was
poised inside his head. A. J. Teagarden had the political instincts of
a German field marshal. He understood the system and its players.
He was fascinated by power and the people that wielded it.

He had created a big stir when he charged into the national Democratic party's office in Washington and accused Ron Brown of cor-
rupting the primary system. Ron Brown had just changed the
timetable of the southern primaries. The South had always been a

fire wall for Democratic politics. The Democrats controlled the South with money and strong precinct organizations . . . that is, until Jimmy Carter. The obscure Georgia governor had managed to come out of nowhere usurping the Democratic National Committee's official choice, Walter Mondale. Carter had carried state after state in the South, riding the wave of free publicity created by the network anchors, or "big feet," and had swept into the White House without the sanction of the party.

In order to keep this from happening again, the Democrats had created Super Tuesday, when fifteen states all had primaries on the same day, eliminating the chance of a Carter-type sweep in the future.

A. J. Teagarden felt that they had made the system vulnerable to a hijacking, and he charged into their offices and told them so. Security had been called to remove him. He'd been blackballed from national politics ever since.

He now languished in his law offices in Providence, handling real estate zoning problems and dreaming of a comeback. He was what was known as a wonk, a political insider, someone who knew the system and the game—a behind-the-scenes player who would rather die than run for office himself. He hid his weaknesses and fears behind a biting sense of humor.

He was a priest of the process. He was also, deep in his soul, a patriot.

He had received a call from a local mobster named Robert Pelico. "The Pelican" had demanded a meeting in a motel ten miles east of Providence. He figured that Pelico wanted him to talk to the governor about some legislative changes in the Rhode Island off-track parimutuel system that his crime family had been getting fat off of for years.

A.J. had been told, on the phone, to go to room 15, and just walk in. He'd receive further instructions once he got there.

The phone was ringing when he entered the empty room.

"This Teagarden?" an unfamiliar voice said.

"The one and only."

"Car is pulling into the parking lot. Go." And the line went dead.

The man driving the car was a bull-necked suitcase with fruity cologne that dulled A.J.'s thought.

New York Tony put the car in gear and pulled out, without speaking. They drove down the road and into a field where there was a bend in a raging river. Most of the snow had melted and the sun was shining. A.J. got out and moved toward a man he had never seen before, who was leaning against a picnic table, his breath fogging the air around his head.

"I'm Mickey Alo," the unattractive man said.

They stood looking at one another, sizing each other up. A.J. knew a lot about Mickey Alo. He'd heard stories about his ruthlessness. The man in front of him was short and fat, but radiated danger.

Teagarden had been in rooms with some of the most powerful men in the world and had never felt a moment's hesitation speaking his mind, yet something about this pudgy man made him feel awkward.

"What can I do for you?" He was off guard.

"I understand that you have some connections with the governor of Rhode Island."

"We're friends."

"How close?"

"Close. Lived on the same street. Took baths together when we were six. Want to see our high school yearbook pictures?" A.J. struggled to regain his confidence.

"We are about to have a conversation that never took place. Are we clear?"

A.J. nodded.

"We're interested in how you feel about running Haze Richards for President of the United States."

"You gotta be kidding."

"Why?"

"He's got no national base, no name identification, no campaign financing, no state organizations, no staff, no voting record, and no time. The Iowa primary is in three weeks. You guys may be able to move local politicians around like pawns on a board, but the national game is played differently."

"Let's say we can influence good national news coverage from a major network. Let's say we can guarantee all the campaign money you need. Let's say we can assist you in creating good name recognition. Let's say all of that can be accomplished in three weeks. . . . What kind of candidate is he?"

"The best."

"Why?"

" 'Cause he does exactly what you tell him. Correct that, he does exactly what I tell him."

"You can control him?"

"Like he runs on batteries." They looked at each other, the rushing river the only sound.

"We want you to talk to him about running," Mickey said.

"Iowa is in twenty days. Skatina and the others have been working the state for months."

"I guess you're the wrong guy." Mickey pushed away from the park bench and started toward his car, which was a short distance away.

"Hold it. I didn't say it couldn't be done. It's just . . ."

"I just told you we had powerful resources. Name identification? You gotta be shittin' me. . . . David Koresh became a national figure in two days. It's simply a matter of how hard you want to push and how big the issue is."

"Where's the money gonna come from?"

"It'll be there. . . ."

"You gonna be sending cash to mail drops in manila envelopes with no return addresses?"

Mickey didn't answer for a long moment, while his eyes did a survey of the unkempt man before him.

"You know who I am. You know what I do. I sell entertainment products that give me certain cash problems. We stack up dough in warehouses in Caribbean tax havens. Two-foot-long rats come out of the jungle and eat the money before we can ship it. Instead of feeding rats hundred-dollar bills, we're gonna send it your way. You set up a finance chairman and sound bank accounts and get ready to stack the money, 'cause it's gonna be coming at you fast in five-hundred-dollar brown envelopes. A campaign is a perfect cash laundry—no way to trace the money. You tell me how much you need and I'll get it to you as quick as the mail gets there."

A. J. Teagarden's mind was reeling.

"I've got to talk to Haze. He might not want to run." Then, brushing past that detail, his mind rushed on. "I'm going to need to put an organization together, set up offices, get advance people on the plane to Iowa."

"I've got some people working on this project now. You can keep them or throw them out. I don't care," Mickey said.

"Who are they?"

"Malcolm Rasher."

"He was working on Paul Arquette's campaign," A.J. said.

"Now he's working for me. You want him?"

"He's good. A great strategist."

"I think he's a yuppie shine with an attitude."

"What could be better than having a black campaign manager? It sends a politically correct message. I mean, Haze looks good with a black running the show, especially since I'll be behind him calling the shots. Who else?"

"I've got two pollsters—Ken Venable and Guy Vandergot."

"They're okay. We can keep them." His mind was racing. "I'll have to oversee them. I have some thoughts on polling and stature strategy. We'll need an issues staff and a press secretary. Maybe I can get Vidal Brown."

Mickey looked surprised. Teagarden had snapped up the offer so fast it was almost frightening.

"One other thing," Mickey continued. "Haze Richards has to know who's behind this. You gotta get him to talk to me at least once before we start. If I'm gonna buy this guy a seat in the Big Chair, I want him to know he's gonna have to do a few things once he gets elected." He handed A.J. a telephone number. "Somebody there can get in touch with me twenty-four hours a day."

Mickey nodded at New York Tony, who walked over to the car and opened the door.

"I'll be in touch in a few hours," A.J. said. He got in the car and New York Tony pulled out, leaving Mickey standing next to the river.

These wonks . . . they're a breed, Mickey thought. The Democratic party had put Teagarden on the beach, and Mickey just threw him back in the water. He was already swimming. "This guy is perfect," Mickey said to the raging river.

* * *

All the way back to the motel, A.J.'s mind was in full advance. It was the offer of a lifetime. Paul Arquette had obviously been a mob candidate. He'd died in the Bahamas and now they wanted Haze. He didn't need anybody to point out the possibilities to him. The underworld had the cash. If they controlled a TV network, like Mickey hinted, it could make a huge difference. A.J. knew that once the campaign got rolling, it could fund itself on national momentum. Mafia money would just prime the pump and get them started. He knew he could get Haze to run. They'd talked about the possibility for hours on end over the years. A.J. already had an election plan. He knew that by front loading the system, the DNC had made it vulnerable to just the kind of highly financed attack that Mickey had described. He could hijack the nomination with just a little bit of luck. His idea hinged on the fact that there were only thirty days between the Iowa caucus and Super Tuesday.

He'd worked it all out in his head a thousand times. All he'd lacked was the money to pull it off. The Mafia was such an obvious answer it made him laugh. He was about to show those fucks at the DNC. The wonks had put the system up for sale and now Albert James Teagarden, the black sheep of the fraternity, was going to steal it from them.

THE MAN FROM PROVIDENCE

HAZE RICHARDS DIDN'T KNOW WHAT TO WEAR TO THE MEET-
ing. He was standing in his closet looking at the array of custom-
made suits and finally chose a charcoal-gray that looked great with a
dark maroon silk tie.

After dressing, Haze stood in front of a three-way mirror and patted
his rock-hard stomach. At fifty-five, he was still square-jawed and
broad-shouldered, with dimples in each cheek . . . pale blue eyes that
contact lenses enhanced to the color of tropical water. He loved the
way he looked.

He flashed his capped teeth and wondered if A.J. really had something. He'd soon see for himself.

He met A. J. Teagarden in the entry foyer of the governor's mansion. They moved past the velvet ropes that separated the public area
from the First Family's living quarters.

Despite the length and duration of their friendship, he and A.J.

had very little in common, except for a love of the political system. They'd grown up living next door to each other. Haze had been the star athlete, lettering in football, basketball, and track. Albert J. Teagarden was president of the debating society, and Haze's campaign manager when he ran for class president. A.J. came up with the strategy and Haze made the speeches, and they always won. But Haze never understood how A.J. could work so tirelessly for Haze's goals.

As they walked out of the governor's mansion, Haze thought, as usual, that A.J. looked as if he'd slept in his clothes, but Teagarden *was* brilliant. They moved into the parking lot and got into a white Chevy, a state plainclothes car with "G" plates. A.J. drove the car erratically, never watching the road, looking over at Haze as he talked.

"Jesus, watch where you're going. We're gonna end up as hood ornaments on a bus," Haze exclaimed.

"Mickey Alo is dangerous. He looks like the Pillsbury dough boy but scary as shit. Just listen to him. He's got an agenda. We don't wanna run him off. I'm not sure this is a done deal, he could be looking at other guys. . . ."

"Lemme ask you something."

"Shoot."

"The Iowa Caucus is in a month. . . ."

"Twenty days."

"How the hell're we gonna go in there and make a showing? Nobody knows who I am. I've got no farm policy, no strategy, no message. . . ."

"I can handle it. Believe me, I know what to tell those Jo-Bobs. I've been polling Iowa half my life. I worked two national campaigns in that state while you were still a DA."

"He's gonna want things. . . ."

"Everybody wants something," A.J. said, flatly.

They pulled up at the deserted gas station ten miles out of town that Mickey had picked for the meeting. A.J. turned off the engine.

"What're we doing here?"

"You haven't dealt with these SpaghettiOs. They thrive on bullshit. For all I know, they're gonna swoop in here in a hot-air balloon wearing Porky Pig masks."

They showed up in a rented motor home, a big, blue and white thirty-seven-foot Winnebago with New York Tony driving.

"See," A.J. said. "We're in a gangster movie."

They got out of the car and New York Tony opened the RV door to admit A.J. and Haze Richards. As soon as they were inside, New York Tony had the rig moving again. Mickey Alo was seated in the small dining booth and didn't bother to get up. Teagarden made the introductions.

"Haze, this is Mickey Alo." Haze shook his hand but didn't sit; instead, he held on to the cabinetry as the vehicle moved along.

"This is a pleasure," Haze said, feeling pretty good already. Mickey Alo was ugly. He knew it was foolish, but he'd learned that his looks gave him a psychological advantage over unattractive men.

"I hope you're enjoying the great state of Rhode Island," he said, turning up the hundred-kilowatt smile.

"Sit down and stop grinning at me," Mickey said to the governor of Rhode Island. "I'm not a fucking broad."

"I beg your pardon?"

"I don't want an autograph. Okay?"

"Okay," Haze said, feeling diminished as he sat down.

"Not there. Sit over there." Mickey pointed to a chair across from him. Haze moved to it and sat. A.J. knew there wasn't much he could do to steer events; he just had to pray and let the chips fall.

"I run an organized-crime family. . . . My father is the boss of the New Jersey mobs. I'm his *consigliere*. We deal in things that are deemed to be illegal by the government. Me an' some friends in several states have decided to become politically proactive and see if we can change some of the shit that's buggin' us."

"Such as . . . ?"

"Such as we want to overturn the RICO Act."

"That's a congressional act. It's not easy to rewrite legislation like that. You'd need two thirds of the House and Senate."

"We want the Supreme Court to overturn it."

"How do you figure that's going to happen?"

"If we elect you President, we expect to help you with Supreme Court nominations. I have an actuarial table on the sitting court that says just on age probabilities alone, four members should retire or be in the ground in the next year or two. I put you in the Oval Office, I want you to pick the guys I want."

"You can't control the confirmation process."

"We'll worry about that when the time comes. The justices I select will have good legal backgrounds. They'll be middle-of-the-road . . . easy to confirm. They just won't like the RICO Act."

"Once they're in, how you gonna guarantee they'll vote the way you want?"

"They're gonna vote the way I say because, if they don't, I'm gonna kill everything they give a shit about, right down to their pets and goldfish."

There was a long silence. A.J. cleared his throat.

"What else?" Haze said, his voice a whisper.

"You neuter the Justice Department. Slow them down, replace the attorney general with somebody who isn't gonna be so contentious."

Haze could feel twinges of fear. A.J. had been right. It's the singer, not the song. . . .

"Also, I want a new head of the FBI."

"Anything else?" Haze wanted to loosen his tie. He was sweating. For some strange reason, he thought he felt heat coming off Mickey.

"That's it. Everything else, you do exactly the way you want. Foreign policy? I could give a shit. Urban renewal . . . ? Bomb the fucks into the Stone Age or give them a block party. I don't care. Everything else is yours, but you fuck with me on what I want, I swear I'll take out your heart with a butter knife."

Haze wondered if the thermostat in the motor home was set too high.

"Here's the deal . . . I finance you for President of the United States, I control media coverage to maximize your success. I buy you the office with cash from my illegal operations. I don't care what it costs. . . . My business makes billions a year, but I can't spend it in prison. You do these few things I want. Simple, clean, no chance of misunderstanding. That's the deal."

"I need some time to think it over."

"You know right now whether this works for you or it doesn't. You tell me in thirty seconds or the offer is off the table."

A.J. Teagarden had to admire the way Mickey was handling it.

Mickey had proven to Haze that he wasn't a man to fuck around with, that he was a man who would push the limits of the game. They were already onto a new playing field, treacherous but so full of promise that it was startling it hadn't happened before.

"Deal," Haze said, his voice shaky.

"We'll be in touch. A.J. will be the conduit for our communication."

When they pulled back into the empty filling station, not more than ten minutes had elapsed.

Haze and A.J. got into their plain wrapper and drove back to town. They didn't speak. It was best to leave everything unsaid. They had just witnessed each other's corruption.

In the motor home, New York Tony closed the door.

"Looks like we got a candidate," Mickey said. Then, almost as an afterthought, he opened the cabinet behind the table, unplugged the video camera and removed the tape that had recorded the entire negotiation.

THE JOB OFFER

"HELLO," HIS VOICE WAS SHAKY.

"Who's this?"

"It's Ryan Bolt."

"Jeez, Ryan, didn't sound like you, buddy. It's Mickey."

"Mickey." He smiled. "Where the hell are you?" Acting now, pretending, needing to be somebody else for a while.

"I'm out here at the Bel Air. Got the presidential cottage. I ran a recon mission by the pool. They put out a bunch a' easy targets. Got twenty-five-year-old skin laying around, half-naked, on chaise lounges. We could score wearing Nixon masks."

"It's just, my car's in the shop. I'm kinda stuck out here," Ryan hedged.

"I'll send a car for you. Stay where you are. The Mick has a tank rolling." And Ryan was listening to a dial tone.

"Fuck." He was too screwed up to leave. Too full of anxiety, but

Mickey hadn't given him a choice. Then he thought maybe what he needed was to fight through it . . . to be with somebody like Mickey who tasted life. Maybe it would take his mind off the mess his life had become. He remembered, Mickey could make stuff happen.

The Bel Air Hotel was a Hollywood aquarium where white swans drifted lazily in the landscaped lakes. Wealthy studio whitefish had private cottages and schooled out by the swimming pool waiting for their divorces to become final. Occasional agents prowled the restaurant, dorsals hissing, little pieces of insincerity stuck in their teeth.

New York Tony had driven Ryan there in a black stretch limo and led him to the presidential cottage which was up behind the pool.

Tony knocked on the door. . . . "Me," he said gently and, in a moment, the door opened and Ryan was looking at the most beautiful girl he'd ever seen. She was in her late twenties with glossy black hair. Her eyes were green and iridescent, her olive skin like natural silk. She was in a tennis outfit and it showed off her exquisite tan legs. Ryan thought, *What is Mickey doing cruising the pool with this goddess on hand?*

"Ryan?" she seemed to know him.

"Yes . . ." his voice tight, stomach acid still flowing like sewer runoff.

"It's me, Lucinda. Mickey's sister. Don't tell me you've forgotten me completely?"

"Lucinda . . ." he finally said, his mind desperately grabbing at rungs on a memory ladder.

"Yeah. We met when I was just a kid. I can tell you this now." She smiled. "Back then I had a terrible crush on you."

He tried for a rakish grin and missed.

"Come in. Mickey's on the phone."

She led him into the antique-laden room. New York Tony stood by the door. Mickey was on the phone, his back to them. He was wearing a polka-dot shirt and Bermuda shorts, with sockless loafers. His Rolex gloated openly.

"Okay, check that out and get back to me." He hung up the phone, turning, his round cherubic face changing gears completely as he broke into a grin.

"Hey, Ryan. . . . Sis turned out pretty good, no?"

"She certainly did." Ryan was having trouble taking his eyes off her.

"She's on her summer break." Mickey put his arm around his little sister.

"You aren't still in college?" Ryan asked.

"I graduated from Sarah Lawrence and I'm doing my doctorate in psychology at UCLA."

"I couldn't get her to go to Harvard." Mickey grinned.

"After the damage you did to the family name, they'd have had me under twenty-four hour surveillance," she joked.

"Hey, come on, I wasn't that bad . . . Was I that bad, Ryan?"

"You were awful." Ryan smiled, remembering a couple of lost weekends when they'd met occasionally in New York during their college years.

"Gotta go, got a tennis lesson at one. Good to see you, Ryan." She stopped in front of him, holding out her hand, looking into his eyes. . . . And then she was gone.

"Come on," Mickey said. "Let's get lunch. I made a reservation in the hotel dining room."

The maître d' led them to the best table.

"Hey, Ryan, don't take this the wrong way, but are you okay?"

"Sure. Why?"

"You look fucked-up. You're not doing drugs, are ya?"

"No. Come on. . . . You nuts?"

Mickey hadn't changed at all, Ryan thought. Always right to the point with no bullshit. He still had that force of personality that drew people to him.

"Lucinda is beautiful," he said, trying to change the subject.

"Yeah, she's a sweetheart. She counsels kids who can't get their belts through all the loops. Spends hours with them."

The maître d' himself brought the menus and pulled out a pad to take their orders.

"Hey, Claude. . . . You 'member those vongole I had here two months ago? With the angel-hair . . . ?"

"Vividly, sir." Claude grinned. "We sent ten gallons to your mother, airmail."

"Can ya whip us up some a' that . . . for two? And the real dry chardonnay, the Acacia." Claude left, bowing out in reverse.

He had ordered for both of them as if what Ryan wanted didn't matter, and somehow it was okay.

"So, how's everything going with you?"

"Tearing up the field," Ryan lied.

"I know a few guys out here and the word I been gettin' is you been stepping on your rep." Mickey frowned. "I hear you're packing an attitude and when they see you coming, they drop the blinds. I'm thinking that doesn't sound like the old wide receiver, so I figured I'd look you up." He was smiling but his eyes weren't. "What's the play?"

"Since Matt died, nothing has worked quite right. I'll punch through it." Ryan remembered how Mickey had flown out when Matt died. He'd lived in the Bel Air guesthouse and handled everything for Ryan. He even picked out the clothes Matt was buried in.

The food came and Mickey ate savagely while Ryan picked at his plate.

"Look, I don't wanna get in your face, man, so if I'm outta line, tell me, but if you wanna change of venue, I maybe have something set up that could work for you. . . . Take you away for a while."

"What are you talking about?"

"There're these guys. We do a little business sometimes, and they're running a guy for President of the United States. . . . I was talking to my friend and he said they needed somebody who could produce a documentary. I know that's chickenshit stuff to a guy like you, with Emmys and everything, but if you're looking to get a little air between you and these L.A. hairbags, I could make a call."

"Documentary?" Ryan said. "I never did a documentary." His heart was racing. Something irrational told him to take it . . . to get the hell out of here. All the memories, the shadow dreams. The self-centered sameness of his life was crushing him. He'd been heaping one lie on top of another to stay afloat, hoping everyone else he knew failed so he might win. He'd never been that way before. He knew that he had somehow poisoned himself. . . .

"You still with me?" Mickey asked, bringing him back. "Like I said, it isn't my boogie, but I know I could set it up. Tell you what . . . I gotta stay out here for a day and fix some things for Pop. I can set it up tonight and we'll fly back to New Jersey tomorrow. I'll introduce you to these guys."

Ryan was frozen with indecision. Mickey read him.

"What happened to you, man? What happened to the guy who used to run fucking Z patterns in front of rabid linebackers? You're sitting here with a complexion gray as spoiled meat. The Mick has gotta pump some voltage in t' you."

Something about Mickey's energy stirred old feelings.

"Why not," he finally blurted. "Make the call."

"I can tell you, now you've said yes, you're saving my ass on this, buddy." Mickey grinned. "I promised these guys I'd find somebody to do this film, and here I end up with Emmy-winning Ryan Bolt. . . . They're gonna shit."

Ryan felt himself blushing, and Mickey looked at his watch.

"I gotta go. Could you do me a favor? I promised Lucinda I'd take her to dinner before this came up. Would you get me off the hook and take her for me?"

"Sure."

"Tomorrow, you and me and Lucinda fly on my dad's jet back to Jersey. It'll be old times."

It was happening so fast, it was all Ryan could do to hang on.

They were sitting on the porch of the bungalow in the yellow sunset. She had changed since her tennis lesson and was wearing shorts and a silk blouse. She was breathtakingly beautiful. There was something so sweet, so simple about her that Ryan felt he was in the presence of royalty. He felt recharged by the light in her green eyes.

Without warning, he heard himself say, "I've been having a terrible time lately. I've been acting irrationally. I'm having . . ." He stopped. Why was he telling this gorgeous girl this? He sounded like a complete head case.

"You have anxiety attacks?" she said, finishing his thought.

"Yes, dreams where I'm chased by dark, evil presences that I can't identify."

"You've pushed your shadow away."

He looked at her. She was staring into his eyes, completely invested in him.

"Whatta you mean?"

"I'll give you a book . . . it's called *Meeting the Shadow*. It's a lotta Carl Jung and Joseph Campbell, but it's fascinating. What it says is, if you deny your dark side, you will stifle yourself. Everybody has a devil in them. These kids I'm working with are so angry, they could almost kill. I try and get that darkness out. I try and get them to confront it. Maybe you have something in your past that you've repressed. If you could find out what it is, it would free you."

"Repressed, you mean something in my past that I don't even remember . . . ?"

She nodded.

"And it has something to do with Matt?"

"It could, but Matt is in your conscious. The shadow is in your subconscious. Losing Matt could be stirring it up . . . like sediment coming up from the bottom."

He looked at her for a long beat. They were sitting here in this artificial lily pond with white swans, in the middle of a riot-plagued city, breathing smog and talking about his psychotic tendencies, yet somehow it seemed perfectly normal.

"Will you marry me?" he joked.

"If you'd asked me when I was seven, the answer would have been yes."

They sat in silence for a long moment.

"Do you ever think of Rex?" she asked suddenly, her face strangely blank.

"Yes, occasionally." He wondered why she had asked.

"That was the weekend we met," she finally said.

GETAWAY

THE LEAR WAS ALREADY OUT OF THE HANGAR WHEN ELIZABETH pulled her Ghia through the gates that were manned by a field attendant.

"I still think you should stick around," she scolded Ryan. "Just 'cause Marty Lanier didn't like the rough cut doesn't mean you can't get an order. What am I supposed to tell Freddie Fredrickson when he calls?"

Fredrickson was the president of the TV Division at Universal. He and Ryan had been allies until the roof caved in on Ryan's career and now Fred glowered at him like temporary office furniture.

"They're not gonna call. I'm dead, Elizabeth. They just haven't put the headstone up yet. You know it, I know it."

She had parked in the heat by the side of the hangar.

"Look, Ryan, I got an offer from Mel Thomas. He's doing the new

Judd Hirsch series. They want me to start next month. I told them I couldn't leave you, but . . ."

"Liz, take the job," he instructed her. "We shouldn't go down together."

"I feel like I'm deserting you."

"I deserted myself, hon. You gotta look out for yourself."

She leaned over and kissed his cheek.

"You know how much I care for you?"

"Me, too. Take the job, Elizabeth. It'll make me feel better."

Lucinda was seated in the back of the plane, her feet up on the gray upholstered seat, as Ryan came aboard smiling.

"Hi," he said, waving at Milo, the pilot, and moving back to join her. She was wearing jeans and a work shirt; a blue blazer lay on the seat next to her. He moved her jacket and sat down.

"Where's Mickey?" he asked, looking around.

"He has to stay over two more days."

She reached into her purse. "I got something for you," she said and pulled out a paperback book. The title was *Meeting the Shadow*.

"You remembered."

"Yep."

"Look, about yesterday . . . I think I came off sort of like a head case. I'm sorry. I don't want you to think I'm out of control."

"Vulnerability is more attractive than invincibility.'

"Is it?"

"For me. Somebody who isn't afraid to show his weakness is always more interesting than some showboat with all the answers."

Soon they were in the air, heading out over the San Gabriel Mountains, leaving the L.A. nightmare behind.

Ryan looked at Lucinda, struck by her composure and beauty. He tried to see Mickey in her, but there was absolutely no family resemblance. Silence hung like a velvet curtain between them.

"So you're working on your doctorate," Ryan said, pushing it away. "What's it on?"

"Bereavement. Guess you know a little about that."

"More than I need to, I think."

Suddenly he was very, very tired. Something about being here with Lucinda relaxed him. Within a short time, he fell asleep.

He awoke some time later and saw that she was looking at him. He turned his eyes away and thought, "God, could I be getting this lucky?"

The answer was waiting in New Haven.

THE SHADOW RETURNS

AT FIRST, IT WAS JUST A VOID, AN ALL-CONSUMING NOTHING-
ness, and then the dark shape passed him—bigger than before—evil
and deadly, trailing pieces of Matt's clothing in the currents behind
it. The Florida Sea World T-shirt from the trip last summer, curling
in the blackness, wafting in emptiness. Matt's shirt, then his tennis
shoes caught on something. The shape went by him in silence but
the roar that followed was the blood pounding in his ears. A simian
eye swept past, seeing him, seeing the shallow desires that guided
him. He didn't think he could stand another pass, another look into
that eye, but the shadow turned and came back.

"Are you ready, Daddy? Here we come."

Ryan bolted up out of a sound sleep, his heart racing. He didn't
know where he was but finally put his thoughts in order. Pool house.
The guest room. He was at Mickey's father's New Jersey estate. It
was eleven-thirty in the evening.

He got up and moved slowly to the bathroom to look at the now-familiar mask that greeted him after bouts with the shadow—hollow eyes, tight lips, a look of desperation.

He dressed, left the pool house, and went wandering out on the grounds. It was cold, but at least the chill made him feel alive. A full moon turned the landscape silver. And then he saw her by the garden. She sensed him before she could have known he was there.

"Couldn't sleep," he said, as she turned.

"Me neither."

They stood in silence.

"Isn't Rex buried around here someplace?"

"He's over there." She pointed to the right.

"You warm enough?" he asked.

"I don't get cold. It's a family trait. Good circulation or something."

"Whatta you doing out here?"

"I was . . . I was talking to God." It had never occurred to him that she was religious. Ryan had no formal religion. He believed that something out there governed things, but he found his church in a field of flowers or a beautiful star-filled night. Ryan had never felt close to God in formal settings.

"What were you telling Him?"

"None of your business." She grinned. "Come on, let's go inside. You look frozen."

They moved through patio French doors into the living room. She turned on one light, and they sat down on the couch in front of the unlit fireplace. She picked up a pillow and put it in her lap. It was funny how comfortable he felt with her. He didn't have to be anybody. With Linda, he always had to help create an image of perfection for others. Only occasionally were they focused on something else, like the night they found the bird in the house.

"You look sad," she said, reading him again, perfectly.

"I guess."

"What are you thinking?"

"Nothing, really."

And then suddenly he wanted to tell her—share it with her—even though it made very little sense.

"It will probably sound odd."

"How will I know unless you tell me?"

He smiled and let a long-protected thought go free. "In our Bel Air house, Linda and I were about to go to bed when we heard this chirping sound," he started slowly. "I walked into the entry and there was a robin sitting on the chandelier. Linda and I knew we had to get it out. We had to save that bird. It became the most important task on earth. So we opened the doors and all the windows and we tried to flush it out . . . Linda waving a towel at the poor thing, me swinging a broom, and then it would take off, flying into walls, landing on the floor. Every time we'd almost get to it, the bird would take off and fly into another room."

"What happened?"

"Finally, after at least an hour, she caught it. The robin was so tired, it just let her pick it up. She carried it outside and set it on the ground. We watched for an hour, but it wouldn't fly. Finally we went to bed. In the morning, it was gone."

"Was that before or after Matt died?"

"It was the night he left. The next day, we went to Santa Barbara and he died. How'd you know that?"

"Because of the way you said it."

"It was like an omen," he said. "He was in our life. We put him out and the next morning he was gone."

"It will get better, Ryan. All things change and become something else. Pain often forces us to grow."

She reached out and took his hand.

"I'll see you in the morning." He stood as she got to her feet. And then he kissed her. It was a quick kiss and not quite on the mouth.

"Don't leave without saying good-bye," she said as she turned out the lights and started up the stairs. He walked back to the pool house and stood there in silence. Something was different. It took a moment before he could identify what it was. It was a sense of calm, the first peace he'd felt in months. He turned off the light and stretched out on the bed. He thought about the shadow. He would fight it. He felt some of his confidence return. Like in college when it was third and long and they called his number. Back then, he knew if the ball came near him, he would catch it. For the first time since Matt died, he looked forward to what tomorrow would bring.

LOOKING FOR A PONY

THE DOOR OPENED AND RYAN WALKED INTO A FLURRY OF ACTIV-
ity. Twenty people were milling on the small concrete floor, which
had few offices, little furniture, and no carpet. A volunteer was pulling
campaign fliers of Haze Richards's last gubernatorial election out of
a box. The Haze Richards Presidential Campaign Headquarters in
Rhode Island was a study in organized confusion. Ven and Van were
on phones trying to get airline schedules to Iowa.

"I need forty seats, minimum . . . to Des Moines," Ven said. "How
'bout Iowa City or Cedar Rapids?" He listened for a moment, then
said, "Okay, book it," and slammed the phone. "Hicks," he said,
glancing up at Ryan.

"I'm Ryan Bolt . . . looking for Malcolm Rasher. He's expecting me."

"Mal," Ven yelled at the top of his voice.

A door opened twenty feet away and Malcolm Rasher looked out.

He was handsome, a tall, black yuppie, with a Polo wardrobe and rimless glasses. "What?" Malcolm yelled back.

"There he is," Ken Venable said. Ryan introduced himself to Malcolm Rasher and they shook hands.

"You gonna make the documentary?" Malcolm asked.

"Tell you the truth, Mr. Rasher, I don't know what I'm doing here."

"We're pulling the troops together right now. This is a scoot an' shoot operation. You got a crew, equipment, anything?"

"Before we pay for all that, don't you think I oughta know what I'm trying to say?"

"Probably right. Come on." He led Ryan into a conference room with a scarred wooden table. There were half a dozen people sitting around talking.

"Sit down and buckle your seat belt, Ryan."

In a few minutes, the other members of the team had arrived and Malcolm closed the door. There were ten including Ryan.

"Okay, everybody shut up and turn on your tape recorders," Malcolm started. "All of this is only gonna get said once. I'm available for questions, but try and steer clear of bullshit. We're gonna sink if we don't get the Big Mo immediately."

Nine small tape recorders came out and got turned on. Ryan wished he'd brought one.

"Okay, let's start with introductions. We're going to have a name and job test tonight at six. Everybody has to know everybody else, what they do and their phone numbers. If any of you thinks this is stupid, you haven't worked a campaign where people don't know each other. I've made out my fact sheet with my job definition and phone numbers—it's on the long table outside. Let's go around the room. . . . To my right is our campaign chairman, Albert James Teagarden, A.J."

A.J. waved. "I'm going to be working on strategy, message, and polling with Ken Venable and Guy Vandergot. Anybody has any ideas, I want to hear them. I'll have more to say in a minute. My fact sheet is on the table."

Then a pretty woman sitting next to Teagarden stood. Her ash-brown hair was silky and her figure showed the hours she'd spent in the gym.

"I'm Susan Winter, the body woman."

Ryan had never heard the term before and wondered what it meant.

Malcolm caught his look of surprise. "A body woman or man, for those who don't know, is someone who is with the candidate constantly. She will handle hotel rooms, extra phones in the suite, making sure the hotel refrigerator has the right stuff. She's also in charge of minute-to-minute scheduling. If the governor needs to be out of a press conference and on a six o'clock plane, she's the one who tugs his sleeve."

Ryan was scribbling it all down on a yellow pad.

"Vidal," Malcolm said.

Vidal Brown stood up. He was striking looking. Half-French and half-Paiute Indian, he'd been educated at Colgate. Ryan recognized him; he'd run press conferences for other Democratic campaigns.

Brown said, "I'm press secretary. I'm a twenty-four-hour commando-type Injun. No time is the wrong time. I love suggestions. Fact sheet, same table."

Next to him was a blonde with a bunch of rubber bands around her wrists, under which she had stuffed phone messages.

"Carol Wakano, and yes boys, I've heard all the Wacko Wakano jokes. I'm campaign finance. You hear of anybody with money for Haze Richards, I want the name. By the way, all mailed campaign pledges over five hundred need to be cataloged for the election review process. Anything less is exempted from that restriction."

"Rick and Cindy Rouchard," Rick said as he and his wife stood. They were Mr. and Mrs. Middle America. "We're Iowa Advance. We're going to be setting up the funders and booking the local TV in Iowa. I don't need to tell you that the *Register-Guard* Convention Center debate Tuesday is going to be critical to our news coverage, so I hope the candidate is ready for it."

"When we get to Iowa, Haze isn't going to stay in the Savoy Hotel with the rest of the candidates," Rasher said. "He's going to be at a farm someplace." He turned to the Rouchards. "Find an Iowa farmer who's about to go broke. Some guy with a sad story. Haze is going to sleep there."

"Great idea," Rick said.

Then it was Ryan's turn. "I'm here to make a documentary. I don't have a fact sheet but I'll get one on the table immediately." He sat down, not knowing what else to say.

"I want you, with a crew, filming the news conference in Providence when Haze announces," Malcolm said. "I'm gonna get the local blow-dries and live-at-fives from here and Providence." Ryan knew he was talking about local TV field reporters. "Get blanket footage on the press conference. What're you going to call this documentary?"

"I don't know . . . I hadn't thought."

"We need a flashy title like . . . like . . ."

"Blizzard in Iowa?" Van said from the end of the room.

"Yeah, that's the right idea," A.J. said. "But blizzards are cold, our guy is hot. Haze is on fire."

"Prairie Fire," Ryan heard himself saying.

"Perfect. 'Prairie Fire.'" A.J. grinned. "That's the documentary. We're gonna be the only ones with good Haze Richards footage and the networks will be forced to use our stuff. If they want it, I'll make 'em use it uncut."

Then Ven and Van stood up and said they were the pollsters. "You know what we do," they said and sat down. Ryan didn't know, but made a note to find out.

The two other people were staff and media relations, Ryan scribbled on his pad, making notes about their appearance so he could keep them straight for the six o'clock quiz.

Malcolm leaned back in his chair. "The candidate is Governor Haze Richards. All of you here are professional campaign workers being paid for your services. Some of you have only a marginal understanding of what the candidate represents. Our campaign chairman, A. J. Teagarden, will be able to fill you in on 'the message.' A.J. has known Haze since childhood. . . . A.J."

Teagarden lumbered up out of his chair. Most of these people he knew; some he'd worked with before and hired for this campaign.

"When I was a little boy," he started, a smile on his face, "Every Christmas I asked my parents for a pony. . . . "

Some in the room had heard the story before and started to smile.

"Christmas morning, I'd look under the tree, but no pony. I'd look in the kitchen, maybe he'd be in there. . . . After all, ponies got hungry. No pony. I'd look in the garage—everybody knows ponies need room. . . . but no pony. I looked and looked. I wanted to ride him to school . . . feed him, pet him. But what I got was roller skates. So I'd put on the roller skates and you know what would happen . . . ?"

"Would you get a blister, A.J.?" Vidal asked, grinning.

"Bet your ass, Vidal, I'd get a fucking blister. And you know why I got the blister? Because I was so upset I didn't find my pony, I would skate and skate to get rid of my disappointment. Now what does this tale of my youth have to do with this campaign?" He grinned at them, stroking his bushy beard. "I'm still looking for ponies. A pony is anything good. A blister is anything bad. We need to avoid getting blisters.

"I did a survey ten years ago. I asked focus groups all over the country a bunch of questions, and then, last year, I asked the same questions to other groups made up of the same social and demographic cross sections. Ten years ago, when I asked people if national politicians cared about them, ninety percent said yes. Even if they didn't always agree with the result, they felt elected officials had their best interests at heart. Just ten years later, astonishingly, eighty-five percent said no—a complete reversal. Eighty-five percent of this country doesn't believe in the system anymore. They don't think politicians give a shit. They don't perceive any difference between the two parties. They're fed up and, hear me on this . . . angry. . . . They're angry as hell, yet in the face of this groundswell of anger, there isn't one voice out there saying, 'I can fix that. I can make the system work.' The press doesn't write about this frustration. It's not a story because everybody accepts it." He looked around the table. "This massive opinion shift has gone virtually unnoticed, unreported, and unresolved. We are in the midst of the second great American revolution and nobody's talking about it. Well, people, this is about to change. We have the strongest, most potent message imaginable.

We're going to tap into that anger, tap into that frustration. We're going to be the candidacy of change. Haze has never run for national office, but every single one of these other candidates has been sucking on the national tit for years. They're a part of the system that the American public is furious with. We're gonna lump all these guys together and we're going to make them wear the clothes of that discontent. So . . . what's the message? It's simple, and it's gonna be as clear and beautiful as an Iowa sunrise."

He looked around the room, taking a minute for the dramatic impact.

"Haze Richards is going to make America work again for you."

They were scribbling it down on pads.

"No more meetings where Congress votes through their own pay raises at midnight. No more limos in the Senate garage. No more budget-stimulus packages. No more check kiting on the House bank. No more billion-dollar peanut-farm aid programs. No more presidential air force. No more horseshit, lying, stealing, taxing and spending. No more! No more! *No more!* Haze Richards, the man from Providence, an outsider who hates what's happened as much as all of us. . . . Haze Richards is going to take America back. He's gonna make America work, goddammit. He's gonna make it work again for you!" His voice was thundering off the back wall of the small room.

He looked around at them, all of their faces turned up at him. "And that, my friends, is the pony every American has been looking for. That message played right wins us the presidency."

They started nodding and smiling.

"We run above the issues," Malcolm said, his voice seeming small after Teagarden's impassioned oratory. "It's not about gays in the military, or health care, immigration, abortion, women's rights, or minority programs. It's about Americans losing control of the system. We want America back and Haze is going to give it to us."

"Haze Richards is going to make America work again for you," A. J. Teagarden finished. "That's the message. Malcolm will give you the strategy." And he sat down.

The room was silent and the lean, black yuppie spoke.

"I've talked strategy with most of you," Malcolm said, "It's sim-

ple. We've got to score big at the Des Moines *Register Guard* debate next Tuesday if we expect to get national press coverage.
Right now, Leo Skatina is polling over fifty percent in Iowa, but it's
on name identification alone. He's a familiar face, but we can cut
into him. The other three guys have modest and equal chunks of
the rest. About twenty percent is undecided. Our goal is to beat
the shit out of them at the Des Moines debate and then get the
press to run with it."

Vidal said, "I got some bad news there. Because of budget problems, most network news shows have cut back their live coverage in
Iowa. The only network sending out a live team is UBC," Vidal continued. "Koppel, Jennings, Brokaw, and the rest of those media big
feet are gonna chill it. CNN will be there, as usual, but even their
coverage will be cut down."

"All we need to do in Iowa," Malcolm said, "is get twenty percent
of the vote and run a strong second to Skatina. If we do that, we're
gonna look like we're taking off like a rocket. Everything, every bit of
our effort, the whole banana goes into Iowa."

"What about New Hampshire?" Susan Winter asked.

"Without Iowa, there won't be a New Hampshire," Malcolm said.
"Right now, Iowa is the whole ball game."

When the meeting broke up, Vidal came over to Ryan.

"Do you know anyone over at UBC?" he asked.

"Cole Harris was married to a friend of mine."

"Cole Harris is dust. They axed him two months ago. He was doing
an underworld crime series that was killed by the news committee.
He accused Steve Israel of collusion and they sacked him the next
day."

"Really?" Ryan said, surprised, remembering the intense black-
haired newsman who had been in L.A. for a while. "I also know the
political editor for Steve Israel on the Rim in New York."

The Rim was a room on the twenty-third floor at the black tower
on lower Broadway that housed UBC. It got its name because of its
circular shape; news staffers and segment producers had desks looking
out toward the floor. The center was the set for the nightly news with
Brenton Spencer.

"Good. You check out your contact. I'll call Brenton Spencer," Vidal said.

Brenton Spencer was the star anchor and executive producer for the UBC nightly news. His ratings had been falling for almost six months. What Brenton didn't know was that he was destined to become the campaign's first big pony.

A COME-TO-JESUS MEETING

BRENTON SPENCER WAS SCARED TO DEATH. THE COLD JANU-
ary wind was tugging at the corners of his cashmere overcoat, chilling
his legs, freezing his balls. He stood in front of his Fifth Avenue
apartment building, waiting for the UBC limo.

The man he'd been summoned to meet was short and repulsive
and didn't give a shit about news. C. Wallace Litman owned the
network and he wanted happy talk. Just yesterday, they'd been fed
a segment about whale pups being born at Marineland, California—Shama and Heidi. The network satellited the footage from
the West Coast at five thousand dollars per minute, and they'd
rolled off two and a half minutes of whales and their trainer. Steve
Israel had put in some jokes, and Brenton had to turn to his co-
anchor, Shannon Wilkerson, and say, "There's a whale of a tale,
Shannon," and she said, "Oh, Brenton . . . that's very fishy. . . ." All
of this while homeless people were freezing to death in Central

Park and the Middle East was teetering on the edge of destruction. When he complained, they pulled out the November sweeps book, which showed a 10-percent erosion in the nightly news ratings, and Brenton had to swallow hard and hope to hell they weren't going to drop his option.

He had a contract coming up for renewal and the business affairs department at UBC hadn't even opened negotiations yet. A very, very bad sign.

Brenton dreaded the meeting with C. Wallace Litman. He knew if he lost the anchor job on the heels of this last rating book, he would be on the plane back to Cleveland and his old job at WUBY-TV, if he could even get it.

The limo finally arrived and took him to Litman Tower. The billionaire financier had the entire top floor.

On the way up in the private elevator, Brenton looked at his reflection in the antique mirror. He had a square jaw that jutted slightly, even white teeth, black hair graying at the temples. At sixty, he had that elder statesman look that should make viewers want to believe him, but somehow they were deserting him.

Now there's a whale of a tale, he thought to himself in abstract panic. The door opened onto a marble entry hall that was decorated with original artwork from world renowned masters.

A butler was waiting to take his coat as C. Wallace Litman moved briskly into the foyer.

C. Wallace Litman was always dressed for work—even in the evening or on Sunday he wore a three-piece suit and tie. He never removed his jacket. He had ramrod posture that held up his little frame to the very last millimeter of his five-foot, six-inch height.

"Nice you could come," Litman said as if the invitation had been open to refusal.

"I always love our visits, Wallace," Brenton said, realizing that he had started out with a wheedling lie.

"Have you seen this new art we just bought? Sally and I have been working through a broker in midtown." He strolled down the hall where paintings of various sizes hung in ornate frames under spotlights. "That's a Remington," he said. "That one there is a Renoir."

He reeled off the famous names but never looked at the art. Brenton realized that the paintings weren't there to enjoy; they were there to impress.

They moved into the den and Wallace sat down. Brenton noticed that his expensive suit didn't wrinkle or ride up on his shoulders as he settled back in the red leather armchair. His eyes finally came up and fixed on the frightened anchorman.

"Brenton, we have a problem."

"Most problems can be solved."

"Maybe not."

Brenton's heart did a two-and-a-half gainer and flopped against his diaphragm. He held his face steady, years of on-camera training working the miracle.

"I don't pretend to know what makes people watch TV," Wallace continued. "Since I bought United Broadcasting, I've been shocked at what the public tunes into. But we're in an advertiser-driven medium. If we don't sell aspirin, we've gotta take it 'cause we're gonna have headaches."

"You don't want to take the November ratings too seriously, Wallace. You know we were facing football runovers on ABC on the West Coast on weekends and Monday, and our local lead-in in New York and L.A. is that dreadful syndicated *Animal World* program. It skews young and we're not getting a good flow into news. . . . Those two markets are ten percent of the country. That really hurts." Brenton had gotten the research department to knock together this argument for him and he had the demographic research in his pocket. He started to pull it out, but Wallace stopped him.

"Brenton, I don't want to see research, I want to see ratings. The cold, hard fact is, you're trending down. How do I see my way clear to renew a two-million-dollar-a-year player who has suffered a rating decline of ten percent in six months? That's my problem, Brent." Litman rubbed his chin in theatrical thought.

"Where's this leading us, Wallace?" Brenton finally asked, dreading the answer, beginning to get one of his headaches.

"We're losing money on the news. The news is supposed to be a profit center. I'm in business to make profits."

"Then don't cover the Iowa convention. We're going to send two SNG satellite trucks and a sixteen-wheel control room out there.

We're the only network sending live coverage. It's crazy. Whoever decided to do that should get his IQ checked." Brenton suspected Steve Israel had made that call.

"I think Iowa is important. It was my decision," Wallace said, "and I think my IQ may be at least as high as yours."

This fucking meeting could not be going worse, Brenton thought. I'm about to get sacked. Then the little financier got to his feet, moved over to the anchorman and put a fatherly hand on his shoulder.

"How would you like me to renew your existing contract?"

"Huh?" Brenton said, his accustomed elegance disappearing.

"Whatta you say we sign you up for two more years at the same salary with a ten-percent bump in the second year. That would take fiscal '98 up to two-point-two. Let's say you retain your executive producer and anchor status, and we put a new magazine show in work for you. I've asked Steve Israel to start developing it. I want to call it *Above the Fold*—that's an old newspaper term for important stories carried above the fold of the paper."

Brenton had been in news half his life. To have this rich asshole explain that to him was mildly irksome, but he let it fly past, his mind locking on the lifeline that seemed to have been thrown out to him.

"I think the show should be you and maybe five young on-air reporters, all of them sort of looking to you for advice on angles for the stories. It could be sort of a cross between *Sixty Minutes* and *West Fifty-seventh.*"

Brenton had been working on a hard-news magazine format he was calling *The Spencer Report.* He started to say something but Wallace waved him off. "If I'm going to do all of this for you, especially in the face of your slipping ratings, I'm going to need you to do something for me, and the favor I am going to ask might impugn your journalistic integrity."

"Integrity is simply a line that gets moved around to fit events," he said lightly, wondering what the billionaire had in mind.

"Have you heard that Haze Richards is going to run for President of the United States?"

"The governor of New Hampshire?" Brenton said, grasping for the right state.

"Rhode Island."

"He's got no national Q. He'd be a hopeless long shot."

"I want to get him elected. So you go on television the day after he announces, which will be tomorrow. I want you to start attacking him. Israel will give you the copy."

"I attack him and that gets him elected?" Brenton was smiling.

"I want you to be all over him. Beat him up . . . for two or three days. You ask America, What do we know about Haze Richards? What qualifies this man to be President? And we'll give you some negative facts about his tenure as governor. They're going to be slanted facts and very unfair to him. Really pile it on."

"If you're trying to get him elected, why would I attack him?"

"I've arranged for you to be the moderator of the Iowa *Register-Guard* debate from the floor of the Pacific Convention Center. We carry it live, and we'll script it for you to ask him something unfair and absurd like what qualifies him to run for the highest office in the land? How could he think he had the 'stuff' to run the country? Then he is going to come back with a demand that you apologize not only to him, but to the other candidates on the stage, for your attack. And then you're going to lose it—you're going to walk off the stage, right there, in the middle of the debate, outgunned by this little governor. It's going to make every local news break, every network lead story, it's going to put him in the race."

"But Mr. Litman . . . Wallace . . . You can't ask me to humiliate myself on TV. If I lose respect on television, I'll have no constituency. I can't do this. It's out of the question."

"In that case, it's been nice having you at UBC. I'm sorry we won't be able to continue our relationship." C. Wallace Litman went to the door and opened it. "Good night, Brenton."

Brenton didn't move. "I'm an asset to the network. You don't want to destroy an asset."

"You'll have two years to recover from one night and a prime-time magazine show to help you do it. The public forgets. By next Christmas, most people won't be able to recall exactly what happened and you'll still be in charge of the nightly news. All you have to do is have one bad moment, one public failure. Bush did it to Rather and he's still on the air. Only difference is, we're going to script it."

"Please, Wallace . . . don't make me do this."

"This is not a negotiation. You make this deal now, or I replace you." He looked at Brenton sadly as if he were calling up the memory of a dead friend. "I'd still rather have you, Brenton."

Wallace led him out into the entry hall, where they waited for the elevator. Wallace looked past the anchor to the elevator door as it opened.

"I need an answer, Brenton."

When Brenton finally spoke, his voice sounded as if he were on life support. "Can we call the new show *The Spencer Report?*" he asked, weakly.

C. Wallace Litman patted him on the shoulder but didn't answer the question. "Nice having you up. I'll have Business Affairs pick up the two-year option. Give my best to Sandy." And he reached in and pushed the down button.

As the door closed, Brenton looked at himself again in the antique mirror.

He looked older.

SOLOMON'S JOURNEY

SOLOMON KAZOROWSKI HAD BEEN IN NEW JERSEY FOR TWO days. He'd been sleeping in a down sleeping bag in his Budget rental car which he couldn't afford.

On Saturday, he'd found a good place in the woods above the Alo house. He'd had to cut down a few medium-size trees with a handsaw he'd bought, in order to get the small Chevy Nova up a hill to a place where he could park it and watch the house from inside the car. It was too cold to keep getting out and taking pictures with the starscope camera he'd borrowed from an old pal who was still working for the Vegas "Eye." The agent had also loaned Kaz five hundred and told him to please not get his ass shot off spying on the Alos. Kaz was determined to accept this advice.

From this spot, he could look down over the driveway and entry of the Alos' castle-style house. He figured unless somebody down there was really looking hard, they wouldn't see him. He'd gotten some good shots of a tall, blond, very handsome man who arrived on Sunday night with Mickey's sister. He didn't know who he was. He looked like an aging surfer.

On Monday morning, Mickey Alo arrived home. He went directly to his father's room. Kaz could see him through the starscope moving excitedly back and forth in front of the window. He was wondering what was going on.

Mickey was in his father's bedroom when the doctor left, having given Joseph a shot. Joseph was breathing in labored gasps. "Who's downstairs?" he finally asked.

"It's Ryan. He came down from Princeton for the night. He's in the living room with Lucinda."

His father grunted. Mickey had begun to regret having let Ryan and Lucinda fly east together. They had obviously started something up. Mickey had never dreamed Lucinda could get interested in Ryan.

Mickey had always been fascinated by Ryan. He never viewed him as a friend, because Mickey had no use for friends. Ryan played a different role in Mickey's life. Ryan was handsome and athletic—everything Americans worshiped, but Mickey had found that he could dominate him. As a boy, that had intrigued and entertained Mickey, made him know he was stronger, better. Now all these years later, that hadn't changed. Ryan's friends were a bunch of dipshits whose brains ran out their noses. It proved to Mickey he had been right to have no friends. He cared about no one.

At Harvard, he had learned that he was a clinical sociopath. The instructor had outlined the condition smugly before an abnormal psychology class. Sociopaths were highly intelligent psychopaths who felt nothing—not love, hate, gratitude, or jealousy. All his early life, Mickey had wondered, when his friends spoke of their emotions, what they were talking about. He had never felt anything. To cover, he had become an exquisite actor, learning to mimic emotions he didn't feel. Once, to test the depth of his hollowness, he had fantasized about killing his mother. Could he look her in the eye and blow her head off? Could he watch her brains and blood splatter on her upholstered headboard while she slept, or listen to her beg and plead for her life and still pull the trigger? He realized that he could easily perform the act. Except for a mild sense of gratitude, he had no feelings for her.

Lucinda came the closest to provoking any emotion. Lucinda was special to him, but he doubted if it was love as much as pride. She was his sister and she was beautiful. He took a perverse pleasure in that, as if she was the receptacle for all the beauty that had escaped him. He would not have his sister involved with somebody like Ryan Bolt.

Joseph was asleep now, and the phone rang in the bedroom. Mickey picked it up. A. J. Teagarden was calling from Providence.

"Everything's set for tomorrow," the wonk said. And then he went on to fill Mickey in on the status of the campaign.

Downstairs, Ryan and Lucinda were sitting in the living room. They had been talking about Ryan's first day in Princeton. He was trying to explain how exciting it was. There was the feeling of something about to happen. He liked the youth and enthusiasm.

"I still don't quite know what I'm doing there," he admitted, "but I'm hiring a crew to film the announcement tomorrow." He glanced at his watch. "The Film Commission said I should call back at six to get a confirmation."

"You can use the phone in Daddy's office."

Ryan moved out of the living room into the darkened hall.

Joseph Alo's office was next to the den, but Mickey had been using it for almost a month. Ryan moved to the desk and picked up the phone. He heard a strange hissing sound through the receiver. He tried to punch up a line but couldn't, and saw that the phone was attached to a large, black box labeled "TelaCenturia." There was a button on the box. He reached down, pushed it and immediately heard A. J. Teagarden speaking. The voice had a strange, tinny resonance.

". . . money coming in fast from the Bahamas. We're going to use it to buy TV spots in Iowa."

"Just a minute," he heard Mickey say. And then there was a click on the line. Ryan tried to get another line. This time he got a dial tone.

Seconds later, the door of the den exploded open and Mickey was standing there.

"What the fuck you think you're doing?" he said, spitting the words at Ryan.

"I'm calling this guy about confirming my film crew for tomorrow."

Mickey moved across the office, grabbed the phone, and smashed it down in the cradle. "You were listening in on my conversation."

"Calm down, will you?"

"This is my fucking office!" Mickey's voice was now controlled, but his demeanor was deadly. Ryan felt a strange energy coming off of Mickey, almost a kind of heat.

"Lucinda said I could use the phone in here."

"You were on that line. What'd you hear?"

"Nothing. Just A.J. talking about the Bahamas or something. What's wrong with you?"

Mickey moved around the desk and got close to Ryan. When he spoke now, his voice was a deadly hiss. "You're a guest here. Okay? You're in my house. You stay outta my office. You don't listen in on my calls."

"Mickey, I wasn't listening in. I was just trying to get a line."

There was a long moment while they stood facing each other, and then Ryan put his hand on Mickey's chest and pushed him back gently. "What the hell's wrong with you? You act like something's going on here."

"Just don't spy on me."

"What's this thing . . . some kinda scrambler?"

"I do a lot of sensitive transactions. We've had some business espionage, Pop had that installed." Mickey tried to evaluate Ryan. Then his expression softened.

"Look . . . I'm sorry. I guess my nerves are a little frayed. It's kinda hard watching your father die right in front of you."

"I shouldn't have been in here. I didn't know . . ."

"Naw, it's okay. You can use this phone." Mickey gave Ryan a sad smile. "The doctor just told me Pop is out of time. Maybe a month, maybe less. I just . . . I'm sorry."

He turned and moved to the side table where his open briefcase lay. He hesitated for a moment, then snapped it shut and took it with him, leaving the office and closing the door behind him.

Ryan stood for a long moment, his heart smashing against his chest. There had been a deadly glow in Mickey's dark eyes that scared him. Then Ryan dialed the Film Commission in Providence and was told that the film crew was booked. Ryan gave his own American Express card number to seal the contract. Then, as he hung up, without warning he saw the little redheaded boy again swinging high on a swing. This time, he heard a voice faintly in his memory.

"Ryan can't do this, I bet," the little boy said, pumping his knees, rocketing the swing higher and higher; then just like before, he was gone. . . . Ryan stood in Mickey's office wondering who the hell he was.

CHAPTER 16

EXPECTED ANNOUNCEMENT

THE GOVERNOR OF RHODE ISLAND WAS ABOUT TO THROW HIS hat in the ring. A. J. Teagarden was in Haze's bedroom in the governor's mansion. He had all of the campaign literature and news clippings about the other Democratic candidates on the unmade bed. Haze's wife, Anita, wasn't living in the master bedroom. A.J. knew she didn't sleep with Haze anymore; their marriage was a carefully orchestrated sham. He saw Haze, who was in the bathroom looking in the mirror, checking out his pearlies.

"I've been going through all this stuff since four this morning and I gotta tell you, these guys are running on special interest platforms. Every one of them. Dehaviland, with his environmental policy; Savage, with his liberal, New Age reconstruct-the-workplace-to-fit-the-work-environment horseshit; Gulliford is Mr. Labor, Mr. Old-Time Religion. Leo Skatina has his women's issue. All of them are Washington insiders; all are drinking from the same pail."

Haze came out of the bathroom, running his tongue over his teeth. "Yep." He looked at his watch—forty minutes till the press conference. He looked out at the glass enclosed rotunda where he gave most of his TV interviews and where the press conference would be held. There were a few news vans pulling in, not nearly as many as he expected.

"I hope I'm not gonna be singing to an empty church."

"It doesn't matter. I don't want this announcement to be too big. Since we're coming in late, I'd rather take them by surprise, hit them from the blind side at the *Register-Guard* debate in Des Moines tomorrow. Keep it short, stay on the message, no issues."

"Come on, A.J., I wanna talk about issues. I've got a great thing on immigration." He stopped because A. J. Teagarden had buried his bushy head in his hands and was groaning in mock misery.

"Don't pull that shit, A.J. I've seen that routine a hundred times."

"We're going to run above the issues," A.J. said, taking his meaty hands down and looking at Haze. "I don't wanna talk about the issues. You talk issues, I'm the fuck outta here."

"What else can we talk about?"

"We're gonna run on the message. The message is: Haze Richards feels the anger, America! He feels the frustration! He feels the disenchantment, the alienation, the sense of loss. And you know why he feels it? He feels it because he's one of you! Haze Richards is a fucking American citizen before he's anything else and, like every American, he is angry about all these special interest gurus . . . angry because, damn it, all these guys have been bought. Haze Richards never spent a day in Congress, never had a lobbyist buy him a free meal . . . never cut a deal with special interests that he had to pay back. Haze Richards is pure, man. He is the only goddamn candidate in this race who hasn't been bought."

"You kidding me?" Haze said, thinking back to the meeting in the motor home.

"Okay, but that's what you're going to say. You're gonna lead the second revolution in America, Haze. A revolution for the discontented. You're gonna make America work again, goddammit. And if you say a word about abortion or gay rights, I'll fucking kick your sorry ass off the stage."

There was a silence in the room.

"If you do this the way I tell you," A.J. said, softly, "I'll get you into the White House."

Ryan had taken a cab to Providence early that morning and met his camera crew. A tall, Oriental girl with a bodybuilder's physique, a plain face, and long black hair stepped up to him with a bone-crushing handshake.

"I'm Rellica Sunn," she said, grabbing the fifty-pound Beta-cam in one hand, her shoulder muscles flexing in a sleeveless shooting vest that held camera equipment. The temperature was in the mid-thirties and this girl was walking around in Palm Springs clothing. Standing with her was a narrow-shouldered sound man with a Nagra unit and a directional mike.

"Ryan Bolt," he said, introducing himself.

"Quite a party; what's going on?" Rebecca asked.

"I think Governor Richards is going to announce for President."

"Of what?"

"Funny."

The announcement was short and Ryan got blanket coverage. Haze stepped to the podium at exactly eleven o'clock and looked out over the crowd of friendly faces that A.J. had paid to show up as window dressing.

"I detect, in America today, a sense of loss and frustration . . . a sense of profound anger. The American dream, for many of us, has died. We no longer have a national purpose. We are reflections in a fractured mirror. We are fighting with each other and tearing the fabric of our nation to shreds. Why is this happening?" His voice rang in the rotunda. "Prices have gone up. Our GNP is down. Blacks and whites are rioting. Our products are inferior. We are losing out to foreign interests. In World War Two, we had a goal . . . and we won that war. The war we fight today is no less a war . . . no less about preserving America. But we are losing this war. It's called the war of economic survival. I don't think America is about losing. I'm mad, like all of you, because we've become second-rate. I'm mad that our system of government has been stolen by special interest groups. I want to take America back. I want to make America work for you.

This is your country and mine. Let's stop being angry. Let's change things." He took a long moment and looked at the cameras with resolution. "With that as my goal, I am announcing my candidacy for President of the United States."

The national big feet and local blow-dries packed up their equipment and got back in their vans as Haze moved off the rotunda into the statehouse.

"How did it go?" Haze asked A.J.

"Truthfully, you were all over the road. Riots? The economy? GNP? Don't bring up issues unless asked, then you shift back to the message. But it's a start."

Republic Airlines had twenty seats roped off for the Haze Richards campaign. They were all in the back of the 737.

Ryan and Rellica just managed to make the flight. To save money, they had sent the sound mixer home. Ryan could run the Nagra recorder. Rell said she'd work with available light. They shook hands to seal the deal. They buckled their seat belts and were off to Des Moines.

Ryan knew where the plane was headed but had no inkling where he was going.

NIGHTLY NEWS WITH BRENTON SPENCER

"LOOK UP," THE MAKEUP LADY SAID, AS SHE APPLIED **BREN**-ton's eyeliner. They were in his office on the Rim a few minutes before "Air."

Brenton's office was on the east side of the floor. White pile carpet, oak walls, and abstract art fought for center stage with a roomful of steel-and-glass furniture. The interior glass wall was fitted with electronically controlled drapes so he could close off the Rim if he needed privacy. He had an array of TV screens built into the far wall so he could monitor the other network news shows and a computer bank that was hooked into a Nexus program to update breaking stories worldwide. Brenton usually kidded with Cris from makeup but tonight he was distracted.

As he was getting ready for his broadcast, he went over some of the copy he had been given on the Haze Richards announcement. He had looked at the file film on the governor earlier in the day, and noted that Haze Richards was extremely handsome, a growing requirement in American politics. United States political campaigns had become beauty contests where men with capped teeth and two-hundred-dollar haircuts claimed to be just plain folks—the only tangible result of this that Brenton could see was America had the best-looking Presidents with the best haircuts in the world. The governor from Rhode Island fit the profile perfectly. Haze Richards had nothing in his backstory to recommend him. He amassed an undistinguished voting record while in the Rhode Island State Legislature; he'd gone right on some issues, left on others. The pattern continued after he became governor. He seemed, to Brenton, to be externally directed, a man who would chase public opinion.

"Little lip gloss?" Cris asked as she put some on with a Q-Tip. She was finishing the touch-up when Steve Israel, VP of the nightly news, stuck his twenty-nine-year-old bald head in, unannounced, and said, "You're on in two minutes."

Brenton heaved out of the chair, grabbed some aspirin for his dull headache, and winked at Cris.

"Break a leg." She smiled.

"Only if you'll nurse me back to health," he said, his heart not in the interplay, his temples throbbing.

"And now, a political commentary from Brenton Spencer," the P.M. announcer said. And then Brenton was on camera, seated in front of the world map in the center of the Rim while news staffers ran around in the wide shots with arms full of empty folders. The newsroom look had been Brenton's idea. Then the camera moved in close for his political update section of the newscast.

He looked seriously into the lens. "What New England governor is mad as hell and about to do something about it?"

The shot switched to some edits of Haze Richards. They'd picked his "angry as hell" sound bite.

The film clip started. "I'm mad that our system of government has been stolen by special interest groups. I want to take America back," Haze said from the rotunda.

In the control room, Steve Israel hunched in his seat behind the director looking at the "line" monitor as the "B-roll" footage on Haze's press conference was running. On the "preview" monitor, he could see Brenton fidgeting with his tie. "Tell him to sit up. He looks shitty," Steve said as the director hit the "God Button" and repeated the instructions to Brenton who sat up and put his hands to his temples and massaged them briefly. "Coming back from the B-roll on camera one in five-four-three-two take one. . . . "

The shot switched back to Brenton, who looked into camera as they made a slow push-in. "With that startling declaration, Haze Richards, a man unknown to most of America, hurried out of Providence and became the last Democratic candidate to head to Iowa and the big show that is scheduled to open tomorrow with the *Register-Guard* debate. So who is this man and why is he so angry? We know very little beyond the fact he was born rich, the son of a doctor. He has had a life of privilege. His government watch in Rhode Island has been marked by inconsistencies, failing even the most modest list of prerequisites for the greatest office in the world. How can a man with no outstanding achievements join a select group of qualified, tested politicians seeking the Democratic nomination? Unfortunately, in these times of media-created candidates, his lack of credentials seems of little consequence. He has no stated position, policy, or point of view. He wavers on important issues, even in his own state."

He went on to say what he'd been told to say. He'd never taken on a candidate so directly, and it scared him. He had moved outside his role of news reporter and entered the fragile territory of participant. And tomorrow he would fly to Des Moines, where he'd take a dive on national TV.

After the show, he felt light-headed and queasy. He went back into his office, pulled the curtain, and poured himself a shot of whiskey to calm his nerves and relieve the pounding pain in his head. Then, without warning, before he could drink it, he threw up into his wastebasket.

SLEEP-OVER WITH A JO-BOB

FORTY MINUTES OUT OF DES MOINES, THE HUGE JET TOOK A
series of bone-jarring, fifty-foot drops off of air ledges, throwing open
overhead luggage compartments and spilling their contents. The
flight attendants had their smiles fixed with adhesive insincerity, their
lips pulled tight against dry teeth. "It's okay. We're just experiencing
a little turbulence."

"Turbulence, my ass," Ryan thought. "We're in a Mixmaster."

Haze Richards lost his cool completely. Ryan had been trying to
film him sitting in the coach section. Rellica Sunn had been kneeling
in her seat, facing backward, gunning off footage of the governor,
who was sitting a row behind her studying Iowa grain-export reports.
But when the plane took its first huge kaboom, Richards's eyes went
wide.

"What's that? What's happening?"

Susan Winter tried to soothe him from the seat next to his. "Just turbulence."

Rellica went flying and would have hit the ceiling if Ryan hadn't grabbed her belt. She never took the camera off her eye. Ryan continued to hold her as the plane hit another deep air pocket.

"Turn around," Haze whispered in panic. "We have to turn around."

The plane lurched to the right, winged over, and dropped five hundred feet, free-falling . . . the engines screaming, handbags and briefcases showering down out of the overhead compartments like calfskin raindrops.

"Turn around, that's an order," Haze barked, his voice suddenly strong. "I'm the governor of Rhode Island. Turn around!"

A. J. Teagarden was slowly making his way to Haze, holding on to seat backs, pulling himself up the aisle, once losing his footing and falling to his knees with a painful whack. Finally, he reached Haze's side.

"Just Iowa Republicans throwing up a little antiaircraft." He grinned.

"I want us to turn around." Haze was pale as a Russian princess, his eyes darting around the plane in panic. And then the plane rolled left, falling sideways in a wing slip, both engines screaming as they sucked in the light, vacuous air.

"This is a direct order from the governor of Rhode Island. Turn us around immediately!" His voice was shrill, terrified.

Rellica Sunn was still shooting. Ryan was holding her around the waist with both arms, trying to keep her from flying around the cabin. A. J. Teagarden leaned over to speak to Ryan and Rellica.

"Turn that camera off. I don't think we're gonna wanna use much of this." When Rellica shut off the camera, Haze appeared to be sobbing.

"Damn it, Haze, stop it!" Finally, A.J. slapped the startled governor.

Miraculously, at that moment, the plane found stable air and they were all sitting in the cabin with the blank expressions of condemned prisoners, their luggage and papers strewn around in the aisle.

They landed twenty minutes later in Des Moines, Iowa, and piled out of the back door of the Republic 737, dragging their luggage, like refugees from a Texas flood.

The Rouchards met them at the gate.

They went to the Iowa Feed and Grain Show, where Governor Richards had his picture taken with the 4-H pig, sold kisses in the kissing booth, and watched prize Herefords on show in the small ring. The Rouchards had found a farm in Grinnell, Iowa, owned by a near-bankrupt couple named Bud and Sarah Caulfield, where Haze would spend the night.

The meeting between Haze Richards and the Caulfields was captured by Rellica Sunn on film. Haze hugged the ruddy potato farmer's wife on their sagging front porch.

"It's so kind of you to let me stay in your beautiful, beautiful home." He sounded like Robin Leach, bowing slightly at the waist, holding Sarah Caulfield's hand for a second too long to show he really cared. They all went into the house and Haze looked around the shabby living room with a picture of their dead son on the mantel. He'd been a casualty in Vietnam. Haze picked up the picture, looked at it for a long time, then set it carefully down as Rellica tightened the shot.

"Hunert-an'-sixth Airborne," Bud said, reverently, "Young Bud died during Tet tryin' to help get his buddies out." His voice cracked with proud emotion.

Later that night, A. J. Teagarden and Haze Richards huddled in the small master bedroom and talked about tomorrow's debate.

The room was done with no-frills simplicity. Faded yellow drapes faced a handmade wooden bed and dresser. A colorful quilt made by Sarah Caulfield's mother was folded over the foot of the bed.

"There's no mirror in the bathroom," Haze quibbled as he moved around the small room.

"We've got to go over this stuff," A.J. forged ahead.

"Shoot," Haze said, finally resigned to the small room. At least he wouldn't have to share it with his wife. Anita wasn't arriving until tomorrow.

"We're gonna stick to the message. Haze Richards is going to make America work for you."

"Come on, A.J., I gotta say more than that. . . . They're gonna demand to know where I stand. What if they ask me about gays in the military? I'm gonna say, 'I'll make America work for homosexuals'? ... That's nuts!"

"No, you don't say that. You look appalled. You look right into the camera and say, 'I think every American should have the right to serve his country if he wants to. I understand there are problems and I think we can work out those problems satisfactorily. But, damn it, this is just another example of special interest divisiveness. We're standing around arguing about gays in the military when the real argument should be, what is the role of the American military? Are we going to continue to spend one fifth of our gross national product on defense while people in this country are starving? Do we stand guard over every democracy in the world and, if so, what is the cost of that experience? Who pays for it? Do we bill rich nations we're protecting, like Japan and Germany and Kuwait? Or do we make hardworking American laborers pay? Those are the questions that the Haze Richards presidency will address. I'm going to make America work for all of you again.' "

"That's fucking gobbledygook and you know it."

"Pound the message home, Haze. It's the sure route to the White House."

Haze looked down at his glossy, pale fingernails.

"Okay, you want an issue? I'll give you an issue. All of these other guys are pandering to the Iowa voters. They're saying what they think Iowans want to hear, and none of 'em have a clue. Iowa's a farm state, so they're all supporting farm protection. Every damn one. So, let's go the other way. Let's take on farm subsidies."

Haze looked at Teagarden like he'd lost his mind. "Attack farm subsidies in a farm state? What're you smoking?"

"I've researched it. It's perfect. It makes you look courageous. Haze Richards talks the truth. You know this is political suicide, but fuck it, if you can't speak honestly, then this country is farther up shit creek than you thought."

"We come out against subsidies, we're dead."

"I don't think so. There's a big difference between the farm program, which you're going to support, and farm subsidies, which you're against. The farm program helps the little farmers, people like the

Caulfields. They're all Democrats. It gives them low-cost loans and pays them to let their fields lie fallow. We support that. But subsidies only help the big corporation farms and those guys are all Republicans anyway and wouldn't vote for you if you were giving away flathead tractors. It's a perfect issue. You make the other guys look like pandering assholes, and the real Iowa farmers will know you aren't hurting them because, believe me, these guys know the difference between the farm program and farm subsidies. I'm telling you, it's a perfect issue. I'll give you all your lines. Just do it the way I say . . . okay?"

A.J. thought Haze looked tired. Not a good sign for the beginning of the campaign.

"Something else . . . Brenton Spencer is going to harass you during the debate. He's going to characterize your candidacy as unqualified and unsound. Mickey Alo says they've gotten to him. When the time is right, I want you to shoot him down. I'll talk to you about it tomorrow when I've got something written up."

A.J. left Haze alone in the Iowa farm room. Haze looked out the window at the desolate farm that Bud and Sarah Caulfield had put their lives into and were about to lose. Haze thought they would be well rid of it.

The Caulfields had given over their house to the Haze Richards for President Campaign and, after dinner, had driven off to spend the night with a neighbor. Haze had their bedroom; Malcolm and A.J. had borrowed their dead son's room. Susan Winter got a couch in the side room. Ryan had been given the couch in the den. Rell Sunn had elected to sleep in the back of the van, which was parked in the barn. Ryan had worried about her sleeping out there in thirty-degree weather but she shook him off and bundled up Bud's down sleeping bag, grabbed a pillow, and moved to the door.

"Ain't ya heard . . . ? Wild rice won't freeze." She put a hand on his arm and smiled. "I like it cold. See ya in the morning." And she left, walking across the cold ground toward the wood barn.

Ryan spent a while wandering around Bud Caulfield's tiny den looking at the books. He pulled down one about crop rotation and flipped it open. Parts had been underlined and there were margin notes.

He was suddenly someplace else. In his mind, he saw another study with books all around. The red-haired boy was with him. "Come on, Ryan, come on," the boy said. "Race ya to the swing." Suddenly, he knew his name. . . . It was Terrance Fisher. And then the memory ended. He sat on the sofa in Bud Caulfield's cluttered den.

On the coffee table, there was a photo album. He opened it and found pictures of the Caulfields in better days: There were shots of Bud junior growing up. The last one showed him at a bus station in his new army uniform going off to war.

Ryan knew the pain of their loss.

He closed the album and thought about Matt. Then he turned out the light and lay back in the darkness. He felt he was close to something important—close to the shadow. Soon he was asleep.

And then he had the dream. . . .

He was standing by a swing in a backyard he didn't recognize. But he knew he was seven years old. He was watching while the red-haired boy named Terrance pumped back and forth on the swing. "Race you, Ryan," he yelled and jumped off the swing and ran toward the house. Ryan was after him, both boys running for all they were worth. In the dream, Ryan was everywhere, as in a poorly edited movie. . . . First he was behind Terry; then he was watching from the side; then he was back in his own body, chasing. His laughter came, tiny and hollow, as Terry rounded the pool. And then . . . Terry's feet slipped on the pavement and he screamed—splashing, floundering. Ryan saw it now in black and white—crude still frames blurred the memory. Ryan stopped and looked down, his feet frozen. He wanted to reach out to Terry but he was held by an invisible force—he couldn't move.

"Help!" Terry screamed, as he went down, gulping air and water, choking, fighting his way back up. The still-frame memories exploded in Ryan's head like emotional land mines. . . . "Help," Terry yelled . . . and then he sank below the surface.

In the dream, Ryan was standing at the pool's edge. He watched in terror as the red-haired boy sank deeper and deeper. The last thing Ryan saw was Terry's green-and-red paisley T-shirt as it flapped lazily against his dead playmate at the bottom of the pool.

Ryan woke up.

He was strangely calm and could remember the dream vividly. He was immediately certain it had really happened. And he knew he needed help. He moved to the phone, took out his AT&T card, and with hands trembling, punched in Lucinda's private line and then his charge number. The phone rang.

"Yes?" she answered, sleep in her voice.

"I've met the shadow," he said.

"That's great," she said, trying to grasp his mood.

"A boy named Terry. We were seven . . . playing in the backyard. He drowned. I let him drown, I didn't try to save him."

Lucinda sat up in her bed. She knew this might be one of the most important moments in Ryan's life and she didn't want to screw it up because her mind was blurred with sleep.

"Hold on a sec," she said and dashed into the bathroom to splash cold water on her face. Toweling it off quickly, she moved back and sat down on the bed. . . . Then she took a deep breath and picked up the phone.

"I'm sorry, I had to close the door. You still there?"

"I killed him," he said in a subdued voice. "Terrance Fisher lived next door, I think . . . or two doors away. I let him drown. I never told anybody." It was all flooding back into his head. He remembered running home, crying in his bedroom . . . afraid to tell anyone that his friend was at the bottom of the pool. His breath was now coming in gasps. He was starting to sweat.

"I just stood there and let him drown and I didn't tell anyone."

"Ryan . . . stop talking for a minute and listen to me. . . ." Her voice was smooth and controlled. After a moment, he stopped babbling.

"Take a deep breath."

She could hear him inhale.

"I want you to tell me, did you know how to swim?"

"I don't know. I guess so. . . ."

"When did you learn to swim? Do you remember?"

"At camp."

"How old were you then?"

"I went to camp in the summer after fourth grade."

"Fourth grade. How old were you in fourth grade—nine, ten?"

There was a long moment while Ryan thought about that. "Yeah," he said forlornly, "ten."

"If you were seven when he drowned, you didn't know how to swim. If you couldn't swim, you couldn't have saved him."

Ryan let that thought play in his mind.

"Ryan. . . . Listen to me, I'm coming out there to be with you. I'll get on an early flight tomorrow and be there after the debate, but I want you to think about something. I want you to think hard about it."

"What?"

"You watched your friend die when you were seven. You didn't save him because you couldn't, but you feel guilty . . . so guilty that you pushed it down in your subconscious . . . so far down you buried it completely. Then, thirty years later when Matt died, you tied the two events together." She stopped, wishing she didn't have to do this on the phone, hating the fact that she couldn't look in his eyes, see the reaction her words were having. But his mind was completely open to suggestion now. She had to get to him now. "Ryan, do you think that Matt was drowned as some kind of divine retribution for the fact that you didn't save your friend when you were seven?" she said. She could hear him breathing.

"Ryan," she pressed, "is that what you think?"

"Yes."

"If you couldn't swim, you couldn't save him. One event is not attached to the other," she said, hitting the words for emphasis. "Do you hear me, Ryan?"

"I hear you."

"You've met the shadow. You've met him, now you can slay him."

They listened to the silence between them for a long time.

"Could I be in love with you?" he finally asked.

"I hope so," she said softly.

They talked for another half hour about other things. Lucinda was afraid to hang up until she knew he was steady. The dream had crushed Ryan's tender grip on reality, but she knew it was a beginning for him . . . maybe for them.

Ryan never dreamed about the shadow again.

*   *   *

Rellica Sunn had been awakened at two A.M. by the sounds of grunting and moaning. She had been sleeping in the of the van and she got to her knees to look out the window into the barn.

Haze Richards was lying on top of Susan Winter. They still had their clothes on, but they had pulled their pants down to allow for coupling. They were pawing and rolling in the hay like two teenagers. Rellica watched for a few minutes, then settled back silently in the sleeping bag and listened as Susan ran the octaves, ending in a high, breathy squeal. Then Haze and Susan crept out of the barn, but Rellica Sunn couldn't get back to sleep. If someone like Haze Richards could get elected President, she thought, then something was desperately wrong.

When the Iowa dawn broke at 5:55, she was still awake.

DEBATE

BY FOUR IN THE AFTERNOON, THE SINGLE BLOW-DRIES, OR POD
people, as A.J. called them, were setting up their equipment in front
of the nondescript Pacific Convention Center in Des Moines. The
boxlike auditorium had been built in the 1950s to house rodeos and
farm events.

Each candidate had been assigned a place on the rostrum according
to a draw that had taken place earlier. Malcolm Rasher had drawn
number 4, which put Haze in a black leather chair between Florida
Senator Peter Dehaviland and New York Senator Leo Skatina on the
right side of the stage.

While Malcolm had been pulling the chair number out of a hat, A. J.
Teagarden had gone off with a small overnight case he'd brought with
him from Princeton. He was in search of the second-tier lighting box
that was the control center for the stage lights. He climbed a metal staircase into the auditorium attic and finally found the lighting booth. He

watched, in silence, as several technicians adjusted the carbon arc lights, aiming them through a glass window at the stage below.

"When're you guys on your union break?" A.J. asked casually.

"Who's asking?" a heavyset lighting technician wanted to know.

"Bob Muntz, regional shop steward from six sixty-nine in Iowa City," A.J. said, consulting his watch for effect. "You guys are entitled to fifteen-minute breaks every two hours."

"Break's in 'bout ten minutes, sir. . . . ''

A.J. sat in a metal chair, put his feet up on the rail, and looked out of the little glass booth, down at the stage fifty feet below. He saw Malcolm Rasher pointing at one of the chairs on the right side of the stage. A.J. tipped back in his chair and waited until the three lighting technicians looked at their watches and moved out of the booth on their break.

A.J. got up and walked over to one of the follow spots and turned it on to see which chair it was aimed at; then he opened the lens covers, exposing the carbon arc bulb. He licked his fingers and unscrewed the arc, replacing the 250-watt spot with a 500-watt halogen light he pulled from his bag. Then he closed the lens cover and moved to the other lights and changed them, too. The only light he didn't touch was the one aimed at the second chair from the right. He put the old bulbs in the bag he'd brought and left the booth quickly, whistling as he walked down the stairs.

Brenton Spencer arrived backstage early from his suite at the Savoy. He'd had a dull headache all day. They'd given him what they called the best dressing room. It turned out to be a yellow concrete dungeon with no windows and a brown-stained sofa. The makeup table had six lights out. He was going to complain but he thought, *Fuck it*; this was a suicide mission, no matter how he cut it. He'd brought his gray suit and his black bold-striped tie, which always looked good on TV. He took it out of a garment bag, along with a terry cloth robe, and stripped off his shirt and jeans. Before slipping into the robe, he stood in front of the full-length mirror in his boxer shorts and black socks and looked at himself skeptically. He felt funny, light-headed. The throbbing in his head started to build. Then, without warning, a blinding flash of pain hit his forehead and his vision went white. He sank to his knees in the dressing room, both hands went to his temples. It felt as if an evil beast had taken a bite out of the inside of his head. He sank lower onto the cold concrete floor and moaned. The pain in his head was so intense that he almost passed out, fighting to remain conscious, some survival instinct telling him to hang on to his consciousness. . . . If he let go, he knew he would fall into cerebral nothingness. He grabbed a towel off the chair and held it to his mouth, breathing in gasps through his nose. Whatever it was that caused the ripping pain started to subside. His forehead was throbbing horribly, but he no longer felt the razor-sharp cutting pain. He sat in terrified silence for almost ten minutes. Then he pulled himself up onto his feet and looked in the mirror. He was white and waxy. He moved on unsteady legs to the bottle of aspirin on his dressing table, shook half a dozen into his hand, and gulped them down with water from a pitcher on the adjoining table. Finally, he moved to the sofa and lay down, putting his feet up. He took several deep breaths.

"What the fuck was that?" he finally asked himself in wonder. He lay there, afraid to move, until it was time to get made up, dressed, and go on stage to meet the candidates.

Outside, the candidates started pulling up at the convention center, arriving like stars at a Hollywood premiere. Across the street, standing behind curb barricades, was a gallery of Iowa voters. The pod people were ready, microphones and cameras at port arms. Each candidate stopped to pose for pictures, and make a few remarks.

Then the front runner pulled up in a black limousine with six people in the back of the car, including the president of the Iowa Democratic Committee. Skatina was the Party choice and they had orchestrated the arrival.

The senator was confident. He was way ahead in the tracking polls and knew he was going to kick ass in Iowa.

"Tonight is gonna be a very special night because tonight we're going to make some promises to the women of America. And I think it's time those promises were made and kept. . . . "

The pod people had already started to pack up when a red pickup truck with the Caulfields and Haze Richards pulled up to the front of the auditorium. The fenders were muddy; the windshield was dirty.

Bud had wanted to wash the truck before they left the farm but A.J. stopped him.

It pulled to a stop and Bud and Sarah Caulfield got out; then Haze Richards stepped down on the concrete apron in front of the convention center. Single blow-dries looked up. Pod people turned. And then it dawned. . . . Oh yeah, that governor . . . from Rhode Island. Reluctantly, some of them got their cameras out again and back up on their shoulders.

"Arriving last is candidate Haze Richardson," Lon Fredericks from WXYO-TV said into his pillbox mike. "Governor Richardson, Governor Richardson," he shouted. Haze paused in the TV glare to hug Sarah and shake Bud's hand, then moved over so that all of the cameras could focus on him.

"Good evening," he said.

"Governor Richardson, you have almost no voter recognition in Iowa. Do you have any hope to win?" Lon Fredericks said.

"It's Richards . . . Governor Haze Richards. I don't know if I can win. I came here at my own expense to try and say what I believe."

"Governor Richards, Governor Richards, over here," Ken Venable called. He had wedged himself in with the press.

"Yes . . ." Haze said, looking into the eyes of his own campaign pollster.

"Who are those people you came here with?" Ken asked, throwing Haze the slow, chest-high pitch.

"That's Sarah and Bud Caulfield. They own a farm in Grinnell that is mortgaged to the hilt and about to go back to the bank. I spent the night with them. Bud and Sarah are the reason I'm in this campaign. I'm in it for them and for all the people like them. I want to make America work for people like the Caulfields."

He moved into the convention center.

UBC had parked their sixteen-wheel control room around the side of the auditorium. Nestled in beside it was the satellite news-gathering truck.

Brenton Spencer walked onstage and stood for a moment. He had a lavaliere radio mike hidden behind his bold tie and had pushed the audio receiver into his ear so that the cord ran down the back of his neck and into his shirt collar to a battery transmitter on his belt. Ted Miller, the director, hit the intercom switch.

" 'Evening, Brent. This is Ted in the truck. We're gonna be going live in two-twenty."

"Okay," Brenton said.

"We'll be giving you any political facts you need through your angel," he said, referring to the earpiece.

"Whatever," Brenton said.

Ted hit a switch in front of him, cutting Brenton out of the audio loop and turned to his sound man. "Is he okay? He sounds terrible."

The sound man shrugged.

Ted Miller hit the intercom, putting Brenton back on with him. "Brent, anything we can get you? Want any water?" But Brenton had taken the angel out of his ear. It was hanging down the back of his collar. "What the fuck?" Ted said. He leaned forward and spoke into his mike to the stage director. "Tell Brenton his angel is out of his ear. We need to talk to him before air. We're up in ninety seconds."

They could see the stage manager on the camera 2 monitor as he ran to the stage and said something to Brenton, who nodded but didn't replace the earpiece.

"He said okay," the stage manager said in desperation over the headset, "but he didn't stick it back in."

"Seat of the pants TV," Ted said. "We're up in five-four-three-two-take one." And the line monitor showed the wide shot of the stage with five empty chairs and a center podium. "Roll music and cue Bob," Ted said. And they pointed at the announcer through a glass wall in the remote trailer. As the bumper music played loud for a few seconds, then was dropped down, Bob Banks, in his rich, round voice, kicked off the 1996 political season and then went on to make the candidate introductions.

Malcolm Rasher sat with Ryan, Ven and Van in Haze Richards's cramped dressing room. They had the UBC-TV feed hooked into an eighteen-inch monitor. A.J. banged through the door with a slip of paper in his hand. "Just got the last Iowa poll. Came in twenty minutes ago. Skatina is at fifty-five percent. His people are down the hall opening the champagne already. They think in five days they're gonna landslide the election." He looked at the slip in his hand,

"Dehaviland is polling ten percent. He's got good internals. They want to like him but they don't get what he's saying. Savage is at fifteen percent, mostly because of young voters. And Gilligan is at fifteen. Good internals but his message is stale. Five percent unde-cided."

Ryan was adding it up in his head. "That's a hundred percent. Where's that leave us?"

"We're in the asterisk division. The Jo-Bobs don't even know we're running, but we're about to change that."

Brenton Spencer moved onto the stage. As the light hit him, he seemed to straighten, to come more alive.

"Good evening, I'm Brenton Spencer and I'll be asking the ques-tions tonight. First, let's meet the Democrat from New York City. Two-time U.S. senator, one of the shining lights in the Democratic party . . . Senator Leo Skatina."

Skatina walked out and took his chair. When he looked up, he started squinting as the blinding follow spot hit him. He tried to shade his eyes, then realized his mistake and lowered his hands.

"What's going on with the follow spot?" Ted Miller said in the control room. "He's burning up."

"We checked the lights this afternoon," the technical director said in a panic. "Jesus, they musta put halogens in there after we set up."

Skatina continued to squint, looking sinister in the TV monitor.

The next three candidates were introduced, and they, too, were blinded by the punishing lights.

"What's with the lighting?" Ryan asked. "These guys are on fire."

A.J. grinned. "Bunch a' shifty-lookin' fucks, if ya ask me."

Then it was time for Haze to make his entrance.

"And from the state of Rhode Island . . . a two-term governor, who only announced last week, a new name in national politics, Haze Richards."

Haze walked out slowly, completely at ease. Since his follow spot had not been altered he had no need to squint. He looked composed and alert as Brenton began the debate.

"Gentlemen, the agreed-upon rules are . . . I'll ask a question and I'll be allowed a follow-up. If any of you wants to make a comment after that, I'll recognize you, but there will be a two-minute time limit on all responses."

Brenton was moving now, prowling the stage, revitalized. A jungle cat in a silk suit and striped tie.

His opening questions were contentious, his responses argumentative, and the candidates were clearly unprepared for an assault by the moderator.

In the truck, Ted Miller agreed. "He's supposed to be moderating this debate, not joining it." Steve Israel's voice came through the speaker from New York.

"What's Brenton doing?" Steve asked.

"I don't know," Ted said into the mike. "His earpiece is out, we can't talk to him."

On stage, Brenton was striding over to Leo Skatina.

"Senator, you have made a lot of showy promises to women, yet I have the demographics of your own Senate staff. Only twenty percent are females."

"To show my sincerity on this issue, let me make a promise to the American people. If nominated, I intend to choose a woman to be my running mate."

In Haze's cramped dressing room, A. J. Teagarden leaned forward and spoke to the TV screen. "There's your opening, Haze. Go. Jump on it," he said, hoping his candidate would seize the offensive. He'd prepped Haze for that one. He was not disappointed.

"I'd like to address that issue, if I might," Haze said.

"Okay, let's hear from the governor of Rhode Island."

"It's this kind of needless divisiveness that is destroying our country. How many women are on Senator Skatina's staff is not the issue. The issue is, How many intelligent, hardworking staffers has Senator Skatina employed—Staffers who will strike at the waste in our government? Our country is being torn apart by this sort of needless conflict . . . men against women, blacks against whites, rich against poor. It's one thing to have a free exchange of ideas, but another to divide our country by creating needless controversy in pursuit of votes."

"All of which doesn't say much about what you think."

"I think to make a vice presidential choice based on color or gender is the high point of political insincerity. How 'bout we get back to what this country is all about and put the most qualified person in the job, regardless," he said softly.

A.J. leaned back in his chair and shot a fist into the air. "Yes! Pony!"

Brenton moved on to the domestic economy and military spending, with a sidebar on gays in the military.

Again, Haze was prepared and interrupted the discussion. "The size of the defense budget and gays in the military just aren't the issues that should concern us."

"You seem to have a lot on your mind, Governor," Brenton sneered. "If these aren't the issues, what are?"

"I think every American should have the right to serve his country, regardless of his sexual orientation. But, beyond that, the real issue should be, what is the role of the military in American society? Are we going to continue to put one fifth of our gross national product into defense and, if we do, what are the economic responsibilites of the user nations like Japan, Germany, and Kuwait, who take our help and pay us nothing? Is it right for the factory worker in Detroit to have to pick up the tab to provide military protection for a Japanese car industry that is putting him out of work? I say no. I'd like to take this government back from the lobbyists and lawyers and see if I can make it work again for all of you."

"Pony," A. J. Teagarden said. Now he was out of his chair, striding around the room.

On stage, Brenton turned to the camera and announced the commercial break.

The stage manager ran down the aisle and confronted Brenton.

"Put your angel in. Ted needs to talk to you."

He reached up and grabbed the angel that was hanging on the back of his collar. "You mean this?" he yanked it free and knelt down, handing it off the stage, then he walked back to center stage as the break ended.

"We're back at the Democratic candidates' debate here in the Pacific Convention Center in Des Moines, Iowa," Brenton started. Then he turned to Senator Dehaviland and asked a tough question about keeping illegal aliens out of border states.

A. J. Teagarden moved to the TV screen. "Kick that one in the ass, Haze. Come on, knock it into the cheap seats." He was so animated that Ryan couldn't decide whether to watch the debate or the overweight wonk who was eating the oxygen in the dressing room.

On stage, Haze turned to the audience. "I don't know how many of you sitting in this audience today were given an engraved invitation to come to America, but my parents sure weren't."

"Pony!" A.J. said.

"I think, again, we're talking about the wrong issues. Immigration? Come on. I'm not interested in attacking people who risk their lives to come here on leaky boats to make a new life. Every family, except for Native Americans, got here the same way. The real issue is a whole generation of children with no hope, no skills, and no dreams. Millions of minds and bodies being squandered because this country can't teach them to be productive. Immigration? I'm not gonna scare you with the demagoguery of fear. But I'll tell you what some members of the Congress won't talk about . . . they won't talk about the people who are really killing this country. Every Wall Street lawyer or special interest lobbyist who has been taking them out to lunch or on Florida jaunts, buying their influence in Congress, contributing fifty or a hundred thousand dollars a year in PAC money, buying their votes. Do you realize that while every American is trimming his or her budget, this government has voted to squander billions of dollars on useless giveaway programs? We actually spend one hundred million dollars a year to store gas surplus in Senator Dehaviland's home state of Florida. Two hundred million for new office furniture in Congress, half a million to build a replica of Egypt's great pyramids . . . one hundred and fifty thousand to study the Hatfield-McCoy feud . . . It gets sillier. One hundred and forty-four thousand to see if pigeons follow human economic laws . . . While you're all cutting back, Congress is funding all this, and then in midnight sessions, they gather in secret and vote for congressional pay raises. I don't understand this. I guess it's because I'm not a Washington insider. I don't owe anything to anybody. I'm just a governor from the smallest state in the nation who's fed up with this corruption. I want to make America work again for all of us."

A. J. Teagarden could feel the *connect*. He could feel it over the tiny eighteen-inch TV screen. "This guy . . . I love this guy," he said, pacing the dressing room in excitement. After the commercial break, they came back for a discussion of farm policy. All four of the Washington candidates took the expected road. Farm subsidies are good, support the farmer in a farm state. Haze went the other way, delivering his speech with wholesome sincerity.

"I know this is gonna sound like heresy in a farm state, but damn it, when is all the pandering going to stop? The farm program, and all of you in Iowa know what that is . . . The farm program is a magnificent program that helps farmers grow their crops; but farm subsidies, which all of my fellow candidates seem to support, is absolute government hypocrisy. We're paying honeybee farmers billions to buy their unused honey. Peanut farmers get subsidies and throw the product away. The federal government doles out billions to California farmers to grow a cotton crop that has to be flooded in a desert, drought-ridden state. All of this just causes products to be too expensive. We can't compete. I'd rather open new world markets . . . force Japan to take down trade barriers . . . create a demand for U.S. farm goods abroad that will stimulate farm growth. I'm against subsidies. If that means you won't vote for me, so be it, but I'm here to speak the truth as I see it. I want the system to work for you. Stop dividing this nation. Let's bring labor and management to the same table. We can control our destiny if we choose to. I want this system to work for everybody."

In the truck, Ted Miller threw his pencil down. "This is turning into the Haze Richards Show. Brenton's gotta cut this guy off."

"Bring labor and management together?" Brenton sneered. "What about the Teamster strike? You think you could fix that?"

"The Teamster strike," Haze said, clearly not ready to discuss it.

"Yeah, the Teamster strike . . . heard about it up there in Rhode Island? No trucks are rolling in this country, it's choking everybody. You say you want to make America work, get everybody together. . . . How 'bout the Teamsters and the Truckers Association? Wanna take a shot at that?"

"Let me tell you something, Mr. Spencer . . . I've been watching your demeanor all night. You're parading around up here, berating my fellow candidates. I think you owe every man on this stage an apology."

Here it comes, thought Brenton . . . the end of my career. His temples were throbbing. "You think I need to apologize?"

"Who elected you to anything?" Haze shot back. "You're supposed to be moderating this debate, not joining in it. If you think you have the answers, get up in one of these chairs and tell us what you'd do."

"I'm not a candidate," Brenton said, falling completely out of his anchorman demeanor.

"These men have put themselves on the line, and I think you should apologize to them for your patronizing attitude, your sense of disregard for what they represent and what they stand for. You're a perfect example of what's wrong with this whole process. You seek to divide us to create a controversy that will get ratings. In my opinion, Mr. Spencer, you're the worst this country has to offer. You seek to divide us for personal gain."

Brenton Spencer stood in center stage, his mouth flapping, gulping air.

In the truck, Ted was screaming at his camera people. "Get loose. He looks like a fucking trout in a bucket."

They racked back fast.

"I don't have to take this," Brenton finally said, and he turned and walked off the stage, leaving all of the candidates sitting there, agape. Haze got up and moved to the podium.

"What was that last question again?" he said to a room full of tense laughter.

"Oh yeah," Haze said, "the Teamster strike. Well, if I was in that room in Mr. Skatina's hometown in New York, talking to the participants, I would find a way, some way to forge a compromise because it's time that Americans stop fighting with Americans. The strongest, greatest nation in the world is being trounced—not because we can't compete, but because we can't focus . . . because we can't agree. I want to change that. Last night instead of sleeping at the Savoy like the rest of the candidates, I stayed with Bud and Sarah Caulfield on their farm in Grinnell. The Caulfields are about to lose that farm to the bank. Not because they haven't worked or planned. Not because they haven't put their heart and soul into that acreage, but because the federal government has elected to ignore their plight, preferring to invest its time writing bills to improve their own salaries while two people in Grinnell, Iowa, lose their dream. I want more than anything in the world to make this country work again, to make America work for Bud and Sarah Caulfield—to make America work for you."

"POOOOONNEEEEEEEEEEY!" A.J. shouted in the little dressing room.

Mickey watched the debate in his father's den while Joseph slept upstairs. Everything had worked out just as they had scripted it. Haze had won. He was tempted to call C. Wallace Litman and congratulate him on Brenton Spencer's performance, but he always found conversation with Wallace Litman irritating, so he withstood the urge. He moved to the bar to pour himself a glass of port when he heard somebody set something down on the marble floor in the hall. He moved out to find Lucinda putting on her coat. There was a small overnight bag in the entry hall. She had an airline ticket in her hand.

"Where you going?" he asked.

"Hi. Didn't know you were in there. You see the debate?"

"Where you going?" he repeated, moving to her. He took the airline ticket out of her hand and glanced at it.

"Iowa?" he said, his voice registering genuine surprise.

"Gonna pick some taters," she said, grinning.

"Can't you see what he is, Lu? Can't you look at him and see?"

"I don't know what you're talking about."

"Ryan has his head so far up his ass, four of his five senses aren't working."

"How can you say that?"

" 'Cause it's true. Ever since I've known him, he's been a fucking charity case. I even hadda get him laid when we were kids. I hadda get him this job 'cause nobody would hire him. Look at him, every fucking decision he's made in his life is flawed. And now he's almost forty and he's a joke in Hollywood. How the hell do you become a joke in a town full of butt-wipes, fags, and actors?"

"I thought he was your friend."

"Lucinda, come here. It's time you and I had a talk." He took her hand and led her into his den. He motioned her into a club chair, then sat on the ottoman opposite her. She placed her hands on her knees, waiting.

"We're Alos. All our lives, we've had to wear that name like a prison number. At first, that pissed me off. Now I'm proud of it. It forged us, Lu, made us stronger. Made us different, special. There's no room in this family for weaklings."

"He's just a friend, Mickey. He's . . . he's going through a rough time right now. I'm trying to help him."

"I'm your brother. It's important to me that I can count on you."

"This is nuts. You brought Ryan home when he was just fifteen. If you felt that way, why did you invite him?"

Mickey leaned back; then he stood. He moved to the window and looked out. "I brought him home because I liked having him around."

"Why?"

"I liked to watch him fail." He turned around and saw a look of surprise on her face.

"He was what everybody wanted to be . . . good-looking, athletic. He's my poster boy for failed expectations. He was never my friend. Lucinda, people like us can't afford friends. Friends are points of weakness. You have a friend, you run the risk he will betray you."

"You must be very lonely."

"Loneliness, friendship, love, hate . . . are just words. They define nothing. I have to know that I can count on you, that you're here for me when I ask. It's the only thing that matters between us."

"Mickey, this is scaring me."

"Pop is going to die soon. It's just gonna be you and me. I'm asking you not to go see this guy. I have very strong reasons. Do I have your word?"

"If you don't want me to, Mickey, then I won't."

He leaned down and kissed her on the cheek. "Good," he said, then turned and walked out of the den.

She heard him go upstairs. She was determined to see Ryan. She would not let Mickey make her choose between them. She ran out, got into her car, and drove to the airport.

EDIT BAY

RYAN AND RELLICA HAD FOUND AN EDIT BAY AT DES MOINES
University in the journalism school. The monitor flickered as they set
to work editing *Prairie Fire.*

"Look at this asshole," she said as a shot of Haze appeared on her
monitor.

"Stop bitching and help me cut this together, will ya? We have to
have it by morning." Both knew he had won the debate. Both felt
they were on the wrong side, helping a man with no moral convic-
tions. The thought caused the atmosphere in the cluttered room to
be thick and cold.

"Doesn't it bother you that this guy is just reading lines A.J. stuffs
in him?"

"Fuck yes, it bothers me," he snapped. "But I'm a TV producer,
not a political scientist."

"Last night I was sleeping in the back of the van and this piece of sour shit jumped on Susan Winter's bones in the barn. There they were grabbing each other's buns, pants down around their knees, huffing and woofing. And I kept saying to myself, 'This guy could be my next President.' " She turned and focused a withering gaze at him. "You know what really pisses me off, Ryan?"

He waited, knowing there was no way to stop her.

"What really pisses me off is I'm helping this asshole."

He felt the same way but he was trapped.

They looked at each other in the very small room on the second floor of the J. Building. A winter wind was blowing outside and the bare branches of a deciduous tree tapped softly on the window, disrupting the heavy silence between them.

She shut off the editing machine.

"I'm outta here," she said softly. "You don't have to pay me because I didn't finish the job. Matter of fact, I don't want to be paid. I wouldn't be able to spend the money with a clear conscience." She picked up her purse. "Lemme ask you a question. . . . If Haze Richards doesn't do his own thinking, doesn't have any courage, and is morally corrupt, how can you make this documentary, how can you get up in the morning and look at yourself in the mirror?"

He had no answer for her.

"You're a good guy, Ryan, but if you stay on his campaign, you're going to regret it," she said, giving words to his exact thoughts. Then she walked out of the edit bay.

Ryan stood there thinking about what she said.

He had gone through his life with emotional blinders on. He had been a golden boy to whom everything had come easy—athletic fame, career success. He had never looked directly at any hard reality, choosing instead to avoid the conflict. And now, at age thirty-five, with his son dead, his marriage and career shattered, it was all bubbling up, the molten residue of all of the ugliness in his life that he'd refused to deal with. He felt surrounded by his life's mistakes, picking up and examining each charred piece. What was this? Oh, yes, Christmas Eve. I realized I didn't love my wife but never dealt with it for five years. What was this? Oh, yes, that was my boyhood pal, Terry, floating at the bottom of the pool. And this . . . Matt was taken from me because I didn't deserve him. And this . . . this piece of emotional poison . . . Ryan Bolt is not about anything.

Ryan Bolt is not about anything. Ryan Bolt is about what other people think. And Mickey Alo, my old friend from prep school, is probably a Mafia hood. Ryan had always suspected it . . . He had even read an article in *Newsweek* on organized crime in which Joseph Alo had been mentioned. He'd brought it up to Mickey, when they were just out of college. Mickey had flown into a rage.

"My father owns restaurants. His family is from Sicily. Sometimes, mob guys eat in his places. That's not a crime. He's never been indicted. It's bullshit."

Ryan had let it drop. It was easier not to push it. What did it matter to him? But now he couldn't avoid it. Mickey got him this job. A.J. had been on the phone in Mickey's den talking about money from the Bahamas. Offshore cash. It didn't take a genius to figure out where it came from or where it was going. If organized crime was behind Haze Richards, if he was their handpicked puppet, then the implications could be devastating.

He sat down on the edit bay desk and listened to the gusting wind outside that brushed the tree limb against the window. Tap-tap-tap. He glanced out at the empty branches swaying in the wind and wondered if he could face these old emotional grenades—wondered if he could deal with his new suspicions—wondered if he was strong enough to try.

The bony-finger twig at the end of the branch hit the window, trying to get his attention. Tap-tap-tap. Tap-tap-tap.

DEFINING EVENT

THE IDEA WOKE HIM UP.

"Shit." A.J. struggled to a sitting position. "How could I have been so dumb." He was still half asleep, in his single room at the Des Moines Holiday Inn. He tried to clear his head. Then he swung his feet off the bed and went to the phone. "Alo, Alo," he said out loud, looking for Mickey's private number. He found it on a card stuffed in his wallet.

"Hello?" a voice growled through the receiver.

"Need to talk to Mickey Alo."

"He's sleeping."

"Tell him A. J. Teagarden is on the phone."

"Just a minute." And he was on hold.

He used the moments to collect his thoughts. He started tapping his foot, nervous energy burning like battery acid. He had been looking for a defining event, one that would score with the electorate at large. A defining event was any event that instantly told the public who the candidate was. Jesse Jackson bringing the Middle East hostages home or Clinton getting his hair cut on the L.A. runway. Both were a defining events. People instantly got it. The debate had set Haze up. He would be in the national eye in the morning. While he had the nation's attention, A.J. needed something tangible to show that Haze's message was true. He'd come up with it while sound asleep. After a moment, Mickey came on the line, his voice choked with sleep.

"Yeah . . ."

"It's Teagarden."

"Yeah . . ."

"This Teamster problem, this strike, are you involved with that?" he asked, knowing that the Teamsters and the mob were generally in bed together.

"Not on the phone."

"I need to talk first thing in the morning. You won't regret it."

"Where you staying?"

"Des Moines Holiday Inn, room four seventy-six."

And the line went dead. A. J. Teagarden lay back on his bed.

Shit, he thought, *it was perfect.*

At seven A.M., New York Tony knocked on his door. A.J. got up and opened it, looking at the hatchet-faced bodyguard through the chain lock.

"Get dressed. Mickey is in a car downstairs," he ordered.

A.J. threw on his clothes, combed his hair with his fingers, and followed New York Tony down the hall and out into the cold Iowa morning.

New York Tony led A.J. around the side of the hotel and into an overflow parking lot where two large men in black overcoats were standing in front of a white windowless van. Their eyes metronomed the parking lot, like wary tank commanders in a fire zone. The bodyguard swung open the van door and A.J. was suddenly looking at Mickey Alo. Mickey had a box of Winchell's doughnuts on his knees and a cup of coffee in a paper cup.

"Seen this?" Mickey asked as he handed the *Des Moines Register-*

Guard to A.J. The headline was in thirty-six-point sans serif boldface
type and screamed:

RHODE ISLAND GOVERNOR TURNS PRIMARY RACE HAZEY

Under that, the subhead read:

RICHARDS SCORES DEBATE KO

A.J. already knew this would be the reaction. He'd stayed up for the
late newscasts, and all four networks had called it for Haze. All of
them had shown Brenton Spencer walking off the stage and Haze's
brilliant move to the mike, followed by his take-back-America closing
while the other candidates sat behind him like a bunch of back-up
singers.

"You were right," Mickey said. "He did great."

"We're on our way. We're going to be the story in Iowa for a few
days, but it will fizzle if we don't build on it. We have to keep par-
laying, trading up. I've got a great defining event, but you're gonna
have to pull it off for me."

"Whatta you need?" Mickey asked.

"Before he walked off the stage, Brenton Spencer challenged Haze
to bring management and labor together in the Teamster strike."

"Yeah? So . . . ?"

"I don't know what the sticking points are in the negotiations, but
wouldn't it be nice if tonight or tomorrow the Teamsters could invite
Haze to come to New York." The wonk started to grin in nervous
excitement. "Haze gets on the train. I want it to be the train because
it's the commuter's vehicle, the way the common man gets to work.
Then he rides into New York . . . like fucking Caesar into Rome.
While the world watches on TV, he walks into some room with labor
and management, and the doors close. Everybody thinks he can't pull
this off . . . He's dust. Then—voilà!—the door opens and he walks
out two hours later with the head of the union—that fat guy, Bud
Rennick—on one arm and the head of the Truckers Association on
the other."

"Tom Bartel," Mickey said.

"Right. And there's a deal. They've buried the hatchet. Everybody is smiling. The Peterbilts are going to roll; there's joy in Mudville. If we time it right, I can ride that pony right on through New Hampshire, into Super Tuesday two weeks from now."

Mickey looked over at Teagarden.

"There's a lot of money at stake. These guys are locked up over mileage and hourly rates. They're way apart."

"I'm sure there's problems, but you told me you wanted Haze in the White House. You didn't care what it cost. I need this."

Mickey looked at his watch, then studied the wonk. "Okay, lemme make some calls. I'll get back to you."

"You gotta do this. I don't care what you have to promise the Teamsters, we'll take care of them on the other end once we get Haze in the White House. Listen, this is made for us. This defines Haze as a doer. This is Haze making America work again. It's right on the message. Make it happen."

"Anything else you want? How 'bout I arrange for Haze to be elected pope?"

"He won't take a job where he can't fuck the secretaries." The wonk smiled. "But I got another idea."

"Let's hear."

"After we do good in this state, we're gonna start getting sniped at by Skatina. He's gonna look over his shoulder and see Haze coming up in the polls and he's gonna start playing rough . . . He'll go after Haze's uninspired legislative record in Rhode Island. He's gonna maybe dig up a woman who had a nice weekend with the gov and now wants to be on the cover of *People* magazine. We gotta keep that from happening."

"How we gonna do that?"

"We got a guy here named Skatina. That's a wop name . . . no offense . . . a wop from New York. Might be nice if maybe the world begins to wonder if maybe Leo has some mob ties. That gets Skatina on the defensive for two weeks while the press paws through his garbage looking for ravioli sauce."

"Really?" Mickey said, beginning to have serious respect for the unkempt man sitting beside him.

"Yeah, really, like it maybe somebody you know wants to come clean, make a public confession."

"How 'bout somebody who's already on trial for bribing a public official? Maybe he confesses the Skatina connection from the stand, under oath . . . ?" Mickey was thinking of an ongoing New York trial where he had good contacts with the defense.

"Sounds promising," A.J. said, grinning.

CONFRONTATION

THE TWELVE O'CLOCK PRESS CONFERENCE WAS A VIDEO RODEO.
Power cables spaghettied around the crowded hotel ballroom.

Vidal Brown was on the stage in front of a microphone podium as correspondents screamed for hard news on Haze Richards.

Ryan was watching from the back of the ball room thinking somebody has to stop this! And then A. J. Teagarden's voice was in his ear.

"I need the documentary. I got a deal with ABC. They're gonna run it on *Nightline* unedited."

A. J. had slipped up beside him in the milling crowd of blow-dries. "Come outside," Ryan finally said.

He led the wonk out of the ballroom and they found a small alcove in the hotel where the din was manageable.

"I'm not sure I like what's happening here," Ryan said.

"What's happening is Haze Richards. Where's the tape?" The wonk leaned in and pushed his bushy face toward Ryan. "Gimme the tape, Ryan. I need footage on Haze. I'm cutting deals on that tape. We've got networks fighting for it. They can't just run clips of the debate; they wanna know who he is . . . the man from Providence, the Prairie Fire. Where is it?"

"This guy is just hype. He doesn't stand for anything."

"That's the system. Reagan wasn't overwhelmed with original thought, either. Now give it to me."

"Why is the underworld backing Haze?"

A.J. had been leaning forward, trying to get in Ryan's face. The question froze him.

"The underworld isn't involved with this candidate. It's horseshit."

"The Alo family is supporting Haze. I overheard you tell Mickey on the phone that cash was coming in from the Bahamas. If the mob is backing all this, what does Haze Richards have to give back once he gets in the White House?"

A.J.'s face turned to stone. His expression told Ryan he had scored a bull's-eye.

A. J. Teagarden spun away, leaving Ryan in the little alcove, alone.

Ryan moved to the elevator and pushed "7." . . . He rode up alone while "Sons of the Pioneers" warbled through the Muzak. He got out, went down the hall, and opened his room. The edited master tape was on the desk. He grabbed it, along with three other tapes of raw footage it had been cut from and one duplicate master he'd made. He put them away in his suitcase, locked the case, and moved quickly out of his room. He took the stairway down to the mezzanine and handed the overnight bag to the concierge. "Could you put this in your lockup for me?"

While Ryan was locking up the tape, A. J. Teagarden was across the street from the hotel on a pay phone talking to Mickey Alo. Mickey had flown back to Manhattan and was in a restaurant where he was having lunch with Bud Rennick, president of the local Teamsters.

"It's A.J."

"Can this wait? I'll call you back on a hard line."

"You better hear it now. I gotta get back inside. We're having a feeding frenzy. I got press crawling up my ass, and I got nothing to chum the water with. And this old friend of yours, this Ryan guy—he's got the tape but he won't give it over."

"I'll look into it," Mickey said slowly.

"Another thing . . . I thought you told me nobody but me, Haze, and Malcolm were gonna know you were involved in this."

"Nobody else does."

"Ten minutes ago, Ryan Bolt told me that the Alo family was financing Haze. This guy could scuttle the whole deal. You gotta wave him off."

"I'll take care of it. Thanks." And Mickey hung up.

"Everything okay?" Bud asked.

"Yep." Mickey made two quick decisions and then he turned his full attention back to Bud. "You invite Governor Richards to New York, let him solve it, but you gotta cave on your hourly wage demand."

"You guarantee you'll give it back to me somehow later, I'll sell it to my board."

Outside the restaurant, Solomon Kazorowski had heard the call from A.J. to Mickey Alo. He had borrowed an ICOM scanner that could intercept cell phone calls from a friend. When Mickey's phone had rung, he eavesdropped on the call. After A.J. hung up, Kaz picked up the picture of the blond man who had come to the Alo house with Lucinda. He pulled a Magic Marker out of his pocket and wrote the name "Ryan Bolt" under the picture. And then, after a moment of thought, he put a question mark next to it.

The first Iowa post-debate poll came in at six P.M. A.J., Ven, and Van were in Malcolm's suite, which was on the tenth floor of the Savoy. A.J. was in the bedroom getting results over the phone. He hung up and came through the door, grinning.

"That was my guy at UBC. Haze is on the map. We're polling ten percent. From zero to ten percent in one day. Fucking unbelievable."

Malcolm got to his feet. "Let's hear the rest."

A.J. looked down at the slip of paper. "Okay, this thing in Iowa is gonna be between us and Skatina. Forget the other three. They're already dust. People aren't quite ready to say they'll vote for Haze yet, 'cause they just heard about him yesterday, but the internals are amazing. Haze is leading Skatina three-to-two on integrity. Skatina has a three-to-one edge on 'Qualified.' We'll have to build on that. Haze scored big on the farm program. That was fucking brilliant if I do say so myself." He bowed at the waist before going on. "The question, 'Does the candidate care?'—we're solid winners. 'Leadership'—we're ahead. 'Trust in a crisis'—they don't know Haze, so Skatina is still the guy they'd trust with the bomb, but I'll figure out a way to overcome that. Get this . . . When asked, 'Which candidate excited and inspired you?'—it was Haze by fifty-two percent." He dropped the paper on the table.

"We need to follow this up with that documentary. Where the hell is it?" Malcolm asked.

A.J. wondered what Mickey had in store for Ryan Bolt.

THIRTEEN WEEKS

JOHNNY FURIE WAS HIS GIVEN NAME, BUT ON THE PIER IN AT-
lantic City, they called him Thirteen Weeks. He worked as a collector
for Charlie "Six Fingers" Romano. If you failed to pay the greedy
little Sicilian loan shark the vig, or worse still, if you tried to take off,
then Johnny Furie was called into action. His specialty was nonfatal
injuries which would leave you hospitalized for specific amounts of
time—thirteen weeks in County Hospital being the sentence Charlie
Six Fingers deemed right for a seriously delinquent account.

Thirteen Weeks prided himself on his ability to dole out the exact
number of hospital days he was aiming for. He worked with a cut-
down, wood Louisville Slugger and had actually audited some medical
courses at City College to help him refine his skills. He had learned,
for example, to stay away from the kidneys, because they could cause
complications that would leave a delinquent account in a wheelchair.
He avoided the head and focused on appendages because they were

hospital-time reliable. Knees were almost always good for two weeks; feet were favored targets if the sentence was longer. Foot injuries could leave a "no pay" on his back with his leg in a pulley sling for months. Johnny Furie rarely missed by much.

His boss, Charlie Romano, operated a loan shark business on the boardwalk in Atlantic City, funding bars and restaurants as well as casino losers. His operation was on Alo turf, so he gave the Alo "buttons" a taste of his action in exchange for protection from range wars with freelance operators.

Mickey Alo called Charlie. He explained the situation and Charlie picked Thirteen Weeks for the job. The six-foot-two, two-hundred-sixty-pound collection consultant boarded a plane to Cedar Rapids, rented a car there, and drove over to Des Moines. He stopped at a sporting goods store in a small town on the way and picked up an eighteen-ounce Louisville Slugger. Then he stopped at a hardware store and bought a drill, a hacksaw, and two feet of nylon rope. He shortened the bat in the front seat of his car while eating a Mc-Donald's Double-Double burger, drilling a hole through the handle and tying a loop in the cord so he could hang the bat under his armpit beneath his overcoat.

Thirteen Weeks got to the Savoy Hotel in Des Moines at seven-thirty P.M. and called Ryan Bolt on the house phone.

"Mr. Bolt? This is the concierge desk. We're holding a package for you. We'd send it up but it's very large and I think, perhaps, you're going to want to store it."

"Who's it from?"

"Uh. It doesn't say." Thinking, *Come on, shithead, just come down, will ya?*

"Be right down."

Johnny Furie moved over to a lounge chair and waited for Ryan to show up. After a few minutes, a handsome, blond man, about six-two, approached the desk and had an animated conversation with the concierge. Johnny sized up the target. He looked athletic, with quick movements. Take him from behind, he thought. . . . An Achilles tendon shot to slow him, then work the lower extremities. He watched as Ryan looked around the lobby with a puzzled stare, then Ryan moved back to the elevator. Johnny Furie moved with him and got in the same elevator.

Tanya Tucker harmonized with the hydraulic lift as they zoomed up.

"Evening," Johnny said, feeling the Louisville Slugger under his coat.

"Hi," Ryan said.

The door opened on seven.

"My floor, too," Johnny said, walking behind Ryan who headed for his room and took out his key. Johnny Furie slowed down, unbuttoning his coat. Just as Ryan started to enter his room, Thirteen Weeks brought the Louisville Slugger out, pivoted, and swung. The bat whistled, aimed low. Johnny Furie couldn't believe it! Even as he swung, he knew he was going to miss. Ryan still had his back to Johnny, but he moved so quickly that the blow glanced off the side of his left leg, doing almost no damage. Ryan dove into his room and rolled on the blue plush pile carpet.

Ryan Bolt had managed to stay healthy through four Division A-1 college seasons as a wide receiver. He ran his share of blind short-outs, during which linebackers got to unload free shots while his back was to them. Ryan had always been able to feel them behind him. He learned from the conditioning coach that he had exceptional peripheral vision. His focal vision was 90 degrees, his gray vision was 75, but he could sense motion for 10 degrees on either side of that.

He'd sensed the man in the gray tweed overcoat moving fast behind him, and he'd lunged forward, getting partially out of the way before the blow hit. He rolled up in time to see his assailant moving into the room after him, swinging the bat again. He dove to his right and the second swing missed him completely.

"Shit, stay still," the frustrated accounts receivable specialist muttered.

Ryan got a foot under himself and charged low. He dug a shoulder into the huge man, driving him back against the wall. The wind went out of both of them.

Johnny Furie pushed Ryan back and swung his meaty right hand, hitting Ryan in the temple. Ryan saw stars, felt consciousness slipping away so he dropped into a partial crouch, his hands up by his head to block two of Johnny Furie's best lefts. Ryan tried to circle, but he was dizzy from the first blow and went down to one knee. The big man was on him, raining blows on his face. The bat was no longer in Johnny's hand; it was swinging wildly under his arm from the rope, banging him helplessly in the side. Johnny turned his attention momentarily from Ryan to the bat, trying to find it and grab it with his left hand. Suddenly, from behind him, a heavy glass ashtray hit Johnny Furie on the back of the head. He turned around and saw a beautiful girl with black hair standing there, the ashtray still in her hand, a terrified look on her face.

Lucinda had just arrived from New Jersey. She'd seen the big man in the gray tweed coat swinging the bat at Ryan just as she'd gotten off the elevator and watched in terror, not knowing what to do. Then, she'd grabbed the heavy glass ashtray and hit the man in the gray coat on the head as hard as she could.

Johnny Furie grabbed Lucinda by the right wrist and hurled her across the room, but when he turned, Ryan was back on his feet. His head had cleared and he hit Thirteen Weeks with a straight right hand.

Johnny felt bone and cartilage exploding, spreading his nose over his face. He reeled back and Ryan hit Johnny again. This time, Johnny's lip split.

"Shit," he said, blood flowing down on his collar. He grabbed the bat and swung it again at Ryan, missing. Ryan scrambled right and grabbed a heavy pole lamp with a metal base, ripped the plug out of the wall, and faced the huge man. People in the corridor were screaming.

A fat man in a T-shirt and suspendered pants stuck his head in the room and looked at Ryan and Johnny, faced off with blunt instruments. Johnny Furie's face was covered with blood. "My God," the man cried and ran up the hall. "Call the cops," he yelled as he went.

Thirteen Weeks knew the mission was blown. He cursed himself for trying to do it in the hotel. He figured the tapes were probably in the room and that by doing the job here, it would eliminate the need to come back to get them. Now that decision was working against him. He could hear people running in the hall, calling to each other. He reached up and tried to wipe the blood off his face. When his hand came down, it was completely red. Ryan started moving toward him, the metal lamp ready to swing.

"Fuck it," Johnny said, then he spun and ran out of the room.

He used the stairs, got out into the parking lot and into the car. His mind was reeling. What would he tell Charlie Romano? Worse yet, what would he tell Mickey Alo?

*   *   *

Ryan was sitting on the corner of the bed in his room at the Savoy, looking at Lucinda, trying to decide what to think. She was bruised and shaken but collected. He stood up and began to pace around the room.

"Was he trying to rob you?"

"I don't think so," Ryan said, reluctant to tell her what he really thought.

"Ryan, what's going on?"

"I didn't give A.J. the tape I made. I refused to let him have it."

"Why?"

"I didn't want to be a part of what they're doing, so I said no. I think that guy was sent to take it from me." He was still not looking at her. He didn't want to tell her about his suspicions concerning her brother—that Mickey was trying to buy the presidency.

Ryan had called Alex Tingredies just that morning. Alex was a friend in the FBI who had been a technical adviser on one of Ryan's TV projects. Ryan had asked Alex about the Alos and gotten a distressing report. He hated to tell Lucinda what he'd learned, but knew if they were going to continue to see each other, he had to take that chance.

"I called a friend in the FBI. He told me that they were getting set to file an indictment against your father for criminal conspiracy."

"So then why didn't they?" she asked angrily. "My father has never had any charges against him."

"They know he's dying and don't want to indict him and never be able to bring him into court. They're switching the indictment over to your brother. It's going to be filed in two months."

She'd always been taught that her family was more important than anything. All her life, she'd fought against believing ugly rumors, but ultimately she suspected they were true. To protect herself, she had looked away, avoiding that reality just as surely as Ryan had buried the drowning of his childhood friend. But it had all crashed in on her one afternoon when she was coming home from college her sophomore year. A taxicab had dropped her off at home.

"You know who lives in there?" the driver asked.

"Huh?" she said dumbfounded.

"Joseph Alo," He said in a reverential whisper. "He's head of the

Jersey mob." It had been said with such awe and trepidation that somehow she instantly knew it was true. Her brother had followed in her father's footsteps.

The conversation with Mickey was still resonating in her head—*I keep Ryan around to watch him fail. The Alo name is like a prison number.*

"Lucinda, we've got to, somehow, deal with this," Ryan said, bringing her back. "I think your brother is trying to hurt me, maybe kill me."

Her mind went back to a time years before when she was just eight. Her mother had left her in a park while she ran an errand. Mickey was sixteen and was there to watch her. Lucinda had been over by the swings playing when a boy about eleven had pushed her off. Mickey had seen it and he'd come over. Lucinda stood in terror as Mickey grabbed the younger boy and hit him in the face. The little boy went down, but Mickey hadn't stopped. He'd kicked him and then rolled him over on his back and sat on the young boy's chest. Mickey was still hitting him when a park policeman ran over and pulled him off. While the policeman attended to the boy, Mickey grabbed Lucinda's hand and led her out of the park. She'd remembered the look in Mickey's eyes, an evil, glowing look of excitement. She knew, even then, he had loved hitting the boy. It was a corrupt memory, half-buried by time. She looked at Ryan and wondered if he could be right . . . wondered if her big brother had sent the man in the gray coat.

"Mickey's at our beach house on Cape May. I think you need to go and talk to him," she finally said. "You need to find out. We both do."

"Yeah." He nodded. "It's time."

He packed and then retrieved the tapes from the concierge, putting them in his ostrich briefcase. On the way out, he saw A.J. in the bar. He was tempted to leave without saying anything, but some sense of propriety seized him. He moved into the Buckeye Bar and tapped A.J. on the shoulder.

"Well, how ya doin', buddy?" A.J. slurred. He was slightly drunk. He led Ryan over to a booth where a curvaceous blonde was sitting. A.J. made an elaborate introduction. "Miss Veronica Dennis, may I present Benedict fucking Arnold."

"Pleased to meet you, Mr. Arnold," the girl said, displaying a staggering lack of knowledge in American history. "Do you work for A.J.?" She was smiling, showing her small, perfect teeth.

"Yes. Mr. Arnold is our campaign turncoat."

"Knock it off, A.J."

"Whatever you want." A.J. slumped down into the booth, put an arm around Veronica Dennis. "Veronica likes Haze, but she says he seems cold. That's what our fine data tells us, too. Old Vonnie, here, is better than a tracking poll," the wonk said drunkenly.

"That's right." Veronica was smiling at Ryan, whom she found attractive. She was working her dimples, arching her back, giving him her D-cup profile. "I thought he was very impressive on TV, but he was sorta . . . Y'know, like he's not very warm or something."

"Ryan, here, he used t' write and produce TV. Didn't ya, Ryan . . . ? So he knows the medium. Is old Haze coming off like a block of ice, like Vonnie says?"

"A.J., I'm gonna be gone for a couple of days."

"Hey, what the fuck good are you anyway? You ain't helping me."

"I'll leave a number where I can be reached."

"See, here's the problem . . ." A.J. went on, looking at Veronica. "Ryan, here, he takes our money and he shoots our film and then he won't give it to us when we need it."

"I'll see ya, A.J." He started to leave and A.J. grabbed his arm.

"Let's say you have this problem in a TV script. . . . You got a character who's hard to like 'cause people think he's cold. How do you warm him up?"

Ryan wanted to get out of the bar, but A.J. was holding his arm.

"Create a tragedy for him," he finally said. "Something that makes people feel sorry for him. I gotta go." He pulled his arm free.

"S' long, Hemingway," A.J. sneered.

"Hemingway? Are you related to Mariel Hemingway?" Veronica said, desperately fighting for field position.

"Nice to meet you, Miss Dennis."

"Listen, I'm in the book," she said quickly, wishing he wouldn't leave.

A.J. watched Ryan go. "Create a tragedy," he said to himself. "Pretty fucking smart."

BUDDIES

"REMEMBER THAT GIRL . . . WHAT WAS HER NAME? FROM COOS Bay . . ." Mickey was grinning at Ryan over a plate of pasta. They were in a booth in the back of the original Mr. A's steak house on Cape May. Large windows overlooked the black Atlantic swelling with winter cold on the south Jersey shore.

"Susan? Sharon? Yeah, it was Sharon something." Mickey was happy! Funny! Having a ball! His fat, round cheeks pulled up in cherubic delight. All around them, people were drinking beer and eating dinner, as the sound of silverware on crockery mixed with conversation and laughter.

The old-time waiters stopped to say "Hi" to Mickey on their way into the kitchen. Mickey had bussed tables in the restaurant every summer when he and Ryan were in prep school.

"Sharon," Mickey continued the reverie. "The bitch had bugs in her rug. Gave me crabs. No shit, Ryan. I had to shave my pubes an soak my Johnson in vinegar."

"Lucky I never got around to her."

Mickey waved at the bartender who sent two more frosted mugs of beer over with the waitress.

Ryan had been dreading the meeting all the way from Des Moines, but the minute he saw Mickey at the beach house and Mickey threw an arm around him and suggested they have dinner together, he'd felt more relaxed. Ryan had asked Lucinda not to join them. He still wasn't sure how this meeting would end. They'd driven to the restaurant in a black Jeep Mickey kept for the beach and on the way they'd never once mentioned the campaign or the documentary. They had been shown to a table like visiting royalty, and then Mickey had gestured at the restaurant at large.

"First Mr. A's, right on the tip of Cape May. My dad picked this location after he bought the beach house. Pop pointed to this spot and said we're gonna build a steak house right here, overlooking the bay."

"Really?" Ryan said, thinking, *How could they afford a beach house before the restaurant had become a success?* But that had been hours ago, and that sober thought had now been replaced by memories of dick jousting tournaments. Mickey's demeanor and friendliness made Ryan's earlier concerns seem foolish.

Two hours later, they had moved into the bar and were wrecking the atmosphere with bone-shattering harmony.

"From the tables down at Morrie's to the place where Louis dwells . . ." The "Whiffenpoof Song" rang off the rafters, with Mickey roaring out the words off-key. The bartender kept the shooters coming.

At two A.M., they stumbled out into the cold January night and pissed in the snowbank, leaving yellow craters in the fresh drift. Laughing, they piled into the Jeep. Mickey was all over the road. "Whooooo," he yelled as the right front tire hit the curb in front of the Cape May Inn, where Ryan had elected to stay.

Mickey pulled up to unit 6 and set the brake. The engine purred. Exhaust made rich noxious steam.

"Man, we had some times, didn't we?" Mickey said, looking at his friend of more than twenty years. " 'Member that first day at Choate when we were roommates and we fought over the window bed? You were the first guy I couldn't pin. You counted with me, Ryan." Mickey shook his head in wonder. Then abruptly the smile was gone. "So, how come you're fuckin' me now?"

"What're you talking about?" Ryan was trying to get his head to stop spinning.

"I got a call from those guys in Iowa. They tell me you ain't co-operating with them. They say you're calling me a hood. I can't believe it. I recommended you." Mickey was looking at the dash.

"I was gonna talk to you about it tomorrow. I'm drunk, man. I can't do this with my brain steeped in shooters."

"These people, they're real upset."

"I thought you hardly knew them," Ryan said, struggling to focus his vision, cursing himself for getting drunk, letting his guard down.

"I do you a favor, I don't expect to get butt-fucked."

"I can't do this drunk. Okay?" Ryan struggled out of the car. "We'll talk about it in the morning."

Mickey leaned forward and swung his head toward Ryan. Ryan was staring into the eyes of the devil. It was hard to even explain what he saw there. He'd never seen such hatred. He felt searing heat as Mickey's glare shot through him.

"I was helping you and you fucked me. Now I gotta fuck you back."

Then Mickey put the car in reverse, yanking Ryan's arm off the door as he went, leaving him awash with fear and liquor.

Ryan opened unit 6 and went inside. He stripped off his clothes, cranked the shower up to cold, and stood shivering as icy needles of water raked his skin. He got out and, still naked and wet, dropped to the threadbare carpet and started doing push-ups.

It took him two hours to get sober.

When he dialed the Alo beach house, it was almost four A.M.

"Yeah." Mickey's voice was heavy with sleep.

"It's Ryan. I need to talk to you."

"I'm through talking to you."

"I have something I need to show you. I'm coming over. Tell the turret gunners not to shoot me." Ryan hung up and called a cab.

He arrived at the beach house just as the sun was coming up. He got out of the cab and paid the driver to wait.

New York Tony was sitting in the Jeep out front in the driveway. He said nothing but watched with feigned disinterest as Ryan rang the bell. Mickey opened the door almost immediately. He was in a maroon bathrobe and slippers and his wet hair was slicked back.

"Out here," he said and led Ryan through the house, to a boat-house on the ocean side of a rolling grass lawn that fronted the shore. Ryan followed Mickey across the brown winter-burned landscape. Mickey unlocked the door and they entered.

The boathouse was painted glossy white and smelled of fresh paint and mildew. Inside, a blue Hobie Cat and two red Sabots were on trailers.

"Whatta you want?"

"What did you mean when you said you were gonna fuck me back?"

"It's in English, you figure it out."

"I'm not supposed to have any thoughts? I'm just supposed to do what I'm told, regardless of what I feel?" Ryan said, searching Mickey's eyes for that deadly glare.

"No, Ryan, you do exactly what you want."

"Mickey, I have a friend in the Organized Crime Bureau of the FBI. He says the Alo family is engaged in criminal activities."

"Fuck him," Mickey said, his hands in his bathrobe pockets.

"Haze Richards is a sham, Mickey. We hit some rough air flying into Des Moines and he turned to Jell-O. He was screaming and begging them to turn the plane around. He doesn't have a thought that A. J. Teagarden doesn't have first. Look at this."

He'd made an extra copy of the tape before he'd left the journalism school. He flipped it to Mickey, who jerked a hand out of his robe and caught it. Mickey had heard from A.J. about the incident on the airliner . . . He didn't know Ryan had it on tape.

"What do I care?" Mickey said softly.

"You're running him for President. Why?"

"Maybe you need a few more facts." The evil look was back, searing heat mixed with emptiness. "Fact . . ." Mickey continued, "When I want something, I get it. I never fail. Anybody gets in the way, I bury them. Fact, the only reason you're still standing here breathing my air is I've known you for twenty years. If you hadn't been my room-mate, if we hadn't screwed a few of the same girls, if you hadn't given me a few laughs, I would a' floated you already."

Ryan had miscalculated. Because he'd known Mickey half his life, he'd thought he could bargain with him. The mask was off. He now saw Mickey for what he really was.

"Now, get the fuck outta my house and my life before I decide to do the job right now. I'll tell you one more thing . . . You mess with me on this, you try and make trouble for this campaign, and you're not gonna be prepared for the shit I'm gonna dump on you. This is your only warning, Ryan. Nobody else would even get one. Chalk it up to old times, but don't ignore it or you're dead."

Ryan knew he had to repair the moment. He had tipped his hand carelessly. "There's no reason it has to be like this," he said. "I didn't mean for this to happen. I'm sorry, Mickey. I'll just go home and forget everything."

Mickey looked in Ryan's eyes and knew he was lying. To Mickey, the lie was more dangerous than anything else Ryan had done.

Lucinda had been awakened by the phone and saw Ryan arrive from her upstairs window. She threw on an overcoat and followed them to the boathouse and listened through the thin wood walls while her brother uttered words she could not comprehend.

Chalk it up to old times, he'd said to Ryan. *Don't ignore it or you're dead.*

He had threatened to kill Ryan. There was very little doubt in her mind that he would go through with it.

She knew she had no choice. She had to stop her brother.

RUBOUT

MICKEY WATCHED THE TAXI LEAVE THROUGH THE WINDOW IN THE den. Then he put the tape Ryan had given him into the VCR.

It was devastating. Mickey watched as Haze Richards sobbed and cried from his seat in the Republic airliner, then ordering, begging to have the plane turned around. Mickey knew he had to get the original and all copies of the tape back. He also knew for certain that Ryan was his enemy. He called to New York Tony who was in the kitchen getting coffee.

"I gotta problem here," he said to the hatchet-faced trigger man. "You gotta do a rubout for me."

Rubouts were New York Tony's specialty. He had skagged almost twenty guys over the years. He followed quietly as Mickey led him out the front door to the Jeep.

"Don't do it around here, and I don't want pieces of him floating up, so make sure when he goes away he stays away. Also make sure he gives you all the copies of this video he made. I don't want this thing to ever surface. Got it?"

"Done."

New York Tony drove the Jeep into Cape May and parked it on the street there. Two blocks over he found an unlocked, green '81 Country Squire station wagon. He got in, slipped on a pair of gloves, hot-wired the ignition, and drove the wagon away. He pulled up at the Cape May Inn just in time to see Ryan Bolt coming out, carrying his bag, and climbing into a waiting cab.

"Perfect timing," New York Tony muttered as he watched the cab pull out. But instead of going south toward the airport, as he'd expected, it headed back into town and stopped in front of the Hertz agency. New York Tony waited while Ryan paid the cab and went inside.

A few minutes later, Ryan got into a white Land Rover, pulled out of the parking lot onto the highway, and headed up the peninsula road toward Princeton. New York Tony was behind him in the wagon. Ryan Bolt was driving very slowly, almost as if he was afraid to be behind the wheel. New York Tony looked at his watch; it was only seven A.M. He figured he was fifteen minutes ahead of the morning traffic . . . now was the time to make his move. He was on an open stretch of road where he could make a pass and crowd Ryan over. The shoulder slanted down into an empty snow ditch. He checked the highway for traffic, then edged up behind the Land Rover, waiting for just the right moment.

New York Tony had learned his trade as a teenager, working for his father in the kill shed of the West Jersey Cattle and Meat Packing Company. He stood four-hour shifts in the blood and dust with a .22-caliber pistol loaded with dumdums. He would calmly fire behind each Hereford's ear, obliterating the animal's thoughts in a spray of red. He perfected his technique with a few cool disco moves. Several of the plant workers had been horrified to see the stocky teenager execute spinning pirouettes, followed by loud bangs. Cows slumped heavily. Tony loved the job. Loved the copper taste of blood in his mouth.

When New York Tony killed men, he thought of them with the same lack of passion. They were just meat, two-legged Herefords. He still worked with a short-barrel .22. His trademark hit was a dumdum in the head and then a .22 long in the heart. He'd been told that trick by one of the legendary street hitters, a mob assassin named Jimmy Hats. A second shot in the heart prevented bleeding, the old man said, and it was true.

Ryan was surprised at how easy it was to start driving again. The bone-numbing panic that had crippled him every time he got behind the wheel in L.A. had left him, just like the shadow dreams.

On this stretch of road, he could see ahead for a quarter mile, so he picked up speed. The two-lane highway looked empty, but then a station wagon accelerated past him, swerved, and tried to push him into the ditch. Ryan yanked the wheel, crashing into the wagon.

The cars traded paint. Tires squealed.

Ryan saw New York Tony behind the wheel, his thick neck muscles bunched, his teeth bared in determination. Then the Land Rover dove right, its wheels falling into the snow ditch, where it skidded along and finally lurched to a stop. New York Tony was out of the car fast. He pushed a gun through the driver's window, into Ryan's face.

"Out," he barked. "Get in my car, behind the wheel."

Ryan was looking into the barrel of the .22. He moved slowly toward the station wagon, hoping a car would pass, anything he could use as a diversion. His adrenaline was pumping, his senses tingling. He was afraid, but something else was mixed in with it. . . . He was angry. He'd had enough.

"Move faster," Tony barked.

Ryan got into the driver's seat as Tony threw his briefcase and bag into the backseat.

Tony got in on the passenger side, holding the gun out. "Okay, get going. Drive slowly."

Tony wanted to get far away from the Rover, then find a secluded spot off the road where he could pull the stolen station wagon in. He'd tie Ryan up and work him over—find out where all the tapes were. He'd do the kill, then get a bag of lye, a blanket, and a shovel. Burial and last rites would be finished before noon. He'd leave the car unlocked in the Trenton ghetto. Some hucklebuck piece of shit would undoubtedly steal it, leaving his prints, putting Tony in the clear.

For the last ten minutes, Ryan had been surreptitiously unscrewing the metal turn indicator. It was almost off when Tony said, "Turn right there." They were ten miles west of Melville on Interstate 47. A heavy stand of cypresses bordered the two-lane highway on both sides. Tony spotted a dirt road that led through the trees.

Ryan made the turn, his gaze flicking to the pistol in Tony's hand. He was trying to gauge whether he could risk trying to crash the car to gain some advantage. The small-bore pistol was aimed right at his head, never wavering. Tony spoke in a rasping whisper, as if he were reading Ryan's mind. "Don't. This thing is loaded with dumdum bullets. It'll turn you into guacamole."

Ryan decided to wait.

"Pull up there," Tony said, indicating a clearing at the end of the dirt cul-de-sac. Ryan stopped the car and set the brake and reset the turn indicator, twisting it. The small chrome rod came off in his hand. Feeling its light weight, he wondered what possible good it was going to do him.

Tony gestured Ryan out of the wagon. "Stand there, by them cut trees," he said, indicating a pile of logs that had been stacked at the end of the dirt road. Ryan moved to them. Somewhere he could hear a stream running.

Tony took the suitcase and the briefcase out of the wagon and dropped them on the ground. "Okay," Tony rasped, "get something straight. Mickey said don't hurt ya 'less you get stupid. You got videos of Governor Richards. I need 'em."

"I gave the tape to Mickey. There aren't any more," Ryan lied. Without warning, Tony fired the pistol over Ryan's shoulder. The dumdum entered the tree near his head; the exit hole was the size of a grapefruit, blowing tiny chips of the bark everywhere. Ryan looked at it in horror, astonished by the devastation.

"Come on, Mr. Bolt, I'm not some dipshit in a TV script. Where are the original tapes?"

Ryan knew that each time he cooperated, he was just moving closer to his own death. Tony leaned down and tried to open the briefcase. The originals were inside. Once Tony found them, it was over, but the combination locks were set and it wouldn't open.

"How do you get this open? What's the combination?" Tony asked.

"I don't remember," he said, lamely. Tony turned the gun at the case and fired. The briefcase blew open and three videotapes rolled out on the ground.

Tony held them up and looked at them.

"This everything?"

"No, I made copies."

Tony was smiling at him, and then he put the tapes on the ground and stomped hard on each one, shattering the cassettes. He pulled the tapes apart and unwound them. Ryan considered charging him while both of his hands were busy with the broken cassettes, but Tony read him again and pulled the gun up.

"Nothing says you gotta die here, Mr. Bolt, 'less you make a mistake." New York Tony took out a cigarette lighter and set fire to the tapes. They didn't burn at first but finally started to blacken and curl as the small flame licked at the edges.

"Know what I think?" Tony said as the tapes were smoldering between them.

Ryan's body felt weak.

"I think this is the whole deal, right here. I don't think there's any more copies."

"You're wrong," Ryan said.

"Turn around, Mr. Bolt."

"What're you gonna do?"

"I'm just gonna ask you to face the other way while I get outta here," Tony lied, thumbing back the hammer on the .22, getting ready to do the kill shot, wishing he were back in the West Jersey Cattle and Meat Packing Company where he could work close, feeling the heat of the animal against his leg. He liked doing his disco shots while the big bovines stood, waiting. But this guy was quick, so he kept his distance.

"Come on, turn around," he ordered.

Ryan knew he was out of time. He turned, planting his right leg, then pivoted back and hurled the turn indicator at New York Tony, who saw it coming too late. It hit him above the right eye. Tony fired prematurely. His first shot went wild; his rhythm was off. Ryan was scrambling for the trees and Tony fired a second time, hitting Ryan in the left thigh. A large chunk blew out of his leg, causing him to spin around and land on his back in the wet leaves. In a flash, Tony was upon him, wiping the blood from the small gash over his right eye. He held the .22 on Ryan.

"We're gonna skip the closing prayer, asshole." He thumbed the hammer back, pointed the gun at Ryan's head, moving the sight up so it was aimed at a spot between his eyes.

Then New York Tony's head exploded.

Red mist, bone, and original thought flew into the air and rained down on Ryan, a wet salad of destruction. For a horrible moment, Tony's headless torso was still standing over Ryan, the gun gripped in its hand. And then New York Tony made his last cool disco move. His left leg buckled and he spun around in a tight circle and fell sideways, landing two feet to the right of Ryan.

Ryan felt numb all over. Then he saw movement in the trees and a stocky, middle-aged man moving slowly toward him. The man was wearing a Hawaiian shirt under an overcoat. He had a huge .357 Magnum in his hand and a chewed-up cigar wedged in the side of his mouth. He came over and looked down at Ryan.

"Hi, I'm Kazorowski. You looked like you was in need of a dust-off," the grizzled ex-fed said.

DR. JAZZ

KAZ GRINNED AT THE HEADLESS CORPSE. "TONY, YOU'RE BEAU-
tiful, babe. . . ."

Ryan tried to focus on the big man in the Hawaiian shirt, green
and purple palm trees strobed on yellow Dacron. Ryan was bleeding
badly as Kaz looked into the wound and whistled.

"You're missing a pound a' hamburger and a quart a' ketchup. We
gotta get you fixed up, then I'll come back here an' take care a' this
hard-on." He grabbed Ryan by the elbow and helped him up.

Heavy arterial blood started to ooze. Kaz got him in the back of
the station wagon, stripped off his Hawaiian shirt, rolled up the florid
monstrosity, and tied it above the wound. He looked around in the
dirt for something to make a tourniquet and found the turn indicator
that Ryan had thrown at Tony. Kaz stuck it through the knot and
twisted it.

Ryan was gritting his teeth and felt himself starting to go into shock.

"Let this loose every minute or two. I know a guy in Trenton who can fix you up." Kaz put on his overcoat and got behind the wheel of the stolen wagon and pulled out, leaving his tan rental behind.

The "guy in Trenton" was an ancient, stringy black man named Dr. Jazz. He was in a ghetto wood house with boarded-up windows that seemed to be growing out of a bed of broken household appliances. Dr. Jazz had an Adam's apple the size of a handball. He was shaved bald and his black dome glistened. Bicuspids flashed in 24-carat gold. His black eyes were always laughing.

"I'm sittin' here feelin' the jazz and along comes an ugly fed name a' Kaz," he intoned, grinning and showing more shiny yellow metal. His voice was high and reedy with a singsong West Indies lilt. He was looking at Ryan in the back of the wagon. "Man, you be comin' real close t' glory. So come on in, tell Dr. Jazz the story."

Ryan was getting cold—he assumed, from loss of blood. He leaned up on his elbows, shivering as he looked at the black man standing on the porch with rotting wicker furniture sagging behind him.

"Ryan, this is Dr. Jazz," Kaz said. "He's gonna sew you up."

The old man grinned wider, showing two holes in his lower bridge. Ryan looked over at Kaz. "What kinda doctor?"

"Dr. Jazz has zipped up more than one outlaw an' more than one lawman. Any time a man's got a hole in him, he thinks it's better not to report, Dr. Jazz has the pizzazz."

"I put mor'n one stitch on yer tired, ugly ass," the doctor said. "Bring him inside 'fore he pumps hisself dry."

Kaz pulled Ryan up out of the back of the wagon and threw him over his shoulder in a fireman's carry. He lumbered up into the old man's house, across the porch, stepping over a sleeping cat, into the tattered front room.

"Bring you back here where we got the big mirror and set ya upright under the big light," the old man rhymed to his bleeding patient.

The guest bedroom was a doctor's office. There was a steel medical table, immaculate under an enormous surgical light. There were medicine cabinets and steel tables; syringes in plastic wrappers were laid out on a white towel. A drug cabinet full of metal-topped bottles was on one wall. Ryan took some comfort from the equipment in the room.

"Kenetta," Dr. Jazz called out.

In a few seconds, a beautiful black woman, about twenty-five, with her hair braided in dreadlocks, moved into the room.

"Hey, Kaz, you look better than the last two times you was here."

"Kenetta, this is Ryan Bolt. Kenetta is Dr. Jazz's daughter."

She looked at Ryan for a beat while Dr. Jazz scrubbed up at a big sink in the adjoining bathroom. Then she leaned down and looked at the wound.

"Jeez, what did this?"

"Twenty-two dumdum," Kaz said.

"Come on, chile," Dr. Jazz yelled from the bathroom where he was scrubbing up. She took a green surgical smock out of the sterile wrapping and moved over to her father and opened it.

Kaz looked at Ryan, who was still not convinced. "Dr. Jazz was a surgeon in Kingston, Jamaica. He had some political trouble in the seventies and had to leave. The trouble chased him and he wasn't able to get licensed in this country. He knows what he's doing. Believe me, you don't wanna go to the hospital. Mickey will find you there."

Ryan was too weak and in too much pain to wonder who this huge, disheveled man was, where he had come from, and how he knew about Mickey.

He watched Kenetta get into her surgical gown and pile her braided hair up under a green paper cap.

"Think we better put da boy ta sleep," Dr. Jazz said.

Kaz nodded. "I'll be back once I take care of Tony."

Kenetta moved to Ryan and stood over him. "This is ether. We don't have lidocaine, but I have Adrenalin here and I'll monitor your vital signs. I'll bring you up if I have to. I'm sorry, but that's the way we do it."

"Shit," Ryan said, thinking he was a long, long way from the U.C.L.A. Medical Center with its pastel rooms and hermetically sealed breakfast trays. She poured the ether on a sterile cloth and held it under his nose. Dr. Jazz cut away the rest of his pant leg and studied the wound.

"Those dumdums sure do make a fucking mess, don't they, sugar?"
he said, less poetically, as Ryan slipped under.

It took Kaz twenty-five minutes to collect what he needed. He also
stopped and bought a flannel shirt at a surplus store.

He got back to the clearing in the stand of cypress trees at about
eleven A.M., he dug the hole in a ravine fifty feet behind the tree
line. He worked for almost three quarters of an hour with a shovel
he'd found in Dr. Jazz's garage. Finally, he dragged the Jersey killer
over and rolled him onto a blanket. He ripped open the bag of lye
Tony had bought and poured it over the body, closed the blanket,
then powdered the top. It was time for the last rites.

"Dear Lord," he said in mock seriousness. "Blessed are the truly
unwise for they bring hope to those destined to pursue them! Amen."
Then he kicked the powdered burrito containing New York Tony into
the shallow grave.

RECOVERY AND BETRAYAL

WHILE RYAN WAS STILL IN RECOVERY AT DR. JAZZ'S HOUSE, KAZ had rented a small room in a hooker hotel in Trenton called the Blue Rainbow. He had learned long ago that hooker hotels made great hideouts because the desk clerks and the staffs had no inclination to talk to the cops or anybody else, for that matter. Money was the only language anybody spoke. He had prepared the dingy, threadbare room, bringing the medication that Dr. Jazz had prescribed, along with clean sheets and blankets he'd bought that afternoon in a department store. He also bought an ice chest and four six-packs of Gatorade to restore Ryan's fluids and electrolytes. He bought two six-packs of Coke for himself. He put all the provisions in the room.

He picked up Ryan from Dr. Jazz at twelve-thirty A.M. Ryan was still out of it, mumbling incoherencies as Kenetta and Dr. Jazz helped get him into the Nova rental that Kaz had picked up that afternoon.

"Ain't gonna be much fun for a while," Dr. Jazz said. "He lost

half of his adductor longus and I hadda rebuild his iliotibial tract. . . .
I sewed what's left of the adductor to his vastus lateralis. He gonna
be gimpin'."

"I'm gonna have to put this on my account," Kaz said, "but I'll
get it to you."

"I don't work for cash," the old man said, the handball bouncing
up and down in his stringy neck. "You watch for infection and give
him dem antibiotics till they all gone."

He watched with old eyes as Kaz kissed Kenetta good-bye, then
got behind the wheel and drove Ryan away into the moonless night.

They arrived at the Blue Rainbow Hotel and Kaz pulled around to
the alley in the back and parked. He had already unlocked the fire
door. He got Ryan out of the seat and supported him so that he
wouldn't have to walk on his damaged leg. Kaz struggled to get Ryan
up to the second floor and down the hall. He passed a heroin-ravaged
hooker with striped orange hair, who smiled at Ryan through broken
teeth.

"Lookin' fo' some good times, baby? I buff yo' pink helmet, make
yo' Johnny feel so nice. . . ."

"Why don't we wait till he stops bleeding, sugar?" Kaz said pleasantly, wondering if she was blind or just brain-dead. Kaz got Ryan
into the room and onto the bed. He locked the door and put a blanket over him.

"Zoooo nooth. Luvvvv wingggg," Ryan said.

"You're very welcome," Kaz responded and he went to the cooler
and popped open a cold soda, sat down, and looked at Ryan, who
had already drifted back to sleep.

The Alos had put Ryan Bolt up on waivers and Kaz had claimed
him. He still didn't know why or how he fit the puzzle.

While Ryan was lying in the hooker hotel unconscious, Lucinda
had dressed and waited for New York Tony to come back. At eleven
o'clock, it was certain something was very wrong. Her brother had
been stomping around downstairs and had started using the phone.
She had tried to call Ryan at the Cape May Inn on her private line,
but there was no answer. She had gone downstairs and moved quietly

into the living room so that she could overhear her brother in the kitchen.

"Where the fuck is he?" Mickey was saying into the phone. "Look, not on the phone, okay? I think we gotta figure it didn't happen. I'll talk to you in an hour." He hung up and spun around and caught his sister standing in the living room ten feet behind him, listening.

"Whatta you doing?" His eyes had that same shiny, glazed-over look she remembered from the park, twenty years ago.

"I just came down to get something to eat."

Mickey moved quickly, covering the short distance between them in less than a second. She tried to turn and run, but he grabbed her arm, spun her, and held her in a vise grip by both wrists.

"Where's Ryan? I tried to call him at the Cape May Inn," she said.

"Ryan doesn't exist anymore."

"Mickey, don't," she said weakly. "You're hurting me."

Finally, Mickey shoved her back. She stumbled and fell on the beach house carpet.

He moved to her and stood looking down. There was something absolutely soulless in the stare. "I told you not to see him. You chose to ignore me. . . . You went to Iowa anyway. If I can't trust you, Lucinda, I can't leave you in my life. Pack your stuff and get out." Then he turned and walked out of the room.

She packed and, half an hour later, left the beach house in the old Mercedes station wagon that was there for the servants.

She knew as long as Mickey was there, she would never return.

BONDING

BUD RENNICK ISSUED THE INVITATION ON BRENTON SPENCER'S
six o'clock news. It was a TV remote from the union headquarters
on East Fifty-seventh Street. Bud was standing on the steps of
the Teamsters headquarters dressed in a black suit. "We welcome
any help in this negotiation that we can get. If Governor Richards
thinks he has a solution, we'd be more than happy to hear it."

Ryan had been asleep for hours and the newscast woke him up.
He was now watching the TV propped up in bed, his leg on fire,
while Kaz sat in a straight-backed chair, drinking Coke out of a long-
necked bottle.

"This has A.J.'s fingerprints all over it," Ryan finally said under his
breath.

"Who's A.J.?" Kaz asked nonchalantly, hoping he would open up.

"Better question is, who are you?"

"We'll get around to that. First I wanna know what you're doing with Mickey Alo."

"Why?" Ryan answered, feeling dizzy.

"If you keep answering questions with questions, we're not gonna get far."

"Why should we get anywhere?"

"Am I remembering this correctly? Weren't you about to get dum-dummed off the fucking planet when I showed up?"

Ryan felt too weak to answer. He wished somebody would get a chain saw and cut his leg off.

"So, who's A.J.?" Kaz asked again, as if no time had passed.

"Teagarden. He's Haze Richards's campaign chairman."

"You feel strong enough to answer my other questions?"

Ryan studied the man who had saved his life and decided he owed him something.

"You're Ryan Bolt, right?"

"Right."

"What's your connection to the Alos?"

"I was Mickey's roommate in prep school," Ryan said as Kaz's expression went flat.

"Don't shit me, Bolt. I'm looking for comedy, I'll go watch pigeons fuck."

"He and I went to Choate School in Connecticut twenty years ago. We were roommates. I didn't pick the room assignments." The two traded empty stares.

"So why are you hanging with him now?"

"When you get through with this interrogation, are you gonna let me know who you are?" Ryan's leg was getting worse. He looked down at the bandage, still seeping blood.

"Depends on whether I like what I hear."

"When my son died a year ago, Mickey came out for the funeral. I hadn't seen much of him since college, but he helped me get through it. And then . . . I hit a rough patch, careerwise, this year, and he said he'd help me out."

"What career? Whatta you do?" Kaz asked, but he already had a pretty good idea. He'd been shopping in Ryan's wallet and found his

Writers Guild card and his T.V. and Motion Picture Academy memberships. Unfortunately, there were no picture IDs.

"I'm a writer-producer in television."

"So, Mickey calls you up, asks you to come out here. Why?"

"To make a documentary film on the candidate."

"Must a' been a pretty shitty film."

Ryan looked at him blankly.

"Mob guys don't like a movie, they generally just walk out. They don't take the filmmaker into a field and try and blow his head off," Kaz explained.

"Yeah, it was a bad movie, especially if you want to put Haze Richards in the White House. It showed Haze to be a coward. Mickey wanted it back."

"It's a wonder you only got one hole in ya. You been stomping around in a mine field wearin' snowshoes." He set down the empty beer bottle. "My name is Solomon Kazorowski. I used to head the Vegas Organized Crime Unit of the FBI. I lost my job and my tin for trying too hard to put the Alos out of circulation. They got to my bosses, but Mrs. K. didn't raise no quitter, so I'm still in the hunt."

"FBI?" Ryan said, not really believing that this unkempt, sagging monster had ever been a member of the Bureau.

"Been off the job for ten years."

"You know Alex Tingredies?"

"The Tin Man? Yeah. Alex is good people. He's still wearing his asshole behind him. One of a dying breed down there."

"Mind if I call him and ask him about you?" Ryan asked, trying to forget the rising agony that was now consuming his whole left side.

"Don't trust me?"

"Just trying to get the snowshoes off."

"Last I heard, Tingredies was in Atlanta."

"He's back in D.C. I called him a couple a' days ago. I got his home number in my wallet."

Kaz found the number. He sat in the chair next to the bed and dialed. On the third ring, Alex Tingredies answered.

"Hello," the agent said.

"Is this Rin Tin Tingredies?" Kaz said, a smile forming on his face. "Who's this?"

"It's fucking J. Edgar Hoover, calling collect from Dead Fed Heaven."

"Gotta be Kaz. Don't tell me you're still vertical. I figured somebody would a' put a 'nine' through you by now."

"Gonna take more than nine millimeters to put me outta service." They both laughed, then: "Listen, you know a guy named Ryan Bolt?"

"Why?"

"He says he knows ya. I'm trying to find out who he belongs to. New York Tony put a round through his leg."

"Is he okay?"

"Yeah, but Tony's gotta bad headache. I sent him to harp class."

"Nobody's gonna miss that piece of shit."

"This guy Bolt . . . can you describe him?" Kaz said, looking at Ryan, who was trying hard not to move his throbbing leg.

"If he's six-two, 'bout one-eighty, pretty-boy good-lookin', California blond, it's probably him. He used t' be an all-conference wide receiver at Stanford. He's got some edge."

Kaz looked down at Bolt and nodded. "I'm gonna put him on. Tell me if this is the guy." He handed the receiver to Ryan, who took it and looked at Kaz.

"I thought I was checking you out."

"Hey, we're checking each other out, we're not getting married, so relax."

Ryan put the receiver to his ear. "Alex?" he said, weakly.

"Yeah. You okay?"

"Sorta. Who is this guy?"

"You know I don't throw compliments around, but Solomon Kazorowski was the best agent I ever worked with. I don't know what trouble you're in, but if it's got anything to do with Mickey Alo or any of that stuff we talked about yesterday, you better listen to him, Ryan. Anybody gets you outta the tunnel, it's Kaz. . . ."

"Thanks," Ryan said. "I'll put him back on." He handed the phone to Kazorowski, who put it up to his ear.

"He sounds trashed."

"He is, but he'll come back."

"Anything I can do for you?" Alex asked, worried.

"Yeah, send me a Hawaiian shirt. I'm walkin' around looking like Paul Bunyon. And if you got a wire on your phone, burn the tape. It wouldn't do either of us any good."

PRAIRIE FIRE

"**THESE TRACKING POLLS ARE UNBELIEVABLE,**" **A.J.** WAS SAY-ing. He was in Haze's hotel room in the Savoy. A.J. wanted Haze to stay with the Caulfields, but Haze was adamant, and in the long run, A.J. figured, it wasn't worth the effort. So they'd moved him into a suite on the seventh floor.

It was ten A.M., the morning of the Iowa Caucus. The campaign staff was gathered in Haze's room. . . . Besides Haze, Carol Wakano, the Rouchards, Ven and Van, Malcolm and Susan Winter were scattered around the suite in blue jeans and T-shirts, while A.J. moved back and forth in front of the window that framed a gray Iowa morning.

"Over all, we're tracking at twenty-one percent. We've knocked Skatina down to forty. He's not even gonna get a majority if this is accurate. The rest of these clucks are out of it. Gulliford is at ten, Savage at seven, Dehaviland . . . Get this—he's tracking at four percent after spending a whole two months kissing blue-ribbon pigs and getting tractor-seat hemorrhoids. Undecideds are down to twelve percent and leaning our way."

"How are the internals?" Malcolm asked.

"We've got a net plus of nine percentage points. On values, we're plus seven. Economy, we're plus fifteen—and we haven't said one thing about how to fix it, change it, or deal with it. Fucking amazing." A.J. was bouncing around the room. "I'm telling you, the message is a winner, a major pony. We're gonna come in second tonight, just like we planned. Then we're gonna get on that commuter train and ride down to New York and we're gonna fix what ails the Teamsters and the Truckers Association."

"How 'm I gonna do that?" Haze asked. "I don't even know what those guys are arguing about."

"I got it worked out, babe. Don't I always have it worked out?" He moved over and patted Haze on the cheek like an adoring parent.

Haze slapped his hand away. "Cut the shit, A.J. I need to talk to you."

"Okay, boys and girls, everybody go get brunch."

They all trooped out except Susan Winter, who was lounging in short-shorts and a halter top on the chair next to Haze. She made no move to leave, and Haze didn't shoo her out as the others left. Once they were gone, Haze got to his feet.

"How 'm I gonna solve the Teamsters strike? I walk in there with those guys, with the whole world watching. I look like a fool if I don't pull it off."

"Would you mind leaving us alone, Susan?" A.J. said to the twenty-five-year-old body woman, who was flexing her naked thighs seductively as she wiggled her toes in white, beaded moccasins.

"She can stay."

"I'm not gonna discuss this unless we're alone."

"You must of forgot, I'm the candidate for President of the United States."

"Shit," A.J. said, spit-spraying across the room. Some of it landed on Susan Winter's bare legs and she wiped it off with a grimace. "You actually think this is about you?"

"Of course it's about me. It's not your face, not your reputation that they're talking about."

"But they're my ideas, Haze. I'm the guy who comes up with the bullshit."

The argument arose so fast, it startled both of them.

"You wanna know how you're gonna solve the Teamster strike? I'll tell you, but get her out of here!"

The tension in the room multiplied again before Haze finally moved to the door and opened it. "Give us a minute, Sue."

She got up and moved out, taking her time, showing how she felt about it. When the door closed, Haze spun on A.J.

"I've had it with this shit! I won't be treated like some dumb asshole. I don't need you to tell me what I think."

"Hey Haze, if I wasn't here, you'd be selling twenty-year life policies for Aetna, and if you don't think I'm right, give me the gate and see how far this campaign goes."

"You're pissed off because I took Susan and you wanted her."

"No, I'm pissed off because every good idea, every piece of worthwhile strategy that ever happened for you came outta my head. And now we're sitting here, ready to make the biggest play of our lives, and you start sounding like you're actually responsible. I put Mickey Alo in the picture. I set up the debate. I came up with the defining event. Me! Not you! Me! And if you start to read the newspaper and think this is about you, then you're the stupidest son of a bitch on the planet!"

They glowered at each other across a threadbare carpet. Finally, Haze took a deep breath.

"How does this Teamster thing work?"

"I don't know. Mickey is working it out. He told me it's a done deal; all you gotta do is go down there, walk in that room with those two guys, spend an hour, walk out and announce that you made it happen. You brought management and labor together. You made America work again."

"I wanna know the terms of the agreement first."

"You wanna ratify the fucking contract?" A.J. was stunned. "All you know about trucks is they're hard to get around on the turnpike."

"Trucking wages and mileage fees affect the cost of goods. It's an expense that's passed on to the consumers. It directly affects the economic viability of our products in the world marketplace."

"Haze, stay out of it. You don't know shit about it. Let Mickey do the thinking. All you gotta do is take the credit."

Haze reached out and poked A.J. in the chest.

"Don't you ever humiliate me in front of my staff again. Don't ever treat me like that again."

"Or . . . ?"

"Or you're gone. I'll replace you."

"And who will do your thinking for you?"

"I will."

"I've known you since you thought it was funny to blow up Coke cans with firecrackers. Lemme tell you something, bubba. . . . You'd have trouble thinking your way out of a parked taxi. If it wasn't for me, you'd be nothing. If you wanna throw me out of the campaign just so that piece of ass outside thinks you're hot shit, then go ahead, but you won't be going to the White House."

A.J. turned and walked out of the room.

The Iowa Caucus results came in slowly that night because of a problem with the counting machines, but it was clear by nine o'clock that Haze Richards had done extremely well . . . and he'd done so at the expense of the Democratic front-runner, Leo Skatina. The headline in the next morning's *Register-Guard* was:

RICHARDS ON THE MOVE
IOWA VOTERS GIVE RHODE ISLAND GOVERNOR 25 PERCENT

It was a huge showing. He had gone from nowhere to second in just twenty days, a seemingly impossible task. The networks were already beginning to call it "The Iowa Miracle."

"Who is this political phenomenon and why did he strike such a chord in Iowa?" the NBC newscast said.

UBC declared Haze Richards the candidate to watch. Steve Israel included man-on-the-street interviews from Des Moines and Cedar Rapids, choosing only the ones that gave Haze the best boost. A UBC exit poll estimated, without any hard data to back it up, that had the Iowa Caucus taken place a week later, Haze would have actually won. In the last two days, Haze had acquired a press contingent of almost a hundred pod people and blow-dries. They were now following him around in two Greyhound Strato-Cruisers.

Vidal Brown held a press conference at the airport the morning after the election, just before they left on a charter flight for New Hampshire. Haze stood behind him, looking pleased. Also on the platform were Bud and Sarah Caulfield, who hadn't seen Haze, except on TV, for almost a week.

"And now," Vidal said, "I'd like to present to you the man from Providence, Rhode Island, who is destined to bring Providence to America . . . the next President of the United States, Haze Richards!"

Haze stepped forward on the small luggage platform that they were using as a makeshift stage. TV cameras panned and zoomed; his smile was washed in a halogen glow.

"Thank you. I want to thank the Iowa voters for their support." He turned to the ruddy farmer standing to his right. "And I want to promise Bud and Sarah Caulfield I'll be back. And when I get here, I intend to have legislation pending that will help them. We're about to take this country back and we're gonna do it for Americans like the Caulfields." Sarah reached out and grabbed his hand.

Japanese cameras recorded the event.

"Governor Richards," a reporter called from the crowd. "Bud Rennick and Tom Bartel have issued an invitation for you to come to New York and talk to them about the deadlocked Teamster negotiations. Is that something you're planning to do?"

"I intend to go to New Hampshire and fulfill two days of my campaign schedule; then I'll go to New York on Tuesday, if I'm still invited, and I'll see what I can do to help fix that situation."

A.J. had timed the meeting so the Teamster victory would guarantee New Hampshire. He thought the afterglow should last for two weeks if they worked the media right. The late momentum should carry them through Super Tuesday.

They boarded the plane and took off at four in the afternoon. Iowans waved good-bye till the plane was out of sight.

*   *   *

By the time they landed in New Hampshire, Brenton Spencer was already reporting the evening news. "A bombshell exploded in the Democratic presidential primary today as a small-time underworld player on trial for contract tampering in New York testified that Leo Skatina had made promises to the mob." The shot switched to a courtroom videotape where a street villain named "Too Fat" Jack Vasacci was sitting in a paneled witness box, his jowls dripping sweat on Armani lapels. "So we calls this guy in Albany who could get the job done."

"And who was the man in Albany?" the prosecutor's voice said, off camera.

"His name was Christopher Deleo. He's an aide to Senator Leo Skatina."

"And this man told you, you had the freeway contracts sewed up before the bids were filed?"

"That's what Deleo said. He said it went all the way to the senator for approval."

The shot switched back to Brenton Spencer, who looked solemnly into the camera from his anchor chair on the Rim. "The senator had no comment. As a matter of fact, he was unavailable today. His press secretary said that Mr. Deleo was no longer an aide of Senator Skatina, and that the testimony given under oath in the federal courthouse was totally untrue. He said further that Skatina as a U.S. senator was not involved in the issuance of state contracts. We'll be tracking this story as it develops."

Haze watched the late report from his suite at the Manchester House in Manchester, New Hampshire. He smiled as Leo Skatina was damned by the unsubstantiated charge.

He had no idea that A.J. had arranged the whole thing.

JOURNEYS

HE HAD BEEN STRUGGLING TO BREATHE AND THE OXYGEN BOTTLE
wouldn't help. Penny had called the doctor, but he hadn't arrived
yet. Joseph Alo's lungs were filling slowly with fluid. He was drowning from the inside. He had tried to cough, but the pressure on his
chest was too severe. He closed his eyes and wished the Lord would
take him.

The priest from the Trenton archdiocese arrived at noon and entered the dark room that had the sweet smell of death and medicine.
He kneeled by the bed and said a prayer of contrition. As he held
Joseph's hand, the dying Mafia don opened his eyes and looked at
the priest whom he'd never seen before.

The priest knelt and began the anointing of the sick. He put some
holy oil on Joseph's forehead, then anointed each of Joseph's palms.
"May the Lord who frees you from sin, save you."

Joseph did not view his excesses as sin. He had simply fought to provide for his family. He had taken on a world that showed him no mercy from the time he was a child, and now he lay in a bed, listening to his lungs filling, knowing he was at the very end.

He closed his eyes and he was a boy again. He was lying on his back in a beautiful green field. He was listening to the birds singing. The breeze was cool and strong . . . it ruffled his thick black hair. He had so much ahead of him, his life was just starting. And then, an old man in white robes and a long flowing gray beard leaned over him, taking the sun away.

"Are you ready?" the old man said to Joseph, the boy.

"For what?" Joseph's voice was the high soprano of his youth.

"Your next journey. I will help you up, but you must go alone."

As the old man offered his hand, Joseph reached up to take it.

In the bedroom, the praying priest became aware that Joseph's hand had just risen above his head. It seemed to be reaching out for something, but then it dropped slowly back to his side.

The priest looked over, but Joseph Alo had passed on.

While Joseph Alo took his last journey alone, Haze Richards began a much shorter one, accompanied by a hundred reporters. It started on the rail platform in downtown Manchester. He said a few solemn words about the need for a unified country before he got on the train. It was the way A.J. wanted it. A common man going into the jaws of certain defeat to help a nation he loved. He took the two-hour train ride into Manhattan with the skeptical press in the seats all around him. Pod people whispered behind their hands, saying he had almost no chance to succeed. Haze sat with his briefcase on his lap, looking out the train window. The rushing Connecticut landscape played like a travelogue with broken sprockets. He wasn't focused on the scenery.

He was imagining what it would be like to actually achieve his dream—what it would be like to be the *forty-third* President of the United States of America.

RECKONING

BRENTON SPENCER HAD BEEN FEELING TERRIBLE FOR A WEEK. HE had almost no energy and it was beginning to show on his newscasts. He couldn't sleep because his headaches were getting worse, waking him up in the middle of the night. He would stagger into the bathroom on unsteady legs, close the door so his wife, Sandy, wouldn't hear, and throw up in his decorator-approved black onyx toilet. He had made an appointment to see his doctor but he was dreading the visit. Something was terribly wrong.

The day that Joseph Alo died, his lead story was Haze Richards's trek to New York. He carried the story on the five o'clock newscast, using a field remote from reporter Doug Miles. Brenton sat at his anchor desk on the Rim, his concentration shot, while a worried Steve Israel talked him through the newscast with the ear angel.

"Come on, Brenton, you're up in five. Stop drifting. You've got to tag the remote," Steve was saying as the B-roll footage of Haze on the train platform was concluding. The floor manager gave him four fingers, then three, two, then pointed at Brenton who looked into the center camera, reading his copy in the lens TelePrompTer.

"Haze Richards has begun a train ride to New York in what is viewed by most as a futile attempt to solve one of the most complicated labor issues in America. He will be staying in Manhattan tonight at an undisclosed location and, in the morning, will try his hand at unlocking the struggle between America's truckers and the businesses that employ them." Then Brenton seemed lost as his copy ran out.

"Throw it to Hal," Steve coached.

"And now to Hal Reed for a campaign update," Brenton said.

While Hal was rattling on about local races, Brenton was wondering if he had brain cancer. What was causing these headaches? He got the broadcast back five minutes later for the last story, which was a brief reference to Joseph Alo's death. Steve Israel had elected to give it a light play for reasons that Brenton could only guess.

"Come on, Brenton, your copy's up," Steve said, and as Brenton read the lens TelePrompTer, a file shot of Joseph Alo was Kyroned over his shoulder.

"Joseph Alo, the founder of the national chain of steak houses known as Mr. A's, died at two-thirty this afternoon in his New Jersey home," he read. "Doctors say he had suffered briefly from a pulmonary respiratory disease. He was seventy-three." No mention was made of his alleged mob connections.

Ryan and Kaz watched the newscast on a black and white TV that was bolted to the dresser in the dingy hooker hotel. Neither one of them said anything until after Brenton Spencer finished his closing. Both were lost in their own thoughts. Ryan was worried about Lucinda, wondering where she was, how her father's death would affect her, how he could find a way to get in touch.

"I need to get out of this room for a while," Ryan said, looking over at Kaz.

In the three days since Kaz had brought him there, he'd never left the bed except when Kaz helped him to the bathroom, which was down the hall. That trip was a twice-a-day adventure that left him light-headed. Ryan's life had been slowed to a crawl. He had counted the water-stained tiles on the ceiling of the room several hundred times, making pictures out of the jagged brown shapes. A Rorschach nightmare that was warping him. He found that *The Mechanic* was rerunning at four A.M. on channel 6. He watched it twice, trying to regain some of the excitement he had once felt for the Emmy-winning show, but it seemed dull and shallow to him now. His own pretentious dialogue echoed insincerely across a landscape of personal excesses. Kenetta had dropped by once and changed the dressing. After she had finished, she smiled at him and told him he was doing great. Then she and Kaz had gone into the hall and whispered. When Kaz came back, he had avoided Ryan's eyes. Now Ryan just wanted to get out of the stifling, cum-stained hotel room.

"The doctor said you're not supposed to get up."

"Fuck it." Ryan sat up, carefully swinging his damaged leg off the bed and resting it on the floor. He tried to stand and put weight on the leg, but as soon as he did, it collapsed under him. He fell awkwardly back on the bed as Kaz ran and grabbed him.

"I'm getting outta here for a while if I have to crawl. You can help me or you can watch." His leg didn't have the sharp pain of a few days ago, but it never stopped aching. He was afraid he'd lost a lot of muscle that he'd need to walk. Kaz helped him up and looked at the heavy bandage on his leg, hoping Ryan hadn't broken the stitches loose.

They avoided the prying, vacant eyes of the resident hookers by moving out the back through the narrow, dirty corridor. Kaz left Ryan leaning on the doorjamb as he went and got the car, brought it around, and helped Ryan into the front seat. The cold January night air perked Ryan up.

They drove around Trenton until Kaz found a bleeding meat joint that was empty and out of the way. Kaz helped Ryan out and got him into the back booth of the diner. They ordered rare steak and coffee while a waiter set the table. After he left, they took stock of each other.

"I may not be the smartest guy on the planet, but I don't figure you came outta that stand of trees and blew up Mickey's driver be-

cause you needed target practice. I also don't think you're taking care
of me because you want a career in nursing."

"Why don't you keep talking and I'll tell you when you stop making sense."

Ryan filled him in on how Mickey had approached him; how
he'd decided to get out of Hollywood and give his battered career
a rest. He told Kaz about going to work in Princeton for Malcolm
Rasher, about the confrontation in Joseph's study, and the overheard conversation between A.J. and Mickey during which A.J.
mentioned cash from the Bahamas. He told him about Haze Richards and the Republic Airlines flight . . . the tape Kellica shot and
the man who attacked him in the Savoy. He ended with the troubling argument with Mickey in the boathouse and the feeling that
he'd overplayed his hand. When he was finished, Kaz sat there di-
gesting it all.

"What's your connection with Mickey's sister?"

"She's a friend. I've known her since I was fifteen, she was seven."

"Bullshit. You've got a case on her," Kaz said.

"Mickey is probably going to take over now that his father is dead,"
Ryan said, trying to change the subject.

"So the Alos are trying to put Haze Richards in the Oval Office.
. . . Ain't that a fucking nightmare?" Kaz thought for a minute. "A
campaign would be a great laundry, the money can't be traced."

Ryan picked up his coffee. It was cold.

"When you saw the story about Haze going to the Teamster meeting, you said A.J.'s fingerprints were all over this. What'd you mean?"

"A. J. Teagarden doesn't let Haze do anything where he doesn't
already know what the result is going to be. If Haze is going to New
York to try and solve that strike, then you can bet it's already a done
deal," Ryan said.

"Mickey could set that up easy."

They sat in silence and thought about it.

"'Y' know what doesn't figure?" Ryan finally said, bringing Kaz back
from his thoughts. "Here, we got Brenton Spencer, this prime-time
network anchorman who's got this bulletproof TV persona, always in
control. He's hosting a nationally televised debate and, because one

of the candidates calls him to task for his attitude on stage, he completely loses it. I don't buy it. People like Brenton Spencer don't act on random emotions. I think Spencer may be in on it."

"Why don't we talk to him and find out?" Kaz replied, realizing he finally knew what his next move should be.

FOOL'S ERRAND

THE PRESS HAD BEEN MILLING THERE FOR HOURS, ADDING THEIR gum wrappers and cigarette butts to a sidewalk already littered with beggars and pigeon shit. A.J.'s plan had been for Haze to go in alone and emerge from the room a few hours later, victorious.

Haze moved into the old building on East Fifty-seventh Street. The press swarmed. Sun guns went on, directional mikes were unsheathed like Wilkinson swords, questions were fired in an overlapping flow of hyperbole and skepticism.

"No comment," Haze said to the clattering motor-drive lenses. "I'm trying to find Bud Rennick."

A door opened and Bud stuck his massive head out.

Camera lenses focused.

Shutters grabbed milliseconds of pictorial truth.

Bud grabbed his jacket, put it on as Tom Bartel came out of the same room and joined him in the hall.

"Anybody expecting me?" Haze asked dryly. CNN had elected to go with the story live and their "on-site" producer was pushing his cameraman forward.

"We're live," he was saying as if his fellow newsmen cared. "Outta the way."

"Come on in," Tom Bartel said, shaking Haze's hand. They moved into the room and closed the door, leaving the press in reportus interruptus.

The high-ceilinged conference room was a rectangular war zone. Paper cups, empty Winchell's boxes and crumpled yellow legal sheets littered the battlefieled, dead reminders of the struggle. The room had been cleared of business agents and lawyers for Haze's visit.

"We have a deal," Bud said. "I caved on all Tom's points."

"I'm a happy camper," Tom Bartel said, grinning.

Haze sat down at the table, opened his briefcase, and took out a deck of cards. He finally grinned. "Anybody wanna play gin rummy?"

Two hours later, they walked out into the glare of the TV cameras. Bud put up his hand for quiet over the din of shouted questions.

"Excuse me, excuse me . . . be quiet. We have a statement." They waited until the news crews settled down.

"We've reached an accord," Tom Bartel said. "We've signed a tentative agreement, which I'm sure we'll be able to get ratified within hours by the association."

A loud gasp went up from the pod people and the live-at-fives.

"Speaking for the Teamsters," Bud concluded, "I want to say that we're happy. I've been empowered by my board to accept this tentative agreement and I'd like to tell the brotherhood . . . Get back in your trucks, guys, this thing is over."

Through it all, Haze said nothing. He stood between them, looking grateful.

"Governor Richards, Governor Richards . . . Stan Hooks, *CBS Business Report*," a tall, bald reporter yelled. "What did you bring to these negotiations to produce this amazing result?"

"I didn't settle this dispute, I want to make that clear. I simply brought to the table some new cards and an open mind," he said truthfully. "This was not a dispute where labor and management couldn't come to terms. This was simply an example of ending the divisiveness and making good things happen because good people on both sides of the issue are trying diligently to solve problems. I was glad to be part of it. I believe America can work again if we let it."

In his park-view room in the Sherry Netherland Hotel, A.J. watched the live coverage on CNN while he ate his room-service lunch. He had a smile on his face and pasta sauce in his beard.

"Un-fucking-believable." He grinned at the TV screen.

CHECKING THE BOX

THEY STARTED SHOWING UP AT NOON. SAD-FACED VISITORS IN black suits with silk shirts and hand-painted ties. First to arrive were the Medinas. With his son beside him, the don from New York sat in the back of his maroon, custom-made Rolls-Royce with the bulletproof door panels. His two creepy Vietnamese bodyguards were riding in the front seat.

Bart "the Doctor" DiAgusta arrived at one, with his wife and three sons. They'd flown commercially from Chicago. The Doctor had made his name by dismembering his enemies with a chain saw in a sixties business dispute with the New York Colombos. He rolled down the window in his rented limo and looked at the two Alo guards under the supervision of Pulacarpo Depaulo, who was a cousin of Mickey's and fresh off the boat.

"DiAgusta," he said to the recent arrival from Palermo, who found the name on his guest list and checked it, asking politely in his fractured English if the driver could let DiAgusta off at the main house and bring the car back down because it was going to get crowded up there.

Penny was in full mourning and greeted them all, thanking them for their condolences.

Mickey was in the study, receiving each guest separately, talking softly, assuring every one that his father had died in peace, that the family would endure.

Some had come out of respect, but all were looking forward to the open-casket funeral where they could make absolutely sure Joseph Alo was one-hundred-percent stone-cold dead. Then they would deal with Mickey and decide whether he was strong enough to hold on to what the Alos had.

Lucinda was upstairs. She had heard about her father's death on television and had come home to the big house to be with her mother. She had been trying to avoid her brother. They both happened to be in the kitchen at the same time and looked at each other without saying anything. She moved around him and out into the hall. People spoke to her and expressed condolences but largely ignored her. This was a time of sorrow, but it was also a time for politics. Any shift in power affected them all. New alliances were already being forged and tested. Lucinda had gone upstairs to be alone, trying to come to grips with the mixed emotions she felt about her brother's anger and her father's passing.

The funeral was at six. The church Mickey had chosen was a Gothic Catholic cathedral in downtown Trenton. Mickey had selected the church because it was large, but also because there was a protected side entrance that would make it difficult for the OCB surveillance cameras to get clear shots of the mourners.

At five in the afternoon, the pipe organ played a dirge for Joseph. Long-lens cameras rested on doorjambs of federal sedans. Blank-faced agents with buzz cuts watched, not bothering to disguise their presence.

The church was full. Late arrivals stood in the back, in silence. Many of the mourners crossed themselves and thanked God that Joseph Alo was really in the box.

Mickey spoke to them from the carved pulpit. The light refracted from the stained-glass Jesus on the cross threw a river of red across the floor in front of him.

Mickey spoke of the loss a son feels when his father passes, of the pure love that exists in a bloodline. He praised the guidance his father had given him. He said his life would never be as full as when his father was there to explain its inconsistencies and fight against its corruptions. It was a moving eulogy and would have been even more heartwarming if Lucinda hadn't been close enough to see Mickey's eyes. They were shining with excitement. Mickey Alo was finally in control and anyone who thought they could take his turf would be watching the parade from a skybox.

They put Joe in the ground as the sun was setting and returned to the Alo estate, where a tent had been set up over the tennis court. The space was warmed with party heaters. A band played peasant songs from Sicily. Penny and Lucinda roamed the periphery of the gathering feeling oddly out of place.

Penny went up to her room at nine, leaving Lucinda alone. After a minute, she found herself again face-to-face with her brother. This time, he smiled at her.

"Hi," he said.

"Hi."

Mickey took Lucinda's hand and led her out of the tent and around the side of the house. They stood listening to the music and laughter coming from the tent.

"That was really nice, what you said about Daddy."

"Thank you. Are we okay?" he said, looking at her carefully. "What I said the other day, I didn't mean it. I've been upset because of Pop. Can you understand that?"

"Yes," Lucinda said, realizing that she was now desperately afraid of her brother, that she was choosing her words instead of speaking her mind, that she wanted to get away from him.

He reached out and hugged her, but his eyes were cold and impersonal. "We're a team," he said. "I'd never let anybody hurt you. I'd never do anything to make you unhappy." He kissed her cheek. "I gotta get back. We'll talk after everybody leaves," he said, moving away.

She watched him go and then looked down. At her feet, she saw a faded wooden cross. She had made it when she was seven. She had knelt in her bathroom, crying, and nailed the wood together. She had painted the name on with her mother's nail polish. She had crept outside late at night and pounded it into the ground with a rock. She had prayed to God to take the soul of Mickey's dog. She had promised herself never to forget the puppy's happy face.

Her brother's voice rang in her ears. . . . *I'd never do anything to make you unhappy.* But he had laughed after his dog had been shot. Somehow he found that funny.

She looked down at the weathered cross and knew everything he said was a lie. "What about Rex?" she finally whispered.

ROUST

KAZ WAS GOOD AT ROUSTS. EVERYBODY STARTED OUT WITH A pile of attitude—"I got my rights"; "I'm gonna call my lawyer." What you had to do was get the bandits to buy into the concept of fecal gravity.

"Shit runs downhill," he used to shout at the frightened felons who were trying to tough it out in Vegas in front of his elite "mob squad" of feds.

Usually he could turn them. He'd convince them they had a better chance with the Vegas DA than their own asshole buddies. Of course, most of them weren't very smart.

Brenton Spencer would be a lot tougher, but the thing about people involved in a criminal conspiracy was, they were always sure they were gonna get found out. That thought haunted them. Their own imaginations were what finally busted most of them. Brenton wasn't used to being interrogated, so Kaz had to get him away from his normal surroundings, find a place where he felt uncomfortable, and convince him he was involved in a federal crime.

Kaz had spent the last day setting up for the roust. He'd called a friend in the federal prosecutor's office and explained what he needed. The closest thing they could find to a suitable crime was in Statute 348.7 of the Federal Election Code, which governs ballot box tampering and illegal voter registrations. Kaz had done a cut-and-paste job on the document, matching typefaces, inserting a paragraph saying that any person who attempted to unduly influence the outcome of a national election could be charged with felony malfeasance of the political process and violation of federal election law. Then he'd photocopied the document so that it was on one sheet of paper and looked official. He had that little jaw-breaker in his pocket as he took the elevator up to UBC and got out on the Rim.

The first thing that struck him was that there were one hell of a lot of young people running around in a hundred different directions with no apparent destination. He grabbed a young man who was flying past.

"Looking for Brenton Spencer," he said.

"Oh God," the young man said, and ran off.

Kaz soon realized that this wasn't a room full of overeager yuppies. This was a room full of panicked people. He saw a crowd around an office door and elbowed his way in through the staffers until he saw a bald man in his late twenties, bent over the form of Brenton Spencer, who was lying unconscious on a white carpet. Steve Israel had his ear on Brenton's chest, listening for a heartbeat. Kaz was being pushed aside by some late arrivals trying to get a better look.

"It's okay," Kaz said. "I'm a doctor."

They immediately let him through and he moved to the fallen newsman.

"Anybody call the paramedics?"

"Three minutes ago," Israel said.

"What happened?"

"He's been having horrible headaches. He walked off the set, back to his office. When I came to get him, he was like this."

"Okay, gimme some room . . ."

Kaz had done his share of field triages, both in the Korean War and a couple of major Bureau shootouts. He started with vitals. Brenton had a reedy heartbeat, weak and irregular, and his breathing was rasping and shallow. Kaz opened his mouth and pulled his tongue free, clearing the throat. He thumbed open Brenton's eyes. The right looked normal but the left pupil was dilated to the size of a small-bore pistol.

"Brain hemorrhage. Get on the phone and tell the paramedics to alert the hospital they're gonna need a head cutter with a catcher's mitt. This guy is critical."

The paramedics arrived a few minutes later. Kaz helped them get Spencer on the rolling gurney and load him in to the ambulance. They tried to leave Kaz behind, but he flashed his lapsed credentials.

"FBI," he said. "Man's a material witness in a homicide. I'm coming." He didn't want to let Brenton out of his sight. The ambulance accelerated away from the curb and rushed across town, its siren hee-hawing at the traffic.

In the back of the ambulance, the vital signs were being relayed, by radio, to New York County Hospital, where the neurosurgeon was getting the operating theater ready. Kaz was concerned about the decreasing blood pressure and the irregular heartbeat.

The ambulance slowed down in traffic as critical minutes ticked by. The increasing pressure on Brenton Spencer's brain began to shut down precious nerve centers, obliterating memory, personality, and thought.

They screeched to a stop at the back door of the emergency room, the siren still wailing. Two attendants ran with the gurney, pushing it ahead of them into the waiting elevator.

"This is that news guy," one said as the elevator door closed, cutting them from view.

Kaz looked at his watch and pulled the phony criminal statute out of his pocket, ripped it up and sprinkled the shreds into the waste-basket.

He felt tired and angry. But the job was like that, he thought. Sometimes you were just too late with too little.

* * *

Ryan heard about Brenton on a news brief on TV and guessed it must have happened before Kaz got to him. He had been trying all afternoon to get in touch with Lucinda. He waited to call until Kaz left because he knew how the man felt about Mickey's sister.

He had tried the Alo house three times, but an unfamiliar male voice answered, so he'd hung up without saying anything. Then, on a hunch, he called his own answering machine in Malibu. After a few routine messages he heard her voice.

"Ryan, it's Lucinda. I need to talk to you. I borrowed my mother's cell phone, the number is: 609-555-9056. 'Bye." Her voice had sounded fragile, hesitant.

With nervous fingers, he dialed the number.

"Hi, I got your message," he said, his heart in his throat when she answered.

"I need to see you, Ryan."

"I'm at a hotel in Trenton called the Blue Rainbow. It's a little downscale, so don't be surprised. Room five-oh-six."

"Can't we meet someplace else?"

"No. You'll see why when you get here."

"I miss you," she said, tentatively. The sentence hovered somewhere between a statement and a question.

"I miss you, too. And, Lucinda, don't let anybody follow you."

There was a long pause on the other end of the line before she said, "Okay."

He lay in the small room, unarmed, and hoped he hadn't just invited his own death. He knew Lucinda wouldn't betray him, but Mickey could have someone following her. An hour later, he heard a light rap on the door. He pulled himself up and, using the desk chair as a walker, moved slowly across the room.

"Yes?" he asked through the paint-peeled door.

"Ryan, open up, it's me," she said.

He fumbled for the lock and swung the door open, throwing caution aside. She rushed into his arms, bumping into the chair, almost tipping him over.

She kissed him on the face, on the mouth. She was crying, tears streaming down her cheeks.

He held her tightly. It was the first time since Matt died that he could feel pieces of himself start to come back together.

She closed the door and looked down at his leg, wrapped in gauze, colored by seeping blood.

"What happened?"

"It's a long story."

She helped him to the bed and sat beside him. "Was it Mickey?" knowing already that it was.

Ryan nodded. "He sent Tony after me and, if I hadn't run into this ex-FBI agent, I'd be dead."

She turned and faced him, her expression grave. "I've done the same thing you did with that little boy, Terry. I've pushed ugly thoughts about Mickey away. I've refused to deal with what I always knew was in him. And now I've looked into his eyes and seen things that scare me."

"I know."

"I want to be with you, Ryan," she said, charging ahead, thinking if she didn't say these words now, she might never find the chance. "I know this is right."

He reached over and held her hand. She paused for a moment before adding, softly, "I'm afraid now that I've found you, you'll be taken from me before I get the chance to make love to you."

He kissed her on the mouth and drew her to him. He had never felt such longing. She sat up, unbuttoned her shirt and removed it. Reaching behind her, she unsnapped her bra and let it fall. Her breasts were full and round and her nipples were thrusting out. She stood to unhook her skirt and stepped out of it. Then she turned to him, wearing only her panties. She unbuttoned his one-legged jeans and eased them carefully down over his bandaged leg. Then she moved into his arms, holding him tightly.

Ryan had been aching inside for so long, he couldn't believe the feeling of comfort, the loss of pain, just holding her gave him. She told him she would never leave him, that she was his for the rest of her life. He started to taste the salt from the tears that were running down her cheeks.

The lovemaking was slow and more consuming than he had ever believed possible. She moaned with pleasure as they exploded together in climax, reaching secret places he had never explored before. And then they held each other in silence, listening to their hearts beating in combined rhythms. No words could describe their feelings, but in that moment, without needing words, they pledged themselves to one another.

ANOTHER WAY TO GO

KAZ CAME BACK TO THE ROOM AT THE BLUE RAINBOW HOTEL to check on Ryan. He'd been told by the intern on the fourth floor of County Hospital that the results of Brenton's surgery were problematic. The anchor had a dime-size aneurysm that had ruptured and knocked him flat. They'd opened Brenton's skull and tied off the bleeding vein, but until he woke up, or didn't, they would have no way of knowing how much damage had been done. Kaz had tried to press the intern for a prognosis, but the young doctor had refused.

"Each one of these is a whole new deal," he'd fudged. "We can't tell how much damage was done before we released the cranial pressure."

Kaz had learned that the practitioners of the fine art of sawboning hated to be wrong, more than they hated socialized medicine. They also panicked over the possibility of a malpractice suit. Therefore, they rarely gave prognoses. So Kaz had learned to ask medical questions differently.

"If you saw ten cases with about the same degree of cranial hemorrhaging, how many of those ten would ever regain any reasonable sense of normalcy?"

By asking the question that way, Kaz was allowing the doctor to avoid comment on a specific case and, at the same time, allowing him to exhibit his vast knowledge of cerebral hemorrhages without running the risk of being wrong.

"I'd say about two or three in ten would get back to something resembling a normal life," the intern said, giving Kaz the answer to the question he'd asked in the first place.

Brenton Spencer had less than a 30-percent chance to wake up and start talking—not very good odds.

The lobby was filling up with the press, so Kaz had gone back to the hotel to wait for news.

When he arrived, he found Ryan sitting up in bed, dressed in new clothes. Seated next to him, smiling, was Lucinda Alo. Kaz looked at them with disgust.

"Lucinda's going to help us," Ryan said, as Kaz scowled.

"I'm fucking delirious about that." Kaz moved to the window and, pulling the curtains aside, looked out into the alley, half expecting to see a dark sedan with two goombah hitters oiling silenced Sig-Sauers. The alley was empty.

"I assume you're Mr. Kazorowski. . . . "

"That's right." Kaz closed the curtains. "Where'd you get the new duds?"

"Lucinda bought them for me."

"You don't get it, do you? Her brother is trying to kill you. Why should she help you? Sicilians teach family loyalty from birth. . . . Nobody is ever allowed in between. But because you've got great teeth and sun-bleached hair you think this Mafia princess is gonna throw her family away so she can play house!" He started to collect his few belongings and jam them into his duffel bag.

"What'm I doing hanging with you? Good luck, but I'm outta here."

Ryan changed the subject.

"What happened to Brenton?"

"Brenton looks like a science fiction experiment. Got enough tubes comin' out of his head to plumb a duplex. We're probably not going to get anything outta him, but right now, he's all I've got."

"I had another idea. Cole Harris."

"Who's Cole Harris?"

"Cole Harris is a guy I knew in L.A. a while back. He used to be a reporter for UBC. Vidal Brown told me he was canned because UBC wouldn't run a series of stories he did on the underworld. Apparently, he accused Steve Israel of collusion with the mob and he was out on his ass before the end of the day."

Kaz stood looking at Ryan for a long time, not sure how to grade it. "That doesn't mean he knows anything about Brenton's connection to the mob or Haze Richards."

"Cole is one of those humorless bastards who thinks he's always right. If he thinks they fucked him, he'll be digging through their trash looking for evidence until he proves it."

"Where is he?" Kaz said, getting a little more interested.

"I don't know, but I'm gonna find out."

"Gonna take her with you?"

"Yes. I need help. I still can't walk."

"But you still can fuck, I bet," Kaz said, wishing immediately he hadn't.

"You're really something of an asshole, aren't you?" Lucinda said.

"You got that right. It's why I'm still alive. Assholes are hard to kill," Kaz fired back.

They glared at each other as a hooker screamed an insult through the wall.

"How do I reach you?" Kaz asked, relenting.

"I have my mother's cell phone," Lucinda said. "I'll loan it to you."

"And I have credit cards," Ryan said. "I'll buy another cell phone."

Kaz looked at the phone in Lucinda's hand, then took it from her. "I'm going back to the hospital," he said and walked out of the room, leaving Ryan and Lucinda alone.

"He's pleasant."

Ryan stood up, using the chair for balance. "Let's get outta here."

Lucinda bought a pair of crutches for Ryan at a hospital supply store. Ryan took the last of the antibiotics that Dr. Jazz had given him, hoping he had passed the danger point for infection. They picked up a cell phone at a Radio Shack with Ryan's credit card and gave the clerk an extra twenty to get it programmed immediately. Then they went to a fast-food restaurant and Ryan hobbled on his crutches to the pay phone. He dialed Steve Israel's assistant on the Rim in New York.

"How's Spencer doing?"

"Not good. He's still unconscious," she said.

"Listen, . . . I know this is a bad time, but I'm trying to reach Cole Harris. You got a number on him? We were friends in L.A. I'd like to look him up."

"He's an asshole. Steve fired him 'cause he was accusing everybody in the 'morning meeting' of killing stories for the wrong reasons."

"Did you ever see the stories?"

"No, but Steve said he didn't have corroborating sources. We'd've been sued if we'd run it."

"So, you don't know where he is?"

"Haven't heard from him. Wait a minute. I think he had a brother in Rye. Carson. Carson Harris. He's probably in the book."

"Thanks. See ya around." And he hung up.

Steve Israel met his assistant at the elevator and they got in together.

"Remember Cole Harris?" she asked.

"Do I ever," Steve responded.

"I was just on the phone with Ryan Bolt. He's trying to get in touch with him."

C. Wallace Litman had spoken to Steve the day before about Ryan Bolt. Wallace said that Ryan had left Haze's campaign and that nobody at UBC should cooperate with him. "Did you give him Cole's number?"

"I didn't have it, but I remembered he had a brother named Carson. I told him maybe he knows where Cole is."

The elevator stopped in the lobby. Then Steve snapped his finger. "Damn," he said. "I forgot something. Go ahead, I'll see you later."

Steve went back up to his office on the Rim and called C. Wallace Litman and told him what he had just found out.

PAYBACK

CHARLIE "SIX FINGERS" ROMANO HAD MADE THIRTEEN WEEKS see Mickey personally to explain how he'd fucked up the job on Ryan Bolt.

He met with Mickey at the gangster's home in New Jersey, just a few days before Joseph Alo died. Thirteen Weeks sat on a carved wood chair in the entry hall, his nose still taped together, hoping that Mickey wouldn't go apeshit and do something crazy. He was facing an oil portrait of a beautiful girl who looked a lot like the one who had hit him on the head with the ashtray. He walked over and looked at the painting more closely.

"That's my sister Lucinda," Mickey said, coming out of the den behind him. "You're Johnny Furie?"

Thirteen Weeks bowed his head as if he were standing before the Blessed Father.

"Don Alo, I apologize for making a mess of this. . . ."

"Did Ryan do that to your face?" Mickey said, amazed that Bolt could inflict such damage on a professional hitter.

"Uh . . . well, he's real quick." Thirteen Weeks cursed himself for blowing the first assignment Mickey Alo had ever given him. "Don Alo, I pray that you would allow me a second chance. I wish to make amends for this terrible mistake I have made," he said, sounding like a courtier in front of a feudal lord, but he wanted desperately to convey his respect for the Alos and his shame at his own failing.

"Don Alo, if you would give me the honor of a second chance, sir, I will finish the job and put Bolt away. I ask no payment, only that I be allowed to redeem this loss."

Mickey remembered the few times he and Ryan had fought as kids. He'd been surprised at Ryan's quickness. He also remembered watching a televised game in college. Ryan had caught four passes right in front of an all-American D-back from Ohio State, had burned him all afternoon with his speed and quick moves. It was this thought that allowed him to go easy on the bone-breaker standing humbly in front of him. Finally, Mickey nodded his head.

"Maybe I'll give you another chance. Leave your number and stick around close."

When Thirteen Weeks left the house, his knees were shaking. He stood on the Alos' huge porch, waiting for his car to be brought up by the stocky Sicilian greaseball who parked it. He made the sign of the cross. "*Bella fortuna,*" the Irish bruiser murmured in Italian. He'd been spared. It wasn't until he was standing on the porch that he remembered the painting and the fact that he'd failed to tell Mickey that his sister was with Ryan Bolt. Then he thought, *Don't get into it, Johnny. . . . You're in enough trouble as it is.*

Five days later, he got the call. A man he didn't know told him to call Mickey from a pay phone. He ran to the pay phone across the street and got through to Mickey, who was waiting at another pay phone in Trenton.

"You on a secure phone?" the gangster asked.

"Yes, sir."

"You know who this is? Don't use my name."

"Yes, sir."

"One-six-seven Hamilton Boulevard, Rye, New York. He's headed there. Get the tapes and then finish the job." And the line went dead.

Thirteen Weeks knew if he could pull this off, he'd get back into Mickey's good graces. He sprinted back across the street and grabbed the Beretta out of his suitcase along with two boxes of shells, ran out the door, and jumped into his rented LeBaron. His heart was pounding. "It's payback time," he murmured to himself as he floored the car.

Ryan found Carson Harris in the Rye phone book and called. Carson's wife told him that her brother-in-law was living there and would be back at five. Instead of calling later, Ryan decided to go there immediately. He wrote down the address: 167 Hamilton Boulevard.

He and Lucinda got back in the Mercedes station wagon and headed for Rye. Lucinda was behind the wheel.

Ryan put his head back and rested as she drove. His leg was throbbing. They arrived an hour later at Carson Harris's house on Hamilton Boulevard. It was five-thirty. The house was in the middle of a tree-lined block of one-story wood-frame houses.

Lucinda parked in the narrow driveway and came around to help Ryan out of the car. He grabbed his crutches and the two of them moved slowly toward the house. Neither of them had any reason to take notice of the LeBaron parked across the street.

When they reached the porch, Ryan saw that the front door was ajar. He rang the doorbell and a woman's voice called from inside.

"Come on in, door's open."

Ryan looked at Lucinda. She shrugged and Ryan pushed the door open, then hiked himself over the doorjamb on his crutches and into the front room of the house.

They were in a small living room furnished in Early American with colonial wood spindle chairs. Over the fireplace, two sabers were crossed over a painting of a white-haired man in a Union officer's uniform. The brass plaque on the bottom of the frame said: COL. RUTHERFORD B. HARRIS.

"Hello . . . Mrs. Harris?" Ryan called out.

"I'm in the back," a woman's voice answered. Something tingled on the back of Ryan's neck. The woman sounded friendly, but Ryan was suddenly filled with apprehension.

"Get outta here," he whispered to Lucinda. He pushed her with his hand.

"Why? What's wrong?"

"Call the cops." He tossed her the cell phone. "Go!"

She turned and moved out of the house.

"Mrs. Harris, it's Ryan Bolt. I talked to you on the phone," he called.

"I've got my hands full," the woman's voice called back. "I'm in the kitchen."

Now he could detect some tightness in her voice. He looked around the room for something to defend himself with, then took the two sabers from the hooks above the portrait. Neither was very sharp, but he picked the better of the two and hooked it into the back of his belt by the hilt. With the sword banging the back of his right leg, he hobbled on his crutches down the narrow hallway through the small dining room to the kitchen.

The kitchen was small, painted white with blue trim on the cabinets.

A plump thirty-year-old woman with shoulder-length brown hair was by the sink with both hands in the dishwater and a terrified look on her face. Suddenly, the pantry door to his right swung open, and the man he'd fought in the Savoy Hotel was standing there with a large automatic aimed at Ryan's chest.

"Good things come to them that waits," Thirteen Weeks said inanely, his mouth grinning under his taped-up nose.

"He forced me," Bea Harris said, her voice tiny.

Ryan could see now that she had tears running down her cheeks.

"Old business first," Thirteen Weeks said. "You got a few video-tapes I need. Where are they?"

"In a locker at the bus station."

"Whatta you going to do with me?" Mrs. Harris said.

"We all go to the bus station. Then we'll see."

Ryan didn't think there was much chance that this monster was going to leave either of them alive.

"Car's out in front. Let's go." Ryan knew if he turned around, the antique sword would be visible. It was his only weapon, even though he didn't think it would do him much good.

"I said, let's go."

Ryan stood in the door, leaning on his crutches, looking for an opening. Johnny Furie moved closer, holding the gun steady, aiming it at the center of Ryan's chest. His smile remained steady as he kicked the bandage on Ryan's bad leg. Ryan screamed in pain and spun to his right. As he went down, he swung wildly with his crutch and hit Thirteen Weeks a grazing, but futile, blow across his cheek with the rubber tip. Johnny jerked his head back and fired the gun, missing Ryan who was now on the floor. Ryan's reflexes took over and he scrambled to his feet. He could feel stitches popping like buttons flying off a ripped shirt. As he lunged to his left, his wounded leg collapsed under him and he landed on his knees. Pain shot up his left side and he almost lost consciousness. Mrs. Harris screamed and ran out the back door. Johnny turned and fired at her. The slug blew a hole in the doorjamb by her head as she fled into the yard.

Ryan pulled the sword off his belt and Thirteen Weeks sensed this movement and spun back toward him. Ryan swung the saber with both hands in a vicious, but careless arc, his vision a blur from the pain.

Johnny Furie was pivoting forward, firing the automatic in front of him.

The sword flashed, hitting Johnny's right wrist with tremendous force.

He screamed as they both heard the sound of his wrist bone snapping.

Johnny watched in disbelief as his severed right hand with the gun still in it hit the floor at his feet. The gun fired once as the fingers convulsed and the recoil caused the hand to skid across the waxed linoleum toward Ryan. Johnny looked on in horror as the stump on the end of his right arm sprayed red blood from the severed artery all over the freshly painted kitchen.

Johnny let out another chilling scream.

Then the back door slammed and Cole Harris ran into the kitchen. He was a Jewish-Italian mixture with blue eyes and black hair slicked back. He looked in amazement at Thirteen Weeks who was now holding the bloody stump in his left hand, screaming, "Fuck! Fuck! Fuck!" in fright and shock.

Ryan tried to get up but his leg was useless.

"Ryan?" Cole Harris said, pulling up the name from memory as his eyes darted back to the 250-pound monster who was hosing down the walls with arterial spurts.

Thirteen Weeks let go of his stump long enough to grab for his gun hand, but Ryan used his good leg to kick the hand across the kitchen. It wedged under the dishwasher, the gun still gripped in the fingers. Thirteen Weeks let out a howl, then turned and ran out the back door.

The sound of sirens approaching could be heard in the distance.

"Cole, I need help. Get me outta here."

"Who was that guy?"

"I can't go to the hospital. They'll kill me." He could feel himself going into shock. Cole helped him up, his leg was bleeding badly. Ryan leaned on Cole and they headed out of the house through the front door.

Lucinda was across the street and ran to help them as Cole loaded Ryan into the back of a VW van parked in the driveway.

"I called the police." She looked at his leg. "What happened?"

"Gotta get outta here," Ryan said, dully, as the sirens got louder. "Follow us. Don't leave your car."

Lucinda tailed the VW van. They turned the corner at the end of the street seconds before two police cars squealed onto Hamilton Boulevard.

The police found Thirteen Weeks's gun hand wedged under the dishwasher. A rookie patrolman gingerly kicked it out and stared at it dumbly. They followed the trail of blood out the back gate and found Thirteen Weeks in the alley a block away, almost dead from loss of blood. They pulled him into the squad car, retrieved his gun from the kitchen floor, and went code-three to the Rye General Hospital.

Johnny Furie was immediately put on the critical list. The bewildered cops stood around, drank machine-brewed coffee, and wondered out loud how Johnny's gun hand had ended up under the dishwasher.

*   *   *

While Thirteen Weeks was being cross-typed for a blood transfusion and pumped full of plasma, Ryan was shivering in the back of Cole Harris's speeding van.

Lucinda had Kaz on the cell phone and told him what had happened.

"Don't take him back to the Blue Rainbow Hotel," Kaz said. "Find a place, but not on a busy street. Get a room in the back and call me with the address."

They picked a downscale motel off the main drag in Rye.

Kaz arrived with Dr. Jazz at nine-thirty. Lucinda couldn't believe they had been waiting two hours for the gold-toothed man, who came jiving and bopping through the door, carrying a medical bag. His bald head was shining, his Adam's apple tromboning up and down in his stringbean neck whenever he spoke.

Kaz tried to get Lucinda to go to the restaurant across the street with Cole Harris, but she refused. She spun on him.

"I've had it with your orders and your attitude," she said, venting all her frustration, fear, and worry about Ryan, in a counterattack on the rumpled ex-fed.

"Hold it, lady." He tried to slow her down.

"No, you hold it. I'm not leaving and I'm not taking any more of your shit!"

Kaz knew she meant business. He finally smiled and put out his hand. "Nice ta finally meet ya, Miss Alo," he said, laconically. She shook his hand, but didn't smile back.

Dr. Jazz was examining Ryan's leg. "He very sick. He pulled out de stitches, he ripped de veins. He in mighty bad shape," the doctor said, shaking his head, too concerned about Ryan to rhyme. He opened his medical bag, filled a syringe, and injected Ryan with antibiotics for infection. Then he gave him an Adrenalin shot to keep his heartbeat up. He took a blood sample in a syringe, twisted the needle valve shut, and put it in his medical bag. He cleaned the wound and resewed it, then bandaged it carefully. The entire procedure took him almost two hours. Dr. Jazz left the motel at some time past midnight.

Ryan slept fitfully while Lucinda held his hand.

He finally drifted slowly down into a deep sleep, where he dreamed of Lucinda, backlit and gorgeous. They were standing on opposite sides of a raging river, yelling to each other. "Don't come across," he screamed in the dream, but she didn't hear him and started to ford the treacherous water. Falling, she was swept away, arms flailing in the bubbling turbulence. He saw Kaz for a moment, drowning in the current, hideous in his green and yellow Hawaiian shirt, going down the stream with her, tumbling, rolling, his face appearing for a moment, the cigar soggy, still clamped in smiling teeth. And then he was on a deserted beach at sunset. He started walking, not knowing where he was going, until he saw Matt and Terry. They were sitting together on the beach, looking out to sea. Ryan came up and stood behind them.

"Can you forgive me?" he said to the two dead boys.

They turned and looked at him. "It was never your fault," they said in unison. And for the first time, still deep in the delirious dream, he believed it.

While Ryan was dreaming and Lucinda was praying, Thirteen Weeks was dying.

Charles Romano was his employer of record and the hospital insurance administrator called him for verification of employment. Charlie Six Fingers called Mickey and told him that Thirteen Weeks was in the Rye hospital, that somebody had cut off his right hand. Mickey and Pulacarpo Depaulo drove up to Rye and arrived at eleven o'clock. They found the back service stairs at the hospital and climbed to the second floor where Charlie Six Fingers had said Johnny Furie was recuperating. Mickey was resolute. A guy didn't get multiple chances to screw up. He wanted the word to go out. . . . You better not fuck up if you were working for Mickey Alo. Some time shortly after midnight, as the medical shift was changing, Mickey slipped into Thirteen Weeks's room and looked down at the huge accounts receivable specialist. Johnny's right hand was now a heavily bandaged stump.

"Hey, *paisan*," Mickey said, touching him on the side of the neck. When he didn't wake up, Mickey grabbed the bandaged stump and squeezed hard. Thirteen Weeks moaned and opened his eyes.

"Talk to me," Mickey said to the hitter.

"Cut off my hand," he stated the obvious.

"Where is Bolt?"

"Don't know. He cut off my hand," he said again.

"This fucking guy can't be working alone," Mickey said softly.

"I saw him coming into the house, through the front window, with the girl in the picture."

"What picture? Whatta you talkin' about?"

"The painting in your house."

Mickey's disgust at Lucinda turned his insides cold and his face empty.

Thirteen Weeks saw the expression and knew he was looking into the eyes of the devil. It was the last thing he saw.

Mickey ripped the pillow out from under Johnny's head, put it firmly over his face, and held it. Thirteen Weeks struggled to get the suffocating softness off his nose and mouth. His stumpy wrist pawed helplessly, trying to grab the pillow with remembered fingers. In a few brief moments, he stopped fighting. Like a light going out, he plunged into blackness.

I R

AFTER DR. JAZZ LEFT, COLE HARRIS WENT ACROSS THE STREET
and got a cup of coffee at a truck stop. Cole had had a few words
with the rumpled, cigar-chewing man whom Ryan called Kaz. His
journalistic instincts told him he was onto a big story.

For most of his life, chasing stories had been Cole's only passion.
He valued it over everything else in his fifty-six compulsive nit-
picking years. At his core he was an investigative reporter, an IR.

He had started doing journalism as a corporal in Vietnam, filing
personal action stories with *Stars and Stripes.* Cole had eventually
taken small-arms fire in his foot when an airfield in the Delta had
been overrun by VC in '63, and he'd come Stateside and mus-
tered out.

Shortly after, he had found a job on his hometown rag, *The Detroit
Free Press*, where he worked the crime beat.

Because of his dogged pursuit of minutiae, Harris had been extremely successful. In the early 1970s, he'd been hired by UBC to try broadcast journalism. He covered everything from the Cold War to Meyer Lansky's failed attempt to get into Israel.

His career had flourished until he'd tried to do a crime series on the mob's secret ownership of Atlantic City's gambling casinos. Cole had found enough hard evidence to call several casino gaming licenses into question. The news desk at UBC had killed the series for unexplained reasons. Cole had refused to drop it, despite a direct order to do so by the senior vice president of news, Steve Israel. Two weeks later, he'd been called into Israel's office.

"Your work is not up to the caliber this news division demands," the bald, young VP of the nightly news had said.

"You kidding me? I got two Pulitzers. . . . "

"Sorry. We had a discussion in the morning meeting yesterday and the executive producers agree."

"This isn't about my professionalism; this is about the fact that I don't want to drop the Atlantic City story," he'd said, his natural newsman's paranoia going ballistic.

"Just clear out your desk. Give your press pass and badge to security."

Cole had left Israel's office and had gone to his office on the edge of the Rim and sat there, thinking about it. He suddenly felt so completely frustrated and outraged that he exploded up to his feet and charged back across the Rim to the conference room where the "morning meetings" were held each day at ten A.M.

The huge conference room, as usual, was jammed. Seated around the large table were the vice presidents of news practice, news coverage, as well as the VPs of business affairs and finance.

Steve Israel, senior VP of news, ran the meeting. Also attending were the senior broadcast segment producers, the director of the political unit, the anchors for the two news mags, as well as Brenton Spencer of the nightly news, the political analysts, and all senior political correspondents.

Cole burst into the room. "You guys oughta be ashamed of yourselves," he said to the startled "big feet."

"Cole, this isn't the time" Steve Israel snapped.

"The Alo family has a silent ownership in two Atlantic City casinos.

I've got good proof . . . witnesses who've seen meetings between Mickey and his father Joseph and members of the Murphy Hotel syndicate. I've gone back and looked at tax records of the Murphy family. These guys owned furniture stores in the eighties. How the hell did they get the money to do a leveraged buyout on two hotels and a casino carpet joint?"

"The decision has been made."

He'd been escorted by security to his office, where his badges and network press pass were removed from his desk before he could even hand them over. A news staffer was sent to get a box and Cole loaded his stuff inside.

"You guys are working for a bunch of assholes," he'd said as he loaded his desk into the cardboard box. "A free press is the cornerstone of democracy," he lectured the uninterested security men, who were watching him closely, making sure he didn't remove any company property. "If this news division won't run valid stories, exposing power brokers and criminal conspiracies, then it's lower than whale shit," he'd said, half shouting, as he slammed notebooks and leather folders into the box. The last things to go in were his two Pulitzer citations and a pen and pencil set given to him last Christmas by C. Wallace Litman, engraved TO COLE HARRIS, THE BEST OF THE BEST. C. WALLACE LITMAN. He grabbed the box and, with one security guard holding each arm, they escorted him out of the building.

He'd tried to get employment at other networks, but Steve Israel had scorched the ground around him. Nobody would touch him.

Cole had run out of money and for two months had been living in the back of his van in the driveway of Carson's house, eating his meals with his brother and sister-in-law in the cramped dining room, wondering whether he should end it all. He had bought a gun and twice found himself holding the weapon in a shaking hand, wondering if he could put it in his mouth and pull the trigger. But something had stopped him. As he sat in the diner, the reason reached up and grabbed him. . . . If he killed himself, they would have won. They would have beaten him. His compulsion to win had somehow saved him.

Cole's ex-wife had told him when she was divorcing him that his strongest link was attached to his weakest and that was why she couldn't stand to live with him. It was the one thing she'd said among all the hurled insults and invectives that had made any sense. Cole was humorless and he was driven. His strong link was his compulsion to be right. That compulsion had made him a tireless researcher and had won him two Pulitzers. His weak link, he had come to find out, was that same compulsion. He drove people crazy. Systematically, he had driven away all the soft, nourishing contacts in his life and was left with the bony remnants.

Then he felt a presence standing over him and looked up to see Solomon Kazorowski, with an unlit, soggy cigar in his mouth, glowering down at him.

"I think maybe we need to share some info." Kaz sat down heavily and looked at the newsman, who was dressed in neatly pleated pants with a blue shirt, tie, matching suspenders, and tweed coat. Despite this perfect ensemble, Cole had only a few dollars left in his pocket. His newsman's instinct took over.

"Let me buy you a cup," he said, pulling out two bills, wondering if he could pump this sorry piece of ex-government beef for some information, without giving up any of his own. Kaz had exactly the same agenda.

They played mind poker for two hours, giving little bits of information to get back little bits, trading shreds like beggars. Each wondered how he could use the other to his own advantage. Gradually and begrudgingly, they gained respect for one another.

HALF-TRUTHS

THAT SAME DAY, A HUNDRED MILES NORTH, NEW HAMPSHIRE
voters were going to the polls. A.J. knew that Haze was going to win
big. The question was, How big? Since the defining event in New
York, Haze was the front-runner, tracking in the high 50 percentiles.
The message had scored. The question wasn't, Would he win New
Hampshire?—but, Would he win it bigger than any candidate in
modern history?

Even better news was that the Super Tuesday states were all polling
their way. A.J. had been told that Senator Skatina was going to drop
out if he did less than 20 percent in New Hampshire, and A.J. was
pretty sure that was going to happen. Skatina had "managed the
damage" stemming from the mob allegations as best he could, but
they'd slowed him down and hurt him. The other candidates were
DOA in New Hampshire and would probably pull out, too. It was
pretty damn hard to get political funding if you're losing elections

and trailing in the polls. A candidate needed over 20 percent to qualify for government matching funds.

The way A.J. had it figured, a week from today, after Super Tuesday, Haze should be running unopposed, except for a few favorite-son candidates. He'd be virtually assured of the Democratic nomination.

A.J. had called a strategy meeting in his Manchester hotel room with Malcolm, Vidal Brown, Carol Wakano, and Ven and Van. He'd left Haze off the list because more and more he'd been fighting with Haze for center stage in strategy sessions. He felt it would also be a good idea for Haze to get Anita back from Providence. A few articles had already appeared speculating about the candidate's missing wife. A.J. knew they were barely speaking, but he was urging Haze to make an effort to patch things up before Super Tuesday. He desperately needed some photo ops with Anita.

There was a knock on the door. He opened it and let his "first circle" in. They spread out in the small room, all of them wearing big smiles. It was fun being on a winning team. The purpose of this meeting was to look past Super Tuesday and start thinking about the Republican Vice President who had been running pretty much unopposed. Vice President James "Pudge" Anderson had been basically selling the regular Republican agenda, not sure whether to take on Skatina, who had started looking like the man to beat, or to shift his focus to Haze.

After the New Hampshire win tonight, and after the latest tracking poll in the Super Tuesday states, A.J. knew the Republicans were going to be looking for ways to knock Haze around, and he had to get some strategy going for that.

"Okay, kids, we've got ponies coming out our ass and that's great," he started. "But we gotta start looking ahead. All winning campaigns communicate optimism, and we've been doing that. Americans are optimistic about Haze, optimistic about the message, but the Republicans are gonna start throwing mud. We've been riding a media wave recently, but we gotta get ready for some white water. Vidal, what have you got for next week?"

"I just got off the phone. We booked Haze on the *Hour of the Living Dead*," Vidal said, referring to what insiders called *Washing-*

ton Week in Review. "We aren't gonna do Letterman or Leno, or any of the entertainment shows yet. They're calling, but I said wait till after Super Tuesday. We're going to stay with a hard news look. Besides *Nightline,* we'll do a *Sixty Minutes* piece. We're still arguing over the correspondent. . . . I want Lesley Stahl to help with our gender gap. Haze knows her and feels comfortable, but they want Bradley. They're probably gonna fold if we give them an exclusive three-day window. That would keep us off *Nightline* till Wednesday. I think with all the free press, I can live with that," he said. "We're also booked on *Larry King Live* for some call-in segments. The way the polls are running, we should do great in that venue," he said, finishing his update.

"Okay, we'll have a separate meeting on campaign spots after this one," A.J. said. "Ven, I need a new two-sentence policy on all the key issues to deal with what the Republicans are gonna throw at us. I also want spotlight teams to work on world affairs. We need Haze to look good on foreign policy 'cause that's Pudge Anderson's strong suit."

The door opened and Susan Winter put her head in. "What's going on in here?" she asked, smiling at them and brushing her auburn hair off her forehead.

"Little strategy meeting," A.J. said.

"Shouldn't Haze be included? Does he know you're meeting?"

"Look, Susan, Haze needs his rest. Today is one of the few days he can just take it easy."

"I don't think he wants to take it easy, A.J. I think he wants to be in all the strategy sessions. If I were you, I'd call him." She gave them a snotty smile. " 'Bye," she said and closed the door.

Ten minutes later, Haze was pounding on the door. A.J. let him in the room.

"I didn't think you'd want to be in on a preliminary strategy meeting, Haze," A.J. apologized. "I was going to capsulize it for you while we watched the returns tonight."

Haze didn't answer A.J. He moved past him, into the room, walked to the window, and looked out. Finally he turned.

"I wanna do Letterman now," he said to Vidal. "Can you get me on? I thought I could do some stuff there to show 'em I'm just a regular guy. . . . Susan thought maybe I should play my guitar."

"Sure, babe, anything you want."

A.J. let the stupid suggestion stand. He knew they were going to win the nomination and he didn't want to get thrown off the bus before it pulled into Washington.

TRAPPED ALIVE

LUCINDA HAD NEVER GONE TO SLEEP. SHE SAT UP, HOLDING Ryan's hand all night. Kaz had begun to think Ryan was going to be no use to him. The leg was a goner as far as Kaz could see. He wasn't going to get anywhere dragging a cripple around. He told Lucinda that she should take Ryan away, someplace where he'd be safe, maybe back to the sun in California. She nodded her agreement. He hoped that Bolt would listen.

Kaz left the motel and drove out of the parking lot to the rail yard, two blocks away, where Cole Harris had elected to park his van and sleep. He said he was used to sleeping in the bus, so that's what he'd done. Cole had a mattress and battery heaters in the back of the VW.

Kaz pulled up as Cole Harris was folding his laundry on a portable table he had set up. He was putting his clean bed linen in plastic bags. Kaz had noticed the night before that everything in the van was spotless; everything fit into neat compartments. There was even a built-in computer with a portable work station. He got out of his car and moved toward Cole, who had one corner of a bedsheet tucked under his chin, pulling the far end up to meet it. He checked the edges to make sure they were exactly even before making the fold.

"How's Bolt?"

"On injured reserve. How 'bout breakfast? I'll buy. I'm going bat-shit watching all this compulsive behavior."

They got in Kaz's rented Chevelle and stopped at a Winchell's for coffee and doughnuts to go. Kaz bought a paper. The front page showed the smiling face of Haze Richards. The headline screamed:

PROVIDENCE COMES TO NEW HAMPSHIRE

The subhead read:

HAZE RICHARDS SCORES KO
WINS RECORD 68 PERCENT

Kaz got on the Jersey Turnpike, heading toward New York City. Then he said, "Bolt says this guy is a mob pawn." A light rain started falling so he turned on the wipers and waited while Cole bit carefully on a sugar doughnut.

"You wanna kick in anything or are you just gonna perform oral surgery on that doughnut?"

"Okay, here's what I got so far. . . . I think UBC is hooked to the mob. I'm not sure how high up it goes, whether it's just Steve Israel in the news division or if it goes all the way up to C. Wallace Litman. When they killed my story on the Alos in Atlantic City, I got to wondering if maybe there was something going on between the mob and UBC. I went back and looked at their news coverage on organized crime. They've killed every single story about the Alos, specifically, and the East Coast crime syndicates, in general. I find that very dis-turbing."

"Where's that take us?" Kaz asked.

"I'm digging around in the Justice Department, using old contacts, but it's pretty damn hard when you don't have any network clout behind you. I figured I'd start at the top, with C. Wallace Litman. So far, I haven't got much that's solid, but one thing seems funny. . . ."

"What?"

"Back in the sixties, he was just this little accounts manager for an investment portfolio company in Florida. He was making twenty-five to thirty thousand a year, and then he quits. Nobody in that firm can remember why. He resurfaced in New York a few years later, and he owned, of all things, two parking lots in downtown Manhattan, and I'm thinking, what a strange investment for this little Yiddish accountant from Fort Lauderdale. 'Course, it's not so strange when you realize the mob is big on Manhattan parking lots and all other cash businesses. Then he parlays the parking lots into some real estate and, ten years later, he tacks that 'C' on the front of his name and he's a big Wall Street gazoonie, buying media companies. I can't prove any of it, but my bullshit meter is in the red."

Cole amputated a piece of his sugar doughnut with his lateral incisors, managing not to get any powder on his clean, blue shirt and matching tie. "By the way, where are we going? I thought we were just gonna get breakfast and have a talk."

"I thought we should go back and have another look at Brenton Spencer. He's in NYC County. Ryan got me thinking, it's very strange Brenton walked off that stage in Iowa."

"Maybe it was the brain aneurysm that made him act funny."

"Yeah, and maybe it wasn't. If he wakes up, I wanna be there."

They arrived at County Hospital at noon and went directly to the Neurology floor. The hubbub had died down and the press had left days ago. Now all that remained was the smell of sickness and Lysol. Nurses moved quietly, like green paper angels, their rubber-soled shoes squeaking on sanitized corridors, while music and doctors' pagings came lightly over the intercom.

Kaz found the same intern he had talked to the day they'd checked Spencer in. He was in the office at the far end of the floor.

" 'Member me?" Kaz said, poking his head in. "How's Spence?"

The doctor had been up all night and was resting on the sofa with his shoes off, stocking feet propped on the arm rest. He sat up and rubbed his eyes.

"Still about the same. Like I told you, it's gonna be a while."

"This is his brother, Carl. He's in the jewelry business. Just flew in from Zurich."

"Brenton and I haven't seen much of one another since I started buying gemstones abroad. It's hard to believe this happened," Cole said, rolling with the improv.

"He's still in the same room. You can look through the glass but don't go in."

They moved out of the intern's office.

"Guy's a doctor, he should wash his socks," Cole mumbled as they walked down the spotless corridor to the room where Brenton was being treated. There was an observation window, but Kaz ignored the instruction, opened the door, and entered.

Brenton had gone camping in an oxygen tent. They stood at the foot of the anchorman's bed and looked at him. His head was wrapped heavily in gauze. To their surprise his eyes were open and staring up at them.

"Is he awake?" Cole asked, looking down into his eyes. "Brenton, it's me. It's Cole Harris." Brenton didn't move his eyes. He was looking up into space.

"Brenton, it's Cole. Can you hear me?"

Brenton Spencer could hear but he couldn't move or speak. His eyes were directed at the ceiling, but saw nothing. He had lost all sight and much of his memory. None of his senses worked except his hearing. Several times a day, people would come and give him a shot and he would fall back into a deep, drugged sleep. But he would always come out of it sooner than they expected. He began to realize, each time he came to, that he was frozen in this body; trapped, unable to see or speak or move. Through the blind patchwork of his crippled brain, he was screaming silently at everyone who came into the room. Screaming, *Help, help, let me out. I'm in here.* He could hear them as they walked in and out.

"Can he understand us?" they would say. "Is he awake?"

Lemme out, lemme out, he would scream in his tortured mind, unable to move, unable to twitch . . . trapped but alive. He lay there while they talked, first to him, then about him.

Brenton Spencer was locked in a nightmare that began anew every time he woke up.

STRATEGY

MICKEY TRIED TO REACH HIS MOTHER THREE TIMES THAT MORN-ing. Finally, he remembered her cell phone and dialed the number off the Rolodex from his office in the Jersey house. It rang three times and then a man answered.

"Who is this?" Mickey said to Kazorowski, who was just pulling his car into the motel parking lot with Cole Harris sitting beside him. Kaz recognized the voice from half a dozen wiretaps he'd heard of Mickey Alo over the years.

"This is the intercept operator." Kaz was flying blind, trying to keep Mickey on the line, not sure what to do.

"Hey, shit-for-brains, there's no such thing."

"Hi, Mickey. How's everything in Goombah City?"

"Who the fuck is this?"

Kaz was out of the car now and moving toward the motel with the phone to his ear. Cole got the door open and, as Kaz moved into the room, Lucinda got to her feet. Ryan was still asleep on the bed.

"This is Solomon Kazorowski."

"Whatta you doing with my mother's phone?"

"Confusing how shit like that happens, ain't it?" Kaz wrote "Mickey" on a piece of paper and showed it to Lucinda.

"Let me talk to him," Lucinda said.

"I've got somebody, wants to say hi." He handed the phone to Lucinda.

"Don't you dare send anybody else to hurt him, Mickey. Don't you dare!"

"I don't know what you're talkin' about, Sis."

"You know damn well what I'm talking about. You sent a killer to try and get Ryan. Leave him alone, he doesn't mean anything to you."

"Hey, little sister, you don't have a clue what means anything to me. You wanna play teacher to a bunch a' retards, I could give less of a shit, but you get in my world, you start fucking with my action, and you're dust. Put Kazorowski back on."

"I never knew you at all, did I?"

"You knew what I wanted you to know."

She didn't have to see him to know that his eyes were shining and blank. She handed the phone back to Kazorowski, trembling with frustration.

"Yeah."

"A million dollars right now, no questions asked, you deliver them both to me."

"Y' know, that's funny, Mickey. You and your friends think the world stops for money—but there's other things that count, grease-ball. You took away all I ever wanted. You set me up ten years ago, because I was costing you money, but I don't give a shit about money. Ya know what gets my dick stiff . . . ?"

"What?"

"Sending guys like you to the asshole academy, and I ain't gonna quit till I put you there." He disconnected the phone before Mickey could answer.

"He offered me a million bucks to sell you out. I think your big brother means business."

"We've gotta get Bolt outta here. Mickey'll send out foot soldiers. He'll find you," Cole said.

"How?" Lucinda asked.

"He's no dummy. He knows Ryan is hurting. He'll look for street doctors like Dr. Jazz."

"I knew a mob guy once who sent button men down a highway with photographs, showed 'em to every gas station on the interstate," Kaz finished Cole's thought.

"Does Ryan still have his boat in Marina del Rey?" Cole asked Lucinda.

"I don't know."

"I'm sure he does. He took me out once when I was in L.A."

"That's perfect," Kaz said to Lucinda. "We get you two out to L.A., you get on that boat and get away. Don't tell anybody where. Drop anchor, stay outta sight. I'll hang onto this cell phone if you need to talk to me."

"Shouldn't I tell you where I am?" she said.

Kaz shook his head. "If Mickey catches either Cole or me, I can't guarantee we won't give up your location. A man tends to start talking when he's doused with kerosene and his clothes are on fire."

"You gotta drive," Cole said. "He'll be watching the airports."

"I can't drive him all the way to the West Coast in this condition. It'll kill him," Lucinda said.

"I've got a way to fly him out of here," Kaz volunteered. "Mickey will never find this airplane 'cause officially it doesn't exist."

Kaz was on the phone for almost two hours, trying to find Deke Metcalf. He finally found him through Deke's sister, who gave Kaz the number of his girlfriend's house in Vermont. Half an hour later, he had Deke on the phone.

"Kaz, I can't steal government equipment," Deke said after he heard what Kaz wanted. "That shit is all over with. They busted all the ranch hands outta Covert Ops.

"Look, Deke, I never asked you for anything, but you've gotta get this guy to the West Coast."

"Who is he?"

"You're better off not knowing. I'm gonna take him to the rabbit farm. You can pick him up there."

"How the hell did I ever end up with you for a friend?"

"We were both fucking the colonel's wife at Fort Bragg, remember?"

"Oh yeah, right. Okay, I'll work something out. Meet me there in two hours."

Kaz doped Ryan up good for the flight, got him stretched out in the back of Cole's van, then called Dr. Jazz and told him Ryan needed more antibiotics. Kenetta met them in a Pay-Less parking lot with the drugs. She checked and redressed the wound while Ryan lay unconscious. Lucinda opened her purse and pushed several hundred dollars into Kenetta's hand. "Thank you; you and your father saved his life," she said.

Kenetta smiled and gave her instructions on how to guard against infection.

The rabbit farm was just that, a breeding farm for medical supply rabbits in the southwestern part of New Jersey. There was a long, paved runway east of the rabbit coops that could handle most MATS propeller aircraft, including the large C-54 that was currently sitting at the end.

Cole pulled the van out on the tarmac under the wing of the four-engine plane with no VIN or tail markings.

Deke Metcalf turned out to be a handsome, forty-year-old black aviator, tall with coffee-colored skin and a roguish air. He flew planes for Air America, the CIA covert ops airline. He and Kaz had worked more than one federal case together.

Ryan never woke up as they opened the back of the van.

"You didn't tell me he was gonna be junk on a bunk," Deke said.

"Drank too much Old Grand-Dad," Kaz said, looking at the plane. "Where'd you get this antique?"

"That's another thing. I can't guarantee we ain't gonna prang it in a cornfield. Bird's a ruptured duck. I volunteered to transport it to Lockheed in Van Nuys for an engine overhaul. Officially, this flight ain't on anybody's board. It's a black ops flight, and to make it interestin', the number-two fan is cooked. This was the only ride I could get my hands on."

"Can you get off the ground with three engines?"

"I already did it once but it's a groaner."

Kaz reached out in a strangely formal gesture and shook Lucinda's hand. "You're okay, Miss Alo. Sorry if I came on strong a while back. You take care of both a' ya."

"I accept the apology." And she leaned forward and kissed Kaz on the cheek.

The three men managed to get Ryan into the cabin. He never woke up. Then Deke helped Lucinda in, pulled up the rear door, and secured Ryan in one of the seats, belting him in. He got behind the controls and, one by one, started up the three good engines. The inboard engine, on the port side, didn't turn on. It stayed feathered as Deke made the run-up, looked at his gauges, tapped a few, and shook his head in disbelief. "I get better odds in Vegas," he said to himself as he pushed the throttle forward and eased off the rudder brakes.

He taxied to the end of the runway, crossed himself, and started the roll. He had filed no flight plan and no radio contact. His transponder was squawking on the CIA frequency, so he would be cleared through military channels, but as far as the F.A.A. was concerned, this flight never happened.

Kaz and Cole watched with concern as the C-54 thundered down the runway and finally lifted off. The cumbersome transport barely cleared the trees on the far end of the field, straining up, over a set of power lines, missing disaster by feet.

He knew it was impossible, but as the plane banked to the east, Kaz thought he heard Deke let out a rebel yell.

AT SEA

MICKEY SAT IN HIS FATHER'S OFFICE UPSTAIRS FOR TWO HOURS running the problem over in his mind, working the angles, exploring options. He was troubled by the fact that Kazorowski had answered the phone. The ex-fed had been with Lucinda and that meant there was a good chance he was also with Ryan. Mickey sat sideways in his father's office club chair with his legs over the arm and looked for solutions. Lucinda might cause some trouble. She undoubtedly knew things she didn't know she knew. She'd lived in the house while her father ran the family. She had to know that Joseph dreamed of controlling a presidential candidate. What if Kaz turned up the campaign funding? Or got to A.J. and scared the wonk into talking? Another unanswered question was, where were the tapes of Haze screaming and pleading in the airliner? If they surfaced, the whole plan could go under. On the other hand, Mickey was beginning to suspect that those tapes were out of the mix. If Ryan still had them, he would have already sent them to a TV station or Kaz would have threatened him with them. The fact that nobody had mentioned the tapes made him wonder if New York Tony hadn't destroyed them before he disappeared. Mickey had to believe Tony was dead.

Mickey finally decided that he needed a front-line mechanic. No more street characters swinging Louisville Sluggers. He needed somebody who wouldn't miss. He'd heard his father talk about an ex-CIA political assassin known only as the Ghost. Silvio Candrate was the Ghost's contractor and booked all his jobs. Mickey leaned over and looked for Silvio's number in his father's Rolodex. When he found it, he closed the office door and picked up the scrambled line his father had installed.

He left a message with Silvio's wife to have the retired gunsel call him once he got home. Then Mickey sat back at the desk and picked up the newspaper with Haze's smiling face on the front page. He remembered how the slick politician had been sweating in the motor home while Mickey bought his soul. He looked down at the picture, finally bringing it up to eye level in front of his face.

"I'm gonna own the President of the United States," he said softly. Power was Mickey Alo's drug of choice.

Elizabeth's phone rang at 2:38 A.M.. She was only in her first REM sleep because the couple downstairs had been doing a headboard rumba on the wall till almost one o'clock. She had rolled over, looked at the alarm clock and thought this had better be good. She fumbled the phone off the cradle.

"Is this Elizabeth Applegate?" a woman's voice asked.

"Who's asking?"

"Did you use to be Ryan Bolt's secretary?"

"Hey, honey, you know what time it is?"

"Ryan is with me. He's not in very good shape. You used to be his secretary . . . ?"

"What's wrong with him?" Elizabeth said, trying to get her thoughts together.

"We need your help. He said you can borrow your brother's station wagon. We need you to come pick us up."

Elizabeth hadn't heard from Ryan in almost a month. She had a new boss who was a raging pain in the ass, making her punch out, then keeping her after hours at the studio and refusing her the overtime. Now her old boss was calling at two in the morning, asking for favors. Trouble was, she couldn't refuse Ryan anything. He was one of those guys she would always help.

"Put him on."

"Just a minute." There was the sound of the phone being passed, then the whispered memory of her old friend.

"Hi," the voice croaked softly.

"Ryan?"

"Sorry , Liz. . . . Wouldn't ask if . . . Can ya help?"

She was suddenly terribly concerned. "Ryan, what's wrong?"

"Zigged when I should a' ducked."

"Don't mix your metaphors," she lectured, trying to sound bright, but feeling dread at the way he sounded. "Okay, I'll get the wagon. Where are you?"

"I don't know. Just a min—" There was a fumbling sound and then the girl was back on the line.

"Sixteen hundred Mountain Road, Valencia."

"That's way out by Magic Mountain." It was at least forty-five minutes away.

"If you have any money, we could use it. I could write you a check, but I'm afraid if you cash it, it could be dangerous for you."

"Why is that?"

" 'Cause when it clears, my brother will see it and . . ." Lucinda stopped, not wanting to involve Elizabeth more deeply. "Forget the money, just hurry."

"The Elizabeth Applegate Rescue Wagon is on the way." She hung up, grabbed her sweats, and slipped them on. She was heading toward the door when she spun around and went into the bathroom, where she combed her hair and put on her makeup. "Damn it," she said out loud as she fixed her face, "I've still got a case on him."

She made the trip in thirty-five minutes because there was no traffic. Mountain Street was the turnoff just before Magic Mountain. She rolled down the off ramp and, as her headlights raked the intersection, she saw that 1600 was a sporting goods store. She pulled into the parking lot. She saw a tall, light-skinned black man standing next to a panel truck with government plates on it. She pulled around the man and parked. By then, he had started removing pins, unhooking the tailgate, and through the windshield, she could see Ryan lying on a blanket in the truck bed. She got out of the car, leaving the engine on. Then she saw Lucinda coming around the side of the truck and her heart sank. She was beautiful with long, glossy hair and delicate features.

"I'm Lucinda Alo," the beautiful girl said.

"Elizabeth Applegate," she responded, turning her attention to Ryan, who was lying on the blanket. He looked thin and unhealthy.

"What happened to him?"

"He was shot in the leg . . . and then he reinjured it. He's lost a lot of blood and he's kinda drugged up."

Deke jumped up into the truck bed.

"Who's truck is this?" Elizabeth asked the handsome coffee-complected man.

"It belongs to the government. Your tax dollars at work for you, but it's not supposed to be off the field. I gotta get it back, pronto," Deke said.

"And who are you?"

"Cat in a Hat." He grinned, doffing his fifty-mission cap. "Open up the back. The three of us oughta be able to get him in your wagon."

Elizabeth and Lucinda got on Ryan's right side and Deke carefully lifted his left, managing not to jostle the wounded leg. They got him into the back of the station wagon, and then Deke looked at Ryan. "Gotta go. Good luck, buddy."

"Thanks for the dust-off," Ryan said weakly.

"Thank Kaz. I wouldn't've done it for anybody else." And he got back into the truck. Without looking back, he pulled out of the parking lot and out of their lives forever.

Elizabeth got behind the wheel; Lucinda got in the rear of the wagon and sat next to Ryan. When Elizabeth turned to check on him, Ryan was looking up at her. The smile was in his eyes, if not on his lips.

"Thanks, Liz. . . ."

"Ryan, what happened?"

"Just take me to the *Linda*."

She put the car in gear and pulled up toward the on ramp. She could hear Lucinda in the back, whispering to Ryan.

When they hit the transition bumps crossing over to the 405 freeway, Ryan moaned and Lucinda whispered encouragement to him.

Elizabeth felt very alone. As she listened to Ryan and Lucinda, she knew she was letting her life slip by.

They arrived at the marina and Elizabeth parked in the darkness, under a broken light at the foot of B dock. She and Lucinda got out of the wagon, leaving Ryan sleeping in the back; then Elizabeth led the way down the ramp to where she thought she remembered Ryan's boat being slipped.

"Shouldn't he see a doctor?"

"I'm going to work on that. First, I have to make sure he's safe."

"Safe from what? From who?"

"Please, just help me find his boat."

They walked farther down until Elizabeth could see the familiar profile of the beautiful fifty-foot ketch. Built in the fifties, she had classic lines. The wood hull had been varnished to a shiny dark brown; the cockpit was covered with white canvas. The boat was named *Linda*, for Ryan's ex-wife, but she had hated the boat and they rarely used it.

When Lucinda looked at the ketch, it was love at first sight. Sailing had been one of her childhood joys. She'd had a Sabot at Cape May when she was seven and had graduated to larger boats, winning some yacht club contests when she was in her mid-teens. She was at home on the sea. Now she jumped down and started to unsnap the canvas, exposing the teak decks and chrome fittings. "Look at this," she whispered as she unwrapped the boat with Christmas morning excitement. She moved below and checked the provisions. There was plenty of canned food and bottled water. She found the chart drawer and the battery selector switch and rotated it to ON BOTH BATTERIES. She turned on the cabin lights and checked the battery condition indicator. She stuck her head up and looked at Ryan's secretary.

"You seem to know something about boats," Elizabeth said.

"I'll manage. Let's get Ryan."

They brought over a rolling dock dolly and loaded the boat seat cushions into it, then got Ryan out of the wagon. He was gritting his teeth in pain as they moved him onto the dolly and rolled him to the boat. It was difficult getting him aboard, but they managed, finally settling him in the forward stateroom bunk. Once the transfer was complete, Elizabeth leaned down and kissed him on the cheek. "Damn, Ryan, take better care of yourself, will ya?"

He put an arm around her neck and whispered in her ear. "Missed you, Liz."

She stood up and held his hand for as long as she could, then moved out to the cockpit where Lucinda was pulling back the small engine hatch and checking the forty-horse Graymarine engine. She checked the oil stick, then replaced the hatch cover, leaving it cracked slightly for ventilation. She turned on the bilge fan and let it run, until it blew the engine compartment clean of fumes.

"You actually know something about this, don't ya?"

Lucinda was removing the canvas cover on the pedestal compass. "I have a boat at home."

"What the hell's this all about? Who shot him?" Elizabeth asked.

"I'm fighting for his life. It wouldn't be safe for you to know more."

"In that case . . ." Elizabeth handed her all the money she had in her apartment. It was $450.

Lucinda took it. "He told me you were one of his best friends."

"Right, so don't fuck up and let him die."

Finally, Lucinda said, "Once I get the main going, can you cast us off?"

Elizabeth nodded and jumped onto the dock while Lucinda pumped the throttle to get gas to the carburetor. Then she hit the start button and the engine roared to life. Lucinda flipped some dash switches and the running lights went on.

Elizabeth untied the four lines and threw them onto the boat. Lucinda backed the ketch out of the slip into the channel. There was no adventure in Elizabeth's life and she envied the beautiful girl. She watched the *Linda* move slowly into the night until the twinkling masthead light disappeared from view. Elizabeth got back in the station wagon, but didn't start the engine right away. She sat in the dark, thinking.

She finally promised herself she'd quit her job first thing in the morning.

T H E   P L A N

* * *

Lucinda made the crossing under power, deciding not to single-hand the big ketch under sail and try to take care of Ryan at the same time.

Once they got past the jetty and into open sea, the *Linda* began to buck and shudder in the close, four-foot swells. Lucinda was afraid that Ryan would roll off the forward bunk and onto the floor, so she ran down to check on him every few minutes. He was sleeping soundly. She propped up pillows around him and tried to take the swells on the quarter to minimize the chop.

There was a half-moon shining in the clear, February sky and she steered the sailboat across the sparkling moonlit water. Then she went below, took the chart of the Catalina channel out of the map tube, clipped it to the navigation table, and switched on the tensor light. She used dividers and parallels to plot the course, the way her sailing instructor at the yacht club had taught her when she was a teenager. She didn't know Catalina, but she decided not to go into Avalon Harbor because she was sure all the day boats went there. Instead she picked Toyon Bay, a small cove a few miles west. She went back to the wheel and set her course by the compass to 176 degrees.

She found Toyon Bay just as the sun was coming up. She got *Linda* into the lee of the cove and then dropped the bow anchor. The chain rattled through the hawsepipe, and once she had laid out fifty-feet of chain, she hit reverse and backed down on the Danforth anchor to set it. She checked for drift, let out some more scope on the chain, then turned off the engine and sat, listening. The rippling water gently lapped against the hull. The island was much more barren than she had expected. . . . Scrubby mesquite plants were hugging rocks that jutted on the low cliffs. But there was a rugged beauty to the place. Across the hundred yards of water, she could see a dark shape of something large on the beach. She found a pair of binoculars under the pilot seat, directed them to the shape, and slowly focused in on a huge, sleeping beast.

"It's a buffalo," she finally said in exhilaration and surprise. She went below to tell Ryan, but he was still out, so she didn't wake him. Instead, she lay down on the adjoining bunk. She loved the gentle sway of the boat at anchor. For the first time in three days, she felt safe.

As the boat swung around in the shifting breeze, she thought about her mother. Penny would worry about her. Lucinda had been unable to reach her before she left.

In moments, Lucinda fell into a fitful sleep.

TROUBLING DECISION

ANITA FARRINGTON RICHARDS HAD NOT TOLD HAZE THAT SHE wanted to divorce him when she'd gone to Iowa. She had intended to, but something had stopped her. It had taken her a few days to understand how complicated her reasoning was. Anita had been raised by upper-middle-class eastern Protestants, who taught their daughter from childhood not to show her emotions, not to make a scene in public, not to draw attention to herself. The thought of having a messy public divorce appalled her, and she realized, after the media swarm at the Iowa debate, that there was no way to do it quietly. So she had not broached the subject with Haze and withdrew instead to reconsider. Anita had left immediately after the campaign victory in Iowa and was now holed up in the safety of the governor's mansion in Providence. She had refused all of the interview requests that her press secretary had tried to arrange. She hoped that Haze's campaign would unwind on its own, that he'd lose New Hampshire so she wouldn't be forced to use divorce to veto his candidacy. Better than anyone on earth, Anita Richards knew her husband wasn't fit to govern. She knew he lacked moral strength. But as the days went by, she realized he was gaining in popularity. Every night, they talked about him on the news. "The surprise candidate," UBC said. . . . "The probable front-runner." She'd started drinking again. She'd had a bout with alcoholism in her mid-thirties when Haze was still a prosecutor. Now she was sneaking into the study every afternoon and taking straight shots of vodka from the little crystal bottle on the marble bar top.

Haze was coming home that afternoon to get packed for a four-day, ten-state swing through the South, and she had finally swallowed enough false courage to tell him she was going to leave. She poured two more shots from the crystal decanter in her hand, sat down on the quilted sofa, and thought about the events that had led her to this dilemma.

She had never been a fighter. She tried to avoid confrontations and so had not been a good moral guide for Haze when he needed one. She had chosen isolation instead. Now she readied herself for what she was sure would be the most ugly event of her life. She was going to file for divorce.

Haze arrived home by limo at six. He found her asleep on the sofa in the study. He looked down at his overweight wife, disgusted at what she had become. He saw the glass on the table and knew she had been drinking again. He started to move out of the den when she heard him and sat up.

"How long have you been here?" she asked.

"Just got in."

"Oh," she said, suddenly not prepared for the fight ahead of her. But it had to be done. He turned and moved up the hall to his private bedroom. She followed him.

"I have something I want to talk about."

"Not now, Anita. They're holding the plane for me."

"I want a divorce."

He looked at her. "Come on, Nita, cut the shit."

"Haze, I can't do this anymore. I'm filing tomorrow."

"You can't divorce me. Whatta you talking about?"

"To begin with, I can do whatever I want. I don't have to ask your permission to file divorce papers."

"But why?"

"To stop you."

"Stop me from what?"

"That's what I wanted to tell you," she said and walked out of his room, back down the hall toward her bedroom. He caught her in the hall, grabbed her by the arm, and spun her to face him.

"Whatta you doing? You know what's at stake? I could actually win this thing."

"I've made up my mind." She pulled her arm free and walked to her bedroom. He started to follow but she slammed the big oak door and threw the deadbolt before he could reach it.

"Anita, you gotta talk to me," he pleaded through the thick door. After a minute, he realized it was useless and walked back to his den to call A.J., who had stopped at his law office a block away to get some papers. A.J. answered on the second ring.

"Jesus, A.J., Anita wants a divorce. She's locked in her room. She's drinking again. You gotta do something," Haze said, turning, as always, to the only man who ever solved his problems.

"I'm on my way." A.J. hung up, dialed the airport, and got Malcolm at the executive terminal. They had chartered a 737 to carry the enlarged staff and the hundred big feet traveling with them.

"We got a problem."

"How big a problem?"

"I can't tell you over the phone. Just hold the flight. If I can't get there with Haze in an hour, I'll call back."

"Shit, A.J., we got a planeful of press. We don't hold to the schedule, they're gonna sense something is wrong. They'll be all over me. First rule in a campaign is don't deviate from the schedule in front of the press."

"An hour isn't gonna kill us. Two hours, we're gonna have to make up something. In the meantime, hose the fuckers down with free booze." And he rang off and sprinted for his car.

At the governor's mansion, he found Haze in the upstairs hall, banging on Anita's door. "Come on, Nita. I just wanna talk to you." He turned and looked helplessly at A.J. "She's locked in there."

"Let me handle it. Go to your room," A.J. said.

"She files for divorce, we're fucked."

"Go."

Reluctantly, Haze moved down the hall to his room, but he stood in the doorway so he could overhear what A.J. said.

A.J. tapped on the door, softly. He had always had a good relationship with Anita. He found her smart and funny and had actually dated her in college, before Haze did. In the old days, they'd had a lot of long, meaningful talks. He had a strong appreciation for her mind and values. "Nita, it's A.J.," he said, tapping again on the door. "Listen, if you don't want to talk to me, say so. Okay? I don't wanna be banging on this door all night. You say 'Get lost, Albert,' and I'm gone. Okay?"

Nothing from the other side of the door. A.J. was a strategist. He always tried to solve one problem at a time. He couldn't get through the door unless he got Anita talking.

"See, if I don't hear anything, Nita, I'm gonna figure you haven't made up your mind and I'm gonna stay out here, banging my poor knuckles on this hard wood," the wonk cooed softly through the massive oak door.

"Go away, A.J."

"Listen . . . uh, I will. I'll go, but first I gotta know you're okay."

"Just go. Leave me alone."

He had her talking; now he had to get her thinking, get her to interact with him.

"You don't wanna be alone, Nita. Haze isn't here, he's in his room. Okay? It's just me. You know I'd never do anything to hurt you. You know I've been your friend since Swarthmore."

A.J. had met her at Swarthmore College at a dance and had brought her back to Harvard where he and Haze were in school. Haze had seen her and that had been it for A.J., a mating ritual that had replayed itself with various women over the years. Haze was the leading man. A.J. always ended up with Dennis Day's part.

"Come on, Nita . . . I wanna make sure you're okay."

There was a long pause, and then he heard the door being un-bolted. He turned the handle and entered the room.

Anita was looking at him with big, brown eyes that were dulled by vodka and lack of sleep.

"What?" she said, angrily.

"What? 'What' isn't the right word. 'What' is an interrogative con-struction asking for information. What we need is . . . 'Why' . . . 'Why' is a word that defines cause, purpose, or reason," he said, his mind racing, knowing that she had majored in English and might find this mildly diverting. He watched her for a smile and got the tiniest response.

"Close the door." He turned and closed it behind him then locked it. "I know what you're trying to do, A.J. You're trying to save his bacon, just like you always do."

"I'm only here as your friend, Nita. I am your friend. You believe that, don't you?"

She had always liked A.J. From that first day at Swarthmore, when he'd showed up at the mixer in plaid shorts and a T-shirt cruising the place, looking for girls. She suspected now she should never have traded him for Haze.

"Why? Why's the word we've gotta go with," A.J. was saying. "Why divorce Haze?"

"I don't want him to be President. You know what he is, A.J. You know he shouldn't be in that job. Why are you doing this?"

"He's not going to win, Nita. It won't happen. If that's your reason, you're doing this for nothing. You're gonna run a divorce on national TV, have paparazzi snapping your picture everywhere you go. You're gonna have to read about it in the tabloids—have Letterman do jokes about it. Right now, Haze is news. Divorce him now, it's gonna be a PR train wreck. But in two weeks, he's gonna be out of it. Nobody'll care."

"I don't believe he's going to be out of it."

"You haven't seen the tracking polls. We're sucking wind south of the Mason-Dixon."

"That isn't what the TV and papers say."

"The press? Come on, Nita. You know better than that. These guys say what we tell them. Fact is, Haze isn't selling down south. Here, look. . . . " He pulled some poll papers out of his pocket that, in reality, showed that Haze was scoring big. But they were confusing unless you knew what you were looking at. He took them over to the desk and turned on the lamp.

"Come here, look at this."

She moved over slowly and looked at the printout. A.J. started a breezy misinterpretation.

"Okay, look here, on 'Likability.' " He ran his fingers across to the coefficient number, which was simply the multiplier. It said fifteen. "Only fifteen percent," he lied, ignoring the real percentage number to the right, which said his "Likability" was 62 percent. "On 'Trust in a World Crisis,' look at this. . . . Are you looking at this, Anita?" She looked down at the page. "Seventeen percent," he said, showing her another coefficient. "They don't like him down there, Nita. We're cooked. It's over," he said, hoping she would go for it.

"Does Haze know?"

"I haven't told him. In two or three weeks, we're gonna be outta the bubble and off the national landscape. Then you can do what you want and it won't be on every newsbreak."

"You promise?" Her voice was now tiny.

"We're gonna get clobbered. The rednecks think Haze is just another fast-talking, New England carpetbagger." He looked in her vodka-dimmed eyes and watched as she bought it. A.J. reached out his arms to her.

"This has been tough on you, hasn't it, Nita?" She nodded and he moved to her and hugged her. He could feel the heat from her body through her clothing. It was cold in the room but, strangely, Anita was sweating. He held her for several minutes.

"Look, I'll stay in touch every day. If anything changes, I'll tell you. You gonna be okay?"

She took a long moment and, finally, nodded again.

Ten minutes later, he got her to lie down on her bed. When her breathing got heavy, A.J. retreated. He found Haze standing just inside his bedroom door.

"What happened?"

"I got us some time."

Haze zipped up his garment bag and they hurried out to the limo. A.J. filled Haze in on the way to the airport.

"Once we win in the South, she's gonna know you were lying," Haze said.

"I know. We're gonna have to figure something else out." A.J. knew that ultimately there was probably only one way to fix Anita's threat of a divorce. But he wasn't sure he'd sunk that low.

SUPER TUESDAY

ON SUPER TUESDAY MORNING, MICKEY MET THE PHONE TECH-
nician in the downstairs entry of the big house in Jersey. Mickey
showed him the phone, where he wanted the Pin Tel installed.

The technician started to attach the wires, hooking the small box
to the den phone. "My supervisor runs stockroom checks. These little
suckers is the latest and we ain't got but a few. They's for government
agencies only, and he's got 'em numbered and listed in this here book
and he—"

"This one gotta printout?" Mickey interrupted.

"Yup. Don't come any better."

It took half the morning to hook the Pin Tel up to all five lines in
the house. The tech had his office call to test it.

"Okay," the tech said as he snapped the plastic console cover back
on the small box. "Anybody calls in, the number is gonna flash up
here on the little screen and it's gonna get recorded down there, in

the memory disk." He showed Mickey a button that scrolled the memory of the Pin Tel. When the phone rang, the Pin Tel flashed the number. It was functioning properly.

"Okay, that there's the number this call is coming in from," he said, pointing to the display screen, "and it goes right in yer file memory, like that . . . there, see?" Mickey nodded and escorted the man to the front door.

"You through using this, you call me, 'cause I gotta pick up the unit 'cause, like I was saying, they keep track of them downtown. An' if one's missing, Lou goes orbital."

Mickey watched as the tech get into his truck, then he took his Mercedes and headed into New York City to meet with Silvio Candrate.

Mickey met the old gunsel in his small flat in Little Italy. Silvio had gone fat with age. Broken veins road-mapped his face, and high blood pressure had cooked his complexion red. In his day, Silvio had been the best. With Silvio, you got two fives for a ten every time. Mickey sat in the small living room, full of pictures of Silvio's family, and they spoke of things that didn't matter, while Silvio's wife brought cakes and coffee. She fussed over Mickey, calling him Don Alo.

After fifteen minutes of polite discussion about Silvio's sons and nephews, they finally decided to take a walk, leaving the stuffy apartment and Silvio's groveling wife behind.

Silvio led Mickey to a gas station that he owned. They moved into the lube rack where one of Silvio's nephews was using a power drill to pull tire lug nuts off a car on a hoist. The drill was screaming loudly in the small concrete garage. Silvio liked to hold business meetings under the lube rack, with the drill playing its horrible music, because he knew that it would be impossible for any bug, no matter how sophisticated, to sift through the wall of noise. Silvio had been holding his negotiations here for twenty years and he'd never yet faced a government recording in court.

"I need your 'Ghost.' I got a problem."

"I'll see if I can find him," Silvio said, pushing his red, chapped lips into Mickey's ear, half shouting over the drill.

"I don't have much time. This is very sensitive. I know what it costs and I got the up-front on me," Mickey yelled back into Silvio's ear.

"Not necessary. You got unlimited credit at the House of Hits. You call back tonight. Ask me if I wanna go to the opera. . . . If I've got a yes, I'll say, 'We should go to the opera.' Gimme a number of a clean phone where I can have him call you."

Mickey wrote down the number of his scrambled line and gave it to the old man. Moments later, they walked out of the lube garage and back up the street to Mickey's car.

Mickey did some business in New York. At six P.M., he called the old man from a social club in Little Italy where his father was once a member. "How ya doin', Silvio? I got some tickets to the opera, wanna go?"

"That's great," Silvio said, never mentioning Mickey's name. "We should go to the opera." It was the message Mickey wanted to hear. When Mickey hung up, he looked up at the TV over the bar. It was Super Tuesday and the six o'clock news was on.

Haze Richards was on camera at his hotel room in Memphis. He had just finished his trip through ten states. The polls had closed in the Southeast and network exit poll data was starting to come in.

"It looks like you're ahead in every state," the network field correspondent said, holding the microphone under Haze's smiling face.

"I'm very encouraged . . . and happy. But let's wait and see what happens when the votes are tabulated."

Mickey smiled from his booth in the back and ordered a glass of grappa. The waiter set it down and followed Mickey's gaze to the TV.

"Whatta you think of this guy, Don Alo?" the waiter asked, respectfully.

Mickey smiled. "I think one day soon, he's gonna be *my* President."

While Mickey was watching the six o'clock news in the social club in Little Italy, Lucinda and Ryan were three time zones to the west on the aft deck of the *Linda*.

It was three o'clock Pacific standard time, and they had the little portable TV placed on the companionway steps to shield the screen from the slanting light. Ryan was feeling dull from an afternoon of lying outside in the sun. He was watching without expression as the network big feet called state after state for Haze Richards.

"Let's switch now to Leslie Wing at Haze Richards's hotel in Memphis," Dale Hellinger said. Dale was a tall, distinguished black commentator with a voice like James Earl Jones's, who had taken over for Brenton Spencer at UBC. The shot switched to an attractive Asian correspondent standing in a roomful of festive campaigners.

"Thank you, Dale. It's a party here at Richards's Election Central and a foregone conclusion that Haze Richards is going to sweep all of the Super Tuesday states by large margins." She glanced off-camera for a second. "I see Haze's campaign chairman. . . . Let me see if I can get him over." She moved with her cameraman in pursuit; then A.J.'s bushy head came into the frame of the small TV.

"Mr. Teagarden, Mr. Teagarden. . . . Leslie Wing, UBC. This is quite a night," she said as the wonk turned and grinned into the camera. People whooped it up and danced behind them.

"We seem to be doing something right, Leslie."

"Haze was a political unknown only a month ago, and now it looks as if he's all but sewn up the Democratic nomination."

"The American people are looking for something. There's a feeling of anger out there, Leslie . . . a feeling that, in the current system of government, there is something desperately wrong. Haze stands for what can be right. He's gonna redefine the process of government. Grab the institutions of power back from the Washington lobbyists. He's gonna get it running the way the people want it to run. It's why I'm with him, and I think it's why America is with him tonight."

"Thank you." And Leslie Wing turned back to the camera. "It's a madhouse here, Dale. People are really enjoying themselves."

"Tell me, Leslie," Dale said from Brenton's old anchor desk. "Is there any word from Governor Richards on when he'll come down and give his victory speech?"

"Let me try and find out, Dale." She tried to follow A.J., but he was dancing a polka with a fat campaign contributor . . . arms and feet flying, off across the floor like two dancing hippos. "I'm sorry, Dale, it's just unbelievable here."

Ryan and Lucinda watched without saying a word as the fifty-foot ketch swayed slowly in the wind at the end of its anchor chain.

"What's for dinner?" Ryan finally asked.

"I was thinking I'd go into town and get us a nice two-inch steak. How about barbecued beef, a green salad, and garlic bread, and the best red wine I can find?"

"I'd like that."

Lucinda went below and changed out of Linda's bathing suit, into a pair of Linda's shorts and a cropped top that she'd found in a drawer under the forward bunk. She jumped into the rubber Avon boat, started the five-horse outboard engine, and went to buy dinner. On the way into Avalon, she wondered if the nightmare was over for them, or just beginning. . . .

PUDGE

VICE PRESIDENT JAMES "PUDGE" ANDERSON WATCHED THE RE-
turns from the vice presidential residence at the naval observatory on
Massachusetts Avenue. He had just finished his own southern swing
through the Super Tuesday states, but had decided to go back to
Washington and watch the returns from there. The Republican primary was not much of a contest. He had no real opposition. He had
the party backing and the influence of the sitting President, Charles
"King" Cotton. What annoyed him was the networks' profuse enthusiasm for Haze Richards, especially from this new black anchor,
Dale Hellinger, at UBC. Pudge had called his own campaign manager,
Carl "Henny" Henderson.

"You watching this, Henny?" Pudge asked.

"Y' mean the Haze Richards runaway railroad?"

"Yeah. This guy was cooking lobsters last month and now he's
gonna make America work again for all of us."

"Don't let it get to ya, Pudge. This is their night. We're not a story 'cause you're running more or less unopposed. The good news is Skatina is gonna drop out. I just got off the phone with his guys. They were told by their backers they hadda win tonight or the money was gonna dry up. So he's out. I'd rather run against Haze than Skatina any day, 'specially since Skatina is from your state, New York, and he could split us there. Let these guys soak in the glory tonight and tomorrow we're gonna start the bimborama."

"I don't like doing that, Henny. We oughta be able to win on our record, on our ideas." Pudge was a rare breed of politician who always kept his sense of honor elevated a notch or two above his need to win. The big problem was that James Anderson was colorless. His own staff joked that Pudge was so nondescript he could lose a tail in an elevator. But, even so, his life had been a steady climb to power.

He had been fascinated by politics since he was a child. His father had been a three-term United States senator. Pudge had gone to Ivy League colleges and had fought in the Korean War, starting in Seoul as a green lieutenant and ending up as a battle-hardened company commander. He won two Purple Hearts and a Silver Star, but after being wounded, he refused to let them send him home, choosing to recover in Seoul and remain with his unit until his hitch was up. That story defined him. Pudge had been his nickname since grade school. He was no longer a plump sixth-grader, but the name still somehow stuck.

Pudge had risen slowly in the party, but eventually people became dependent on him, finally realizing what a steady force the dedicated young man was, and he was elected to Congress.

Four years ago, Charles "King" Cotton asked him to join the Republican ticket. King didn't need a colorful vice president; he had enough color for a Florida sunset. What he needed was regional balance, and the New York congressman got the nod. Then halfway through his first term, King Cotton had developed prostate cancer. Pudge knew that the charismatic, white-haired President was dying. That was how the fattest kid in the sixth grade came to be running, unopposed, on the Republican ballot for the presidency of the United States.

"I don't want to start a bimbo attack," Pudge repeated to Henny Henderson.

"You say that now, but we gotta throw some dynamite, Pudge. I don't think Haze is much to worry about, but we gotta unwind some of this precious bullshit. 'Make America work again,' and then he rides into town like Clark Kent and gets lucky with the Teamsters in your home state. That sets him up for voters. They think he can perform in a crisis, but this guy has a pretty damn good performance record in a bedroom, too."

"Let's get him on his voting record."

"There's nothing to look at. You gotta let me do my thing, Pudge."

"We'll talk in the morning," Pudge said, hanging up and switching around to the various networks, ending on UBC.

"We're going to call the Republican primaries for Vice President Anderson in all twenty states, as expected," Dale Hellinger announced. "But the big news, the roller-coaster ride here at campaign central, is the overwhelming night that Haze Richards has had for the Democrats. We might even call it a history-making event, a landslide Democratic primary victory for Haze Richards in all twenty states with margins that are absolutely stunning."

Pudge wanted to keep from toting out the bimbos that Henny had found. But by ten o'clock, as state after state set record Democratic wins for Governor Richards, he wondered if bimbos might end up being his last line of defense.

Anita Richards felt deserted and lied to. A.J. had told her Haze couldn't win. She took a long gulp of vodka out of the cut crystal glass. She had stopped putting in ice two hours ago, and now, as she swallowed it, she sloshed some of the clear liquid on her pink robe. She looked down at her painted toenails. The last delicate appendages on Anita Richards, they were attached to plump feet and stocky ankles. Suddenly her toes went in and out of focus.

"Shit," she said out loud, "I'm drunk." Then she closed her eyes and got a bad case of bed spin. She opened her eyes and the room swung like a chandelier in a windstorm.

"Anita is elated," Haze was saying happily on TV. "She and I have worked long and hard for this day. It's her victory as much as mine."

Anita held on to the bed and her sanity with tearful desperation.

DISCOVERY

IT WAS JUST BEFORE SUNSET WHEN LUCINDA RAN THE RUBBER Avon up to the dinghy dock in Avalon Harbor. The harbor reminded her of an Old World painting. The bay was a huge horseshoe with red-and-white mooring cans strung in the water in semicircular rows like party decorations. A brightly painted green pier and a turn-of-the-century dance hall stood guard on opposite sides of the bay. It was the off-season and the boat traffic was light. She tied up the dinghy and walked on bare feet into the tourist section of town and asked an island policeman to direct her to a good meat market.

"Tannyhill's, on the corner of Descanso and Third, is my favorite. They're open till ten," he answered.

"Thank you," she said. "And is there a hospital on the island?"

"Right up Falls Canyon Road." He pointed at a narrow street that wound up the hill.

She decided to go to the hospital first. She needed to find a doctor soon to look at Ryan's leg.

The Avalon Municipal Hospital was a Mexican-style one-story structure with an arched front door and a red tile roof. Lucinda opened the screen door and looked into a bare but clean reception area.

"Anybody here?" She heard a door slam, and then a young woman wearing blue jeans and a T-shirt came in from the back and stuck her hand out.

"I'm Dr. Andrea Lewis."

"I'm Lauren," Lucinda said, suddenly deciding it would be a mistake to give her real name.

"How can we help you, Lauren?"

"My boyfriend has a bad leg and it was sewn up by a doctor back east, but it may need to have the dressing changed, and I was wondering if I could bring him in here and you could look at it."

"I'm not a specialist, but I'll be happy to have a look," Dr. Andrea Lewis said, smiling. "What kind of 'bad leg'?"

"He was in an accident a few days ago. It got ripped open and they had to do a lot of reconstruction."

"Sounds like he should be in a hospital. Where you staying?"

"The motel in town," Lucinda lied, beginning to realize these questions could be dangerous if somebody came looking for them.

"Which motel?"

"The . . . uh . . . the little one. . . ."

"The little one," Andrea repeated flatly, the smile fading.

"Okay, look, we're not married and his parents are real strict, and he's afraid they're going to make him come home if they find him," she said, realizing how stupid it sounded the minute she said it.

"If you want, I'll look at him. What's his name?"

"Bill. Bill Williams." She was fucking this up terribly. She felt her face reddening. "Maybe we could come in the morning. . . ."

"I'll be here," Dr. Lewis said. Lucinda smiled, then turned and got the hell out of the hospital. She could feel the doctor's eyes on her back as she moved down the road.

She bought the steaks at Tannyhill's Market, and some frozen vegetables she could zap in the microwave, lettuce, and the ingredients for salad dressing. She got California Napa Valley cabernet sauvignon and watched as the clerk bagged it all and took fifty dollars of Elizabeth's money. As she left the market, she saw a pay phone across the street. Suddenly, she felt she had to talk to her mother. She crossed to the phone, took some change out of her pocket, and dialed her home in New Jersey. She could feel her heart pounding. If Mickey answered, she would just hang up, she reasoned. Her hands were shaking, but she needed to hear her mother's voice. The phone rang five times and she was about to hang up when Penny came on the line.

"Mom, it's me. I wanted to tell you I'm okay and I'm sorry if I've made you worry."

"Lucinda, where are you? I want you to come home."

"I can't, Mom. I just can't. You have to trust me. But I miss you and I love you. And I'll call again, soon."

"Come home, Lucinda," Penny said, her voice cracking with emotion. "I miss you, honey."

"I can't, Mom. Please understand. I gotta go now, but don't worry about me. I just called to say I love you." She hung up quickly, unable to endure her mother's pleading.

She headed the small Avon into the light swells, and after a mile could see the ketch, lit by mastlight and moonlight. She pushed away her worries as she hurried back to fix Ryan's dinner.

Mickey scrolled the Pin Tel until he found the number that had just called. He'd removed the phone speaker from the headset in his office two days ago, so his breathing would not betray him as he listened in on random calls. He had just overheard the conversation between his sister and mother. Lucinda had not given away her location, but the Pin Tel did.

He picked up the phone and dialed the number on the printout screen. Mickey let it ring almost twenty times before a young man's voice came on the line.

"What's happenin'?" the unfamiliar voice said.

"Where is this phone?"

"Pay phone, man. I was walking by, I picked it up."

"Where is it?"

"Catalina Island, across from Tannyhill's Market."

By ten o'clock that night, the Ghost was on his way to California to finish the job Thirteen Weeks and New York Tony had both bungled.

CRISIS

HAZE RICHARDS AND A. J. TEAGARDEN LEFT THE MEMPHIS HIL-
ton at four-forty-five A.M., before anybody was awake. They rode in
silence in the back of the hotel limousine in a dense fog, traveling
down mist-wet streets toward the Memphis International Airport.
They had a big problem to solve.

They arrived at the private jet terminal a few minutes before five
and were let out onto the field. The limo parked under the wing of
their rented 737 and Haze and A.J. climbed the steps into the back
of the empty plane.

"This is fucked," Haze finally said when they were alone.

A.J. was not sure how much to tell him. "How badly do you want
to be President?"

"Cut the shit." Haze slumped down in his window seat.

"If she drags you through a divorce, it's over."

Haze said nothing.

"She doesn't think you're fit to govern . . . Her words not mine. This is a public relations nightmare. The press will feed on it. She'll get forced onto TV. She'll be angry, she'll accuse you of stuff, your female demographics will drop lower than a midget's balls."

"Get off it." Haze glowered.

"I'm not kidding. Your divorce is gonna make Burt and Lonnie's seem like a pillow fight. She's gonna rip you open. The gender gap it creates will be impossible to close."

"Get to the point."

"How bad do you want this? How far are you willing to go?" A.J. could feel his heart beating in his chest. He was powered by high-octane ambition. A.J. knew they were going to win the Democratic nomination, it was as good as secured. They had twenty-three states and two caucuses in Haze's pocket. With nobody left in the race, the nomination was theirs, unless Anita gave hope to the vanquished. If she filed divorce papers, A.J. knew that the four defeated candidates would be tempted to wait him out, to see how the polls reacted. Anita could kill his nomination. They had to stop her.

"You gotta talk her out of it, like you did before," Haze said.

"I'll try, but I lied to her and now she knows it. I probably used up my one ticket."

"So, whatta we do?"

"Delay her."

They sat in silence as the steward stuck his head in the back. "Are you gentlemen buckled up?"

"Yeah, let's go," A.J. said while the engines started and the plane taxied onto the runway.

In minutes, they were thundering past the tower and climbing up, out of the low morning fog and breaking into the sunlight, heading east with the orange ball riding low off the starboard wing.

"We delay her. . . . Why? What good does that do?"

"I called Mickey," A.J. said, flatly.

Haze looked at him, not sure what the ramifications of that call might be.

"He said if we couldn't take care of it, he would."

Haze was looking at the man he'd grown up with, wondering if it was possible they were talking about the same thing.

"What the fuck does that mean?"

"He said he'd take care of it. That's what he said. I can't stop him from doing whatever he wants."

"And I said, what does that mean?" Haze's voice was rising.

"Keep your voice down, will you?" A.J. said, glancing around, but they were alone in the empty cabin.

"You telling me he's gonna kill her?" Haze was whispering.

"I don't know what he's gonna do. . . . Put the fear of God into her, make her do what we want, shake some sense into her. How do I know?"

They sat in silence for a long time.

"Haze . . ."

Haze was looking out the window at the rising sun.

"Look at me, will ya . . . ?"

Haze finally turned, but there was no expression on his handsome face.

"This is what we dreamed of, man. This is what it's been about since grade school. You and me . . . getting where we want to go . . . in the White House, Haze, the Oval Office."

Haze said nothing, his expression hard to read in the orange light coming through the window.

" 'Member what we said when we were kids?" A.J. went on. "The higher the monkey climbs, the more his ass is exposed. Our ass is exposed. We gotta do whatever it takes. The White House . . . that's the prize. Maybe a man can't win a prize like that unless he's willing to step up and take it."

"How does Mickey take care of it, huh?"

"I don't know, Haze, but if you want to be President, we have to stop her. These guys are spending heavy bread. They won't stand around while your wife flushes it down the toilet."

Haze knew A.J. was right. And after the initial shock had worn off, he wasn't sure how upset he felt about it.

The plane touched down in Providence at nine-fifteen and taxied to the executive terminal. Haze and A.J. had not spoken in almost an hour. They got in A.J.'s Land Rover and drove to the governor's mansion. The streets of Providence were still clogged with morning traffic. When they parked in the garage under the mansion, it was almost ten.

"Anita's car isn't here," Haze said as they moved toward the elevator.

Upstairs, the Providence mansion was quiet. Anita's press secretary wasn't in yet. They moved down the hall and into Anita's suite. As soon as they entered, it was obvious Anita had left. Clothes were strewn everywhere, discards from a furious packing session. A.J. went into the bathroom to check the cosmetics counter.

"Gone," he said flatly, as he walked out of the dressing room.

"Whatta we do now?"

"I'll go to the pay phone downstairs and call Mickey. He's gotta stop her." He started digging in his pocket for a quarter. "You got change?" he asked.

"Use this," Haze said, taking his AT&T card out of his wallet.

"You really stink in a crisis, you know that?"

"*What?*" Haze said, angry and confused.

"You wanna call the head of the Alo Mafia family and log it on your AT and T account? I'm never gonna pull a bank job with you, homey."

A.J. dialed Mickey's private number on the pay phone in the lobby.

"This is A.J., lemme talk to Mickey," he said to an unfamiliar voice on the phone. After a moment, he heard the slightly mechanical sound of Mickey's voice. The tinny quality, he assumed, was caused by the scrambler.

"Yeah?"

"She's not here," A.J. said.

"She's in good hands," Mickey said.

"It wouldn't be wise if she were hurt. I don't think it would look good for the man to win the nomination today and then lose his wife, all in twenty-four hours."

"You and I must be having the same thoughts. We might still need her."

"Exactly," A.J. said.

"Tell your friend, I'll take care of everything." And the line went dead before A.J. could say anything more. As he hung up, a strange revelation hit him. He had somehow become involved in a conspiracy to commit a kidnapping. In his wildest dreams, he could never have conceived of a set of circumstances that would lead him to such a venture.

A.J. had always thought of himself in a certain way—gentle and funny, a good friend who always looked for the best in people. His keen mind was his secret weapon. Albert James Teagraden, the little boy who grew up at 234½ Beeker Street would never hurt anyone. That just wasn't part of the plan. Yet here he was, standing in the lobby of the governor's mansion, having just called the head of the Jersey mob to discuss the kidnapping of Anita Farrington Richards, a woman he liked and respected.

A.J. moved to the elevator and pushed the button. He stared at his distorted reflection in the polished brass door. He looked wider— wider and shorter, with shiny, yellow skin. The reflection made him look a lot like Mickey Alo.

"Talk about your defining moments," he said to himself.

The door opened and A.J. stepped into the elevator. It swallowed him like Jonah, into its mahogany, brass-railed stomach, where he wondered, for the first time in years, what had happened to that little boy from Beeker Street.

DARKNESS

THE ROOM WAS SMALL AND DARK, WITH NO WINDOWS, AND THE air was pungent with the smell of mildew and urine.

She was sitting with her hands tied behind her back. Her shoulders ached and she was thirsty. Something like a napkin or dish towel had been wedged into her mouth and her jaws were taped shut. At first she had cried, but her nose became filled with mucus, restricting her breathing, and she almost suffocated. Fortunately, she realized the danger before it was too late and had willed herself, as an act of survival, to stop crying. *Relax*, she had told herself. *Breathe slowly.* After a few agonizing moments, she cleared her air passage.

Anita Farrington Richards was terrified, but she had decided that her only chance to survive was to keep her wits, stay calm, and hope to find a way to communicate with her captors, men she had barely seen.

She had left the governor's mansion at eight-thirty, put her suitcase in the trunk of her car, and driven across Providence to River Street where she intended to meet a divorce attorney named Susan Salter. Anita had set up a nine A.M. appointment, without telling anyone. She had been on her way to Susan's office when a brown Camaro rear-ended her at a stop sign. She pulled over to exchange licenses when a dark shape suddenly filled the window on the passenger side. Before she could even call out, the driver's door had been yanked open and, in an instant, two men were in the front seat with her. She had started to scream, but the man on the passenger side had pushed her down, and jammed a gag into her mouth. He leaned down and whispered into her ear.

"Shut up or you're dead."

And then, with her head held down against the driver's thigh, they pulled out. She could hear the traffic and, occasionally, the man on the passenger side gave instructions to the driver.

"Right up there. . . . Halfway down the block. . . . They'll open the gate."

She had tried once to straighten her legs.

"You move, you're gonna get conked," the man had said. Then the car came to a stop. She could smell something dense and rich, perhaps oil in an open tank. A hood of some kind was put over her head before she was allowed to sit up; then her hands were taped behind her and she was led across uneven pavement. She heard a metal door open; she was pulled up some stairs and, finally, put into this room. The hood had been snapped off her head and the door closed, leaving her in darkness.

Anita tried desperately to hold on, to maintain her reason. Icy fear consumed her, periodically pushing her to the edge of sanity. Each time she struggled back. Her mind wouldn't hold still; it pinwheeled across a landscape of thoughts, sticking on meaningless details of her life, then racing off in search of nothing.

Oh, God . . . oh, God . . . oh, God . . . she chanted in her mind. *What will they do to me? How can this be happening?*

A.J. had sent the plane back to Memphis to pick up the rest of the press and campaign staff. He left Haze at the governor's mansion and walked across the mall to his office. He sat down in his old leather chair and tried to recapture some of the excitement he had felt only a few hours ago when they'd swept Super Tuesday. It was useless. The excitement was replaced by a terrible listlessness.

The call from Henny Henderson came in at ten past twelve. He heard his secretary giving out the usual "Mr. Teagarden is not in right now." But he perked up when she said, "Would you say that number again, Mr. Henderson?"

"I'll take that, Jill," he called out.

"Oh, he just walked in. I can connect you now." And in a moment, Pudge Anderson's campaign chairman was on the phone.

"Well, I guess you're a happy guy this morning," the Republican wonk said cautiously.

"How you doin', Henny. . . . You call to set up a handball game or did you just miss me?" A.J. said to the man whom he hadn't spoken to for ten years, since Henny had called him a loose cannon in the Democratic party.

"Haze really came out of nowhere. Guess it's us against you guys now," Henny said. "I'll bet you've got the DNC spitting tacks into your picture."

"Haze is an astounding candidate. He's got a great vision for America, Henny. He's tapping into a lot of discontent."

"That's not all he's been tapping into."

"What does that mean?"

"Does Haze know a woman named Bonita Moncy?"

A.J.'s stomach flipped. "Is that 'money'—like, 'We're in the money'?"

"Actually, now that you mention it, 'in' is the right word, 'cause she says Haze has been screwin' her. She runs a travel agency in Florida. Apparently, Haze set up some vacations down there where he did more than lie on the beach. Want the vitals?"

"Yeah, let's hear," A.J. said, his spirits plummeting.

"She's five-five, thirty-six, with platinum-blond hair and abdominals you could scrub laundry on. She says they spent two consecutive weekends together last June . . . the seventh through the ninth and the thirteenth through the fifteenth."

"Jesus, Henny, calm down. You sound so happy."

"Before we let go of this, I just thought I'd call and give Haze a chance to say it ain't so."

"That's pretty damn nice of you. Why didn't you just run right to the press with it?"

"I would have, but Pudge wouldn't let me. He said he wanted to give Haze a chance to deny it first. That's why I called. We could fit in some handball, too, if you want, but I think you're gonna be too busy trying to bury this turd before it stinks up your campaign. However, you should know, behind Ms. Money, we have a line of bimbos queueing up."

"You're a real prick!"

"I didn't fuck those girls, A.J. I'm just the poor messenger. If it wasn't for Pudge's sense of fair play, you would have been reading this blind in the papers tomorrow."

"I'll have to talk to Haze. I'm sure this is just a publicity seeker."

"Right. Well, we're gonna take it to the news guys at nine A.M. tomorrow, unless you can give us a reason not to. That's 'reason,' spelled A-L-I-B-I."

"Gimme a number."

They exchanged phone and beeper numbers, then hung up. A.J. leaned back and looked out across the mall at the governor's mansion.

"Shit," he finally said, then lunged out of his chair and headed over to find out what he already knew was true.

Haze didn't deny it. He sat in his office in the statehouse and looked glumly out the window.

"Were you there? those two weekends in June?"

"Yeah. . . . Anita was having the hysterectomy in New York. I flew down to Florida."

"Great. Your wife is getting her uterus ripped out while you're playing tonsil hockey with this platinum-blond travel agent. Jesus!"

"Look, A.J., it happened. Okay?"

A.J. sat down and looked at Haze for a long moment. "I can't believe this. Yesterday, we were sweeping twenty states on our way to the White House, and today, my life is caving in on me."

"Your life?"

"Okay . . . *your* life is caving in on me."

"Look, I can't stop her from talking."

"Were there witnesses?" A.J. asked in desperation.

"I'm not a complete fool."

They sat without speaking and listened to the grandfather clock measure time. Then A.J. pushed himself out of his chair and walked slowly across the room toward the door.

"Where are you going? Whatta you gonna do?"

A.J. looked at Haze, the beginning of a desperate plan forming in his mind. He'd gone this far, he reasoned, why not go all the way? "If we can't stop this girl, then we gotta get somebody else to stop her."

"Not Mickey. You can't have this guy kill half the people I know."

"No, not Mickey. We'll get Henny Henderson to stop her."

"Why would he stop her . . . ? He found her."

"He'll stop her if it's in his best interest to stop her. We have to create a situation to convince him it is." A.J. walked out of the governor's office, leaving Haze confused.

Five hours later, they met at the same gas station parking lot. Mickey Alo was alone behind the wheel of the same motor home.

"This better be good," the mobster said.

"It is," A.J. answered as he climbed in beside Mickey and they headed up the highway.

They pulled off the road at a scenic outlook near the same raging river where they'd first met. Mickey set the brake, got out from behind the wheel, and moved to the back of the coach. A.J. made no effort to follow.

"This is your powwow. I drove all the way from Jersey, I hadda borrow this fucking parade float from Pelico. You wanna tell me what's so important we gotta go camping together?"

A.J. looked up from the tassels on his loafers and out the window.

"Okay," he started slowly, not looking at the mobster. "On the political front, we're doing great . . . but we got problems on the home front. Haze has . . . well, he's been indiscreet. He's had more than one liaison with several different parties. The assignations have been brief but carnal."

"Listen, stop looking out the window. Okay? I'm over here. Second, stop talking like Bill fucking Buckley. Say what you mean. . . . Haze is out banging available pussy. Is that it?"

"*Was.* Haze *was* out banging available pussy. I told him after we met you, and decided to get in this thing, that he'd have to take the cure. And he has."

"Who knows about this?"

"Well, that's the problem. Pudge Anderson's campaign chairman, Henny Henderson, called and told me about some travel agent in Florida that they've got their hands on. He hinted there's more than one woman in the wings. I confronted Haze and he acknowledged it. They're gonna go to press with it in the morning."

Mickey got up and moved to the sofa, his mind playing the angles. "So, what happens?" he finally said.

"You saw what happened to Gary Hart with Donna Rice, and you saw Gennifer Flowers take a bite out of Clinton. This will be worse. The conservatives and the moral Right will crucify him. Unless . . ." He stopped and forced himself to swing his gaze back to Mickey.

"Unless what?"

"Unless we create a reason Henderson and Pudge can't use it."

"What kind of reason?"

"What were you planning to do with Anita?"

"Anita has decided to take a long trip. She's going to be leaving the country. She may come back after the nomination is secured; she may not. It's gonna be up to her. Right now, she's thinking about it."

"What if Anita meets with tragic circumstances?" A.J. blurted out.

"You been watching too much television."

"What if she was chartering a plane and flying to meet Haze in Ohio where we're doing a press conference tonight. The plane could have problems. . . . " He stopped, unable to finish the thought because Mickey was smiling at him.

"Jesus, you're not who I thought you were at all."

A.J. looked away and tried to finish. "Haze will cry on national TV. We'll stretch it out . . . we'll make it play for a month, maybe longer. The funeral is the cover of *Time* magazine. Haze will do the eulogy.

He'll talk about a thirty-year love affair. He'll make trips to her grave and the nation will mourn with him."

"How does that keep them from parading these whores?"

"They can't. Pudge will look like an asshole if he starts to attack a man who is grieving for his wife. I promise you. It'll hurt him worse than Haze."

They were quiet for a minute; then A.J. went on. "It cleans up two problems at the same time. Anita goes away and so does her divorce threat. Also, our internal poll shows the public finds Haze a little distant. This will create sympathy for him and warm up his image," A.J. said, using the logic Ryan had given him in the bar back in Iowa. "Pudge won't dare throw his bimbo grenades," A.J. concluded, suddenly feeling trapped in the motor home, wanting to escape the stuffy environment.

"Okay, rent a plane. We'll rig something that won't look like sabotage."

"What about the pilots?"

"Not even remotely important, Albert. People are meat machines. Sometime they have fiscal or emotional value. If they don't have either, they don't count." He pointed his finger at A.J. and pulled an imaginary trigger. "Bang," he said. "No venue, no value."

"Shit," A.J. said, softly.

Mickey dropped A.J. back at the gas station. The wonk stood next to his car as Mickey looked at him from the steps of the motor home. "Rent the plane with campaign funds. Have it standing by at the executive terminal at the Providence airfield at six-thirty tonight. I'll take care of everything else." Mickey smiled at him. "This bothers you, doesn't it?"

A.J. pulled his coat around him and nodded.

"Lemme give you something to comfort you," Mickey continued. "Right this second, approximately five hundred people are stepping off the planet. . . . Some of them are dying in car wrecks, some are having coronaries, some are committing suicide. Dipshit passengers on the train to glory. While they're leaving, the maternity bus is pulling up, letting off a thousand new idiots. They're screaming and sucking in their first breaths, shitting their first loads. Net gain:

Five hundred people. Ninety percent of them will turn out to be worthless assholes. One less here or there won't make a bit of difference."

"You're a sociopath. . . . "

"Welcome to the dark side of the planet, Albert."

Mickey closed the door of the motor home and drove off.

A.J. stood in the gas station, feeling cold and alone.

CRASH

MILO DULEO HAD SEEN MORE THAN HIS SHARE OF DEATH. HE'D learned to fly in the Navy. He'd had the dangerous but important job of monitoring the Russian-Afghanistan war in his supersonic high-flying Lockheed SR-71 Blackbird. He would streak off at stratospheric heights, the wing cameras whirring as he took surveillance photos along the Afghanistan border. He had been shot at dozens of times but had finally gone down when he got jumped by a squadron of Yakovlev 38s. He'd been taking an adrenaline ride against orders, streaking low through narrow valleys, the huge rock outcroppings racing past on both sides. Before he knew it, he was dodging ASM rockets and, finally, took one up the tailpipe and had to eject over hostile territory. He'd been lucky and run into a Mujahedin scout patrol, and was returned after two months to his carrier. He'd been asked to stand for a naval review and was found to have lost his aircraft unnecessarily. The decision ended his gonzo years. He found a home in commercial aviation, but grew bored with it and took a job flying Joseph Alo's Lear-55. With the Alos, he was occasionally asked to do some dick-puckering work, and he lived for those jobs. . . . Like the time they'd grabbed a black drug dealer with the unlikely name of Napoleon Outlaw and pushed the sorry son of a bitch out of the Lear without a parachute, forty miles out over the Atlantic Ocean . . . Not exactly the same as dodging MiG-29 Foxbat missiles, but at least with the Alos, he still had a chance to pump a little joy juice.

Milo was looking forward to tonight's flight as he packed his jump chute and prized Heckler and Koch MP-5 submachine gun with the retractable stock and rotating rear sight cylinder. He loaded his gear into his black Range Rover and took off for the Providence executive terminal, where Pulacarpo Depaulo and Anita Farrington Richards were scheduled to arrive just after dark. The only tricky part was getting aboard unobserved. He had asked Mickey to rent a Lear-55 because he was familiar with the avionics, and if it was locked, he could access the cabin through the rear luggage compartment. The plane would be parked at the terminal, and because of the cold weather, he figured the pilots would be in the lounge drinking coffee. He should be able to scale the fence and get to the plane without difficulty.

It worked pretty much the way he figured. Milo jumped the six-foot fence and moved quickly across the tarmac and opened the rear luggage compartment. He unscrewed the panel that accessed the toilet. Within minutes, he was in the back of the plane. He shinnied into the small head, sat on the toilet seat and replaced the panel. Once it was secure, he remained there with his parachute and back-pack duffel on his knees.

At nine-fifteen, he heard the door of the plane being lowered and the two pilots talking.

"What's wrong with her?" one of them asked.

Then Milo heard the thick Italian accent that he recognized as Pulacarpo's.

"She's a'got too much'a to drink. I'm'a bring da car out so we get her in'a plane much bett'a."

Sitting in the small rest room Milo pulled the machine gun out of the top of his bag.

"Did you see her out there in the car? What the hell's wrong with her?" one pilot asked.

"If she's sick and gets in trouble while we're flying, we're gonna have an insurance claim, sure as shit. You better call the office and find out what they want us to do."

Milo opened the door and stepped out into the cabin with the H&K MP-5 on his hip. The two pilots turned and saw him standing behind them. Their expressions registered shock.

"Why don't you two sky kings go on up and start the preflight, okay? Anybody gets loopy, I'm gonna take him out," Milo said softly, his adrenaline giving him a rush.

"You shoot that in here, you break this bird's skin; we'll never get off the ground," the taller one said to him.

"Bullshit . . . Guess what, Sky, I'm qualified in this equipment."

He herded them into the cockpit but kept his distance so there was no chance they could spin and grab him.

"Put the seat belts on, fellas, just so nobody'll be poppin' up, un-announced."

Both put on three-point belts; then Milo unplugged the two head-set mikes and took them out of the cockpit. He sat on the jump seat with the machine gun on his knees and waited until the limo pulled onto the tarmac. He saw Pulacarpo leading Anita out of the limo. Her hands were tied and she looked drugged. Pulacarpo helped her to the plane and Milo grabbed her arms to steady her as she came aboard.

"Is she drugged? What's she got in her?" Milo asked, concerned that a body pumped full of chemicals would raise eyebrows at the autopsy.

"She's a'been drink vodka . . . too much, is'a my think."

"Okay, that works. Get outta here." Milo helped her into a seat.

Pulacarpo left the plane and pulled the limo away from the exec-utive terminal. Milo looked at Anita, her eyes at half-mast.

"Having fun, Mrs. Richards?"

Anita didn't answer; her head lolled on her shoulders. He reached down and buckled her in. Her hands were still tied behind her, but he decided to wait until just before the end to take care of that detail. He moved back into the pilots' cabin.

2 6 3

"Okay, let's power up, boys," he said to the two frightened pilots, who began flipping switches. The starboard engine began to whine. As it wound up, Milo plugged the headphone into the jack behind the pilot's head and put it on.

"This is White Lear-55, 7-6-8-9 Whiskey Sierra, requesting first available take off," Milo said into the headset mike.

"Roger, Niner-Whiskey-Sierra. You can proceed on taxiway 1-6 to runway 3-5 south and hold short."

Then Milo tapped the pilot on the shoulder with the H&K. "Wanna do that, Sky?"

Milo got permission from the tower for takeoff; they taxied out onto the tarmac and began the roll. The engine whined as the sleek Lear-55 roared down the runway and took off into the night sky.

Milo signed off with the tower, contacted Hays Field departure, and told the pilots to head toward Cleveland. They punched in the omnirange coordinates and Milo leaned back and watched them with a practiced eye. They flew in silence.

Two hours later, they were over Lake Erie and Cleveland appeared on the color radar, fifty miles ahead. Milo took the H&K machine gun and stood behind the copilot.

"Gonna use the bathroom. Anybody gets up, he's dead." Then, without warning, he jabbed the copilot under the left ear with the stock. The man's head rolled down on his chest. The pilot let out a yell and struggled to unhook his seat belt. Milo swung the weapon back in his direction. It took two hard blows to the head before the pilot stopped struggling and slumped against the side panel of the cockpit.

"Thanks for the lift, fellas." Milo reached into the cockpit and rolled the trim tab forward, putting the plane into a shallow dive. He checked the color radar in the dash and noted the position. They were ten miles from land. His plan was to bail out at about five thousand feet and ride the prevailing winds with his chute, to reach land on the western tip of Lake Erie. He had set the dive so that the plane would hit farmland to the east of Hopkins Field, Cleveland's international airport. There would be questions about the crash, but several flights had gone down trying to land at Hopkins in recent years. The FAA had made extensive investigations and could not explain why the area had become a mini-Devil's Triangle for aviators. Lear-55 Niner-Whiskey-Sierra was going to be the latest in a series of unexplained aviation disasters. Milo untied Anita and checked her. It wouldn't be necessary to knock her out. She was still dazed by the alcohol. He left her and moved to the rear emergency exit, pulled the handle release, yanked the hatch open, and threw it on the carpet behind him. The wind screamed through the opening and Milo could feel the joy juice pumping through his body. Then he lunged out into a blast of cold night air.

Milo was falling. His face freezing. The bitter cold was biting his skin. He counted to ten and then pulled the rip cord. The chute streamed out, then snapped open and he was yanked up, the shoulder straps pulling at his body. Off to the right, he could see the shoreline of Lake Erie and the lights of Cleveland. He pulled on the guidelines, gently leaning the chute in that direction. He saw he would easily reach the shore.

Inside the Lear, Anita was awake. She had been in a stupor, but when Milo pulled the emergency hatch, the cold air brought her to her senses. At first she couldn't figure out where she was and then it came to her. . . . The trip in the limo, the stop at the liquor store, and the whispered instructions by the man with the heavy Italian accent. He had forced her to drink the vodka while he poked her in the ribs with an automatic and held the bottle to her lips till she passed out.

Now she was in a plane. . . . She could hear the screaming engines, much louder than normal and, when she turned, she saw the emergency exit gaping. She unsnapped her seat belt and stumbled forward, where both pilots were unconscious.

"Oh, my God," she said out loud. And then she could see the ground. They were very low, streaking over moonlit farmland, fields, and occasional buildings.

She looked in horror out the windshield, as a brick building rushed headlong toward her. *This can't be right,* her struggling mind was saying, as the Lear obliterated itself into a concrete and brick grain locker.

The flames shot three hundred feet in the air. The concussions of the explosion rattled the windows of farmhouses miles away. Pieces of the plane were on fire and burning all over the surrounding fields. The main fuselage was a twisted, charred framework of burning metal.

By the time the first fire unit arrived, there was very little left.

SYMPATHY

KAZ WORKED ALL AFTERNOON IN A SMALL OFFICE IN THE JUSTICE
Department in Washington, D.C. He was working off a computer
printout and his eyes were beginning to cross as he rummaged
through the corporate shadow box that was C. Wallace Litman's tax
return. Kaz was beginning to suspect that he wasn't going to get
anywhere. In front of him on a scarred metal table was a confusing
web of interlinking holding companies, tax loss corporations, foun-
dations, and charitable deductions. It had turned his mind to putty,
but he plowed on. He wasn't even sure what he was looking for. He'd
been cashing so many tickets with old federal buddies, he'd developed
the leprosy effect—when they saw him coming, they'd start walking
in the opposite direction.

The file in front of him was called ICCI (Intertel Communications
Corporations, Inc.). It was a cluster of what looked like tax-loss corporations that were sheltering an investment in Atlantic Telephone

and Telegraph. Litman had been gradually increasing his holdings in telephone companies for the last two years. Kaz had phoned Cole Harris and asked if he knew why. Harris explained that the telephone company would probably end up being the main supplier of TV programming sometime down the road. Every house in America, Cole said, was already wired for the telephone and, with fiber-optic cable, it was possible to use phone lines to provide entertainment and news, thus eliminating the need for traditional over-the-air broadcasting. An intriguing thought, but all it had gotten Kaz so far was a headache. He was scheduled to meet Cole that night for dinner. Cole had been digging into connections between UBC and the mob, a subject he was already passionate about. Kaz had urged him to be careful and discreet—two words that apparently had been left out of the IR's vocabulary. Cole Harris had a tendency to come at problems with the subtle urgency of a wrecking ball.

At seven, Kaz closed up shop and left by the side door. Kaz and Cole had been meeting in a dingy restaurant in Virginia called the Spotted Calf. It advertised beef in secret barbecue sauce. The beef was tougher than an NHL goalie and the secret sauce was baked to the shade and consistency of road tar. Cole arrived after Kaz had already been there for half an hour and was working on his second Coke.

"I won't bother to ask you, 'What's up?' " Cole said. "You look like you've been hit by a logging truck."

"Litman has companies inside of companies. His tax structure is designed like a Bangkok suburb. I'm lost."

"While you've been stuck in tax hell, I managed to sniff up a little something interesting."

"What's that?"

"Got through to a guy who worked with Litman at Harcort, Lowe and Smith in Chicago. C. Wallace Litman, as you'll recall, was an account manager for them as a young CPA before he quit and came north to seek his fortune in television."

"What about it?" Kaz asked.

The waitress came over and Cole glanced at her. "I'm celebrating. Martini, two olives." She moved away, a hefty woman who looked ridiculous in her farm girl skirt and fluffy white apron.

"We gotta find another place to meet," Cole said. "This place fails on every level, from placemats to pussy."

"Get to it. What did you find?"

"Well, this guy says that he remembers C. Wallace saying that he was handling Meyer Lansky's wife's personal accounts after Meyer moved to southern Florida."

"C. Wallace was Theodora Lansky's investment adviser?"

"That's what this guy says."

"Jesus, how the fuck we prove that?"

"I figured if he filed her tax returns, he hadda sign 'em. Instead of going through C. Wallace's taxes, why don't you dig up Teddy Lansky's and see what you find? I can almost guarantee there won't be any interlocking companies."

It was then that the TV in the bar showed a picture of Anita Farrington Richards. Kaz caught it out of the corner of his eye. "Look 't that."

Cole swung around as the waitress brought the martini.

"Were you watching the TV in there?"

The waitress nodded. "Haze Richards's wife just died. Went down in a plane crash on her way to meet him in Ohio." She walked away.

Kaz and Cole exchanged looks and clambered out of the booth. They galloped into the bar like two water buffalos after a cow.

"There isn't much left of the plane," a field correspondent in a checkered coat was saying. "Apparently, several other flights have undershot Hopkins International Airport in recent years. The Lear-55, carrying Mrs. Richards, the wife of the certain Democratic nominee for President, crashed into a grain locker and exploded. The FAA is on the scene and they will be moving pieces of the debris to a hangar at Hopkins Field for inspection. So far, three bodies have been retrieved from the wreckage and the flight plan filed in Providence showed them to be David Horton, the pilot; Sam Shelton, the copilot; and the candidate's wife, Anita Richards. Dental identifications will confirm that, probably sometime tomorrow."

Then Vidal Brown was on camera in a shot that had been taped earlier.

"Haze Richards is under sedation. Anita was Haze's life mate, they met in college and she shared all of Haze's hopes and dreams. He is simply devastated by this loss."

"How you wanna work this?" Cole said.

C. Wallace Litman saw the story while he was monitoring the ten o'clock news. He always stayed up until the late newscast was complete so he could make notes to be passed out at the morning meeting. The UBC affiliate in Cleveland had supplied the footage of the Lear jet crash and the confirmation word that Anita Richards was dead. C. Wallace dropped his pad and called Steve Israel, at his desk on the Rim, hoping he would give him the broad strokes.

"I don't know," Steve told him, after he'd asked what the political ramifications would be. "This has never happened before. The closest we can come is James Buchanan in 1857. His fiancée, who he was going to marry before the inauguration, committed suicide, so his niece, a woman named Harriet Lane, ended up serving as the first lady. Of course, this is completely different. We're conducting a telephone poll right now, but my guess is Haze is gonna get a huge wave of sympathy."

C. Wallace moved to the window after he hung up and looked out over the New York skyline. A troubling thought hit him. Could Mickey have had anything to do with the crash? Then he brushed the idea away. What would he possibly have to gain?

The men at Pudge Anderson's Washington, D.C., election headquarters were gathered in a small room in a suite of offices they had rented for the campaign. They were waiting for Pudge and Henny, who arrived twenty minutes late. Pudge dropped his overcoat on the table and they all sat down. Henny turned to Justin Davis, the campaign pollster.

"Justin, you have the results?"

Davis, a heavyset man with brooding good looks, had already done a quick telephone tracking poll. He had the results in front of him. It looked horrible for them.

He got to his feet with the slip of paper in his hand. "To begin with, I feel bad for Haze's loss. . . . But we've got to deal with the political fallout. It could affect our strategy, so forgive me if this sounds a little cold-blooded."

"Understood," Pudge said.

"Okay. This is just a three-hundred-call survey, so its accuracy is moderate, but representative. It is also random, so it is demographically scattered. The people we called felt immense sympathy for Haze. When asked if the loss of his wife would affect his ability to be President, most people said no. That didn't surprise me. The thing that I found surprising was that this has somehow lifted his internals. The spot percentage is almost fifteen percent higher than when we asked the same character questions a week ago. Same on the crisis questions and the economy. How this plane crash could improve his ability to deal with a national military crisis or the economy baffles me, but there it is. Of course, this is just a preliminary survey, but we've gotta deal with the fact that Haze is a recipient of a helluva lot of goodwill right now. My guess is this will build, not ebb. The question is whether it's a two-week phenomenon or whether it drops to the bottom line and becomes part of his baseline goodwill coefficient." Justin sat down and looked at Pudge and Henny.

"What do you want to do with the bimbo?" Stan Dershman said from the back of the room, asking the question they were all thinking. Dershman was the press secretary and he had a big kiss-and-tell tournament planned for tomorrow in which Bonita Money was going to get up and put Haze in the Philanderers Hall of Fame.

"If you go through with that, we're gonna get backlashed into oblivion," Justin said.

The room was silent.

"How 'bout we just change the timing?" Dershman continued. "They're not going to mourn this woman for long. . . . Maybe in a month, we can trot Bonni out and she can sling her shit-burger and it won't blow back on us."

"After his wife is gone, the fact that he had an affair with a woman two years before sort of loses its impact, doesn't it?" Justin said. "If Anita's not on stage to bleed for the TV cameras, I don't think we get the same energy out of it."

"The man has lost his wife," Pudge's voice interrupted them. He had rested his chin on steepled fingers. "I can't believe you guys are saying what you're saying. I always hated this Bonita Money thing. I never was sure she was telling the truth. It's over. We're not going to use it."

"What if she decides to go public on her own?"

"You go to her, Justin. . . . Do whatever you can, just make sure she stays quiet. Let's get out of this sewer and get back to running a campaign." He picked up his coat and walked to the door, then turned and looked back at the roomful of people. "There are times when the end doesn't justify the means."

Pudge walked down the hall, where he found an empty office, and wrote Haze Richards a personal note of condolence.

Mickey got the news directly from Milo, who had called him on the secure line from a gas station minutes after the crash. The conversation had been brief.

"Catch it on the news," Milo said and hung up.

Mickey waited around for the first news report that came in as a special bulletin at nine-thirty. He watched, without emotion, as the newscaster talked about the flaming wreckage and the curse of Hopkins Field in Cleveland—a curse that had already claimed three other aircraft in eighteen months. Mickey Alo shut off the set, then went downstairs to the kitchen and fixed himself a sandwich and a cold beer.

Lucinda had heard people from two boats discussing Anita's death on the marine ship-to-ship radio. She pulled out the old black-and-white and adjusted the rabbit ears so that she and Ryan could watch the newscast on the aft deck. Ryan felt his heart sink as the story unfolded. He had heard rumors inside the campaign that there was trouble between the candidate and his wife. . . . Then his mind went back to the bar at the Savoy House, where he had told A.J. that the way to create sympathy was to create tragedy. Had he been the unwitting architect of this tragedy? At that moment, he promised himself that he would devote his energies to Mickey's destruction.

"What is it?" Lucinda said, noticing a strange look on his face.

"Tomorrow, I want to go into town and see the doctor you found. I need to get better."

Lucinda reached out and took his hand. They both knew the vacation was over. What they didn't know was that the Ghost was already in town, waiting.

CHECKUP

THEY ARRIVED AT THE DINGHY DOCK IN AVALON AT EIGHT-TEN the next morning. It took another ten minutes to get Ryan off the boat and up onto the bench on the wooden dock.

Lucinda left him sitting there while she went off to rent one of the electric golf carts that were used by everyone on the island instead of cars. Ryan sat on the bench looking at a pay phone across from him. It was only twenty feet away, but he wondered if he could make it. He stood on his one good leg, reached in his pants pocket for some change, then hopped across the wooden deck, grabbed the phone, and, teetering precariously, fed some quarters into the slot and dialed a number from memory.

The phone in the Alos' New Jersey house rang five times before Pulacarpo answered it.

"Yes," he said.

"Lemme talk to Mickey."

"He's a'no here right now. You wanna leave a'you' name an' a'you' number?"

"Tell him Ryan Bolt is on the line." He could hear the other man breathing. "Go get him. He wants to talk to me."

Ryan was put on hold and then, in a few seconds, Mickey was on the line.

"Hey, Ryan, buddy, how you doin'?" Mickey's voice grinned at him through three thousand miles of phone cable.

"Not so good, Mickey. Every time I turn my back, some overbuilt slice a' pizza is swinging a bat or a gun at me."

Mickey pulled the Pin Tel out of the desk drawer and was scrolling it while he talked. The number Ryan was calling from was different from the one Lucinda used, but he saw that the area code and prefix were the same. . . . Ryan was in Avalon with his sister.

"Listen, Ryan . . . I don't know what you think is going on, but you got it all wrong."

"Yeah? How's that?"

"I'm your friend."

"You're nobody's friend."

Mickey put down the Pin Tel, then slowly sat back in his swivel chair. "You have something on your mind or you just trying to get your balls to swell?"

"I called to tell you you're going down for this."

"For what?"

"For Anita Richards. I know why her plane crashed. I know why you killed her. I also know you're behind Haze Richard's candidacy. You had two tries at me when I wasn't ready. Now I am."

"You threatening me?"

"It's not a threat, it's a promise. I'm gonna put you away, Mickey."

"I invite you to try, shithead."

"You remember when we were kids at school? I was always better than you, Mickey. I always won. In sports. In school. Pick a category, I'm better."

"The category is killer. You're not a killer, Ryan. I'm a killer. For you, it was always games with rules. Fifteen yards for clipping, no hitting after the bell. I got only one rule: Win at all costs. So you take your best shot, asshole. I ain't worried 'cause nothing's ever stuck

2 7 4

to me yet." And he hung up, leaving Ryan balanced on his good leg, feeling stupid.

When Lucinda returned to the pier, he was back on the bench. "Does it hurt?" she asked, seeing the tight expression on his face.

"No . . . no. Let's go."

She helped him to his feet and down to the end of the pier, where she had parked the rented cart. After Ryan was seated, she moved around and got behind the wheel. They zipped off toward the island hospital.

Armando Vasquez watched them go. His wiry body advertised twenty-eight years in South Central L.A. Knife scars and the names of old girlfriends were scratched onto his muscled arms like bridge graffiti. He looked down at a small picture of Ryan he had in his hand, then got up off the bench near the end of the pier and stood watching as they headed up the hill. He reached into his pocket and pulled out a small, razor-sharp curved linoleum knife. He leaned against the rail with the knife in his palm and waited for them to return.

The hospital was busy when they got there. Schoolchildren with sinus infections sneezed and sniffed in the waiting room as they were given medicine and complained about shots. Several of them stole glances at Ryan and Lucinda. By nine-fifteen, the morning preschool sick call was over and Dr. Andrea Lewis came out and looked at them waiting patiently on the tan vinyl sofa, holding hands.

"So, this is Bill . . . ?"

"Huh?" Lucinda said.

"Lauren and Bill . . . remember? That's you two. I wrote it in the logbook." Then, not waiting for a reply, she reached out her hand to Ryan, taking in his blond good looks.

"I'm Dr. Andrea Lewis."

"Hi, I'm Bill."

"Sure you are."

"Would you mind taking a look at his leg?" Lucinda said sharply.

"Can you walk?"

"I'm a good hopper."

With Lucinda on one side and Dr. Lewis on the other, they pulled him up and helped him into the doctor's examining room. The room was painted yellow with a wood cabinet full of medical supplies and a metal examining table covered with sterile paper. Ryan struggled up onto the table as Dr. Lewis took a pair of scissors from an instrument tray.

He unbuttoned his trousers and Lucinda removed his tennis shoes and began to tug gingerly at the jeans until they were off. The bandage had turned brownish red from additional seepage. Dr. Lewis looked at it carefully.

"Is the wound on the front and side?" she asked, noting the stains on the bandage.

"That's right."

She slipped the scissors under the bandage on the inside of his leg and cut it off, peeling it back slowly. She pulled the bandage free and looked at the repair job done by Dr. Jazz four days before.

"Who did this work?"

"A doctor in New Jersey," he said. "Is it bad?"

"No, it's very good . . . tight stitching, good surgical knots. Have you had a fever?"

"No . . . "

"You've been taking antibiotics?"

"He gave me a heavy dose of penicillin."

Dr. Lewis turned away, got an alcohol swab, and cleaned around the wound.

"This is a gunshot wound, isn't it?"

Neither Ryan or Lucinda responded, so she went on.

"I can't treat you unless I call the sheriff and tell him."

"Don't do that, please. There are people trying to kill him . . . powerful people. If they find out he's here, they'll come, they'll kill him."

"Why?"

"They just will."

"You're wanted by the police," Dr. Lewis said, feeling a momentary fear rising up in her.

"We're not," Ryan finally said. "I'll make a deal with you. We'll get out of here. . . . You don't have to do anything. If you don't treat me, you don't have to report it."

Dr. Lewis didn't know what to do. She had been an intern for only six months. It was her first job since graduating from UCLA Med

School. The Avalon Hospital made arrangements with the university to take one doctor a year. She wanted to be a GP so she had applied, thinking it would be a great adventure, but she hadn't bargained for anything like this. On the other hand, some irrational urge made her want to help them. They didn't look like criminals. They didn't sound like criminals. She guessed they were both college-educated, both were clean-cut and extremely attractive.

"It's not that easy. The law doesn't say, if I don't treat you, I don't have to report it. The law says, I have to report any gunshot wound that I see whether I treat you or not."

"It's not a gunshot wound. I got stabbed accidentally with a barbecue skewer." Ryan grinned at her.

"You two come in here with cornball aliases. You don't want the police advised . . . and I can see the dimple here where the slug entered the thigh. All that's missing is a videotape of the shooting."

Ryan turned to Lucinda. "Gimme a hand, let's get outta here."

Lucinda started to pick up his pants but Dr. Lewis put out a hand to restrain her.

"A barbecue skewer. That's the story?"

"I guess so, unless you can come up with a better one," Ryan said.

"It's pretty cold this time of year to be barbecuing in New Jersey."

"We're compulsive," he said. She shook her head and looked at the leg again. She put on latex gloves and gently spread the edges of the wound to see how it was mending. She could tell it was less than a week old, but it seemed to be knitting well. "Okay, I'm going to redress it. You're gonna need to watch for infection. I'll give you two week's worth of antibiotics. Take them twice a day until they're all gone."

"I take it you're not gonna want a follow-up visit?"

"Look, Bill, or whoever you are . . . I could get into a helluva lot of trouble over this. I'm doing it because something tells me you two are on the level, despite the fact you haven't told me one thing that sounds true since you got here. I'll wrap the leg, give you the drugs, leave it off my medical log, and pretend I never saw you. For that, you can leave an extra hundred dollars in the dish out there for the children's playground. If you come back here, I'm gonna notify the police."

Andrea turned to the table and grabbed some sterile pads and disinfectant powder. She shook the powder onto the wound and put the pads over the stitching. She wrapped the leg in gauze first, then with a white, heavy elastic bandage. She gave Lucinda the powder and the rest of the bandage on the roll, along with several sterile pads.

"In four days, cut off the bandage and redress. If he starts getting a fever or if there is oozing or discharge through the stitching, get him to a hospital, fast; otherwise he could lose the leg. You can cut the stitches and pull them out in about a week." Then, as an after-thought, she added, "No more barbecuing till August."

"Will I get back use of this leg?"

"That depends. Since I didn't do the surgery, I can't really tell what's left in there and what's gone. Can you lift it up?"

He tried to lift the leg. It moved halfway.

"Okay, you have hip flexors and abductors. You still have tendons and blood flowing to the muscles. Whoever did this job—connecting the veins and arteries—you should send a thank-you note."

"Will I be able to walk?"

"I don't know. You'll have to try and build up the muscles that are left. You're probably going to have weak spots, like if you pivot the wrong way, you could go down. A leg is supported by muscle, bone, and tendons wrapped in flesh. Blood supplies oxygen to the muscles. Without that, they atrophy. You lose any of the parts, you change the physical equation. You could have a permanent injury or other muscles could build up to compensate. But it will probably never be as good as it was."

Lucinda got Ryan's pants and helped him pull them over the newly bandaged leg.

"I'll get some ampicillin." She moved out of the office and Ryan motioned to Lucinda to follow her. Lucinda left as Ryan pushed his good foot into his tennis shoe, didn't bother to lace it, then stood and pushed the other foot into the left shoe. Then he hopped to the door, thankful for the firm new dressing on his leg. He lowered his foot and tried to put some weight on it, but he knew, instantly, that the leg wouldn't hold him. He hopped to the outer office. Andrea

Lewis got pills out of the cabinet. She put them into a bottle, wrote something on the label, and handed them to Lucinda. Dr. Lewis turned to Ryan.

"You need crutches?"

"I lost mine," Ryan said.

"I have some wooden ones in the back. Just a minute."

Andrea moved out of the office and down the hall. There was a phone in the equipment room and she toyed with the idea of calling the sheriff. His office was only two blocks away. But for some reason she couldn't identify, she knew she wouldn't call. She brought the crutches back and handed them to Ryan. Lucinda reached out and shook her hand. "Thank you," she said softly.

Lucinda dropped five $20 bills into a jar labeled SCHOOL PLAY-GROUND FUND, and a few minutes later, they got into the electric cart and headed back to the harbor, while Andrea watched from the front porch of the hospital.

Lucinda stopped at the market near the payphone where she'd made the call to her mother. She picked up some fresh fish and vegetables and threw in some barbecue briquettes. A middle-aged, red-haired man with a sunburned nose saw her struggling with the heavy grocery bags. "Need any help with those?" he asked. He had a fishing hat pushed back on his sun-raw forehead.

"I think I can manage, thanks."

She moved out and handed the bag to Ryan in the front seat of the electric cart and drove to the wooden pier.

They walked slowly down the pier while Ryan tried to put some weight on his bad leg, but each step was causing more and more pain. He decided to start some sort of self-therapy first thing in the morning. They moved down onto the dinghy dock and, after Lucinda scrambled aboard and stowed the groceries, he threw the crutches into the boat and stood on one foot while Lucinda started to help him aboard.

Armando Vasquez watched from the darkness under the gangplank. He was crouched down with the linoleum knife out and ready. He chose that moment and made his charge, staying low, the knife out in front of him.

Ryan saw him, but without his left leg to pivot, he was helpless, teetering on the edge of the pier. Armando slashed at his torso with the linoleum knife. Ryan jerked back and fell awkwardly to the dock, landing on his elbows, favoring his left leg, trying not to tear out the stitches again. He was on his back as Armando rushed at him and slashed at his throat with the knife, missing again, as Ryan rolled left out of the way.

"Hey! . . . Hey you!" the redheaded fisherman from the market bellowed from the pier above them. "Stop that!"

Armando hesitated. Lucinda was trying to get out of the Avon to help Ryan. The man from the market was now running down the gangplank, his beer belly bouncing in front of him, the hat flying off his head. He had a long-poled fish gaff in both hands as he charged toward Armando. Once he got to the dinghy dock, he swung the gaff. The sharp point buried itself in Armando's shoulder. "*Ayyee puta,*" Armando swore as the fisherman yanked the gaff free, tearing out a hunk of the Mexican's flesh. Armando screamed, and the fisherman swung the gaff again. This time, it hit him in the side of the neck, but didn't stick as deeply. Armando yelled, jumped off Ryan, then turned to face the balding fisherman who had the gaff now in both hands. He swung it again as Armando turned and dove into the water and started swimming the short distance to shore. Once he was at the beach, he ran toward the street, the wound in his shoulder trailing blood down his ripped shirt on his back. They all watched until he was out of sight.

"Jesus," Ryan stammered.

"Looked like he was after your watch," the fisherman said, grinning, pointing at Ryan's Rolex. "That there's a ten-thousand-dollar invitation to get mugged."

"Bill Williams," Ryan said, extending his hand.

"Jerry Paradise." The red-haired man leaned down and held out his hand to Ryan, who was still on his back on the dock. Ryan took his hand and Jerry pulled him up on his good leg. Lucinda grabbed the crutches and handed them to Ryan.

"This is my girlfriend, Lauren."

"Thank you, Mr. Paradise," she said.

"It's okay, y'all take care now and don't wear that hunk a' gold on yer wrist, son."

"Thank you."

Jerry looked at his own watch, then out to the empty water. He sighed, shook his head in disgust, then started back up the gangplank.

"Can we give you a lift someplace?" Ryan said.

Jerry turned and smiled at them. "I was expecting a buddy to pick me up. I'm camping on the beach down at White's Cove, but he's not here."

"We can take you," Ryan said.

"I don't wanna put y'all out."

"Hey, you kidding? Jump in."

Lucinda and Jerry helped Ryan into the boat, then Lucinda followed.

The Ghost was the last to board. He pushed his hat back on his head. He knew it made him look goofy, just another fat fisherman.

Lucinda started the small outboard, and they headed out of the harbor with their deadly passenger.

The Ghost had found Armando in the Island Bar. He'd shown him the picture of Ryan that Mickey had sent him. "He's screwin' my girlfriend," he'd explained to the puzzled Mexican. "*Chingada—mi novia,*" he said as Armando nodded gravely. The Ghost gave his new friend a hundred dollars and told him he'd pay a hundred more after he'd frightened Ryan away. The Ghost told Armando not to kill him, just scare him. It had worked out exactly the way he'd planned. He was alone with the target, heading out to the boat where the Ghost would close his contract. If everything went the way he wanted, he'd be back on the plane to Atlantic City by morning.

RIGHT OF RETURN

AT NINE A.M. THAT SAME DAY, COLE AND KAZ MET AT RUBIO'S for breakfast. The specialty at the Washington restaurant was eggs Florentine, so both of them ordered the dish and told the waitress to keep the hot coffee coming. Neither Cole nor Kaz had been to bed. Kaz had spent the entire night abusing old friendships, making calls to buddies in government. At midnight, he'd awakened Kirk Allen, a friend of many years who was waiting out his federal retirement in the FAA. Kaz told him that maybe there was more to the Anita Richards plane crash than a short landing curse at Cleveland International Airport.

"If you got something, Kaz, you better spit it out. This is the Democratic candidate's wife. Dicks are on the chopping block. You gotta squat to piss around here this morning."

"Just tell the forensics team to look for anything unusual. Explosives, a pneumatic control problem, tampered instruments . . . anything. That plane didn't go down 'cause it was voodooed. The only curse in Cleveland is on the Indians."

"If you got something, Kaz, and you're holding out on me, I'm gonna come after you with a seminary knife."

"If I get anything useable, I'll get back to you."

While Kaz had been sniffing that trail, Cole Harris had driven all the way back to his brother's house in Rye, New York, arriving at midnight. The reason for the trip back to Hamilton Boulevard was in an old black leather suitcase buried underneath his brother's ski equipment in the basement. Cole pulled the suitcase out while Carson and his wife Bea nervously looked over his shoulder. The experience in the kitchen a week earlier had shaken them. They had told the police nothing in an attempt to protect Cole, and, although they didn't want to say it, both of them were hoping he would get his things and leave.

Cole put the suitcase on the tool bench and popped it open. Inside were hundreds of reporter's spiral notebooks. They contained his notes from twenty years of on-site reporting from all over the world. He started looking for the two or three that he had filled out back in March of 1971. He finally found two notebooks that were held together by a large, red rubber band.

On the cardboard cover, he had written:

ISRAEL, 1971
Meyer Lansky

With the notebooks under his arm, Cole climbed the stairs into the living room where he sat in good light and flipped one open.

"You gonna go through that here?" his sister-in-law asked, nervously.

"Yeah, if that's okay."

"Uh, well, I guess," Carson said, glaring at Cole. "It is kinda late, y'know. . . . "

"You probably don't want another news-gathering experience. Why don't I get outta here."

Cole bummed five hundred dollars from Carson; then he stood

and kissed his relieved sister-in-law, hugged his brother, and went to the nearest all-night coffee shop.

He sat in the rear with his back to the wall, away from the window, a survival technique he had learned in Lebanon, then started on the first book, marked "Tuesday, March 10th." His mind went whirling back to that day in 1971. He'd been attached to the UBC European bureau and had been sent to Jerusalem to cover Meyer Lansky's lawsuit against the State of Israel. The world press, about a hundred newsmen, were wedged into the courtyard of the Ottoman Palace of Justice in the Russian section of the walled Old City.

It was stiflingly hot with no breeze and the mood was ugly. They were all there to witness the outcome of one of Israel's strangest legal battles.

The Jewish State of Israel was made up almost entirely of immigrants. Section 2(b)3 of the Israeli constitution said that any man born of a Jewish mother should be granted the "right of return" to Israel. Every Jew deserved a place in the new Jewish State.

Meyer Lansky, after a career of questionable activities in Miami, New York, Las Vegas, and other hard-core mob enclaves, had petitioned the State of Israel for the right to return. Confident that he would spend his final days in the Promised Land eating kippered herring and wearing a beanie, he'd nailed a mezuzah to his door in a Miami suburb and waited for the news of his citizenship. But there was an asterisk on the Law of Return that said if you had a bad reputation or were suspected of criminal activities, the minister of the interior could block your repatriation. This is what happened to Lansky.

But he had one course left open to him. He could sue the Israeli government and attempt to overturn the ruling.

Lansky had hired a lawyer named Yoram Alroy, who had served with honor during the Six Day War. Yoram was joined at the counsel table by a Miami lawyer named David Rosen. They had tried to make the case that Meyer had never been convicted of a crime and had been tried unfairly, without evidence, in the world press.

On the other side of the aisle was the Israeli prosecutor, Gavriel Bach. He was tall and slender with patrician good looks. Gavriel Bach had resolved to keep underworld elements out of Israel, no matter

what the cost. In the middle of the trial, the press heard that three
months earlier the Justice Department had invited Gavriel to Washington and the rumor in the press corps was that some sort of unusual
deal had been struck.

The United States government was setting up a case against Lansky
and feared that, if he settled in Israel, they would not be able to
extradite him. The feds hoped that once indicted, Lansky would turn
state's evidence on mobsters in the United States.

Another rumor said that an undisclosed number of Phantom F-4
jets had been offered for sale to the Israeli Air Force if they would
refuse Lansky citizenship. These leaks had been heavily reported but
denied by "official sources." There was no proof any of it was true.

Lansky's case had been argued before the Israeli Supreme Court
for almost a week, and on that stifling day they were gathered to hear
the outcome.

As Cole reread his twenty-five-year-old journal, memories flooded
back of the skinny, foul-mouthed, sixty-eight-year-old mobster who
had come to hear the judgment. Lansky was dressed in a threadbare
department store suit; his tie was crooked and twisted under his collar. As he came through the side door of the courtyard, the world
press surged, shouting questions.

"Mr. Lansky, over here . . . ABC News . . . We understand that
Gavriel Bach has cut some kind of deal in Washington to force your
return to Miami, where prosecutors say you're about to be indicted."

Lansky glowered at them. Cole was startled by his diminutive size.
Only five-foot-three, he nonetheless generated venom.

"The fucks," Meyer said under his breath.

"What about the suitcase? What is in the suitcase?" somebody
from NBC's Middle Eastern bureau shouted.

"What suitcase?" Meyer glowered. "What the fuck you fucks
talkin' about?"

"Watch your language, please, sir. We can't broadcast profanities,"
the NBC correspondent said, as if Meyer cared.

"What is in the suitcase?" the NBC correspondent pressed, referring to a medium-size metal Haliburton suitcase that Gavriel Bach
had taken to several in-camera meetings with the chief justice of the

Israeli Supreme Court. "We understand the U.S. Justice Department gave Gavriel Bach evidence against you."

"Get me outta here," he yelled at his attorneys, who had been pushing him through the throng. Finally, he reached the double doors leading to the courtroom. Cole followed and physically pushed his cameraman through the door before they were locked out.

Meyer and his two attorneys sat on the wooden bench two levels below the five justices. Gavriel Bach sat alone at the counsel table. In front of him, sat the metal Haliburton suitcase. Like the rest of them, Cole wondered what was inside.

The chief justice read the unanimous verdict in Hebrew. It was translated simultaneously into English. The world press listened over headphones. The Israeli Supreme Court found that it was perfectly legal for Meyer Lansky to take "the Fifth" in front of the U.S. Congress during the Kefauver hearings, as every American citizen had the right under the Fifth Amendment of the U.S. Constitution not to incriminate himself. However, Mr. Lansky did say that his refusal to speak was on the grounds of self-incrimination. The Israeli Supreme Court had weighed that heavily, as it indicated from Mr. Lansky's own mouth that he had viewed his actions as crimes. The judge continued on . . . Hebrew filling the room like rolling thunder.

The reading of the judgment went on for almost an hour. The chief justice finally concluded that the minister of the interior had been right to deny Meyer Lansky citizenship. "If he were allowed to stay, the ugly phenomenon of organized crime, as it exists in America, might be transplanted to Israel."

Cole filed his story with his Paris bureau and pouched the video-tape to his assignment editor there. UBC reported that evening that Meyer Lansky had been handed over to the United States embassy to be returned to Miami, where he would stand trial for tax evasion and casino skimming.

The trial never took place because of Meyer's health.

Two days before Christmas, that same year, Cole read in the *London Times* that twenty-five U.S. Phantom F-4 fighter-bombers had been delivered to Israel.

*   *   *

Cole closed his notebooks about two A.M. and sat alone in the empty coffee shop, thinking. His mind kept coming back to that suitcase sitting in front of Gavriel Bach on the prosecution table. What was in it? Why had it been in court that day? He finished his cold coffee and drove for five hours back to Washington, arriving just in time for his prearranged breakfast with Kaz. Now he sat, tired and grainy-eyed, and watched the gross fed shovel down eggs Florentine. Cole picked at the corners of his own plate, eating the whites only, leaving the high-cholesterol yolks.

"Where are we?" Cole finally asked.

"We're having breakfast at Rubio's, the finest eatery inside the Beltway."

"Where are we in the investigation, you asshole?"

"Well, I got Teddy Lansky's '72 tax return coming up from that dark Cavern of Greed known affectionately as the IRS basement. I should have it this morning."

"Lemme ask you something . . . could you get me any inside information from the Justice Department about a deal that might have been made between Gavriel Bach and somebody in the State Department in '71?"

"Who's Gavriel Bach?"

"He was the Israeli prosecutor defending the government against Meyer Lansky's right-of-return suit in 1971. So, how 'bout it?" Cole asked again.

"Yeah, maybe, but I'm running out of friends in that building. Why do you need it?"

"I got a hunch. I'll let you know if it turns into anything. Things can only get better."

But they didn't; they got worse. . . .

BIG BREAK

BY TEN-THIRTY, KAZ WAS BACK IN THE JUSTICE DEPARTMENT
waiting for Teddy Lansky's tax returns. He sat in a borrowed office
with a visitor's tag clipped to his breast pocked. The small, gray,
windowless office was the type and size generally assigned to a lowly
GS-3. He began leafing through the department's staff phone book,
looking for an old warhorse from the seventies named Abel McNair.

McNair had gone into foreign service after the war, and Kaz
thought he'd had dealings with the Justice Department on Middle
Eastern operations in the seventies. A. McNair was listed in the phone
directory as assistant secretary of the Middle Eastern quadrant and
Kaz dialed the interoffice exchange.

"Abel McNair's office," a man's voice said.

"Tell him Solly Kazorowski's calling."

There was a long moment while he was on hold, then the same
voice came back on the line.

"I'm afraid Mr. McNair can't speak to you right now."

"Can you give him a message?" Kaz said pleasantly.

"Sure, go ahead."

"Will you tell him I'm going to go ahead and buy the ribbed Rough Rider condoms he suggested for tonight instead of the lambskin French ticklers and, if he'll just pick up the champagne, I'll meet him at Lance and Timmy's around six."

There was a long moment of silence. "Maybe you'd better tell him that. . . . Just a minute," the man said, and then McNair was on the phone.

"Kaz, I'm real busy this morning. I'm due to deliver a briefing in twenty minutes. Whatta you want?"

"I need to know if you ever heard of a guy named Gavriel Bach?"

"Sounds familiar. Can't place it. . . ."

"In the seventies, he was an Israeli prosecutor and he cut a deal with somebody in Justice on Meyer Lansky's lawsuit against the Israelis."

Again, there was a long pause. "Yeah, yeah, I remember. Tall, thin guy. . . . I think he died. Matter of fact, I'm pretty sure he did. Cancer I think. I got a mission fax on that."

"Who cut the deal?"

"Something like that would a' had to be under David Robb."

"Where is he? Is he still in the service?"

"Shit, Mr. Robb, he's gotta be eighty-five if he's still among us."

"Thanks, Abe."

"I heard you got fired."

"Yep."

"Too bad. Gotta go."

"When you gotta go you gotta go," Kaz said and hung up.

Ten minutes later, a mail boy hustled in with a rolling basket full of the business of state.

"You Kazorowski?"

"Yep."

"Gotta sign for this." He indicated an envelope on the top of his pile. "It can't leave the building. It has to be returned to the Intake slot by six-thirty."

Kaz signed and pulled the envelope open as the mail boy pushed his load of important world fuck-ups out of the office and down the hall.

Kaz looked at Teddy Lansky's tax return. It was mildly interesting in itself that Teddy didn't file jointly with Meyer . . . probably for reasons known only to the long-dead mob financial planner. He looked at the bottom of the federal form and, in the place reserved for the name of the accountant, there was a tight cramped signature.

In faded blue ink, it said: "Wallace Litman."

Ryan and Lucinda invited Jerry Paradise aboard their ketch just after one in the afternoon. Jerry helped Lucinda get Ryan out of the rubber Avon; then they all sat in the cockpit next to the big, shiny wheel and grinned at each other in the midday sun while they popped open cold beers. Just thirty yards away was a fifty-foot day-fishing boat with twenty men aboard. The Ghost realized the fishing boat was too close for him to "close the contract," so he sat drinking his beer, filling the air with pleasant nonsense.

"Y'all have a helluva nice little yawl," he drawled.

"It's a ketch," Lucinda corrected him.

"Mind if I go below and take a look?" The Ghost wanted to get a look at the layout in case he had to come back after dark. "I love the way they set these things up. I'm a fisherman so I'm mostly on stink-pots. But I'd like t' get into sailing."

"Go on, show him around." Ryan smiled.

Jerry got up and followed Lucinda down into the forward cabin.

Something about Jerry Paradise bothered Ryan. Maybe it was the good old boy half-southern accent. Maybe it was the humorless grin under pig-mean eyes. Maybe it was how quick he moved on the dock as he swung the gaff at the Mexican. Then Ryan saw something on the seat beside him that must have fallen out of Jerry's back pocket. He reached down and picked it up. It was an airline ticket. He could hear Jerry and Lucinda still talking below; Ryan opened the folder. The name on the ticket was Harry Meeks. The ticket receipt said he had come in on United Flight 1628 from Atlantic City yesterday. The return flight was scheduled for six that night. So much for camping on the beach, Ryan thought. He closed the folder and put it back on the seat where Jerry had been sitting and scooted a few feet away so that it was out of his reach. Atlantic City was Mickey Alo's turf. Ryan was pretty sure Mickey had sent him.

"Boy, that's a honey of a layout." The Ghost came up the cabin stairs and interrupted Ryan's thoughts. He sat down, noticed his ticket on the seat, then looked over at Ryan, who was studiously looking off at the day fishers. The Ghost silently cursed his mistake, but it didn't seem that Ryan was close enough to reach it so he slipped the ticket back in his pocket and grinned at them.

"What kinda lures you use?" Ryan asked, turning back.

"Huh?"

"When you fish . . ."

"Oh, mostly live bait. It's best for catching rock cod."

"You oughta try some deep-water lures. I got a steel-head feather lure that's great for albacore."

"Really?" the Ghost said, looking at Ryan with pale, blue eyes.

"Yeah, those tuna damn near jump on the hook. It's got a vibrating thing on it so when you troll, it sets up a humming noise in the water that attracts 'em," Ryan said.

"I gotta get me one a' those." Jerry was looking at the fishing boat, which was pulling up anchor and getting ready to head off to a new position. Ryan was looking at it also.

"Honey, get my tackle box. It's forward in the Coast Guard locker, up in front of the V-berths. The green metal one."

"That ain't necessary."

"No, you gotta see this lure." Lucinda sensed the urgency in his voice, couldn't understand it. "Go on, get it."

She nodded and moved forward. Ryan and the man who had been sent to kill him watched as the fishing boat started to pull away. The Ghost had already decided that he would kill them with his bare hands. He didn't want to leave any slugs behind, because it had to look like an accident. He figured that Ryan would be easy because he was almost immobile with the bum leg. After they were both dead, he would leak gas into the bilge from the engine and pull a spark plug wire loose. Then he would run a cable overboard and start the engine from the dinghy. That should blow the ketch into kindling. It would look, to the Coast Guard, like two weekend boaters forgot to air out the bilge before starting the engine. No crime, no investigation, no jeopardy.

The Ghost watched as Lucinda brought the green metal tackle box up from below and handed it to Ryan. As he opened the box, he angled it so that Jerry couldn't see inside. Under the tackle tray was an Army Colt .45. He had bought it in St. Thomas because of stories he'd heard about pirates in the Caribbean who boarded pleasure boats and killed the owners so they could strip out the electronics.

"This little baby is amazing." He pulled out the steel-head feather lure and offered it to Jerry.

The fishing boat was almost around the point. The Ghost knew now was the time to make his move, so he took the lure and smiled at Ryan and then, without warning, lunged across the open cockpit at him.

Ryan's hand snaked out of the tackle box and the gun was cocked and aimed at Jerry's face before he even got close. The Ghost froze, caught halfway between his target and eternity.

"Who the fuck are you, mister?"

"I told you . . ."

"Mickey sent you down here . . . didn't he?"

"Who's Mickey?"

Lucinda didn't know why Jerry had tried to jump Ryan or why Ryan had the gun on him. It had all happened so fast.

"Ryan?" she said.

"This guy has a ticket from Atlantic City. He's set to go back tonight. He's not camping anywhere. I think your brother sent him."

"How would Mickey know we're here?"

"I don't know, but he sent this guy."

"I saved your life," the Ghost said.

"Did you? Or did you set us up and then attack that Mexican so we'd drop our guard? Now get off my boat!"

The Ghost looked at Ryan and tried to read his eyes. Should he charge him? Would he fire? Some guys are killers, some aren't. Still, the Ghost had a healthy respect for the large-bore automatic in Ryan's hand.

"I see you again," Ryan said, "and I'm gonna drop you."

"I'm just a fisherman. I come out here every year to fish, have been for fifteen years. . . ."

"Yeah? Then you oughta learn there's no rock cod on this coast. Get over the side, Jerry, or I swear I'll open you like a can of creamed corn."

Jerry finally moved back to the rail, gave Ryan a wild, loopy grin, and rolled backward over the side, splashing into the water. Ryan and Lucinda watched him swim away from the boat.

"Get the anchor up. I'll get the engine started."

Lucinda moved to the anchor winch at the bow and turned it on. She could see Jerry Paradise treading water about twenty feet off the port side watching them. The anchor chain snaked up out of the water and the anchor clanged into the metal cleats under the bowsprit.

Ryan had the engine going and they pulled out of Toyon Bay. As the boat swung around, she caught another glimpse of Jerry Paradise. He still had the same wide nightmarish grin on his face.

Lucinda moved back to Ryan and sat quietly in the cockpit.

"He's going to keep trying," Ryan said. "I just got lucky with that ticket falling out. I should have shot him."

"Why didn't you?"

"Gun was empty. Took all the bullets out a year ago when I started thinking about solving my problems with it."

They sat in silence as the small engine pushed them away from the island.

"Even if it was loaded," Ryan continued, "I don't know if I could have done it. Your brother was right. . . . I need a game with rules."

STATURE STRATEGY

THE CALIFORNIA PRIMARY WOULD PUT HAZE RICHARDS OVER THE top mathematically, but after Super Tuesday, there was no way he could lose. All of the other Democratic candidates had pulled out.

Haze was scheduled to make a speech after the California victory. The campaign staff was staying in the refurbished San Francisco Fairmont Hotel and the speech would be in the banquet room, which was campaign night headquarters for the California Haze Richards for President Committee.

A.J. wanted to keep the speech short because Haze was still in mourning over Anita's death, although it was grief that included at least one romp with Susan Winter each day.

Susan had become the campaign's unofficial first lady, and that caused A.J. more than a little concern. It was bad enough she was sleeping with Haze, but now she tended to treat everybody on the staff like dirt. She had resigned her position as "body woman" so that she would be free to work on Haze's body, an irony that gave A.J. no pleasure. She had become cold and imperious. The staff responded by calling her Nuclear Winter.

Worse still, A.J.'s relationship with Haze had soured since Haze had won Super Tuesday—a result of the terrible criminal conspiracy they were both part of.

They couldn't stand the sight of each other.

A.J. decided to use that dreadful event rather than run from it. He demanded a meeting at five with Haze, requesting that they meet alone.

By three o'clock on California Tuesday, the exit polls in both northern and southern counties indicated that the win would be with at least 65 percent. Ben Savage, although technically out of the running, was still on the ballot in his home state, but he had only been polling a tepid 20 percent. Haze would be the Democratic nominee.

A.J. needed a quiet meeting with Haze to go over the text of the victory speech. He had worked with Malcolm Rasher for two hours the night before, trying to come up with the perfect three paragraphs thanking Californians for their support in helping Haze through the horrible days after Nita's death and for giving him the margin of delegates needed for victory. They had decided that Haze should talk about Nita, her memory, what she meant to him, how she was looking down and smiling on this day because it had been her dream as much as his.

The meeting took place in Haze's hotel room as scheduled. The room was the presidential suite of the Fairmont Hotel. The ceilings were twenty feet high with hand-carved frescoes. The plate-glass windows overlooked the magnificent harbor with the red span of the Golden Gate Bridge cutting across the bay to Sausalito. It was a long way from Bud and Sarah Caulfield's humble farm in Grinnell, Iowa. Haze and Susan were wearing matching blue monogrammed robes.

"Whatta you want?" Haze asked brusquely.

"I've got the victory speech," A.J. said as he handed the pages to the candidate who read them, handing each one to Susan after he'd finished it. She was shaking her head in silent disbelief by the time she got halfway down the first page.

"How much longer do you think you can play this pathetic bullshit about Anita?" Susan asked, drilling A.J. with cold eyes.

"Oh, about four months, give or take a day," he said, the bile rising in his throat.

"You're making Haze look weak. He's standing there, blubbering about Anita in front of the world. I think he should look strong. I think we oughta talk about the future, not the past."

"Well, gee, let me run right down and work on that."

"I think Suzie has a point," Haze said.

There was a deadly silence in the room. A.J. started getting angry. "I've got poll stats down in my room that say America's heart is breaking for your loss. They want you to cry for Anita. She was your life mate, she was your partner. They know you loved her and they love you for it. I got you this far, I won Iowa, I came up with the defining event in New York, got the financing, and, goddammit, I'm not gonna stand around here and watch you shtup it away in a sea of vaginal bullshit."

"That's it, Haze. . . . Fire this piece of shit," Susan hissed.

"You can't fire me, Haze, and you know why? Because you and I share a terrible secret. Wanna tell Nuclear Winter here what it is?"

"Cut it out, A.J."

"I'll tell her. Want me to spill it right now, old buddy? 'Cause it's okay with me." The guilt over Anita was wearing A.J. down. He was perilously close to cracking up.

"Shut up," Haze said softly.

"Then tell her to get out! I have something else to say."

"Give us a minute, Susan."

"What?" She was on her feet now, wondering what A.J. had that could possibly outgun her.

"Get out, Susan," Haze said, more forcefully . . . and she got up and started for the bedroom.

"Not here. Tell her to go to her own room." A.J. opened the door and checked the hall for press. Then he motioned Susan to exit.

"Go on," Haze said, and she moved out of the room, pausing for a second to drill A.J. with a venomous look. A.J. had slept with Susan Winter back when she was a law clerk in his office. A.J. had given her the job with the campaign, and now she had become a virulent enemy. After she left, he closed the door.

"Haze, you're gonna ruin this, throw the whole thing away."

"I don't think so."

"Have you even looked at my stature strategy? I sent it up to you three days ago. You haven't said a word." He was referring to a program he'd devised to raise Haze's international stature after winning the primary. Haze had no international profile at all. A.J. wanted Haze to go abroad and have a series of meetings with important international figures like John Major, or Mitterrand . . . with Yeltsin. Get his picture taken with Arafat and key members of the Israeli Knesset. The idea was to show Haze solving world problems with the heads of state in Europe, the Middle East, and the Orient.

"I don't want to go abroad."

"Haze, I can't protect you from the press if you're here."

"I don't need protection."

"You need protection. You're gonna say something stupid, make some blunder. You're not used to this kind of intense scrutiny. If I can get you overseas, we can play it differently. Haze, listen to me. Overseas, you're dealing with delicate shit. You can't discuss it. You can stay above the issues, like we did here. Somebody says, what's your position on the Serbs in Sarajevo, whatta you gonna say?"

"How the fuck do I know? I don't know anything about that. That's why I don't wanna go."

"You say strides are being made between peoples who have been at war for ages, and it is unreasonable to expect a solution overnight. You are working to see that steady progress is being achieved."

"I can do that here."

"No. No, Haze, you're outta slack over here. You can't feed the press platitudes forever. Now, you're the nominee! They're gonna demand specific answers, and every answer you give will create enemies who will cut into your approval ratings. The longer I can keep you abroad, the better chance we have of defeating Pudge in November. In six months, you're gonna be in the White House, Haze. You're gonna make it, but you gotta listen to me. You've gotta do what I say. I've never let you down yet. Have I? Tell me one thing I've told you, didn't turn out the way I said." There was desperation in A.J.'s voice. They both heard it.

The argument lasted for almost half an hour, and in the end, they struck a compromise. Haze would go abroad, but only if Susan could go, too. A.J. agreed, knowing he would regret it, but he made Haze promise no more screwing. Haze was getting tired of the lecture and he finally agreed, but he had no intention of keeping the promise.

Kaz and Cole watched the victory speech in a bar-restaurant inside the beltway. The talk in the bar was all about the coronation of Haze Richards, the candidate from nowhere who had swept in and won the Democratic nomination. Kaz and Cole sat in silence listening to the short speech, which included a moment where Haze talked about Anita and wiped his eyes.

"You see any tears?" Kaz asked glumly.

"Yeah, but it's California. Could be the smog. They got like fifty particles of nitrous oxide chasing every poor little oxygen molecule."

Kaz waved at the bartender to get him another Coke. "We gotta find David Robb. I called around; nobody knows where he is. I guess that means we gotta check out hospitals and nursing homes. And death certificates."

Cole looked down at the empty martini glass in front of him. "Lemme ask you something, 'cause I'm confused."

"That's why I'm here, Cole, to cure your confusion."

"Haze Richards has the Democratic nomination, right?"

"Seems so." The bartender put the Coke down in front of Kaz. Cole waved him off.

"Anita Richards is dead, but we have nothing but hunches as to why."

"Cops go on hunches."

"I need two valid sources to run a story. Why would Haze kill his wife?"

"Sympathy. Could win him the election."

"Come on, he was winning."

"Make him win bigger. . . . Or to stop the bimbo grenades that I'm sure Pudge was set to throw. What else is troubling you?"

"How do we knock the Haze Richards campaign off the track? Seems to me the only thing we have a chance of proving is that the mob financed C. Wallace Litman and that his network is steering on the election. That may not even be a crime, and just because Litman worked on Teddy Lansky's tax returns in the seventies doesn't mean he was bankrolled by the mob. Where's the evidence? We've got no smoking gun."

"Not yet, but if we can prove that UBC is a mob-controlled company, and if we can prove that Mickey Alo wants to put Haze in the White House, then I think we can knock him off. The American people hate to get duped. If we can prove the mob and UBC picked Haze and were trying to manipulate the election, the backlash will end it."

Cole paid for the drinks and they moved to a table for dinner. "Ever since the Lansky trial in Israel I've always wondered what was in that suitcase. It had to be powerful. It kept him out of Israel," Cole said as they were seated.

"My bet is illegal wiretaps of Lansky's private conversations with criminals. Probably stuff Justice couldn't use in the U.S. courts 'cause it was obtained illegally, but it would be perfectly all right to let the Israelis borrow it. If we get lucky, maybe those tapes still exist. They won't be listed in the records 'cause there was no paper behind the bugs. David Robb would have had to approve the deal. That means he has them or knows where they are. If we find him, maybe we get half the equation. . . . Maybe we get old recordings of Lansky talking to Joseph Alo."

"Or maybe he's talking to Wallace Litman."

"I wish I was still boozing so I could drink to it," Kaz said.

The waiter brought menus, but when they saw the prices, they got up and left.

Kaz and Cole had dinner at a crowded McDonald's next to a pinball arcade. As kids screamed and threw ice cubes, they divided up the tedious task of locating David Robb.

DOWNWIND

LUCINDA STEERED A COURSE FOR CABO SAN LUCAS, AND THE fifty-foot ketch headed downwind in a following sea. The course corrections were frequent as she rode the mounds of fast-moving water that were overtaking them from the stern. The sky was filled with high, scudding clouds that turned the day silver in the afternoon light.

Ryan had stayed on deck, hopping awkwardly to port and starboard, reeling in the jib lines with the chrome coffee grinders.

The incident with Jerry Paradise had crystalized the danger for both of them. For Lucinda, it was the final chord in a dark fugue that started playing the day they buried Rex—an orchestrated deception that included the beating in the park . . . the cold, empty warning in the den and the threat in the kitchen where he'd pushed her down and accused her of spying on him. All of these things paled next to Jerry Paradise and the attempt to kill them.

"We should call Kaz and tell him what happened," Lucinda finally said.

Ryan listened to the wind whistling through the rigging. He knew she was right. The cell phone was in the center drawer below. It was dead but Ryan told her there was a charger down below.

Lucinda got the cell phone, turned on the tiny generator that fed power to the cabin, plugged in the charger, and set the unit up on the chart table. She turned to go back up on deck, but hesitated when she saw Ryan sitting at the wheel, looking off toward the horizon, his chin high, his right hand on the helm. Her heart caught as she looked at him. There seemed to be something more substantial about him now—something that was missing before, a strength of purpose, a determination. He looked down and caught her staring at him. She smiled to cover her embarrassment and clambered up the stairs to join him.

"What were you just thinking?" she asked.

"I was wondering what force in the cosmic plan decided to hand us this gigantic problem. How are we qualified to keep the underworld from stealing the presidency?"

She had no answer. The thought overwhelmed her.

A gust of wind caught the mainsail and they both felt the boat lean over as it rushed down the hill of rolling water.

Ryan looked out at a low-flying gull that had its wings spread and was cruising, effortlessly, along behind the *Linda*, never changing its position, riding the same wind so that it appeared to be hovering, while in fact it was moving fast, maintaining the position with only slight adjustments of wing and tail. Ryan thought it would be nice if he'd been able to control the currents of his life with such ease.

In forty minutes, the cell phone was charged and Lucinda went down and got it. She dialed her mother's number. It rang three times, then she heard Kaz's voice on the other end. "Yep," he said, noncommittally.

"Kaz?"

"Who's this?"

"Lucinda. I'm with Ryan. He wants to talk to you." She handed the phone to Ryan, who put it to his ear.

Kaz was still in Washington, parked in front of the Human Resources Office. He was about to go in and find somebody who would buy a line of bullshit he'd dummied up about an overpayment on David Robb's social security.

"How y' doin', Kaz?" Ryan said.

"How you feeling is a better question."

"Coming along. But I have a problem that needs solving."

"Do my best . . ."

"Nobody should have known where Lucinda and I were. We had been there for three days and some guy who called himself Jerry Paradise, or maybe his name's Harry Meeks, showed up and tried to kill us. He was from Atlantic City, so I'm pretty sure Mickey sent him, but the only thing I can't figure out is how Mickey could know where we were."

"You call him?"

"I called him once, but it was from a pay phone and it was the same day we got attacked, so that couldn't be it." He looked at Lucinda. "Just a minute . . ." He turned to her. "Did you call your brother?"

"No." then she remembered the call she had made to Penny. "But I called my mother at the Jersey house two days ago when I went into Avalon for food."

"Lucinda called Penny at the house in Jersey two days ago."

"He must have a Pin Tel."

"A what?"

"A gadget the phone company developed to catch people who are making threatening phone calls. If he's got one, he'd get a printout of the number she was calling from. It's not much of a trick to get the address." Then Kaz added, "I guess I don't have to tell you not to call him again unless you wanna decorate the inside of a pine box."

"Listen, Kaz, I want to be part of this."

Kaz said nothing, so Ryan forged ahead.

"Mickey's already tried to kill me three times. As long as I'm a target, I might as well go ahead and get a uniform."

Kaz really didn't want to work with amateurs, but he couldn't say that to Ryan. "Cole and I are working on something. Get some place where you won't draw a crowd and lay low. Is that a cell?"

"Yeah."

"Okay, gimme the number and stay out of sight If I need any help, I'll call."

Ryan gave him the cell-phone number and they ended the conversation.

After he hung up, Ryan and Lucinda held hands in the cockpit of the ketch as the day turned slowly to dusk. The sun sat on the horizon like an orange cue ball on frothy green felt. It slowly sank from view and then they were in a strange murky twilight, the boat shooting down the sides of the following sea. For almost a minute, the color of the ocean and the sky were an identical shade of dusky gray. Where sky and water met, there was no horizon. It created a strange vertigo, as if the small sailboat were in a colorless vortex, a small shifting platform in a world of invisible, coursing currents.

Then night fell and the moon lit the ocean as they, once again, slipped silently away, heading toward Mexico.

They finally arrived at a protected cove in Mexican waters about six miles south of Ensenada. It was nine-thirty in the morning when they dropped anchor. With sleep still in her eyes, Lucinda got the sail down, gathered it in, and lashed it to the boom with a line. Then they sat in the cockpit and drank coffee. Lucinda turned on the radio for some music to lighten the mood, and while they listened to the distant sounds from a San Diego station, they admired the beautiful, but barren, Mexican coast.

At ten o'clock, the radio station announced what most of the world already knew—Haze Richards had won the California Democratic primary. He would control the national convention scheduled in Denver.

Ryan shut off the radio, then got his crutches and moved forward on the deck of the boat.

"Where are you going?" Lucinda asked.

"I'm going to get this leg in shape."

She watched as he stretched out and hooked his right leg under his left heel and started doing leg lifts, using the right leg to help. He was sweating and grimacing with pain. He did ten reps, counted to twenty, and did ten more. Over and over, he repeated the exercises.

He had no strength in the leg and after a while, Lucinda could watch no longer and went below. In the small cabin, she could still hear the thumps as his heel hit the deck. She had seen the mangled leg up close. She knew that most of his muscle had been lost.

Up on deck, under the Mexican sun, Ryan continued his leg raises. Sweat was rolling off him, but his mind was miles away. He was back at Stanford University on the practice field in the shadow of Maples Pavillion. He was nineteen years old, lying on the ground in his practice uniform doing grass drills with the backs and ends. He could hear the fitness coach, Zoran Petrovich, screaming at them with his German accent, *Lass go. Come on ya lazy pussies, two, free, fo' . . . two, free, fo' . . .*

Ryan struggled with his damaged leg, trying to lift it, using less and less help from the right until he couldn't lift it at all.

Lass go, ya pussies. . . . A bunch a' fooking Fräuleins. . . . Yah?

In his thoughts, he was back in time. He was young and healthy. There was no fear of defeat—only open fields and touchdowns stretched before him.

Come on, let's go. . . . One, two, free, fo' . . .

He had always been at his best on game day. He wasn't going to give up. He wasn't going to let Mickey win . . . not after coming this far.

HEALING

SIX HUNDRED MILES SOUTH OF THE BORDER, THEY FOUND A SHEL-
tered bay listed on the map as Magdalena. They anchored in the cove.

May turned into June, and June became July.

They found a world without worry. Ryan worked out twice a day
for almost two hours, concentrating not only on his leg, but the rest
of his body as well, building muscles long left unused. Lucinda
cooked and swam and sunned herself in the nude on the forward
deck. At night, they made love under the stars.

Weeks passed and their only connection with the world was the
ship-to-shore radio and the occasional Mexican lobster boat that
came into the cove looking for fresh beds. Twice a week, they called
Kaz and Cole, who'd had no luck finding David Robb. Kaz said he'd
worn out his welcome at the Justice Department and could no longer
even get a visitor's pass. They both sounded tired and frustrated.

Atmospheric conditions allowed them to pick up a San Diego all-news radio station one evening in late June and they learned that Haze Richards had gone to Europe and was discussing world events with heads of state. He returned to the United States the third week in July for the Democratic National Convention, which neither Ryan nor Lucinda saw because they were out of TV reception. Kaz told them about it on the cell phone.

"This fucking guy. . . . You should have heard him. He's gonna make America work, my ass. He'll make it work for that bunch of oil cans in the mob. UBC said he was the candidate of the nineties, the Roosevelt of a new era. I was so depressed, I wanted to shoot myself."

After the convention, Haze had picked Senator Ben Savage from California as his running mate, then went back to Europe where he had his picture taken with Arab kings and Balkan presidents. Kaz passed the events along to them. He seemed to get more desperate with each call. To Ryan, it all had become distant—part of something he'd left way behind.

In two months, Ryan had strengthened his leg enough to be able to take short, hesitant steps without crutches. The leg felt spindly and strange under him.

One afternoon, Ryan and Lucinda had taken the Avon to shore. It was warm and they seldom wore any clothes. They were alone in the secluded cove. It was their Eden. All the darkness in their lives, all the shadows were washed away by the ocean, then burned away by the blazing sun. They had taken beach towels and food and the small rail barbecue off the *Linda.*

Ryan was determined to walk the length of the beach. Lucinda looked at him, smiling as he fell out of the boat, twenty yards from shore, and started swimming. His stroke was graceful and his kick getting stronger. She had removed the stitches two months before. Ryan had turned a deep shade of brown, except for the angry red line that marked Dr. Jazz's stitching and cut a diagonal stripe across his leg.

She watched him as he pulled himself out of the water, tan and muscular, his blond hair long and almost white from the sun. She beached the boat and he helped her pull it up. Then she took the towel and ran to the end of the beach.

"Where you going?"

"You can have me if you can get me," she teased.

He chased after her on his bad leg, having difficulty in the sand. She moved backward, laughing. Finally, she threw the towel at him and he caught it and lunged at her, going down hard in the sand. She thought he might be hurt so she ran to him, naked and brown from a month in the sun. He grabbed her leg and pulled her down beside him and they hugged each other.

"God, I love you," she whispered in his ear.

"I don't know why," he said honestly.

She kissed him on the mouth, and then he was kissing her body, her nipples erect with the heat of passion. Both found release once he was inside her. They longed to have more of each other. The penetration of mind and body couldn't seem to fill the ache of love. She pledged herself to him and was prepared to give up her life for him. He vowed no harm would ever come to her and would die before losing her. They marveled at the intensity of their feelings.

"I wish this would never end," she said.

"The memory never will."

That night, they unwrapped the last two steaks from the boat freezer and cooked them over the metal barbecue on the beach. Because there was no town in which to buy groceries, from now on they would live off of the dwindling supply of canned goods aboard, and the lobster and fish that they caught by hand.

After dinner, Ryan and Lucinda lay in the sand holding hands and thought back to the first time they had met, when Ryan had been invited to the Alos' house for Thanksgiving.

"You came through the door and I fell in love with you. How can that be?" she said. "I was only seven years old. It's as if God said to me, this is the one."

Ryan talked about Matt.

"The worst part is all the things that I wanted to do with him." Ryan was looking up at the stars and wondering if Matt could hear him. "Things that will never happen. They're losses that I can't get over because they live in my imagination and change as I do."

Ryan thanked her for making the shadow dreams go away. . . . Thanked her for explaining Terrance's drowning to him. . . . For taking that darkness out of his life.

"If we survive this, will you marry me?" he finally said.

She propped herself up on one elbow and looked at him, the moonlight catching the blue in his eyes. "You better believe it, buddy."

He took Matt's elementary school class ring off his little finger. . . . It was his most prized possession and it had only cost twenty dollars—a powerful example of how meaningless his climb to wealth and power had really been. He slipped it on her finger and they looked at each other for a long time, celebrating their engagement without words.

One evening at the end of August, Cole got the call that changed everything. He was just coming through the door of his Georgetown rooming house when the phone rang and a thin-voiced man from the Phoenix Medical Group spoke to him.

It had been Kaz's idea to check out old-age medical plans in warm-weather states, like Hawaii, Florida, Arizona, and New Mexico. Older people, Kaz said, tended to migrate to warm climates because their skin had gotten thinner and their circulation slower. Something that Cole of course knew, but it was a worthwhile thought when you were down to a few hundred dollars and contemplating the problem of contacting medical insurance plans in fifty states. They were looking for a man who seemed to be out of the system and could very possibly be dead. They had to narrow the search somehow.

"Is this Mr. Harris with Medicare?" the voice said, with a distant twang.

"Yes it is."

"I got your letter and I'm responding about David Robb."

Kaz had dummied up a letterhead for Medicare, using the letter canceling his own federal policy as the prototype. They tapped Carson Harris for the two hundred dollars it cost to get letters and envelopes printed. "This is it, Cole. I can't keep loaning you money," his frustrated brother said. So Cole and Kaz hocked their rings and watches.

Kaz had written a short letter saying that David Robb's account was being reviewed by Medicare, and asking the medical plan to contact them at the enclosed number. They had five hundred copies of the bogus letter printed and sent it off, hoping nobody would notice that the envelope was mailed with a stamp instead of a government franking mark. They'd sent the letter to medical plans in warm-weather states and had received no responses until the call from Phoenix.

"Is this your home?" the voice inquired.

"Private extension," Cole said, trying to move the man along.

"I'm a little confused about your letter. You're doing some kind of check on David Robb . . . ?"

"Who's calling, please?"

"This is Dale Dennison, Southwest Age Benefit Program. We're connected to Medicare and we hold the current policy on Mr. Robb."

Cole had a pen in his hand and was fumbling in the drawer for a piece of paper. "Just to make sure we're talking about the same Mr. Robb, would you mind giving me his current address?"

"Our information lists him at the Wild Oaks Retirement Home in Phoenix."

"Could you give me his age, his underlying carrier and his social security number?" Cole said, figuring it was a possibility this was another David Robb.

"What is this about?"

"We're doing a demographic realignment so that the actuarial shift in benefits won't affect the baseline average for sixty-plus men on Medicare drawdowns," Cole said, hoping some elaborate gobbledy-gook would sufficiently mystify Mr. Dennison so he'd stop asking questions Cole couldn't answer.

"Oh, I see," the confused voice said on the other end of the line.

"You were going to give me his age and underlying carrier and his SS number."

"Uh, right. Well, he's a federal employee on the Blue Cross Plan. . . . He's eighty-six and his Social Security number is 568-52-2713."

Kaz got home at eight. He'd been trying to find David Robb through the War Department and had been shut out. He was in a foul mood when he walked in, but when he heard that Cole had succeeded, his mood changed abruptly.

The retirement home was a low, one-story building on Route 357, the highway that ran through Phoenix.

Kaz and Cole paid the cab from the airport and went inside. What they found depressed them.

Wild Oaks was a vegetable garden where old people did a Thorazine shuffle under the prison-guard stares of attendants. Kaz introduced himself to a stout Navajo nurse named Arleen Cloud, who looked at them with open suspicion.

"I'm Joseph Robb; this is my brother Don. We're David's cousins from Altoona," Kaz said to the woman, who wasn't buying it.

"Who do you two guys think you're kidding? I've got David Robb's file; he doesn't have any relatives. He's outlived the whole clan."

" 'Cept for his uncle," Kaz said.

"Which uncle?"

"Uncle Sam." Kaz pulled his old federal badge and flashed it. "So keep the attitude coming, Nurse Cloud, and I'll drop an obstructing justice charge in your mailbox."

David Robb had tubes sticking out of every conceivable orifice and one or two that had been created for him—like the one in the center of his neck so a ventilator on a timer could pump oxygen into his lungs at four-minute intervals. He had bed sores and couldn't have weighed a hundred pounds. He was in a private room with one window. The best thing about David Robb were his eyes. They were deep brown and still held the light of intelligence. Kaz moved over to him, pulled up a chair, and sat down.

"Mr. Robb?" The man looked at him and nodded his head.

"I'm Solomon Kazorowski; this is Cole Harris." He held up his FBI badge for the man to see. "We need to talk to you about Gavriel Bach. Can you speak?"

The man nodded, then slowly opened his mouth. "Yes." The word seemed fished up from the bottom of a dusty well.

"You talked to him in 1971 about Meyer Lansky. You gave him some material. Is that right, sir?"

Again, David Robb hissed his reply, nodding his head slightly for emphasis.

"Sir, what did you give him?"

David Robb looked at them for a long, heartbreaking moment; his withered eyelids blinked across beacons of despair. He licked his lips, but put no moisture on them.

"Sir . . . what was in the suitcase?"

"Wiretaps," he said in a sandpaper whisper. "Conversations with the underworld."

"Illegal taps?"

David Robb nodded his head in response.

"Sir, do you remember who was on the tapes? Was Joseph Alo on the tapes?"

The old man looked at them and said nothing. Then he closed his eyes for almost a minute. When he opened them again, he looked at Cole.

"So long ago . . ." The ventilator turned on and hissed and sucked as the accordion pump went up and down in a glass tube, forcing fresh air into the old man's sunken chest.

"Where are the tapes now?"

"Gav took the tapes, never returned." He closed his eyes and started to breathe heavily. Kaz and Cole looked across the bed at one another as the old man began to snore. As if to emphasize that the interview was over, the ventilator abruptly shut itself off.

"I don't believe this," Kaz said. "Two months and all we get is, 'Never returned.' Gavriel Bach is dead."

"Gavriel Bach was sort of a lone wolf in the Israeli prosecutor's office. I remember that from when I covered the trial. He had that suitcase on the prosecutor's table the day the verdicts were read. He didn't leave it with the justices. I can't see him giving the tapes to the Israelis. Besides, once Meyer's case was over, what use would the Israelis have for any of that stuff? It was about U.S. criminal activity."

"What're you trying to say?"

"One of two things happened to them. He kept them or threw them away. You're a cop. Would you ever throw away evidence, regardless of whether you thought you'd ever need it again?"

"Of course not."

"So maybe he held on to it. Maybe that suitcase is in an attic someplace."

"In Israel?" His eyes rolled like an Atlantic City slot. "We're down to our last ten dollars. How the hell we gonna get to Israel?"

"I'll do the heavy lifting. You work on tactics," Cole said.

"Oh really?"

"Isn't Ryan Bolt loaded? Maybe we take him aboard, let him bank-roll this pilgrimage."

"He's a cripple and an amateur."

"You got a better idea?"

They left the Wild Oaks Retirement Home and stood outside in the shimmering summer heat while Kaz tried to call Ryan Bolt on Penny Alo's cell phone.

It was after nine in the evening before he finally got through.

PAPER TRAIL

THE GHOST WAS DRESSED IN A SOUTHERN CALIFORNIA GAS Company uniform. Over his right shoulder, he carried a canvas bag with a silenced Ruger Mark II and two 10-shot .22-caliber clips. He was wearing latex gloves and a blue baseball cap. He found the alarm on the side of the valley apartment house and jumped it with alligator clips. After he had deactivated the alarm box of apartment 4-C, he climbed the stairs and stood in front of the door. He slipped a lock pick into the door and opened it. The door caught at the end of a chain, safety-locked from inside.

He listened, heard nothing, so he put his shoulder to the door and pushed hard. The safety chain popped off the door and landed halfway across the living room.

The Ghost closed the door behind him and began a careful survey of the apartment, checking to confirm it was empty. The dresser top paid a pictorial tribute to Ryan Bolt. One photo was taken at the studio; in it he was smiling, sitting in the front seat of an electric golf cart. Nameplate read THE MERCENARY. A few pictures were taken at industry banquets—Ryan and formally attired table mates with their chairs pulled together flashing manufactured smiles. The Ghost found a back door in the kitchen, which explained how the chain could be set on the inside. He checked the closet for men's clothing, checked the bathroom, but found no evidence that anybody was living with her. He discovered a small alcove off the kitchen from which he could watch the rear door. He pulled the Ruger .22-caliber automatic out of his bag and worked the slide, putting a round in the chamber. He made sure the silencer was screwed on tight. Then he settled back to wait.

The key turned in the lock at seven-thirty.

Elizabeth Applegate moved into her kitchen carrying a bag of groceries. The Ghost put the cold steel of the automatic behind her ear.

"Set down the bag and put your hands over your head."

"What . . . ? Who . . . ?"

He pressed harder with the barrel. "Do what I said."

Elizabeth set down the groceries and tried to turn around to see who was behind her, so he grabbed her roughly, threw her onto the floor, then landed hard on top of her. Before she could say anything or scream, he shoved a dishrag in her mouth and secured her hands behind her with plastic strip cuffs he'd brought with him. He rolled her over and she found herself looking into the cold, blue eyes and round face of a red-haired man who she thought looked a little like Jerry Colonna without the mustache.

"Okay, Elizabeth, I don't want to hurt you, but I will if that's the way you want it. Your only chance of surviving me is to do exactly what I tell you. You understand?"

She nodded, her eyes blank with desperation. He smiled at her, then pulled her to her feet and pushed her, on numb legs, into the bathroom, where he closed the door and undid the cuffs around her wrists.

"Take off all your clothes," he commanded.

The Ghost had learned that, stripping a subject before an interrogation made getting information easier. You eliminated resistance and introduced a sexual threat for both men and women.

She started unbuttoning her loose-fitting print dress, then let it fall to the floor. She was in her bra and panties.

"Let's go. All of it. I'm losing patience." With a shaking hand, Elizabeth undid her bra and removed her panties and stood naked in front of him.

"Isn't that better? Look at you," he said, smiling.

He grabbed her roughly and retied her hands with the plastic cuffs. "Now get into the tub." She moved backward and stepped into the tub.

"Lie down, Elizabeth, on your back."

She was about to vomit. Fear had turned her stomach to acid and she started to gag. The Ghost had been waiting for it. It almost always happened. He yanked the gag out of her mouth as she threw up on herself.

Then he forced her to lie in her own stomach fluid.

She was lost in terror. "Don't kill me," she rasped at him through a throat burning with aspirated vomit.

"That depends how good a girl you decide to be."

"I'll be good."

"Wonderful. I'm here to find out about Ryan Bolt."

"Who?" she said, not even knowing why she said it.

He struck her across the mouth with the gun. She screamed as she felt her lip split open. Her mouth filled with blood.

"What did you say?" he asked softly.

"Okay, okay, don't . . . don't . . ." And she started gagging on the blood flowing in her mouth.

"Where does Ryan do his banking? I went out to his condo on the beach; there's no financial records there. I need to know what charge cards he has . . . who pays his bills . . . stuff like that," he said.

"Uh . . . Who pays his bills?"

"That's right. Simple little answer to that question gets you home free, Elizabeth."

"Uh . . . uh, Jerry . . . uh, Jerry, uh . . ." She was beginning to hyperventilate.

"Slow down, take a breath. Jerry who?"

"Jerry Upshaw, his agent. They had like a business managing service where they'd do the bills and stuff for an extra five percent."

"So, where's this guy's office?"

"He's in a private building called The Mayflower on Vine. Jerry dropped Ryan as a client. But he's still doing his bills until Ryan gets back in town." She was looking at the redheaded man hopefully. "Can I get out now?"

"Hell yes. We're through, and Elizabeth, I want to thank you for your splendid cooperation. It's really been a huge help."

She struggled to get up. He waited until she was in a crouch and then fired the Ruger. The silenced automatic jumped in his hand. The bullet hit Elizabeth in the forehead. The back of her head exploded; and her brains flew up onto the tile splash. She reeled backward and hit the wall just under the shower head, then slid down and finally came to rest in her own vomit and blood.

The Ghost unscrewed the silencer and did a quick survey of the apartment to make sure he'd left nothing behind. He left by the front door, got into his car parked a few blocks away, and drove into the summer night.

Upshaw's office was on the first floor of The Mayflower building at Mayflower and Vine. The Ghost found the alarm in an outdoor utility box. *Ridiculous*, he thought. The alarm didn't even have a police dialer on it. He disarmed it and found a back window, worked it open with a screwdriver, and shinnied in. The computer he was looking for was in an office marked CLIENT ACCOUNTING. He turned it on and punched in "Bolt." Magically, there on the screen was Ryan's financial history. He moved quickly through the data bank until he found Ryan's credit card accounts. He started to scan them and then saw something that turned his mood black. Ryan had used his AmEx card in San Diego. He'd withdrawn ten thousand dollars.

"Damn," the Ghost said. With that much cash, Ryan wouldn't leave a paper trail. He scanned the computer for Ryan's airline mileage card numbers and wrote them down. Then he shut off the computer and left the way he came in, closing the window and resetting the alarm.

Back at his small hotel in Hollywood, he went to the phone book and looked up airlines in the Yellow Pages. One by one, he would check them all.

* * *

The flight from San Diego landed at Phoenix International Airport. Ryan walked down the ramp without crutches. Lucinda was at his side. Kaz and Cole greeted them at the gate, and as they shook hands, the ex-fed and the ex-IR were amazed that Ryan could walk at all. Both Ryan and Lucinda were the color of walnut. They made a spectacular couple. With Lucinda's long black hair and Ryan's white-blond, they were turning heads in the airport as they moved down the corridor to the airline counter.

"I wouldn't've believed it if I wasn't seeing it," Kaz said, looking down at Ryan's left leg as he walked with only a slight limp.

"I'm not gonna be making any sharp cuts over the middle, but I'm not bad if I move straight ahead."

Ryan and Lucinda had packed only carry-on luggage, just one change of clothes and their toilet articles. They'd left the boat at a Mexican marina and paid the dockmaster to watch if for a month.

Kaz had the airline schedules in his hand.

"We take a two o'clock United flight to Atlanta and then connect with the El Al transatlantic direct to Tel Aviv," he said as they moved up to the United Airlines desk, where Ryan paid for all the tickets with cash. The ticket agent found Ryan's name in her computer and automatically credited his mileage account without mentioning it. An hour later, they were boarding the first leg of the flight.

"United Airlines," a man's voice said over the phone. "You guys are screwing me on my MileagePlus. I fly on your airline and you don't give me credit?" the Ghost said. This was the fourth airline he'd called.

"Could you give me your name sir and your MileagePlus number? I'll get your account on the screen."

"Ryan Bolt," he said and then gave the number he got from Jerry Upshaw's office. He waited as he heard the computer keys clicking over the phone.

"Well, sir, I have your account here. This is odd. . . . We just credited your account with forty thousand miles."

"That's impossible." The Ghost grabbed for a pen on the nightstand.

317

"No, sir. . . . Four tickets from Phoenix to Atlanta and then continuing on from Atlanta to Tel Aviv on El Al Flight 2356. Is this Mr. Bolt? Where are you calling from?" The man was starting to get suspicious.

"My mistake." The Ghost hung up abruptly.

Then he called El Al airlines. "You have a flight from Atlanta to Tel Aviv?"

"Yes, sir, Flight 2356, leaving at seven P.M. arriving at eleven A.M." a man informed him.

"Can you get me out of LAX so that I can meet that flight in Israel?"

Computer keys clicked.

"Yes, sir. Flight 3476 leaves LAX at four this afternoon and arrives in Tel Aviv at nine A.M. That would be two hours ahead of the Atlanta flight. Do you want me to book you?"

"Yes, please. The name is Harold Meeks."

The Ghost packed his small suitcase, then called a cab. Before he left, he placed a call to Mickey Alo on the scrambled line.

"I just found out they're going to Israel."

"Really?" The mobster had left the dining room table to take the call. He still had his monogrammed napkin in his hand.

"Why would they be going to Tel Aviv?" the Ghost asked.

"Don't know."

"There are four of them traveling together. Do you have any idea who's with them?"

"Just get it done. I thought you were the best. What's taking so long?"

"Mr. Alo, it's much easier for me to take care of it in Israel. I have contacts over there. People die unexpectedly in that country all the time. Don't worry, it's better this way."

After he hung up, he dialed a man named Akmad Jam Jarrar in Paris. Akmad wasn't in, so he left a message in his hotel voice mail that said, "I need to get the old crew together. Meet me immediately in TelAviv, the Hotel American. Same terms as always. The Ghost."

UNEXPECTED PROBLEMS

THE PASSENGER IN SEAT 25B OF EL AL FLIGHT 3476 WENT INTO a convulsion at 7:37 A.M., just as the El Al flight attendants were beginning to set up for breakfast. His name was Leonard Greenberg, he was fifty-six, and he owned a jewelry store in Burbank, California. His legs shot out and kicked the seat in front of him; then he jack-knifed forward and hit his head on the back of the tray table. The woman sitting in the seat in front woke up with a start, turned, and glared around the seat at him. What she saw immediately alarmed her. Leonard Greenberg looked at her with half-lit brown eyes and said, "So sorry." Sitting beside him were Leonard's wife, Hanna, and his sixteen-year-old daughter, Sasha. They were all going to Israel for the first time.

"Get the stewardess! Get a doctor!" Hanna Greenberg shouted at her daughter Sasha, who scrambled out of her seat and ran to get the flight attendant.

"His shunt is failing," Hanna said to the startled woman in the seat in front of him. Hanna had seen this happen twice before and she knew the results would be fatal if Leonard didn't get immediate surgery to relieve the pressure on his brain.

A man from a row behind them, across the aisle, came forward and kneeled beside Greenberg. He carried a small, black briefcase.

"I'm a doctor."

"It's his shunt. I've seen these convulsions before. He has to get to a hospital immediately."

"What is a shunt, for God's sake?" the flight attendant said.

"Everybody has cerebral spinal fluid that surrounds the brain," the doctor explained. "Some people don't have the proper drainage and fluid gets trapped in the brain causing what is known as hydrocephalus. To fix this, we install a plastic tube in the lateral ventricle called a shunt. Occasionally the shunt gets clogged, causing extreme pressure on the brain. This man needs immediate surgery!"

"You need to explain this to the pilot. Come with me." She led the doctor up the aisle, past the first-class passengers.

The Ghost woke up as they brushed past on the way out of the cockpit. He caught a glimpse of the strained expression on the flight attendant's face and knew immediately something was wrong. He grabbed the flight attendant's arm and flashed his goofy, harmless salesman's smile.

"We got a problem?"

"Sick passenger. We're probably diverting to London, Heathrow."

"But that's gonna take hours. I gotta be in Tel Aviv. I have important business. . . . "

"There's a phone aboard. I'm sure you don't want a fellow passenger to die so you can keep a business appointment." She pulled away, picked up the intercom, and announced the change in destination.

The Ghost retrieved the air phone on the wall in the front of the cabin. He used one of his Harry Meeks credit cards and walked back to his seat with the phone.

He dialed the number for the Hotel American in Tel Aviv and asked for Akmad Jarrar's room. In a minute, he heard the Arab's voice.

"Thank God you're there," the Ghost said, without preamble.

"Yes, my friend, I have just arrived. I took the first flight I could get."

"I need help. I'm being diverted to Heathrow because some passenger is sick. . . . Our CEO is arriving at Ben Gurion Airport at eleven on El Al Flight 2356. He's traveling with three accountants; at least one is a beautiful woman. They should be met but not escorted. We're scenario dependent until I can get there. The C-cube is your hotel." This was a code they had used before. "CEO" would sound like chief executive officer to anybody picking up the open telephone signal, but to the Ghost and his team of assassins, it stood for covert elimination objective, or target. "Accountants" or "CPAs" were collateral personal assistants. In espionage circles, they were generally men or women with briefcases who worked with or for the target. "Met but not escorted" stood for follow but don't apprehend. "Scenario dependent" meant they would be dependent on the chain of events. "C-cube" stood for communications command control center. Akmad said he would handle it, and the Ghost gave him a brief description of Ryan and Lucinda, mentioning that Ryan would most likely be on crutches and was blond and handsome, the girl dark-haired. The Ghost said he had no descriptions of the other accountants.

"Are they prepared to do business?" Akmad asked.

"Definitely," the Ghost said, indicating that they were dangerous and should be treated as such. As they rang off, the Ghost felt the plane banking to the left for Heathrow. He would probably be in Tel Aviv four hours later than planned. But he was invigorated by the unexpected problem. He loved improvising. He loved the chase. But most of all, he loved the kill.

Ben Gurion Airport was in Lod, outside Tel Aviv and ninety minutes by car from Jerusalem. The airport was small but modern. Security was stringent.

The planes didn't taxi up to ramps, but were left out on an expansive tarmac, where the travelers deplaned, then got aboard big buses to be taken to the terminal. Cole explained that the process of open tarmac deplaning allowed for tighter security.

Kaz, Cole, Ryan, and Lucinda stepped off the El Al plane and were struck by the heat and humidity. It was over 100 degrees and moist. Their clothes immediately stuck to them as they moved down the steps of the plane to the ground transportation. Cole knew Israel well. He'd covered a lot of stories there. He had decided they would stay in the Hotel Carlton in Tel Aviv. The international bar there had always been a news hangout. Then he would find somebody at Reuters he could pump for information. He needed to find out everything he could about Gavriel Bach's family. . . . Was his widow still alive? Where were his children? Where would his personal effects be? Cole knew they had damn little to go on. They were ten thousand miles from home, looking for a bunch of illegal wiretaps given to a dead Israeli prosecutor twenty-five years ago. Even if they still existed, the tapes might have nothing of value on them. Yet, they were following that feeble lead halfway around the world.

Customs took an hour. Finally, they walked through the turnstiles, past the uniformed Israeli guards with their shiny jackboots and shoulder-mounted Uzis. On their way to the taxi stand, they passed a short, skinny Arab in khaki shorts and a T-shirt, smoking a Turkish cigarette.

Akmad Jarrar saw the four Americans and assumed they were the ones he'd been looking for. The handsome man wasn't on crutches, as the Ghost had said, but he moved with a slight limp. The girl was indeed beautiful.

He followed them out into the sunlight and watched as they got into a Subaru taxicab that pulled out into the traffic, heading toward Tel Aviv. He waved his hand and his own rented blue Mitsubishi screeched up to the curb with two men inside. Behind the wheel was Frydek Mistek, a German terrorist who was ideologically damaged by his love of money. He had worked on several hits with the Ghost in the old days when the CIA was doing covert sanctions. Frydek was a good second man. He was nondescript, average in every way except for his aptitude for violence. In the backseat was Yossi Rot, a slender man with Jewish good looks and dark curly ringlets. He had once been a "powder man" for the

Mossad, but he'd drifted into the netherworld of freelance operators.

They all spoke in English. Akmad pointed to the car with the
Americans. "Stay close. . . . Taxis are easy to lose."

Frydek accelerated and followed the Japanese taxi into the City of
Mirrors.

CITY OF MIRRORS

THE HIGHWAY SLOPED DOWN, LOSING ELEVATION AS THEY headed east toward Tel Aviv. To the south, a jagged coastline framed Jaffa Harbor where the first Zionist pioneers had landed in 1882. Ancient stone buildings stood guard along the coast, baking in the somnolent heat. The city of Tel Aviv blended into the outskirts of Jaffa.

They dropped down farther and soon were on the broad, paved streets of the city. Tel Aviv was as modern as L.A. and as ancient as the Bible. It reflected the best and the worst—a city of mirrors.

They moved down Shenkin Street and turned onto Allenby Road, and, before long, they pulled up to the hotel. The Carlton was a five-story architectural mistake that had been located in what became a business district when the city grew to the north. Journalists liked it because the switchboard was secure, the location was central, and you could get sloshed on two or three drinks at the "international bar," where the policy was to pour doubles for anybody with a press pass.

Ryan handed over the cash and they booked two rooms. In five minutes, they were all upstairs in Cole and Kaz's cubicle, which overlooked the shops on Allenby. An old air conditioner wheezed and coughed tepid air into the threadbare room. Cole was sitting on the bed, using the phone, trying to find somebody at Reuters who could help them. None of the old crowd seemed to work there anymore. He'd tried names of five journalists who were no longer assigned to Tel Aviv when he remembered Naomi Zur, an American woman he'd always had a thing for. She was a photojournalist and he'd tried for months to get her in the sack, but she was in love with an Israeli colonel. The phone was ringing her extension, and after a moment, he heard a familiar husky female voice.

"Photo Ops, Noami Zur speaking."

"I've been trying to get this burnoose on and I can't remember. . . . Do you wrap the east end under the crown or do you hook it behind your ear and tuck it in back?" he said, recalling a time they both had tried to infiltrate a Palestinian refugee camp to get a story. Cole made a lousy Arab and almost got them killed.

"Jesus, Cole . . . If you're back, I'm gonna put in for an immediate transfer."

"Hey, Naomi, it wasn't that bad. How 'bout lunch at the restaurant downstairs in the Kolbo Shalom?"

Reuters was located directly over one of Tel Aviv's largest shopping centers, dominated by the Kolbo Shalom department store.

"Who's buying?" She remembered that Cole had a reputation for never picking up tabs.

"That's why they put those matchbooks in the ashtrays, Naomi, so people can draw straws."

And then he couldn't help himself. . . . "By the way, how's Uri?"

"He died. Land mine," she said flatly.

"I'm sorry." Cole remembered the ruggedly handsome Israeli war hero who had risked his life countless times. "See you in an hour. . . . I'll buy this time."

He lunged off the bed and grabbed his light coat and headed for the door.

*   *   *

After Cole left, Ryan and Lucinda went to their room down the hall. Kaz sat for a long time on his bed lost in thought. He decided they needed to get hold of some ordnance. Something told him that wandering around Tel Aviv, unarmed, was dangerous. And stupid. He figured that buying arms in Tel Aviv couldn't be too tough. He locked the door and headed down the hall to Ryan's room to get some cash. He paused in front of the door when he heard a sound inside and realized it was Lucinda moaning. The breathy gasps were accompanied by the gentle tapping of the headboard against the wall. Kaz, concerned for her safety, almost knocked but caught himself at the last moment.

Jesus, he thought, *it's been so long since I got laid I almost didn't recognize the music.* He decided to find a dealer and bring him back here. A few minutes later, he was out in the bustling street.

Akmad Jarrar spotted him from the front seat of the blue Mitsubishi, then got out and followed on foot.

The restaurant in the Kolbo Shalom Center was on the second level and overlooked the harbor. The food was international and the clientele was strictly business.

Cole could hear four or five different languages and the tenor and tone of the conversations were intense. Spreadsheets were pored over, cell phones rang, while watercress salads and shish kebab were ferried around on pewter trays.

Tel Aviv had become a business mecca, where the emerging Eastern democracies were spreading their wings on the currents of Israeli financing.

Naomi Zur walked into the room wearing a tailored shooting jacket. She had her black hair pulled back in a bun and her shirt tied in a knot at her waist. She wore no makeup. At almost five-nine, she was a truly striking woman. She spotted him and, with black eyes twinkling, moved toward him. They were eye-to-eye as they embraced. She squeezed his hand before sitting down across from him.

"You look like the cover for the desert edition of *Vogue.*"

"You're such a fucking liar, Cole, but thanks." She smiled and grabbed the menu. "So you're buying?"

"All you can eat, as long as you stay under ten U.S. dollars."

"Then we better work the roll basket."

"I'm sorry about Uri."

"Thank you. He's gone . . . and we have to move on." It was very Israeli. She was not about to dwell on it or share her pain with anybody. She asked for no sympathy and wanted none.

After the salads arrived, she started the ball rolling. "Alluring as I am, I don't think you came all the way to Israel to buy me a plate of falafel."

"I need help on a story. I thought the computer bank at Reuters might have what I need."

"What about the computer bank at UBC?"

"They threw me out, Naomi. *Punta de basta.*"

She nodded as if she wasn't surprised. For a second, Cole wondered what effect he'd had on people over the years. Maybe it wasn't the impression he thought he'd been leaving.

"Whatta you need?" she finally asked.

"When I covered Lansky's trial in '71, the lead prosecutor was a man named Gavriel Bach . . ."

She listened attentively as he ran the backstory, ending by saying he needed to find Bach's widow, if she was alive. If not, then his family. He was sure that a major political figure like Bach must have reams of background stuff in the computer. He left out all of the information about Mickey Alo and UBC, his newsman's paranoia still intact. When he was finished, she looked at him quizzically.

"What's the story here? This is more than just a background check on Gavriel Bach."

"Yeah."

"Gimme the lead line."

"He was breeding Persian longhairs. I'm doing a story for *Kitty Litter* magazine," he said.

"Look, Cole, you know how it works. If I help you and it leads anywhere, I need to take the ride."

"Okay, but you gotta trust me to give it to you when I think it's safe. I have certain security considerations. Some dangerous people are after me."

"Your word was always worth something," she said slyly. "I just could never figure out what."

He paid the bill with American money and they took the elevator up to the news bureau. On the way out, they passed a tall Israeli with dark ringlets. Yossi Rot joined them in the elevator and watched while Naomi pushed "14." He got out at 3 and went back to the lobby and looked at the directory. The entire fourteenth floor was occupied by Reuters News Bureau.

Cole was seated in the Background File Room in front of the computer as if he owned it, scrolling information while Naomi stood behind him. There were reams of material on Gavriel Bach. His widow was Mishama Bach, known as Misha. She was last mentioned in a story about an Arab shoot-out in Jerusalem only two months ago. She had been a witness to the shooting. The article said she was living in the Old City and taking care of her sister-in-law.

Cole scribbled down the address on Ben Yehuda Street and promised Naomi he would cut her in if anything happened.

When Cole got back to the Carlton Hotel, Kaz was already there. He had two Uzis with extra clips lying on the bed. A suitcase was open on the dresser with two Desert Eagle automatics and a nine-millimeter Beretta, complete with extra clips and shoulder holsters. Standing beside the dresser, with one hand still on the open suitcase, was a scruffy-looking man in a dusty brown shirt.

"Meet Emir Shamgar," Kaz said.

"Sham*a*gar," the Israeli corrected him.

"Right. And he's your friendly Allenby Street firearms dealer. I figure wc oughta pick out some party favors before we tool around in this jungle. Ken and Barbie are asleep, but once you pick out what you want, we'll get 'em up and conclude the arrangements. Mr. Sham*a*gar is very agreeable to terms as long as we pay one hundred percent up front."

Ten minutes later, Ryan and Lucinda joined them. Ryan decided to risk putting the purchase on his American Express card. It amused Cole that Shamagar had an AmEx charge plate and imprinted the card before picking up the phone and calling the AmEx credit center for verification.

"It's the new Israel," Cole said bleakly.

After Ryan picked out one of the heavy Desert Eagles and two clips, they concluded the deal. It came to just under sixteen hundred dollars. Mr. Shamagar graciously threw in two boxes of ammo before he left.

It was four o'clock in the afternoon when Shamagar left the Carlton. By then the Ghost was seated in the blue Mitsubishi across the street and saw him go.

MISHA

KAZ SLUNG THE UZI OVER HIS SHOULDER AND PUT THE NINE-millimeter Beretta he had selected into his belt, but Cole elected to leave his Uzi in the room. Ryan felt like one of his TV characters with the ridiculously heavy Desert Eagle strapped under his arm in an upside-down holster. He wore his loose-fitting silk jacket over it, but the bulge was still obvious. Kaz stuffed the extra boxes of ammo into Lucinda's purse.

They stepped out into the late afternoon heat and hailed a cab.

The Old City of Jerusalem was only one hundred kilometers from Tel Aviv, but the traffic was miserable and it took two hours. They got out of the taxi at Ben Yehuda Street and didn't notice the blue Mitsubishi that pulled up a block behind. The Ghost, wearing an unmarked red baseball cap and dark glasses, got out of the car with Akmad and followed them on foot.

Ben Yehuda Street had been turned into a pedestrian mall. It was about fifty feet wide and intersected by several streets that were closed to traffic. The yellow stone that paved it matched in size and color the old stone used almost two thousand years ago on the ancient buildings. The shops lining the streets had colorful awnings that hung down like fringed eyelids at half-mast. The mall was teeming with people of all nationalities. They walked downhill, then through the Jaffa Gate, which marked the entrance to the Old City.

The first thing that Ryan noticed was the feeling of holiness about the place. There was a sense of spiritual history all around him . . . Jewish, Christian, and Muslim. They passed the Wailing Wall; above it sat the Dome of the Rock.

"This is amazing . . . like being in church," Lucinda said, picking up Ryan's thought.

"Only two cities in the world feel this way," Cole announced, "Jerusalem and the Vatican."

They moved on along the narrow, winding street and finally found the apartment number.

The building was three stories high, the front door was oiled wood, aged to a rich golden brown by heat and time.

Cole knocked on the door and after a minute, an old woman with a babushka around her head leaned over the balcony and screamed something at them in Hebrew.

"Sorry, ma'am," Kaz shouted. "Don't speak Jewish."

"Hebrew, you dickhead," Cole corrected him.

The woman disappeared, and a girl about twelve came to the balcony.

"Yes? What do you want?"

"We're looking for Mishama Bach. We're friends of her late husband."

The girl spoke to someone behind her, then turned and looked down at them again.

"Just a minute," she said and was gone.

A few moments later, the door opened and they were looking at Misha. She was tall and raw-boned, dressed in loose-fitting clothes. Her steel-gray hair was pulled back and knotted in a bun behind her head. Good bone structure saved a face crushed by disappointment and time. Her best feature was her dark brown eyes. In her youth, Cole imagined, she was probably quite beautiful.

"I'm Misha Bach." Her English was flavored by a slight British accent.

"I'm Cole Harris. I knew and admired your husband. Could we come in for a minute? We've come a long way."

She turned her gaze expectantly to the others. Cole made the introductions and, after they shook her hand, she invited them in. They entered the house and followed her up the narrow wooden staircase to an apartment on the second floor.

"This is my sister-in-law's house. She's been very sick and so I've been staying here the last few months taking care of her."

The apartment was small but neat. Framed prints of Zionist heroes looked down stoically from white plaster walls—David Ben-Gurion, the Israeli flag furled behind him; Menachem Begin in front of the Knesset. In a position of honor was a portrait of Gavriel Bach in the robes of a Supreme Court justice.

"My sister-in-law was very proud of her brother. He became a Supreme Court justice before he died," Misha said as she saw Ryan looking at the portrait. "She's asleep in the bedroom. Let me close the door." She moved across the room and pulled the bedroom door closed as Cole smiled broadly. He was in his news-gathering mode, which, after four months, Kaz had come to loathe.

"Mrs. Bach, your husband was one of the most distinguished legal minds I've ever encountered. I covered the trial of Meyer Lansky in 1971. Gavriel did the State of Israel an outstanding service at that trial, a service that was, perhaps, pivotal to its survival."

"Thank you. I don't believe he ever mentioned you, Mr. Harris."

"Well, I was just one of many admirers. We spoke several times and my respect for him was overwhelming because never once did he sacrifice his ideals for a result. He was a man we could all learn from. A man with such depth of soul and feeling, such commitment to the highest moral standard that I personally was compelled to reevaluate my own career goals and motives after coming in contact with him." Cole was vibrating bullshit.

Kaz, Ryan, and Lucinda shifted their weight awkwardly in the small room.

"You must have known him very well to have understood that."

"Not well enough. And that's why I came all the way here to talk to you, Mrs. Bach. I'm doing a major series of articles for *Time* magazine called 'Silent Heroes.' I'm picking one unsung hero from each of five countries . . . men who changed the course of their country . . . maybe even the flow of history . . . men who served mankind without any special recognition or applause. And because of the absolutely therapeutic effect Gav had on my life, I've picked him as my Israeli." Cole was in hyperspace, orbiting freely over this complex ball of nonsense.

Misha Bach had her hands clasped in her lap and was leaning forward toward Cole, almost as if she was afraid she might miss a word.

"How can I help?"

"Did you know he made a deal with the U.S. Justice Department before the trial and, as a result of that deal, twenty-five F-4 Phantom jets were delivered to the Israeli Air Force?"

She shook her head. "I know he went to Washington before the trial, but he never told me much about his cases."

"I need proof of that historic arrangement or my editor won't publish that part of the story."

"I don't know how I could help you . . ."

"There was a metal Haliburton suitcase and I think inside that case was physical corroboration of the deal. It was left in Gavriel's possession after the trial. . . ."

"What does the suitcase look like?"

"It's metal, about twice the size of a briefcase." He demonstrated with his hands. "Silver-colored, silver handle . . ."

"Why, that's in the storage room over the carport at my house in Herzelia Pituah. It's been there for years."

"It is?" Kaz said, astonished by the revelation. With grudging respect, he thought *The slimy little fuck is gonna pull this off.*

Cole was elated. "I know this is a lot to ask, but could we get in there and have a look?"

"Oh, no problem. The garage key is under the third flowerpot on the left side of the house."

"You don't mind if we just walk in?"

"Well, there's nothing to take. Just old suitcases and boxes up there, some sports equipment." She smiled at Cole.

"Mrs. Bach, you're gonna be so proud when you read this story. I'm gonna tell the world what a hero Gavriel Bach was. In my opinion, he may have saved the very State of Israel." He gushed insincerity like a broken sewer line.

Ryan thought he saw the Ghost as they were leaving the apartment on Ben Yehuda Street. He glimpsed a man, with dark glasses and a red baseball cap, duck into a souvenir shop. He was about the same size and shape as Jerry Paradise and there was something about his quick movements that reminded Ryan of the fight on the dock in Avalon. Ryan grabbed Lucinda's hand and pulled her close to him.

"What is it?" Kaz said.

"Across the street. I think I saw the guy who came aboard my boat."

Kaz saw nothing but said, "Okay, the three of you get moving. I'll check it out."

"Bad idea," Ryan said. "You don't even know what he looks like." Ryan was reaching under his arm for the Desert Eagle. He yanked it out of the quick-draw holster and held it by his leg.

"Okay," Kaz muttered. "Cole, you take Lucinda and wait for us at the Jaffa Gate. Get a car; make it one of those Mercedes taxis. There's thousands of 'em and they're hard to follow. Get rid of the driver and have the motor running."

"How 'm I gonna do that?"

"I don't know. Lay some of your more pathetic bullshit on him. Move it! And watch out, there may be more than one guy on us."

Finally, Cole moved away with Lucinda.

Ryan and Kaz watched to make sure nobody followed, then looked across the street.

"Which shop?" Kaz asked.

"Third one down."

"Put the cannon away. This ain't Dodge City. Pull it just before we move in. I'll go in first and head left. Once I'm inside, you come in behind me. Move fast, go to the opposite wall of the store. Stay low; he'll shoot for your kill zone, around your chest, so don't move at a normal height. . . . The lower the better. If he hits you, you want the slug to go through your lung or shoulder and miss the important stuff."

"Shit, what about my head?"

"It's a small target."

A shot of adrenaline hit Ryan's heart like cold piss. They crossed the street to the shop. Kaz was still wearing the Uzi on a sling on his back, but he had one hand on the stock so he could rotate it up and let a stream of lead fly in seconds.

Kaz moved through the door, fast, low, and sideways. He hit the wall inside on the left. The Uzi was up and trained on the shop.

With his heart pounding and his mouth dry, Ryan went in after him, staying low and moving sideways fast. Before he made the right wall, his bad leg buckled. He went down split seconds before two shots exploded, blowing holes in the wall where his head would have been. Kaz fired the Uzi in an arc across the small shop. Hasidic souvenirs turned to dust. The spent brass spewed out of the eject port and chimed as they bounced on the tile floor. The smell of cordite filled the air. They heard the back door slam shut, footsteps pounding in the alley. Ryan struggled to his feet and started in pursuit, but Kaz yelled, "No! Clear the fire zone first. Could be another one in here."

They raced through the cluttered shop, carefully checking aisles. They found the bearded shopkeeper cowering behind the counter. When they were sure there was no second shooter, they moved out the back door and looked down the deserted alley.

"Let's get outta here. We don't need this guy, we need what's in the suitcase," Kaz said, and they headed toward the Jaffa Gate. Ryan was limping badly and his back felt big and unprotected.

At the gate, they found Cole in a loud argument with an Israeli cabdriver. They were yelling at one another in two different languages. Lucinda was standing nearby, watching the commotion in disbelief.

Kaz moved up and pointed the Uzi at the cabbie. "Get the fuck outta here, shithead."

The man moved back glaring at them, as Cole got behind the wheel. Ryan and Lucinda sat in the back. Kaz piled in the passenger seat and laid the still-hot barrel of the Uzi on the dash.

"Go, man! Boil some eggs!" Kaz yelled.

Cole put the taxi in gear and squealed out of the ancient gate, scattering chickens, Arab shopkeepers, and IDF soldiers as Cole leaned on the horn. Finally, they hit a two-lane road and sped back toward Tel Aviv.

SUITCASE

THE SUBURB OF HERZELIA PITUAH WAS ON THE COAST. IT WAS the Malibu of Tel Aviv. Corporation presidents and high-ranking diplomats owned or rented villas there. Cavriel Bach's house, a sixties A-line, was well situated at the end of a land spit, a quarter of a mile beyond the main cluster of houses, screened off by a row of ficus trees. A pool in the back overlooked the Mediterranean.

The long driveway was shielded by a six-foot-high concrete wall. The ex-TV producer, ex-Mafia sister, ex-IR, and ex-fed parked their stolen cab in front of the two-car garage and got out.

"Rummage around in the glove compartment and pop the trunk," Kaz said to Cole.

"Why?"

"Everybody over twelve is strapped down over here. That cabbie had to have some kinda weapon with him. I want the gun. We need all the firepower we can get."

They found a Russian-made Tokarev TT-33 and a box of seven-millimeter cartridges for a German Mauser. Kaz pulled out the nine-shot clip and turned it over in his hand; then he chambered the slide and dry-fired it.

"Piece of Russian junk. Used to be a nine-millimeter, but you can't get Russian cartridges anymore, so somebody rechambered it. Good luck." He handed it to Cole, who held it like a steaming turd between his thumb and index finger.

"I don't want this."

"I'll take it," Lucinda said, taking the gun, slipping it quickly into her purse.

Cole found the garage key under the flowerpot, right where Misha said it would be. He put it in the keyhole, and the electric door hummed, then opened. The room above the empty carport was long and narrow, about ten feet by four. At one end a series of shelves were stuffed with sporting equipment and old luggage.

On the second shelf, wedged in against the wall, was the Haliburton suitcase. Cole grabbed it and pulled it down.

"Feels light," he said as he popped the latches. They all gathered around and looked inside. It was empty.

"Maybe it's not the same case," Lucinda said.

"No, that's it," Cole said. "These things were very big with agency spooks in the Justice Department during the seventies. It's an odd size, bigger than a briefcase, smaller than a suitcase."

They stood in the small room, looking into the empty case as if the answer were somehow still miraculously inside. Finally, Ryan reached down and closed it. They had come so far. It didn't seem possible that this was the end.

"Whatta you wanna do?" Cole asked.

"Let's take a look around inside," Ryan suggested.

"You think those tapes are lying around in some desk drawer? Come on, this shit is twenty-six years old," Cole said.

"Can't hurt to look," Kaz said.

They walked around the side of the house. Kaz checked the window frames for alarm tape but didn't find any.

"Lemme have a credit card," Cole said.

Ryan handed over his MileagePlus card and Cole moved toward a door that appeared to lead to a pantry. Cole slid the card in beside the door handle and finally popped the lock, then handed the card back to Ryan, smiling. "Thanks for the press pass." They opened the door and went into the house. The last to enter was Ryan, carrying the empty Haliburton suitcase.

Silvio Candrate tracked Mickey Alo down at a business meeting in a Trenton hotel. Mickey had been trying to set up distribution and supply routes for Hawaiian ice, which was a designer drug and the brain wreck of choice with the trendy club crowd in Manhattan. Silvio's call got to him at ten A.M. The sound of a screaming pneumatic wrench and clattering lug bolts provided background for the conversation.

"Mickey," he said "our friend in Israel called me. He thinks you should know that something strange is going on. I got a number you should call if you got a secure line. He's standing by this number for ten minutes."

"Gimme it."

Mickey went to a pay phone in the lobby of the hotel. He jammed in a coin and dialed the number. The operator came on and told him it was eight dollars for three minutes. He always carried ten dollars in quarters in his briefcase. He stuffed the coins into the slot and waited. After the second ring, the Ghost was on the line.

"Hello." His voice seemed surprisingly close.

"Whatta ya got?"

"We secure?"

"More or less; it's a pay phone."

"I found out who everybody is. The two late entries include a guy named Cole Harris, an ex-newsman . . ."

"Never heard of him."

"The other guy's an ex-fed named Solomon Kazorowski."

"Fuck! When's that labonza gonna leave me alone?"

"You know this guy?"

"Yeah, I know him. He's been walking around in my asshole with a government searchlight for twenty years. He got fired for busting everybody's balls. What's he doing over there?"

"I don't know. That's why I called. They're looking into something to do with a guy named Gavriel Bach. Ever heard of him?"

"No."

"They met with an old woman, Bach's widow. I followed 'em to a house in a pricey suburb. They're inside now. I got an Israeli with me says Gavriel Bach was a big shot, ended up as a Supreme Court judge. I just figured before I closed this off, I'd check in with you, see if you got any last-minute instructions. I'm on a package rate. I'll do 'em all. Cost you nothing but the fallout."

"Just a minute, let me think." Mickey held the phone against his chest; something was buzzing around in his head. Bach's name was familiar but he couldn't place it. He put the phone to his ear again. "Tell me more about this judge . . ."

"I'm gonna put the Israeli on." The Ghost handed the phone to Yossi Rot "He wants to know about Bach."

"He was very big here," Yossi said in his soft voice. "He was a Supreme Court justice. Made the news when he died, maybe six years ago."

"Before that . . . ?"

"I don't know . . . prosecutor, I think."

Mickey slapped the buzzing thought down. "Put the other guy on." After a second, the Ghost was back on the line.

"If I remember, this Gavriel Bach tried the case against Meyer Lansky back in '71. He kept Meyer out of Israel, but what could that have to do with anything?"

"You want me to ignore it? I can just hit these people and get outta here."

Mickey wondered what they were after, but decided too much time had already passed. The presidential election was just three weeks away. It didn't matter what they were looking for. And if they died halfway around the world, it would remain a mystery.

"End it," he finally said, not giving a second's thought to the fact that he was ordering his sister's death.

The Ghost hung up the cell phone and moved back to the blue Mitsubishi. He looked at Frydek, Yossi, and Akmad Jarrar, who was leaning against the rear bumper. Inside the trunk was enough C-4 to blow the entire dock at Jaffa.

"Okay, Yossi, I want you to get up the driveway and put a physics package under that taxi. . . . Use a radio detonator in the C-four. When I hit the switch, I wanna shoot that fucking cab into space."

Yossi nodded, opened the trunk, and grabbed a satchel. Then he jumped over the wall at the foot of the property and, after picking a sheltered route, moved toward the house.

THE BIG HOWARD JOHNSON'S

THE PHOTO ALBUMS WERE ON THE COFFEE TABLE IN MISHA'S sitting room and Lucinda flipped through them while Kaz, Cole, and Ryan moved through the house looking for the missing contents of the Haliburton suitcase. There were lots of shots of the grandchildren. Somebody, probably Misha, had written an identifying line under each one and dated it.

The photos were well organized. On a whim, Lucinda started searching for the album that contained pictures taken in 1971. She found it in its logical place, between 1970 and 1972. It started with January but she skipped to March, the month the trial had taken place, where she saw a handwritten caption that said, "Gav builds 'crooked' pillars after Lansky trial." These shots showed Gavriel Bach stripped to the waist and grinning at the camera. In several pictures, he was troweling concrete onto a large pedestal at the head of the drive, next to the house. Lucinda moved with the album out into the living room. She could hear the men somewhere in the house, opening and closing drawers.

"Could you guys come here a minute . . . ?" she called.

Ryan came first, moving out of a guest room. "What is it?"

"I may have found something," she said.

Within seconds, they had all gathered in the living room. Lucinda held the open photo album out to them.

"These were taken right after the trial."

They huddled around the album and looked at the photographs of Gav working on the pedestal.

Kaz was already moving to retrieve the empty Haliburton suitcase from the pantry where Ryan had left it. He returned with it and set it on the coffee table, opened it, and started to look carefully at the inside.

"What're you doing?" Ryan asked.

"If he took the tapes out of here and put them into that pedestal, I was wondering if he got any plaster dust in here." Kaz licked his finger and pressed it on several specks of white powder in the bottom of the case. He pulled his finger out and showed it to the others. "Like this . . ."

They all smiled at Lucinda.

"Pretty damn sharp, honey," Kaz said and Lucinda blushed. Cole had seen some tools in the garage and he and Kaz went off to get them. Ryan was waiting at the open front door. Out of the corner of his eye, he saw movement. He swung just in time to catch a glimpse of a man in a white shirt and khaki shorts running down the drive. Kaz and Cole reappeared with a hammer and tire iron.

"Somebody was just here. I saw him running down the driveway," Ryan said.

"What'd he look like? Was it the guy in the ball cap?" Kaz asked.

"I hardly saw him. He looked slender. . . . In a T-shirt and shorts."

"Let's go check it out," Cole said.

"No," Kaz said softly. "Always assume the worst. That way we don't get surprised. Let's assume we were followed from Jerusalem. If we go down there, they're gonna know we saw him and we're gonna lose what little advantage we have. Hang on a minute." He moved to the taxi and started to look at it carefully. When he got to the front, he saw a handprint on the dusty chrome bumper. Kaz lay down on his back and slid under the car to examine the frame. Wedged in next to the gas tank, he saw about two pounds of plastic explosives connected to a detonator. He carefully reached up and pulled the detonator out of the plastic. It was a sophisticated radio unit with a "hot" wire that ran into the explosives. Kaz took his beeper off his belt. It was a state-of-the-art satellite communication system used by the federal government. He had stolen it when he'd been fired and faithfully replaced the battery every two weeks. It had never rung, but he was ready if they ever needed him. He knew it was stupid but it felt good riding on his hip. He removed the back of the instrument, yanked the hot wire off the detonator and twisted it onto the battery pole of his beeper. He pushed his beeper and the wire back into the plastic, shoved the detonator into his pants pocket, and shinnied out from under the car.

"Find anything?" Cole asked.

"Nope. Let's get that pedestal down."

While each took a turn holding the Uzi and scanning the driveway, the others went to work with the hammer and crowbar.

Little by little, they exposed the core of the pedestal. Finally, there was an opening big enough to reach through. Ryan had the longest arm and he stuck his hand down and grabbed hold of a bag, but he couldn't get it through the hole they had made.

"There's something in here," he said. "Get some more bricks out."

They worked until finally the hole was large enough and Ryan could pull out a large canvas sack. They rewarded the find with tight smiles.

"Let's get inside," Kaz said, his eyes searching the perimeter as they moved back into the house and closed the door.

Even with binoculars, the Ghost could see only the front door through a growth of ficus trees on the west side of the property. He had decided the best way to eliminate all four was to get them into the taxi and take them all out at once. He looked at Yossi Rot and Akmad Jarrar.

"I'm gonna move up and see if we can snipe at them through the windows," the Ghost said. "That oughta get 'em moving. Yossi, once the cab starts to move, blow it. When it goes, we gotta be out of here in seconds."

The Ghost moved to the Mitsubishi, opened the trunk, and took out a blue steel Charter Arms Explorer-II .22-caliber pistol. He thought it was almost as ugly as the old broom-handle Mausers, but the Explorer-II was surprisingly easy to handle. The Ghost liked it because it could be silenced without distorting the shot. He secured the eight-inch silencer onto the threaded barrel, grabbed the twenty-five-shot ramline clip full of dumdums, and slammed it in. Then he attached the scope. He turned his ball cap backward, then jumped the wall, and moved toward the house.

In the living room, they examined the contents of the bag while Kaz kept an eye on the yard through the plate-glass window. The audiotapes, big and unwieldy, were on six-inch plastic reels. Cole remembered the old reel-to-reel odd-size tape recorders from the seventies. There was also some 16-millimeter film on four 800-foot reels. None of it was labeled. Cole held one of the reels up so he could try to see who made them, hoping it was government issue. "I'm really gonna feel like an asshole if these are movies of some kid's birthday party." The light wasn't very good on the far side of the living room, so he moved to the plate-glass window.

Just then, Kaz caught a flash of movement out beyond the pool. Then he saw the Ghost step out from behind a low wall on the far side of the pool with a deadly-looking scoped pistol. Flame shot from the muzzle.

"No!" Kaz yelled, throwing himself in front of Cole, pushing him as the window shattered and they both went down in a shower of glass.

Ryan leaped over the sofa and landed on his bad leg. It crumbled and he rolled on his shoulder. Regaining his feet, he grabbed the draperies and yanked them across the gaping opening, cutting off the Ghost's field of vision.

Cole was sitting up, a puzzled look on his face. He had blood all over him. He looked down at it, dazed, then slowly realized it wasn't his.

Kaz was lying on the floor, his legs splayed out in front of him.

Blood was coursing out of a huge hole in his chest. He had taken the .22-caliber dumdum in the back. It had broken up on impact. The fragments traveled through his upper lung at the manufacturer's guaranteed velocity and exited in a five-inch pattern right below his collar bone. The wound was pulsating with thick arterial blood, draining Kaz's life down his shirt and onto the floor. Ryan pulled the Desert Eagle, scrambled to the window, and cracked open drapes. He saw nobody out there.

"Get a towel," Cole screamed, and Lucinda ran to the bathroom and grabbed some bath towels. On her way back, from the hall window she saw the man who had called himself Jerry Paradise running down the driveway, a baseball cap on backward. She ran into the darkened living room and thrust the towels at Cole.

"I saw him running down the driveway! It was him, Ryan. . . . It was Jerry Paradise!"

"Leaking like a Mexican fishing boat, ain't I?" Kaz's speech was coming slowly.

"Why'd you do that? Why'd you do that!" Cole kept saying over and over.

"I ain't gonna make it. Goin' to the big Howard Johnson's . . . "

"Bullshit," Cole said, desperately.

"Get the car into the garage. Get me in . . . I'll smash into 'em. Give you a chance." He was talking through clenched teeth.

"No, no, you're going with us," Lucinda said.

"Dyin'," Kaz said, slowly. "Got one thing left to do . . . "

Cole had been in the Marines and there was a moral commandment that you didn't leave a soldier in the field to be scavenged by the enemy.

Kaz knew what Cole was thinking, so he pulled his backup piece and pointed the nine-millimeter Beretta weakly at them. "You get the car." Kaz knew they had one chance to win the game, but he was running out of time. He could feel the strength draining from him. "Do it," he said, thumbing back the hammer.

Ryan looked at the dying ex-fed. Something caught in his throat. He couldn't let Kaz die, but he knew he was powerless to save him. All he could do was grant his last wish.

"I'll get the cab," Ryan said.

"You got a bad leg," Cole said.

"Even with a bum wheel, I'm faster." Ryan knew the keys were still in the taxi, so he threw open the front door and ran the short distance across the drive, keeping the car between him and the bottom of the driveway. His leg was throbbing, but as long as he ran straight, it felt pretty solid. He dove into the cab, got the engine going, then backed it into the open garage, and hit the automatic door closer. The garage door came down, cutting the open drive from view.

The Ghost saw the garage door coming down through his binoculars. He summoned Yossi and Akmad. "They're gonna be coming out. Get ready."

Yossi held the detonator and they waited.

Ryan and Cole got Kaz into the front seat of the car. He was propped behind the wheel and looked frighteningly pale. When he coughed, blood oozed through the towel they had pressed over the wound.

"Move over, I'm going with you," Ryan said.

"Listen, damn it. We got what we came for. Mickey's plan is history." His voice was now a faint whisper. They had to lean in to hear him. "This is for our country," he said proudly.

They could take his badge and his life's work, but they would never change what he was inside. He just wanted good to triumph over evil.

"Let's get it done." He faced forward, leaning against the door as Cole turned the ignition. Then, with the taxi idling, Kaz looked at Lucinda. "Gimme your cell," he croaked. There was a death rattle now. His lungs were filling with blood.

She handed him the phone and he punched in the area code and the number for his beeper which was jammed into the C-4 directly under him. "That's my sister's number. Tell her I love her," he said and hit the send button on the phone. He handed it back to Lucinda and then, with his eyes half-closed, floored the gas pedal and drove right through the wooden garage door, turning it into splinters.

Lucinda could hear the cell phone dialing. She was holding it stupidly in front of her as she watched the taxi speed down the driveway. She heard some clicks and then a cable hiss.

The signal shot through the transatlantic cable at the speed of light.

Kaz drove sloppily, his head spinning, his eyes blurring, his hands numb and lighter than air.

The phone call was relayed in Denver and streaked off toward Las Vegas where it went to the FBI Western Regional Exchange, then was routed up to the Telstar geosynchronous satellite that transmitted to all federal agents working in the Northern Hemisphere.

Kaz saw the Mitsubishi parked with three men standing near it at the end of the driveway. Yossi pointed his detonator at the car and Kaz saw him push the button. Nothing happened.

The Telstar satellite shot its ten-volt message down from space toward Kaz's beeper under the stolen taxi just as it jumped the low curb on the driveway and bounced through the trees heading for the Mitsubishi. The three men were scrambling to get into the car when Kaz accelerated. He T-boned the door, rocking the Mitsubishi up on two wheels. The Ghost raised his Explorer-II and fired a stream of .22-caliber yellow jackets into Kaz's face, turning his head to red mist.

"You fucker," the Ghost said, his heart racing. He was wondering what to do next.

The decision had already been made for him.

Kaz's beeper rang.

They felt the concussion all the way across Jaffa Harbor. When the C-4 detonated, it shot fiery parts of both automobiles a thousand feet into the air. Debris was later found a quarter mile from the explosion. . . . But nobody ever found the remains of the Ghost or his associates. And nobody ever found Solomon Leeland Kazorowski. He was gone—off the planet. He was in the crowded bar at the big Howard Johnson's, waiting for his check-in, a smile on his face, having his first Jack Daniel's in ten years.

LISTENING IN

THE BLAST KNOCKED OUT SOME OF THE WINDOWS IN THE BACH house. Cole and Ryan had watched from the garage door. One graphic detail would haunt both of them for the rest of their lives. High above the colony of houses, the black and green hood of the taxi shimmered in the sun, twisting and turning, caught in a terminal updraft. It kited out over the harbor.

"Son of a bitch," Cole said in awe as debris started to rain down in the yard.

Ryan and Cole turned and saw Lucinda standing behind them, her hand to her mouth.

"Let's get moving. We gotta get out of here," Ryan said, coming to his senses first.

They moved back inside the house on rubbery legs, gathered up their things, and stuffed the tapes and film back into the bag. Within a few minutes, they were walking down the long driveway. A small fire had started in the trees and people were beginning to come out of their houses and stare in disbelief at the site of the explosion.

The three of them walked out of the development and finally hitched a ride in the back of a citrus truck.

They rode in silence back to Tel Aviv. All of them were thinking about Kaz.

The corner room at the Carlton seemed littered with Kaz's meager possessions. Lucinda started collecting everything while Cole tried to get Naomi Zur on the phone. It was hard to believe the big, rumpled ex-fed in the Hawaiian shirt was gone. He had saved Ryan's life and Cole's. He had provided them with field savvy none of the rest of them possessed. They felt sad and vulnerable.

Cole finally got one of the Reuters staffers to give him Naomi's home number. She had just stepped out of the shower when she took the call and was dripping water on her floor.

"You need what?" she said to Cole.

"I need to listen to some tapes, transfer some film, and have you get me out of Israel, all as fast as possible."

"Here's how you accomplish that, Cole. . . . First you go to a TV station and pay somebody to transfer the stuff, then you go to Ben Gurion Airport and you buy a ticket."

"Naomi, my partner was just killed. I may have the biggest story of my career. I'll cut you in, but you have to help me and then smuggle three of us outta here on a private bird."

"Why can't you go commercial?"

"Because, every time we travel commercial, some goombah hitter is standing outside the gate with an Uzi."

"Where are you?"

"We'll come to you. Pick a place."

"There's an entrance for Reuters in the underground garage. Park in one of the yellow spaces, go to the elevator farthest away from the parking stalls. There's a keypad there, punch in the numbers three-six, then PYD. That'll get you in. I'll meet you on the fourteenth floor in twenty-five minutes."

"You're a doll."

"This better be the best damn story since Watergate," she said and hung up.

When she finally heard it, even Naomi, who had covered some of the biggest stories of the decade, knew that, if true, it was huge.

The four of them were sitting in the Reuters conference room and she was looking at Ryan and Lucinda, who she thought looked way too pretty to be players in this drama. She listened to the entire backstory. This time, Cole told her everything, including the fact that Haze Richards was a mob-controlled candidate. . . . The canvas bag had been emptied and the tapes and film were on the conference table between them.

"I can transfer the film to videotape but, shit, Cole, I haven't seen that size audiotape in five years. Engineering could transfer it, but it's gonna take a couple of hours. They're gonna have to send it out."

"No fucking way this tape leaves my sight."

She looked at the reels again. "We turned our seventh-floor library into a stockroom for outdated equipment. . . . Maybe some of the old tape equipment is down there."

"Let's go."

As they headed down the hall to the elevator, Naomi found herself walking next to Lucinda. She looked at the strikingly beautiful girl and wondered what she was made of. "Are you our cheerleader?"

"You should always try to eat a good breakfast. It'll keep you from getting bitchy," Lucinda said, deadpan.

Naomi smiled, thinking that they would get along fine. The four of them got in the elevator and headed down to the seventh floor.

The library was a clutter of old machines, desks, and out-of-date supplies. They finally found a Wollensak tape recorder with no cord. The reels were too small, but the tape size was perfect.

"I can straight-wire it," Ryan said, examining it. "We just gotta pray the tubes are all right."

They got back in the elevator and rode up to fourteen, where Ryan grabbed a desk lamp out of an office and, with his pocketknife, cut the cord off. He used the blade to take the back off the tape machine. He found the female electrical feed, stripped the lamp cord, and attached it to the Wollensak. He wrapped the new connection with Scotch tape and set it down on the conference table.

While he had been doing all of this, Cole had been taking the audiotape off the plastic reel and rewinding it on the smaller reels from the Wollensak. He wound it till it was to the lip and then left the rest of the tape on the conference table, strung out in rows. Ryan plugged in the small reel-to-reel recorder and let out a sigh of relief as the red power light went on.

Cole fed the end of the tape into the little Wollensak. "Okay, Ryan, hit Play and pull it through."

They turned on the tape recorder and, miraculously, the little unit worked. The speakers were more or less blown, giving the recorded phone taps a fuzzy quality, but it was possible to hear everything that was being said. The tape ran past the head, and as Ryan pulled, it spooled out onto the floor. Each tape was vocally slated by the agent monitoring it.

"January sixteen, 1966," a long-ago voice said. "Agent Peter Lawson. This is a wiretap on M. Lansky's Fontainebleau Hotel suite. Day shift, nine A.M.," There was a hiss. Then the same voice came back on. "Day shift, ten A.M. No contacts."

Cole explained that the voice slates every hour were for the log and that he remembered his old research said Meyer often checked into the Fontainebleau under an assumed name to do business.

Then another hiss and suddenly the sound of a phone ringing. Then Meyer's voice came on the phone. The mob financier sounded tired and angry. "Yeah," he sighed into the phone.

"Meyer, it's Augustus. Just checking in. How's Buddy?"

"Buddy is Meyer's son who's in a wheelchair with multiple sclerosis," Cole volunteered.

"How's Buddy? Shit, gimme a break with this, will ya? Fucking guy . . . fucking moanin' all the time. I got my hands full." And then he screamed, "Hey, Teddy, turn down that radio, will ya?" And then he was back. "Whatta you need, Augie?"

"This line clean?"

"Yeah. I got a guy comes in every morning and sweeps the place."

Cole picked up Ryan's questioning look. "This kind of bug doesn't put out a power charge unless somebody's speaking on the phone.

It's voice-activated, so it was missed by debugging equipment. Voice-activated bugs are common now, but back in the seventies, the mob didn't know this shit existed."

The conversation continued. . . . "Meyer, we're having some trouble in Philly with Castanga an' all them fucks up there. Every time I wanna move product, he's got his hand in my pocket and I'm thinkin', this here ain't in the spirit of the agreement, so to speak."

"Look, Augie, I ain't a ref. You should talk to Mo-Mo. He's got good ties with Castanga."

"Fuckin' Giancana. I think Mo is behind this whole thing."

"Okay, okay . . . Lemme look into it, but if I get this straightened out, you cut me in for a couple a' points."

"You was already in, Meyer. You know I wouldn't leave you in the cold. You're my rabbi in this deal."

"Shit," the old mobster said for no apparent reason.

"Anyway, I'll call back in a day or so . . . okay?"

"Yeah, sure . . . a day." And the line went dead, with no good-bye.

Most of the calls were like that. They were just wise guys in dispute with other wise guys or deals that were being set up where Meyer was some kind of traffic cop, sorting out differences. Each tape took about an hour to play, and by the time they were through the second one, they were beginning to lose hope. It was easy to see how these tapes had helped the Israeli Supreme Court deny Meyer's "right of return," but so far, they contained nothing that would tie Meyer, C. Wallace Litman, and Joseph Alo together.

They shut off the machine as a Reuters staff assistant brought in some sandwiches and cold beer that Naomi had ordered.

Cole was beginning to think they had come all this way and had lost Kaz's life for nothing. He still had three cans of sixteen-millimeter film in front of him.

"Why don't you let me have engineering transfer the film to videotape," Naomi said, picking up his black mood. He had been so sure the tapes would confirm their theory. Now they seemed valueless. They still had an hour or more of tape to listen to, so he shoved the film cans across to her and she gave them to the staffer.

"Take these down to Engineering and get them transferred to VHS immediately. And don't let them out of your sight." As soon as the assistant was gone, they started the tape again.

They were listening to conversations from the early seventies. The tape started with a conversation picked up in a private dining room above a strip club in Miami called the Boom-Boom Bazoom Room. The club belonged to the Costa family.

Apparently, there was some dispute over Colombian cocaine distribution in Miami. Miami had always been an open city, but as the drug trade grew, tempers frayed, and when the lead started flying, it got dicey. Meyer was trying to hammer out a truce between the Costas and the Delaricos. The only thing the two families could seem to agree on was that they hated the Colombians more than each other.

"We got a deal all set up with Mendoza," Frankie Costa said in a high, nasal voice. "We supply everything, from the farm to the arm, and these guys in Dade are trying to cut in on our distribution. We got the whole drugstore. Got everything from Early Girl to Mother's Helper. And now, at the last minute, Delarico is trying to make a side deal with my Spanish guys to supply their fucking Peruvian Marching Powder at a premium and it's gonna flood the market. We'll have White Lady comin' out our asses."

Cole widened his eyes. "What's this ravioli talking about?"

"Early Girl is marijuana. Mother's Helper is Valium. Some guys take it along with uppers to level out. Peruvian Marching Powder is Peruvian coke," Ryan explained.

Cole nodded. His body was suddenly very tired as he looked at the tape running through the old Wollensak. Hope diminished as each spent reel leaked magnetic tape onto the floor. Cole began to accept that it was probably all going nowhere.

Then it happened, in a conversation between Meyer Lansky and somebody he called Wally. The monitoring agent was named Lee Stein and the verbal slate said Meyer was at a pay phone across the street from his apartment. The date was January 15, 1971. Stein said the feds had cut into the line from a phone pole a block away. Meyer made his calls from this pay phone, thinking it was absolutely safe and he spoke freely, secure in the belief pay phones couldn't be tapped.

"Did you get the package, Wally?" Meyer's voice came on the line, pinched and flat.

"Sure did, Meyer, just like you said. But we're gonna hold it in the paint company offshore till I need it."

Cole knew that Mary Carver Paints was a shell company and money laundry in the Bahamas that Meyer had set up for the Alo family. Then he recognized C. Wallace Litman's voice on the tape. Cole sat up straight. "That's Litman," he whispered. "We could do a voice print, but that's him. This could be it. We could have it."

"Okay, good," Meyer continued. "I think you should level off on the newspapers and radio. We got four chains but I'm much more interested in television."

"I agree, Meyer. I got my eye on United Broadcasting. They're a group of independent stations, but I think they can be bought for the right price. We could expand and create a TV network. We can leverage the buy and I'd recommend that, because we're going to need a lot more cash downriver to acquire additional stations and fund programming."

"How much?"

"I'm not sure. Figure media properties right now are trading at multiples of seven, maybe eight. And it's only going to go up. I'd like to dump the radio stuff to help fund the UBC buy. Maybe Paul Arquette could help us in Washington. He could help push the license transfers through the FCC."

"You wanna talk to him, okay. I don't talk to him 'cause Joe Alo wants us to stay away. Don't want no stink on his candidate."

"I'll talk to him. I'm in Washington next week. How's Teddy?" Wallace said, turning the conversation to Meyer's wife, for whom he had a genuine affection.

"She's fine, Wally. And Mrs. Litman?"

Cole's heart was pounding.

"She's fine. You two are gonna have to meet sometime."

"We can't meet. Joseph wants you in the clear. If he puts his man in the White House, you're the one gonna do it. You and your TV network." There was a long moment of silence, then Meyer added, "Once we own the Man, we're gonna put all these fucks in the Justice Department out of business."

"You take care of yourself, Meyer. I hope you're feeling better."

"I feel like shit, but I'm going home to Israel. I applied for citizenship. I'm gonna go home and die in the Promised Land."

Cole reached out and turned off the tape. He looked at the others in the room. They were all holding their breath.

"Son of a bitch," Naomi finally said. "You were right." And then she leaned across the table and kissed him.

CHAPTER 63

GOING HOME

THE RIDE TO BEN GURION AIRPORT WAS A PARANOID TRIP through the shadows of their imaginations. Every car, every taxi, seemed to hold vicious assassins. They were led onto the field and boarded the private jet. Their hearts were pounding.

Even though Kaz wasn't with them, his spirit permeated the small ten-seat Hawker jet. His bag of possessions occupied an empty seat in the passenger cabin.

The jet belonged to Reuters, and it had taken Naomi four phone calls to get permission to use it. She had pleaded and flirted and, lied, and finally, the Middle Eastern bureau chief had signed off on it.

As soon as the sixteen-millimeter film was transferred, they had grabbed the two VHS cassettes and left for the airport in a Reuters sedan without stopping to play them.

They were soon out over the Mediterranean, headed for a refueling stop at the Azores before crossing the North Atlantic. Cole shoved the tape into the VCR in the plush cabin. They watched the silent film of Meyer meeting men in dark suits on Miami street corners in the sixties. Each shot was identified by location and date by a film slate, written on an eight-by-ten-inch handheld blackboard. The telephoto lens zoomed in to catch the conversations. Sometimes, it was possible to see lips moving.

"We gotta get a lip reader to translate this stuff," Cole said. Naomi nodded.

The film didn't seem ominous unless you knew who the players were. Cole recognized a few notorious figures. There was a shot of Meyer and Joe Colombo coming out of a Miami nightclub; shots of Meyer and Sam Giancana. They watched the ever-changing parade of Mafia princes and then, toward the end of the second tape, Cole jabbed the Pause button. The shot showed Meyer getting out of a taxicab with Joseph Alo. Lucinda saw her father as he was twenty-six years ago, and then, as they ran the tape farther, Mickey Alo got out of the cab. The camera zoomed in; Joseph could be seen talking. After a minute, the shot turned off and the monitoring federal agent held a slate in front of the lens that said: "July 5, 1970, Fontainebleau parking lot." That was the only film in which Mickey Alo appeared. But C. Wallace Litman made a surprise appearance in a shot taken in Las Vegas. An elevator camera in the Frontier Hotel photographed him talking briefly to Joseph Alo. They finished viewing the tapes, turned off the TV, and moved to the four seats that faced one another in the back of the cabin.

"Strategy session," Cole said. "We got Meyer and C. Wallace Litman planning to use UBC to put a guy in the White House, saying Joe Alo is the quarterback. We got Meyer and Joseph Alo on film. And we got Joseph and Litman together in the Frontier elevator. We don't have anything to tie Haze Richards to Mickey Alo."

"I overheard a telephone conversation between A.J. and Mickey talking about Bahamian funding for the Richards campaign," Ryan said.

They sat in silence for a moment. They weren't sure it was enough.

"If the federal government had Meyer Lansky on tape talking about gaining the presidency by using a TV network, why wouldn't they have done anything about it back then?" Lucinda asked.

"Bunch a' reasons," Cole said. "In '71, network TV wasn't the huge political factor it is today. In '60, we had just begun to find out how powerful TV was when Nixon lost the presidency to Kennedy over a television debate. Second . . . these mob guys are always plotting ways to get back at the Justice Department. Most of it is just hot air. And third . . . you gotta remember these were illegal wiretaps. The government couldn't use them even if they wanted to. They might have wondered back then what he was talking about. The plan had a twenty year timetable. That's too long for any fed I ever met. Kaz was the exception. They're looking for quick busts. As time passed and nothing happened, this stuff disappeared into a file and nobody gave a shit anymore; it was forgotten."

Ryan nodded. "Let's say we've got enough proof here. How do we use it? If we put it in the wrong hands, it could get buried or discredited. We've already seen how dangerous Mickey is and how far he's willing to go to get this done."

"We need to give that a lot of thought," Cole said, studiously. But he already knew what he wanted to do. "We don't have many options and I don't want to turn loose control of the story till it's in the right hands."

Naomi knew exactly what Cole meant. They'd have to choose the outlet carefully. What they had was only the tip of iceberg, but it was enough to attract official interest. Once the Justice Department started going through Litman's financial records, with special attention to Mary Carver Paints, she knew, it would all come out. But in the wrong hands, it could be distorted, the story altered. If they didn't spring it quickly, Litman and Mickey would have time to destroy the records before the Justice Department could move in.

"We've only got two weeks," Cole continued. "In two weeks, Haze Richards is most likely going to be elected President and then it'll be too late. That means that in the next fourteen days we have to communicate this to the entire electorate and we have to pick somebody the public will believe."

After half an hour's discussion, they chose Tom Brokaw at NBC because Cole used to play tennis with him and trusted him. He would contact Brokaw once they landed.

Events changed everything.

While the Hawker jet was still over the Atlantic, Mickey Alo pieced together what had happened in Israel.

The Tel Aviv police had recovered Kaz's nine-millimeter automatic, which had been blown through the roof of the taxi and landed not two hundred feet from the site of the collision. The I.D.F.'s Special Investigations Section in Tel Aviv had been able to lift prints from the weapon and matched them to Solomon Kazorowski. The wire services reported that a gardener working next door to the Bach house had seen the taxi, presumably driven by Kazorowski, hit a blue sedan containing three unknown men. He had also seen two men and a woman hurrying down the Bachs' driveway. The gardener had given a fairly accurate set of descriptions. Mickey had called Silvio from a pay phone. Silvio said that they had better meet.

They stood next to a noisy fountain in the park off Third Street near Little Italy.

"I think he's dead," Silvio said, speaking of the Ghost.

"How can you be sure?"

"He told me if he fails to check in every noon, then he is gone. He has already missed one call." Silvio's shoulders were sagging. "I think he was in that explosion."

"He got Kazorowski."

"The others are alive; they got away." He looked at Mickey and wanted to get away from him. When he had set up the contract, he didn't know that Mickey Alo had ordered the death of his own sister. He couldn't conceive of the evil that would allow for that act.

They met in the Rhode Island governor's mansion. Mickey had been told to park in the back, that a state trooper would meet him there. He was instructed to say that he was John Harrington. The trooper would ask no questions once he heard that name. Mickey would be escorted up a back elevator to the den in the governor's suite on the second floor. Haze had been assigned a Secret Service team as the Democratic nominee, but he could still shrug them off since he was being accorded that protection as a courtesy. His Secret Service contingent would be left at the airfield and his old troop of state police officers, who had covered him for two terms in the Rhode Island state house, would take care of the escort to the governor's mansion. It was all done without notifying the press and they swept into the underground garage four hours after Mickey had requested a meeting. Haze stepped out of the limo with A.J. Both men had circles under their eyes, but Haze, just back from Europe, managed to look presidential. His suit fit him perfectly. It was a deep blue with maroon tie and a perfectly folded pocket square. He shook hands with several of the troopers who had been friends over the years, and then used the "governor's lift" up to the family quarters. Once A.J. and Haze were alone in the elevator, Haze looked over at him.

"This fucking guy. . . . You know what we had to go through to pull this off?"

"Haze, don't. Mickey's a killer. Don't fuck around with Mickey."

Haze looked at A.J. coldly, but said nothing. The door opened and they stepped into the governor's quarters. They found Mickey in the den. He turned as they walked into the room.

"I don't have much time," Haze said. The little mobster reminded him of the low road that had brought him to this place of power. "I can only give you ten minutes."

"Really? Only ten?"

Haze missed the ominous sarcasm in the remark. "I have a schedule, I'm on thirty-minute intervals until Election Day. I've allotted two intervals for this meeting."

"Then let me get right to it. You remember Ryan Bolt?"

"Vaguely. He was doing that documentary that never happened."

"He and a guy named Solomon Kazorowski, an ex-fed, and Cole Harris and, of all people, my own sister are trying to prove that I put you in this game and used the United Broadcasting Company to fuel your candidacy."

"So . . . ?"

"So, if they can prove that, it's gonna go down hard. The public is gonna rise up and you ain't gonna be President, chickie."

"How do you know that's what they're trying to do?"

"Forget how I know it. Kaz is dead, but they were messing around in Israel looking for something that could hurt us. I need to find out what exactly they're looking for and what they already have. I need you to call around in the Justice Department and find out what a man named Gavriel Bach could have had that could hurt us. There's gotta be a file down there someplace. I don't know where else to start."

"We're getting our national security briefings from a guy named Gideon Black," A.J. said. "We could call him, see what he's got."

Haze made the call but couldn't keep the impatience out of his voice. He resented Mickey's hold over him. He promised himself that once he was elected, he would find a way to break it.

Gideon Black was at his desk, working late when he got the call. "The head of the Middle Eastern section is a career diplomat named Abel McNair," he said. "I can hunt him up and have him call you, sir."

"If that wouldn't be too much trouble," Haze said, knowing the man would kill himself to get the job done.

Within five minutes, the phone rang and Abel McNair was on the line with the man he was pretty sure would be the next President of the United States. After Haze told him what he wanted, Abel McNair remembered the conversation he'd had with Kazorowski. He had just heard on CNN that Kaz had been murdered in Israel. He knew "the flag was up."

"I think I can help you, sir," Abel said. "Kazorowski called me about two months ago trying to find out about a deal that was cut between the Justice Department and Gavriel Bach to keep Mr. Lansky out of Israel. Apparently, the department gave Bach some unspecified material. Wiretaps, I think, proving that Meyer had criminal connections. Kaz was looking for that material. I don't know what it could be, but I could try to find out."

"That won't be necessary. Thank you." Haze hung up and reported to A.J. and Mickey what McNair had told him.

"Wiretaps?" Mickey repeated, his heart beginning to sink. "Kaz was looking for something to tie Meyer to my father. Ryan was looking for a way to prove this election was rigged by our control of UBC. Meyer was in the plan from the beginning. He and my father hatched the plot in the early seventies. God knows how many times he and my dad might have talked about it. If the feds had any of that on tape, it could be explosive."

"Was there anything else or can I get back to the airport?" Haze said, as if he really wasn't affected by any of this.

"Yeah, there is . . . I need to force Ryan and Cole Harris underground so if they have anything dangerous, they can't use it. I need to discredit them so people won't believe them."

"How're we gonna do that?" Haze asked.

"You're the Democratic nominee for the presidency of the United States. Ryan Bolt used to work for your campaign. He was hired to do a documentary, but he was a little nuts. A.J. had to fire him. Ryan promised that he was going to get even. Tonight, he and this outta work newsman, Cole Harris, called you up here in the governor's mansion. They threatened your life. A.J. was on the extension and heard it all."

"You gotta be kidding," Haze said.

"If they threatened your life on top of being involved in that car bomb explosion in Israel, the Secret Service is gonna go ballistic. . . . It'll drive them underground."

"It's a pretty good plan," A.J. said. "With a nationwide manhunt on, whatever they got is gonna be a lot harder to unload."

By the time the Reuters jet touched down in New Jersey, their pictures were already on the ten o'clock news.

RUNNING

IF THEY HAD LANDED AT NEW YORK'S KENNEDY AIRPORT, IT would have been over, but they touched down at Levit Field in New Jersey, where the customs contingent consisted of two old men in a shed waiting out their retirement. Nobody had been into the fax room for hours to look at recent transmittals. The customs officials boarded the private jet, steaming coffee mugs in hand, looked at the passports, asked a few routine questions, and stamped everybody's reentry forms. In ten minutes, the four of them were in a taxicab, heading into Trenton.

They pulled up at a Days Inn, and while Ryan held the cab, Cole went inside to make sure there was a vacancy. The big television in the lobby was on CNN. As Cole moved to the desk and told the clerk he needed two rooms, he heard Wolf Blitzer mention his name.

". . . fired news correspondent Cole Harris."

Cole turned and saw an old UBC employee photograph of himself filling the screen. In the picture, he needed a shave and looked like an ax murderer.

The clerk was trying not to register shock that the man being called a violent terrorist on TV was standing right in front of him.

Wolf Blitzer continued: "Allegedly, Mr. Harris and an unemployed television producer named Ryan Bolt and the sister of New Jersey underworld kingpin Michael Alo are involved in a plot to assassinate presidential candidate Haze Richards."

"Son of a bitch," Cole said and ran out of the lobby to where Ryan was standing next to the cabbie, talking.

"They're full. Let's go." He all but pushed Ryan into the cab. Cole told the cabbie to get going and take them into Trenton. They pulled out of the parking lot and down the road. Ryan and Lucinda started to protest, but Cole grabbed Lucinda's arm and shook his head in silent warning. Naomi had been on enough dangerous stories to know enough to shut up and play along. A few miles farther on, they passed two New Jersey state police cars with red lights and sirens, speeding in the opposite direction.

When they finally got to the outskirts of Trenton, it was almost eleven P.M. Cole pointed to a bus stop. "Pull up here. We can take the bus to Virginia," he said for the driver's benefit.

They got out, taking their suitcases from the trunk while Ryan paid the fare.

"The bus to Virginia? What's going on?" Ryan asked after the cab pulled away.

"We're on the news . . . not Naomi, but the rest of us. They're saying we're trying to kill Haze Richards."

"We're what?" Ryan said, astounded.

"Yeah. There's an FBI manhunt or something. . . . It sounds big. The clerk back there had his mouth fall so far open, I was counting fillings. I figured I'd better get outta there."

"What'll we do?" Lucinda asked.

"That cabbie will have the cops heading to Virginia and there's a hotel back up this street. Naomi can get us a room . . . make sure it's got a TV. We gotta find out how bad this is."

The hotel was a woodsy, four-story fishing lodge on the outskirts of town called The Angler. Naomi checked herself into a suite under an assumed name, then went down the back stairs and let them in a side door.

Ten minutes later, they were watching the whole, awful story on CNN. It was much worse than they expected.

"Ryan had been very irrational for months," Marty Lanier was saying from the NBC boardroom where he was doing an interview with a glamorous CNN field correspondent. "He had become sort of . . . well, I hate to say it, but anti-Semitic. He attacked me in the screening room and security had to be called to remove him." Ryan thought he detected a slight smile under Marty's grave demeanor. The CNN correspondent turned to the camera.

"The police in Los Angeles now suspect there may be a connection between Mr. Bolt's increasingly violent behavior and the shooting death of his former secretary, Elizabeth Applegate, just three days ago. Ms. Applegate was found in the bathtub of her apartment where she'd been shot in the head with a twenty-two-caliber dumdum bullet."

Ryan dropped his head into his hands. When he looked up, his expression was a mask of agony. Then he went into the bathroom and closed the door.

As they sat in silence, the TV shot switched back to Wolf Blitzer.

"We now have a report from the U.S. Customs Service that the three fugitives arrived from Israel tonight on a private jet belonging to Reuters News Bureau. The pilots are currently being interviewed. They landed at a small airfield in New Jersey. Also aboard was Naomi Zur, a photographer for Reuters."

"Welcome to the club," Cole said grimly as Naomi's picture hit the screen.

Blitzer droned on. "This is all somehow linked to the explosion in Israel yesterday that claimed the life of ex-FBI agent Solomon Kazorowski and three unknown Israelis. Rental car records are being checked to ascertain the identities of the other parties. The three fugitives and Solomon Kazorowski had contacted the widow of the late Israeli prosecutor Gavriel Bach yesterday, lied to her, and told her that they were doing a story for *Time* magazine, and needed to gain access to some old records Bach had apparently saved. They went to Mrs. Bach's house outside of Tel Aviv, where they broke in and were later involved in a shootout with the three Israelis. Justice Department sources close to the investigation say that this appears to be part of a very serious plot to kill the Democratic nominee for President of the United States."

They channel-surfed. There were background stories on all of them, including Naomi and Lucinda.

Ryan came out of the bathroom a few minutes later, sat on the bed, and said nothing. When the stories started to repeat themselves, Cole turned off the set.

"Ain't this a bitch?" he said. "But I got an idea that could get us where we wanna go."

"This I gotta hear," Naomi said.

"I want you to hear this all the way out because I've been giving it a lot of thought. We kidnap the UBC feed. Put our story up on the satellite ourselves. Broadcast it the way we want it. We'll use C. Wallace Litman's own network to destroy his plan. We've got enough evidence and the know-how. . . . All we need is a little guts and ingenuity."

"What're you smoking?" Naomi said.

"They were going to use the network to accomplish their plan. We'll use it to destroy them. We broadcast this, then the other networks are gonna have to pick up on it. They'll force Justice to trace Litman's records.

"If we produce the right broadcast, we can bring them down. . . . It's not impossible hard to kidnap a TV signal. It's doable."

"I still think we should take it to Brokaw, Naomi said flatly.

"Nobody is going to believe us now. We're crackpots. They're going to spend all their time indicting us. Nobody is going to look at what we have."

"You don't know that," Lucinda said.

"I know it. Come on. . . . I was one of those arrogant jackals for thirty years." He spun on Ryan.

"And you gotta come to the party, Ryan. I know you just got a helluva shock, but snap out of it. I can't have you sitting there looking at your shoes."

"Go fuck yourself, Cole."

"I'm just saying we need your help."

"Elizabeth was a friend. She came to my rescue when I was hurting. Now she's dead because of me."

"I'll tell you who shot her . . . that mook in the baseball cap. This is hardball, Ryan."

Ryan moved across the room, and pulled Cole to his feet. They stood there with fistfuls of each other's shirt. "If you wanna swing at me, go ahead," Cole said.

"All you want is to get back at those guys for kicking you out," Ryan yelled. "That's all this means to you. Kaz and Elizabeth were killed because of this. This is about a hell of a lot more than your bullshit career."

"This is about the fourth estate. It's about the hijacking of high-teck communications by a bunch of grease stains. By the time any-body starts listening to us, Richards will be in the White House," Cole shouted back.

Ryan let go of him and turned to the window, still breathing hard and struggling to get control.

"Believe me, we can steal this signal. But we gotta stick together."

Ryan finally looked at Cole.

"We'll need an engineer, and I think I know just the guy to help us," Cole said, seizing on Ryan's renewed attention.

"He won't turn us in?" Lucinda asked.

"I don't think so. UBC threw him out two weeks before he was to get his pension. They claimed he stole engineering equipment from them."

"Did he?"

"Well, kinda . . . He was working at home on a new switching de-vice. They did a random trunk search one night and found all this equipment in his car. He tried to explain but they tied a can to him anyway. Guy's name is John William Baily. Everybody called him Babbling John 'cause he's the quietest son of a bitch you ever met."

"You can still get out of this, Naomi, " Ryan said. "We could say we kidnapped you."

"Thank you, Ryan. I was wondering who was going to suggest that."

"I didn't because I've worked with you. We'd have to kill you to get you off this story," Cole said.

"He's right, but thanks for the suggestion."

The moment seemed to bring them together again and Cole sat at the phone and pulled out his tiny leather pocket phone book, looked up John William Baily's number, and called him.

Baily answered on the second ring.

"I suppose you've seen the TV," Cole said after identifying himself. "Yep."

"Look, John, we're onto something big. But we need help." Nothing came back from John Baily, so Cole plunged on. "We need to put a big story out."

"How?" Baily asked.

"We need to access the Galaxy Four transponder. Take it over." There was a pause. "You know what I'm saying?"

"Yup."

"But before you meet with us I have to tell you that a lot of people are trying to catch us and it could get dangerous."

"Fuck 'em," John Baily finally said. He agreed to be on a street corner in Westchester in an hour.

Cole informed them that they needed to steal a car, but he had no idea how to do it. Lucinda said, "I do. My brother taught me."

Ten minutes later, Lucinda pulled up to the side entrance of the small hotel in a gray Ford Falcon.

Naomi and Cole drove off to meet John Baily, while Lucinda and Ryan waited at the hotel.

RF ENGINEER

JOHN BAILY STOOD ON A CORNER IN A DIMLY LIT SUBURB OUTSIDE
Manhattan. It was almost midnight when he saw a gray Ford cruise
past with a woman behind the wheel.

John remembered Cole Harris from UBC and couldn't stand him.
Cole had been demanding and brusque and treated the people in
engineering like servants. But hatred obeys the law of relativity,
and John hated the brass at UBC worse than bleeding hemorrhoids. He relished the chance to show them how vulnerable
they were. He'd told them that they didn't have adequate security at
Hertz Castle, which is what he had named the roof parking lot
adjacent to the thirty-story Black Tower. The lot, reserved for visiting executives, was loaded with rental cars all parked right in the
shadow of the huge ten-meter dish that was the network's main
East Coast link to the Galaxy Four geosynchronous satellite UBC
used to rain its signal across the United States. "The bird" was

one of the new hybrid satellites that could broadcast C-band as well as K-U band uplinks.

"John, over here," a voice whispered from the darkness, breaking his thought. He turned and saw Cole Harris standing in the shadows away from the streetlight. John walked over to the IR. He noted, with some satisfaction, that time had not been kind to Cole Harris. He had lost some hair and had the sallow, undernourished look of a racetrack lout, but he still wore the yuppie uniform. Tie and suspenders over pleated pants and lace-up wing-tip shoes.

"Great to see you," Cole said, grinning, slapping the tall, skinny engineer on the back, hoping to elicit a response. He didn't get one. The gray sedan pulled up, and Cole opened the back door to usher the engineer into the car.

"This is Naomi," Cole said, introducing the woman behind the wheel.

"Pleased to meet you," she said.

"Yep," he replied and that about covered it, all the way back to The Angler.

They arrived back at the hotel around one o'clock in the morning. Cole introduced John Baily to Ryan and Lucinda.

"John knows all about the network's technical facilities. He's the RF engineer."

"RF?" Lucinda asked.

"Radio frequency," Cole explained.

"So, how do we do it? How do we kidnap the signal?" Ryan asked.

John had one topic on which he was willing to speak in full sentences and that was the physical plant at UBC. He'd designed it, or most of it. He'd kept it running. He'd devoted his life to it. He had repaired, rebuilt, and juryrigged all of the equipment in the early days when money had been short. The switching panel he decided to make at home would have allowed the network to go from the main uplink to the backup with absolutely no phase jitter or flutter. Currently, you had to shut one system down and then turn on the other, waiting for the forty-five seconds of black that was scheduled between each hour of broadcast. That time was used by affiliate stations for local ads and station IDs.

He'd been accused of stealing and had been fired for cause. He lost his job, his pension, and his life's work. He had been unable to get a similar job elsewhere and was now a maintenance man at a junior high school.

"Thing you gotta understand is how it works," he said. He'd often described the system to visiting executives, so he had the speech prepared and could do it on autopilot. "The network owns two transponders on the Galaxy Four satellite. They broadcast on two transmitters simultaneously—one for the East Coast and mountain time zones called the ETB feed and the WTB for the western time band. The satellite is twenty-three thousand, four hundred miles out in space and the signal goes up from the big C-band dish at Hertz Castle to the bird out in space," John continued. "The power to run the transmission is hard-wired from the building and is called shore power. There's two backup five-hundred KVA generators in the basement of the Black Tower that can run the main C-band dish in case the shore power is interrupted; the ten-meter dish runs on a range of four to six gigahertz. If there's a shore-power failure, it automatically switches to one of the backup generators in the basement, which supplies the dish with lower power, something like eight or nine hundred kilowatts, but still enough to get a clean bounce-back signal from space."

"What's a gigahertz?" Ryan asked.

"One gigahertz is a thousand million cycles per second. Doesn't matter, really; all you have to know is we gotta take out the shore power and both generators to put the network off the air."

"We have to do two things," Cole explained. "First, we have to kill the signal at UBC Central, then we have to have our own taped broadcast ready to go. We need to steal an SNG remote truck. That truck has a smaller dish and it runs on a K-U band. We line it up on the satellite and, as soon as we blow the power on the main and backup generators, we transmit our pirate signal."

"In order to do it, we need to shoot our pirate signal up before we blow the main feed while they're still in that forty-five seconds of black," Babbling John said. "The trick is to make it so smooth that the hundred and eighty local affiliate stations can't see the signal waver."

"Why is that?" Naomi asked.

"Every local station watches the signal like a hawk," Cole explained. "If they suspect the network feed is being tampered with, they'll call UBC Central, and they'll find out those guys on the Rim have been knocked off the satellite. Then they'll drop the network feed and put up a 'stand-by.' . . . We'll be off the air locally all over the country." These were problems Ryan had never considered.

"The people in the control rooms are gonna see it if we don't do it smooth," John picked up. "You get an effect called double illumination. They're gonna know somebody is screwing with the signal. If we get on the bird, we're only gonna have about ten to fifteen minutes and then they're gonna find us. They can figure out where we're broadcasting from very easily and we'll have enough cops for a parade."

"Okay," Cole said. "Here's how we do it. . . . " And he laid out the rest of the plan.

As he listened, Ryan had butterflies worse than before the Notre Dame game at South Bend his junior year. That game ended in disaster. He'd dropped the ball in the end zone for the go-ahead touchdown just as the gun sounded. If he dropped the ball this time, the gun would probably be the last thing he ever heard.

"UBC has ten SNG trucks scattered around the country and several mobile control centers," John said. "The trick is gonna be to find one we can get our hands on."

"Okay. Naomi, you and I are gonna produce this special," Cole said, clapping his hands, suddenly energized.

"We need videotape editing equipment. We're gonna have to break in someplace. The show must go on."

"They've got video equipment at the school where I work," John said. "It's one a' the reasons they hired me, to help set up the video lab."

Big stories were like that. When things started to go right, they went right in bunches. Cole had already forgotten all the bad breaks that had been exploding in clusters around them.

MOON SHADOW

MADISON JUNIOR HIGH SCHOOL WAS A ONE-STORY MONUMENT
to brown stucco and bad design. The video lab was on the east side
of the campus in something called the Learning Center. When John
Baily opened the door and switched on the lights, Cole Harris knew
he was in trouble. The lone camera was a ten-year-old Trinitron on
a rolling foot stand. The recording equipment was three-quarter inch
but also very old. The area the students were using as a studio was
just a wall covered with dull green paper.

"Ain't exactly UBC Central, is it?" Cole said. John grunted. All of
the other equipment was outmoded, but John promised he could
make it work.

Cole set up a work table on the far side of the room and handed
John the half-inch cassettes of Meyer meeting with the Mafia princes.

"I need to get this onto three-quarter for editing."

John took the tape and moved to the back of the video lab. Naomi

374

sat behind the desk and turned on an old Apple computer. Ryan and Lucinda moved around the room, feeling useless.

"Want me to write the copy?" Ryan volunteered.

"I'll do it," the IR said. He always wrote his own stories. "This is gonna take an hour, maybe two."

Ryan and Lucinda walked out of the video lab and found a bench outside that overlooked the moonlit playing field. Ryan turned and looked at her for a long moment, not sure exactly how to start what he wanted to say. He had been worried about something for almost two days.

"I want you to know something," he said, his voice blowing away from him in the light wind. "I owe you my life. I can't tell you how close to the edge I was when I got on that plane in Burbank. Somehow, you got the lights back on."

"There's no charge for that."

"I know this nightmare is coming to an end . . . and somehow I know that it's going to come down to Mickey and me."

"Maybe it's just your sense of drama at work . . . the bad guy has to confront the good guy. It won't happen that way." She didn't want that to be the way it ended, because Ryan would lose. She knew nobody could beat Mickey. Nobody ever had.

"Maybe not. But I've been having strange thoughts about it. I'm going to have to stop him. He won't let it end any other way, and I don't think I can do it without killing him."

Somewhere in the darkness a hoot owl sent up a mournful orchestration.

"What are you asking me?" she finally asked.

"If that happens, can you still love me?"

Lucinda reached out and took his hand. It was very cold in the darkness. "Love isn't something you control. It doesn't turn on or off. Love is something that happens. It's there, whether you want it to be or not."

The hoot owl sang a lonely chorus.

"Ryan, two months ago, if you'd asked me that question, I would have had a different answer. Two months ago, I was living in a fantasy, even though the evidence was right in front of me. I'd been protected by my family from everything. And then all of this happened. I've had to say good-bye to that fantasy."

"I'm sorry."

"Don't be. . . . You didn't ask for this any more than I did. I won't say it hasn't been hard. Those first days after Jerry Paradise came aboard your boat, I was waking up at night wondering how my brother could have sent someone to kill me. And I can still remember the good things. . . . He could be charming and funny. . . . He made me laugh when I was little. But, Ryan, he was acting. I know now he feels nothing for me or anybody else." She looked away for a moment before continuing. "He laughed after Rex was shot. He tried to kill us." She turned to look out at the frozen, brown field. "It really hurt. But now I see that all of the things I loved about Mickey and my father were created by them to manipulate me. I know that if Mickey controls the presidency, he'll destroy everything this country stands for."

She looked at him squarely. "But most of all, I know that I love you. More than my life. Or anything in my life. If it ends badly, at least I found you."

They heard the predator's wings beating a whispery cadence. Ryan and Lucinda looked out into the darkness. At first, they couldn't see him; then the huge hoot owl passed for a second between them and the moon.

"There he is," Lucinda said in awe as he drifted by, throwing a moon shadow across the frozen field.

Mickey knew that the final confrontation to save his father's plan was going to be up to him. He had grossly underestimated Ryan. The fact that Lucinda had crossed over and was now against him fueled a strange remorse. . . . It had consumed him for days, and he had finally identified it as anger. Anger was an emotion, and Mickey had never had to deal with emotion before. It sat in his stomach and gnawed on his insides. *Revenge.* Ravenous, uncontrollable. He needed to get even.

Ever since he'd found out he was a sociopath, he had studied up on the condition. He learned that sociopaths often had IQs in the genius or near genius range. He learned that they often became great actors and could fake emotions that others felt, allowing them to manipulate and control people. Sociopaths, he learned, could lie and scheme, even kill, without paying any internal price.

In one book, titled *Aberrant Psychology*, he had stumbled across a strange chapter in which a psychiatrist wrote that past the age of forty, sociopathic behavior tends to disappear. The subject becomes normal. He or she learns to feel, much like any other human being. The doctor called his discovery a hopeful breakthrough, but the thought terrified Mickey. The idea that this gift he had come to cherish above all others might disappear haunted him. He would lose a tremendous edge. He had always been able to select targets analytically, attack them viciously, and suffer no remorse.

He sat in his father's study looking at the paintings Joseph had collected. Oils depicting Palermo Harbor and the fields around Naples. He'd called a meeting to discuss a way to find Ryan. The men waiting downstairs would kill for Mickey.

Mickey walked into his father's bathroom and looked into his own eyes. He looked at the round face, the oily hair, the pudgy fingers. He held his hands out in front of him. The sight of his own trembling fingers shot a new feeling through him. *Fuck*, he thought. Then a new emotion hit him. It made his stomach freeze. An electric charge buzzed his nerve endings. It made his sweat turn cold.

For the first time, Mickey Alo tasted fear.

Haze Richards was having the time of his life. He was at the Imperial Hotel in Vienna, meeting with world leaders at an ad hoc financial conference that A.J. had arranged.

When Haze spoke, people stopped talking. He had a limited grasp of world economics, but A.J. had given him some key facts and observations. Men who already ran their own governments fell silent and made notes while he spewed out prepackaged ideas.

Despite being a horrendous pain in the ass, A.J. had been right. He'd kept Haze on the front pages and on the covers of national magazines. Shots of the candidate with Boris Yeltsin and François Mitterrand or with the heads of OAS and NATO appeared everywhere. He was introduced to the most beautiful women in the world. He signed autographs like a movie star.

But A.J. had been less reliable of late. He was drinking heavily. He'd missed a staff meeting two days before. They'd found him passed out in the hotel bar. A.J. was going to have to go.

Haze was in the Imperial's presidential suite with its twenty-foot-high ceiling and ornate paintings. The arched windows commanded a view of the picture-book city. The floor of the main room had an inlaid wood surface and was half the size of a basketball court. Ten-foot-high portraits of various Hapsburgs hung on the walls. Napoleon, he'd been told, had slept in the huge bed in that very room when he'd been in Vienna in 1797. . . . Kennedy, Eisenhower, DeGaulle, and Churchill, as well as just about every famous ruler in three hundred years, had wandered these floors and looked out of the arched windows. And now it belonged to Haze Richards, the next President of the United States of America.

The election was two weeks away, and Haze was scheduled to return home the next morning. The staff wanted him to make a quick swing through the farm states, where they were showing a slight weakness; but everywhere else, he was way ahead. It looked like Haze was going to chair a blowout over Pudge Anderson.

He went into the bedroom, flopped down on the canopied bed, and started doing his daily regimen of fifty stomach crunches.

Two more weeks. Thirteen days. Three hundred twelve hours and Haze Richards would be the forty-third President of the United States of America. "Whatta fucking country." He grinned.

He was flat on his back, doing aerial bicycles, right in the middle of the bed where Napoleon had once slept.

TRUCKS

THE SATELLITE NEWS-GATHERING TRUCK AND MOBILE CONTROL
center were easier to find than Cole would have guessed. When Ryan
flicked on the morning news, the sportscaster announced that the
UBC NFL *Game of the Week* was tomorrow at Giant Stadium. The
truck was probably already there with the setup crew.

They found the two trucks parked on the service road just inside
of the stadium. They had switched cars and pulled a gray station
wagon into the parking lot and parked. It was just past midnight on
Sunday morning. They sat looking through the windshield at the
portable satellite news-gathering dish that sat in the back of a six-
wheel pickup and the enormous eighteen-wheel mobile control center
attached to a Peterbilt tractor.

"There she is," Babbling John said, fondly saluting an old friend.

Ryan had worked construction during summers when he'd been
playing ball and he had some experience driving heavy equipment.

The eighteen-wheel MCC truck had one extra axle but he thought he could handle it.

"Think you can hot-wire a Peterbilt?" Cole asked Lucinda.

"If the ignition wires are under the dash by the key box, I can."

Ryan had suggested that he and Lucinda should steal the trucks. If they failed and got caught, that would leave the experienced TV journalists Cole, John, and Naomi still at large to try another broadcast tactic.

They watched in silence for about twenty minutes to make sure nobody was guarding the equipment. Then Ryan got out of the station wagon. His leg had stiffened and he felt awkward as he walked around to get the tire iron out of the back. Then he and Lucinda moved across the parking lot toward the trucks.

The service gate was unlocked and they moved inside. Ryan climbed up on the running board and looked into the cab. There was an Acme sleeper behind the front seat with the curtain pulled.

Ryan stepped down and whispered to Lucinda. "I'm gonna break the glass and open it up. If there's somebody in the sleeper, I'll try and handle him. Stand back," he said. He hadn't bargained for hitting an innocent driver on the head with a tire iron. He hoped he could control the situation without violence. If there was an alarm, he'd have to turn it off fast.

Suddenly he was flooded with doubts. He thought about Kaz and, once again, wished the ex-fed was with them, growling and chewing the unlit cigar, telling them what to do. Ryan knew it was now up to him.

He swung the tire iron at the window, shattering the glass and the alarm went off, hee-hawing in the still night. The curtain behind the front seat was jerked back and Ryan found himself a foot from a startled man in jeans and T-shirt with a gray beard.

" 'The fuck?" the driver said as Ryan reached in and grabbed him by the front of the T-shirt and yanked him onto the front seat, holding the tire iron at the ready.

"Shut off the fucking alarm," Ryan demanded.

"Huh?"

Ryan slammed the tire iron viciously into the doorjamb for effect.

"Okay, okay, buddy, take it easy." The driver fumbled for the genie and shut off the braying alarm.

"Gimme the keys," Ryan commanded, and the man handed them over. "What about the other truck. . . . You got those keys?" Ryan asked. The man shook his head in fright.

Lucinda ran to the SNG truck and pulled the ignition wires loose. Then she touched them together and the engine started on the six-wheel Dodge pickup with the 4.1-meter K-U band satellite uplink in back.

Ryan helped the frightened driver out of the cab and climbed in behind the wheel. The truck was different from those he'd driven years ago, but he hoped it worked roughly the same way. When he turned the key, the big brown Peterbilt rumbled to life. The driver turned and sprinted away in the dark.

From the station wagon in the parking lot, Cole watched in amazement as the big eighteen-wheeler pulled away from the fence with the SNG truck behind it. Both vehicles started a slow, lights-out roll along the interior service driveway.

Cole followed both trucks as Ryan turned right, past the tennis courts where the U.S. Open was held every year. Finally, lights on, they pulled onto the expressway, heading toward Kennedy Airport.

Inside the Peterbilt, Ryan's heart was pounding. He looked over the shiny brown hood at the cars below. He downshifted and the big engine growled.

He realized he was smiling.

Earlier, they had spotted a truck sales lot right off the freeway two miles from Giant Stadium. A sign advertised: THE TRUCK MART CLOSED SUNDAY. They had decided to hide in plain sight, to park there with all the other used trucks. They would disguise the SNG truck with its telltale satellite and hope to get through the day and into the evening.

John and Cole decided to broadcast on Sunday night for several reasons. First, there were relief crews on duty then and they would be more confused when the signal went down than the regulars. Confusion would buy them a few extra minutes. Both Cole and John were concerned about the ATIS. Once they started broadcasting, it would give their position away, but they didn't tell the others about

it. It was a problem they hadn't solved. A second reason they chose
Sunday night was that viewership HUT levels were high and they
wanted a large audience. Third, the streets were less crowded and
chances of getting across town to UBC's Black Tower with the stolen
trucks were marginally better. Cole wanted to get on before *60
Minutes* aired on CBS, so that they would maximize viewership. They
ended up deciding to take Brenton Spencer's old *Six O'clock News*
spot on UBC, an irony no one seemed to enjoy.

They found the off ramp and pulled the truck up to the sales lot
that was decorated with a red and white fence. Cole grabbed the tire
iron from Ryan and broke the padlock, then opened the gate, and
Ryan pulled the stolen truck in between a white Kenworth and a blue
Mack. Lucinda backed the SNG truck into a protected spot behind
the office. Their hearts were pounding, their adrenaline flowing. No
sooner were the trucks' lights off than two patrol cars screamed by
on the expressway, going code three, toward Giant Stadium.

IMPORTANT MEETING

C. WALLACE LITMAN GOT THE CALL SUNDAY MORNING AT FIVE A.M. Steve Israel woke him up.

"Sorry to wake you, sir, but somebody stole an SNG truck and a mobile control center from Giant Stadium," he announced without preamble.

Wallace was still deep in sleep as the information hit him. He didn't want to wake Sally, so he put Israel on hold, then moved into his den and retrieved the blinking line.

"Okay, somebody stole the trucks," he said brusquely. "Go on."

"The driver gave descriptions of the man and woman to the police. I got the small control room and a K-U dish coming down from Chicago and I'm making arrangements to borrow one of CNN's trucks, so we're okay for the Jets game this afternoon."

C. Wallace Litman nodded. It didn't seem like something that should have pulled him out of bed at five A.M. The equipment was insured. It would be pretty hard for anybody to get very far with them. An eighteen-wheel remote truck with UBC in five-foot-high letters on the side, and a four-meter satellite dish in a pickup were going to be damn hard to hide.

"I don't suppose this could have waited, Steven?"

"I just thought you'd want to know."

"And now I do," C. Wallace Litman said and hung up abruptly. He wondered briefly why somebody would steal a satellite uplink and a mobile control center. He got into bed and within minutes was asleep.

Another phone call woke him at seven-forty-five. He fumbled the phone off the cradle as he glanced at the clock. "What the hell is it now?" he growled into the phone.

"You know who this is?" Mickey said sharply.

Litman scrambled up into a sitting position, struggling to get his bearings.

"There's a car waiting for you in front of your building. Be in it in the next five minutes."

"I have plans for the day."

"Cancel 'em." And the line went dead.

C. Wallace Litman got out of bed as Sally sat up and looked at him with concern.

"Business," he said, and moved into the bathroom to take a quick shower.

Ten minutes later, he stepped out into the cold, fog-covered New York morning and walked a few yards to a black Lincoln Town Car with the engine running. Inside he found a swarthy man with too much hair wearing a shiny green suit of horrible design. He was sitting behind the wheel smoking a cigarette. C. Wallace Litman had never seen him before.

"You waiting for me?" he asked, silently cursing Mickey. Litman wasn't used to being dragged out of bed or operating on another man's timetable.

"I'm'a here, pick'a Mist'a Litman up," Pulacarpo Depaulo said.

C. Wallace Litman got into the backseat and closed the door. "You mind not smoking?" Wallace said, and Pulacarpo flipped the butt out the window and put the Lincoln Town Car in gear.

*   *   *

The meeting was held in a deserted barn at a farm outside of Trenton. It took them an hour to get there.

When they pulled up, Wallace could see four men standing in a semicircle, their breath hanging in a mist above their heads. They approached the car and escorted him to the barn. Once he was inside and his eyes had adjusted to the light, he saw Mickey Alo sitting on a stool in front of a workbench reading computer printouts from a folder. He stood as Litman moved toward him, but didn't cross to meet him. He held his ground and forced the financier to come to him. It was a test of power. It was important to know who was fucking whom. They had spoken on the phone many times and seen each other's pictures on the news or in the paper, but, for reasons of security, they had not met since Mickey was a boy.

"We got a problem," Mickey said.

"How's that?"

"Last night, your guys lost a remote truck and a satellite dish. It's already been on your seven A.M. Sunday news."

"I know. I was told at five this morning."

"I think it was stolen by Ryan Bolt, Cole Harris, my sister, and that photojournalist from Reuters."

"I hardly think that they could . . ." But then Wallace stopped because Mickey's expression hovered between exasperation and contempt. His pig eyes were hard and C. Wallace felt some sort of heat coming from him. He changed course, softening his tone. "I assume you have reasons."

"What I have is an educated guess, which could be wrong, but if it's not, then we're all in a fuck of a lot of trouble."

"Let's hear."

Mickey filled C. Wallace Litman in on the whole story: the suitcase full of Justice Department wiretaps given to Gavriel Bach; the trip to Israel; the break-in at Bach's house; the explosion that killed Kazorowski and the three assassins; and his assumption that they would try to broadcast the story on UBC. When he was finished, the two men stood in silence. A slight wind hit the empty barn, rattling the door and sprinkling hay dust from the loft above.

"You ever talk to my dad about buying the network in the seventies?"

"Once or twice a year. But we were careful about using pay phones. You think they stole the K-U dish and the mobile control center so they could broadcast our old conversations?"

"I think it's possible. If I'm wrong, we've wasted a few hours. If I'm right, we have to stop them."

Mickey's eyes left no room for argument. If, as they said, eyes were the windows to the soul, then C. Wallace Litman had just seen all he needed of Mickey's twisted psyche.

"Are you asking me how to stop them?"

"What the fuck do you think, Wally?"

"I . . . I'll have to ask engineering. If they try and kidnap our signal using that uplink, I think we can triangulate them. Mind you, I'm not an engineer. I don't really understand how they do it, but I'll find out."

"I want you to monitor this personally."

"How do you know they're still in New York?"

"It's a guess."

"A guess?"

"I often get lucky with my guesses. I have ungodly senses and demons who direct me," Mickey said, sounding way too creepy for C. Wallace Litman.

"I see."

"Good. Call me on the scrambled line when you know the answer," he said.

The two men stood facing each other.

"That's it. That was everything I brought you to hear." Mickey dismissed the fifth richest man in the world as if he had just delivered a pizza.

C. Wallace Litman could feel Mickey's eyes still on him as he walked the short distance to the door. It was as if some invisible force had reached out and touched him between the shoulder blades. He quickened his step and was almost jogging when he went through the barn door.

Wallace went directly to the news director's office in the Black Tower, on the Rim. He got hold of Red Decker, the chief engineer who had taken over from John Baily, and laid out the problem.

"Actually, it's gonna be pretty easy. Every uplink has an ATIS," Decker said.

C. Wallace shot an annoyed look at his chief of engineering, who quickly explained that ATIS stands for automatic transmission identification signal. "It goes up to the satellite and indicates that the signal is coming from a particular ground system. We know the ATIS number on the stolen unit and it can't be changed. The satellite also registers the GPS, which is the global positioning system on the dish. The GPS has to be activated to position the uplink and lock on the satellite. We can determine the location of the SNG truck with a handheld GPS receiver. It will give us the location of the dish they're using within a few yards."

"Good. Get it ready before nightfall."

Decker left wondering what the hell had gotten into Wallace Litman—to have the owner of UBC personally direct a recovery operation on a stolen satellite dish seemed unusual. He didn't know that the presidency of the United States was hanging in the balance.

Wallace called Mickey back on the scrambled line at three-thirty that afternoon. He had everything set up and had some additional information.

Mickey picked up the phone on the second ring. "Yeah?"

"It's me," Wallace said, preferring not to mention his name, whether the line was scrambled or not.

"Let's hear."

"We're set to pick up the signal. If they try and hit the satellite and if they're in New York City proper, we'll get a printout on the location to within a few feet. Also, engineering says they would be able to tell if a pirate signal tried to hit our transponder on the bird in space. They can see it in the control room. It's like the image wavers; they call it double illumination. They can notify stations to drop the feed. It would take us off the air, but it takes about four minutes to do it."

Mickey had considered ordering UBC to go dark but had eliminated the idea. It would be a big national news story and he didn't want that. . . . Also, he couldn't keep them from hitting another network's satellite. He felt pretty sure that Ryan and Colt would pick UBC for poetic revenge. People were like that. . . . They made decisions based on emotion.

"Tell them to be ready. That material can't get on the air," Mickey said.

Wallace sat in the news director's office on the twenty-third floor looking out at the activity on the Rim. Joseph Alo didn't frighten Wallace. But his son, this little fat boy Mickey, he scared C. Wallace Litman more than impotence or death.

The New York City police and the FBI had thrown up a perimeter on all of the roads leading out of the city immediately after the police got Ryan's description from the truck driver. They figured Ryan and the others were the terrorists who were trying to assassinate Haze Richards. Why they had stolen the satellite dish, they couldn't fathom, but the federal government had told the NYPD to spare no expense. The new standing order was to shoot the fugitives on sight.

Sunday morning they camped in the mobile control center in the back of the eighteen-wheeler. They listened to the Sunday traffic on the turnpike a hundred yards away and tried to get some sleep.

At two in the afternoon, they huddled around the small desk in the mobile control center under dim red submarine lights while Babbling John Baily drew the floor plan of the basement of the Black Tower at UBC. He showed Ryan and Lucinda where the two backup generators were located. Then he drew the roof of Hertz Castle and began filling in the position of the satellite dish and the staircase. John labeled everything precisely in large print. He explained that the eighteen-wheel Peterbilt and its forty-foot box were too tall to fit into the parking structure. They'd have to park the mobile control center on the street below. The SNG trucks had been designed to fit in the parking garage and had once been kept on the roof there. Cole and John decided that if they parked the dish on the corner of the roof and the big truck on the street, they would have enough coaxial cable to hook the two units together if they strung a line down the fire stairs four stories to the street below.

Naomi took pictures of them grinning like Bonnie and Clyde Barrow before a Kansas bank job.

At five, they synchronized their watches. Ryan climbed into the eighteen-wheeler and Lucinda got in the seat beside him. They pulled the forty-foot box out of the Truck Mart. Babbling John Baily rode in the back with the control center equipment. The SNG truck with Cole and Naomi followed.

They had decided to stay on secondary streets to avoid being seen by the New York highway police. The huge truck rumbled through residential neighborhoods in Queens. The streets were strangely quiet as families gathered together for Sunday dinner.

As the sun set, New York City was washed in a red glow that clung to the underbelly of the threatening iron-gray clouds. They moved with the traffic along FDR Drive toward the financial district. A mile away, they saw the Black Tower of UBC rising thirty stories into the night sky. It seemed to Ryan to be beckoning them in black-glassed silence.

Or was it just giving him the finger?

THE ASSAULT ON HERTZ CASTLE

RYAN PULLED THE EIGHTEEN-WHEELER TO THE CURB ON JOHN Street. The two-block-long street was perpendicular to Broadway and the lighted entrance of UBC was around the corner and half a block up. Ryan shut down the engine and got out of the cab, then knocked on the side of the truck.

Babbling John threw open the door and glared out at him. "You hadda hit every damn divot and pothole in the city? This is high-tech, delicate shit back here."

"I'm gonna go help Cole and Naomi. We'll come down and open the fire door."

"Don't forget this," John said as he handed Ryan a canvas bag full of tools he'd collected from the control center tool supply.

Ryan moved to the front of the parking garage, where Cole was out of the SNG truck, examining the bar arm that required a parking key card to raise. He and Ryan selected two wrenches from the canvas bag and began to unscrew the bolts on the arm.

Naomi was behind the wheel of the SNG truck and had pulled it up in front of the gate to help disguise what they were doing. Finally, the last bolt came off and they pulled the metal arm out of the bracket. Naomi pulled the truck into the parking structure while Cole and Ryan reattached the arm. Three minutes later they were standing on ground zero at Hertz Castle. A half-moon threw a shaft of light through the clouds on the empty parking stalls. The forty-foot UBC satellite dish pointed its "flow gun" into space, looking like a huge, discarded umbrella.

Ryan and Cole looked up through a hole in the clouds at the stars. Somewhere, twenty-four thousand miles out there, a five-foot transponder was speeding through space at several thousand miles an hour in a geosynchronous dance with the earth.

If all went well, they would hit it in less than thirty minutes. . . . An electronic shot heard around the world.

They had parked the satellite truck in a spot where it could be lined up in the same trajectory as the main uplink. The smaller dish was dwarfed by the ten-meter uplink.

They went to work in silence. Cole unhooked the one-inch coaxial cable that was wound like a fire hose on a wheel on the back of the SNG truck. Cole opened the fire door on the roof, and, while Naomi made sure that the line didn't kink, Ryan grabbed the heavy two-inch plug and moved into the concrete-enclosed staircase. The metal stairs rang as he moved down, pulling the heavy cable after him. He was down two flights when his leg began to feel wobbly under him. He stopped for a minute to rest. The wounded leg seemed almost healed but sometimes the muscles didn't work right. It weakened at unpredictable times.

"What's wrong?" Cole whispered down at him.

"My leg. I'll be okay," he whispered back. He started down again, moving slower this time until he got to the fire door at ground level. "You better take a look at this," he called up to Cole, who came pounding down the red metal staircase to where Ryan was standing.

"Some kinda alarm on the door." They looked at the pewter fire handle that opened the door.

"Shit," Cole said. The control truck was ten feet away on the other side of the door, but they couldn't get to it without setting off the alarm. Cole looked at his watch; it was seventeen minutes to six. Ryan still had to get to the basement in the building half a block to the east. He had to get the exterior service door open, disable the shore power, and destroy the two back up generators—all in less than a quarter hour. They didn't have time to screw around with a fire door.

"We gotta risk it," and, without waiting, Cole pushed it open. Immediately a bell started ringing somewhere in the parking complex.

"Kaz, you're a shitty guardian angel," Cole said, ignoring the alarm, as he handed the cable to Babbling John, who hooked it into the side of the truck. John and Cole moved into the darkened control room, leaving Ryan outside.

Inside the big truck's control room, John started to heat up the equipment. Cole sat in the director's chair while Babbling John looked at the monitors as, one by one, they lit up.

"Okay, let's see if we can get a downlink," John said.

He turned on the global positioning systems, which told him on a computer readout exactly where they were on earth, printing out the latitude and longitude. It also told him in what direction the dish on the roof was pointing and the axis of the trailer that it sat on. All of this information was stored in the computer. Then John punched in the Galaxy Four access code and the GPS interfaced with the satellite in space. The portable dish four floors above began to rotate, slowly changing its position, aiming its "flow feed" antenna at the satellite.

On the roof, Naomi jumped as the little dish began to move beside her. She photographed it with her Nikon motor-drive while it first elevated then rotated to the east, looking for the UBC transponder on the Galaxy Four satellite. She could hear the alarm bell still ringing far below, but she tried not to let it bother her. Naomi Zur had been trained in covert operations. She knew nothing ever went the way it was planned. Half of being good at fieldwork was being able to improvise.

In the control room, John Baily was waiting for the dish on the roof to access the satellite. He was looking for the UBC signal so he could pull it in on a downlink—none of which could be traced. The ATIS only registered when they transmitted. Once he had the network feed, he would make minor manual adjustments to get rid of electronic noise. Once he'd cleaned up the signal, he would have the same images on his five monitors in the truck that the Sunday crew in the Rim control room had on their monitors. Then he and Cole heard the three electronic beeps that told them that the GPS had found the transponder on Galaxy Four. A few seconds later, the typed words they were both waiting for appeared on the main line monitor:

"Satellite Acquired," it said in white block letters at the bottom of the screen. In seconds, they were watching the *Game of the Week* postgame show from the Jets locker room. Ahmad Rashad was interviewing a defensive back named Calvin Hobbs:

"We was just getting good reads and tryin' to keep interior containment. . . . It was a team effort," Hobbs said, grinning on all five monitors.

Ryan and Lucinda had fifteen minutes to get the rest of the job done. They had gone over the plans earlier that afternoon with John and Cole.

Babbling John had been hunched over his schematic drawings in the dimly lit control room at the Truck Mart. He showed them where the exterior door at UBC would be located. It would be locked. "But," he said, "I still got the key. Assholes forgot t' take it from me."

He had pulled his heavy ring out off his belt. *Why,* Ryan wondered silently, *did X-over-Y geeks always carry fifty keys on giant key rings attached to their belts? One of life's mysteries.*

John removed a key and handed it to Ryan. "I can't guarantee they didn't change the locks on this door, but knowing them guys, my guess is no." Ryan put the key in his pocket. "They got two big exhaust ports coming out about ten feet over the door that leads down there. Those ports are for the two generators in the lower basement. When the shore power is pulled, the generators kick on automatically. They're both air-start, five hundred KVAs. They get turned on by a blast of air instead of a starter motor. Between the time the shore power is out and the building goes dark, these things will be up and running in less than six seconds, turning the power back on throughout the building. You gotta take the gennies out first, then go for the shore power. Do it the other way and you're gonna give 'em time to phone out. All the phones in there are on computers. You blow the power and those assholes're gonna have t' shout out the windows to get help."

Nothing in Ryan's experience prepared him for what he was about to do. He and Lucinda moved around the side of the building, finding a small alley that separated UBC from the Federal Bank building next door. The space between the two huge high-rises was the size of a lane just wide enough to allow service trucks to pull up to the doors. He looked up as he felt the first drops of icy rain hit his neck.

"It's raining," he said to Lucinda.

"Probably isn't gonna change much."

He marveled at Lucinda and her courage. She was right there beside him. If nothing in Ryan's existence had prepared him for this, he wondered what it must be like for her.

They found the door John had told them about. Ryan took out the key and stuck it into the lock. It slid in smoothly and turned. Ryan opened the door and, just that easily, he and Lucinda stepped onto the ground-floor service entrance of UBC.

The stairwell was well lit, the poured concrete walls shiny and smooth, reflecting the banks of humming overhead fluorescent lights. They moved slowly down the wide medal staircase. Ryan felt his leg tightening but he pushed on. John had said that the power room was in the lower basement. They would have to go down a long, lighted corridor, and the double doors at the end of the hall should open with the same key that had let them in from the alley. They could hear constant humming from ten servo-mechanisms, as air conditioners and elevator motors turned on and off, whining to life and then thumping off with pneumatic precision.

At the bottom of the stairs, Ryan opened the duffel bag. Inside were two blankets and two big battery-powered flashlights and tools to disconnect the main power handles. Ryan checked both flashlights and then, holding one, they moved down the long corridor to the service doors. Ryan slid the key in this lock, and again, it worked.

The power room occupied almost a quarter of the basement. The west wall was dominated by six huge circuit-breakers, all with large levers with red rubber handles. The two enormous 500-KVA backup generators sat side by side in the center of the room, screened off by a low interior wall so that nothing could fall accidentally into the machinery. Ryan saw that the ceiling was almost thirty feet above them. The basement in this portion of the building was two stories high. For some strange reason, Lucinda laughed. He cocked his head in a silent question.

"Nerves. Either that, or I'm slipping over the edge."

He took her hand and squeezed it.

"Let's get these handles loosened." He handed her two pairs of square-bit, rubber-handled pliers and took two pairs for himself. Then he moved to the first lever, and clamping the teeth of the pliers to each side of the bolt that held the handle, he started to unhook it. The idea was to get all six of the power levers loosened so that they could throw them and shut off the power. Seeing by the flashlights, they would then unscrew the bolts with their fingers, remove the handles, and take them with them when they left, making it impossible for UBC security to turn the power back on.

It was here that they encountered their first major problem. . . . All of the bolts had been spot-welded into place.

COUNTER MOVES

RED DECKER WAS IN HIS CHIEF ENGINEER'S OFFICE AT UBC WHEN Wallace Litman called and told him to go directly to an office in midtown Manhattan. He had packed one of the little Sony GPS hand units and a large electronic satellite map of New York that gave latitude and longitude accurate to feet and inches. It filled a small suitcase. The map had been developed by Lojack, a car alarm system that gave precise electronic locations of stolen cars through a radio signal. It would also work for the portable GPS.

Red found the office in a turn-of-the-century building decorated by ornate columns and pigeon shit. The office he was looking for was on the third floor and the fogged-glass door said DIMARCO AND SON, FREIGHT FORWARDING. He had been told to be there at five P.M. and was right on time. He tried the door and found that it was unlocked, so he moved slowly into the little room.

"Is'a okay, I'm'a wait for you. . . . "

Red spun around and saw Pulacarpo Depaulo leaning back in a swivel chair, a Sony Walkman on his curly, black head. Pulacarpo flashed a broad, white smile across iridescent green lapels.

"You from'a TV?"

"Yeah. From UBC. I'm here to help find the stolen equipment," Red said, demonstrating his total lack of understanding of the real mission.

Pulacarpo pulled the headphones down around his neck and got up. "Everybody, they next door. . . . " Red Decker followed him down the hall to the rickety lift, which groaned like an old whore as it rattled and lunged down four flights to the underground garage.

A blue van pulled up and Red was ushered into its plush gray interior. Once inside, he found himself looking into the four faces that C. Wallace Litman had confronted that morning. Two of them sat on jump seats. The other two made room for Red on the back seat. They were all dark-skinned men, with hooded eyes and five o'clock shadows.

" 'At'sa my cousins." Pulacarpo waved a green-suited arm at his four *cugini*.

"Nice to meet you," Decker said.

They didn't respond.

"They no speak'a no English just now. 'At'sa my pretty good, in'a school, I'm'a think," Pulacarpo explained, getting the idea across badly.

They pulled out of the underground garage into the cold, New York twilight. The sun was just going down as they headed across town.

Everybody wasn't next door as Pulacarpo had said.

The blue van went east four blocks. It pulled up in front of sixty stories of poured concrete and mirrored glass. The marquee said LIN-COLN PLAZA. The building was half owned by the Alo family. Joseph Alo had always liked to put American names on his real estate prop-erties—Lincoln Plaza, Hancock Square—but everybody in New York called it the Pasta Palace because the building housed crooked unions and mob front businesses.

Red was accompanied by Pulacarpo and his cousins into the ele-vator and taken to the top floor with such speed that his ears popped. He was led out toward a staircase and eventually found himself on the roof, which was covered with AstroTurf.

The center of the roof was dominated by a heliport and a gray and red Bell Jet Ranger. Six men were standing in the misty rain on the raised heli-platform, but Red's gaze was drawn to a short, round-faced man with oily hair who stepped forward.

"You got the doohickey?" Mickey Alo said, not introducing himself.

"Right here." And Red pulled the small Sony GPS receiver out of his pocket and opened the suitcase with the electronic map.

"That's it?" Mickey said, surprised at the size of the thing.

"Yes, sir." Red had a funny feeling about this little round man. Something told him to be respectful.

"Fucking-A. I thought it was gonna be like some kinda big deal."

"No, sir, it's very miniaturized."

"What's your name?"

"Russ Decker."

"Decker? Like the chain saw company?"

"People call me Red."

"Okay, set up where you want. This okay, up here?"

"It's great. Good place, no interference. I should be able to receive if they send." Then Red noticed several automatic weapons lying on the seat in the back of the Jet Ranger. Some survival instinct told him he should just keep his mouth shut, get the job done, and go home.

"Hey, Chain Saw," Mickey said, "You want a special?"

"No, sir."

"Nickadoma, give him a meatball special."

A tall man with broad shoulders handed Red the chunky sandwich.

"Thank you," Red said, taking it even though he didn't want it. He tuned in the GPS, and wondered what C. Wallace Litman could possibly have in common with this bunch of thugs.

They found a sledgehammer in a tool cabinet under a workbench. Ryan hefted it. It had a ten-pound head.

"What're you gonna do?" Lucinda asked.

"I don't know, but we gotta stay on schedule. We disable the generators, then we'll turn off the shore power and try to break these handles."

They both knew that if security guards came down and the handles were still attached, the guards could simply shove them back into place and knock Cole's broadcast off the air. The UBC ten meter C-band dish on the roof next to their SNG truck was more powerful and could cut right through their transmission. They had to break the handles somehow. Lucinda spotted two carbon dioxide fire extinguishers hanging in brackets near the door.

"Maybe if we cool them down first, it will make the metal more brittle," she said.

"Worth a try."

Ryan looked at the closest generator, the air starter perched on top of the unit like a giant prehistoric insect. The starter would drive a heavy blast of air down into the motor and turn it on. By blocking the intake, John had said, they could stop the process.

Ryan climbed up on the generator and looked at the intake. It was about two feet by one. "Gimme a blanket," he said to Lucinda. Ryan took it and jammed it down into the air intake.

"Get the fire extinguisher." He looked at his watch; they were almost out of time. The network would be in the forty-five seconds of black in under two minutes. "We gotta throw the switches," he said, as he climbed atop the second generator, and stuffed another blanket into the intake.

He climbed down as Lucinda set the flashlights up, turning them on and pointing them at the circuit breakers in the brightly lit room.

"Thirty seconds," he said, his voice tight with tension. "Start cooling down the handles."

Lucinda began to spray the ice-cold carbon dioxide gas from the fire extinguisher onto the handles of the circuit breakers. Ice crystals began to form.

On the Rim, Steve Israel came out of his office to supervise the changeover from the NFL remote broadcast of the *Game of the Week* to their regular network programming, *The Nightly News* with Dale Hellinger.

Dale was behind the anchor desk, slipping his ear angel in as they were getting set to go into the forty-five seconds of black. The camera operators adjusted their shots.

Rick Rouchard settled into his director's chair in the control room and pushed the "God button" that let his voice boom out over the set. "Okay, Dale, we're in black in fifteen seconds. Coming out of black in a minute. Everybody stand by, we're fifty-nine, forty-nine to straight-up."

They all watched the clock in the control room tick down.

"We're in black," the director said. "Coming out of black in forty-five seconds . . . " And then the entire room, including all of the monitors and cameras, went dark. "What the fuck?" the director said as Steve Israel grabbed for the computer phone—the only thing on the Rim still working.

"Gimme Engineering," he shouted into the phone.

The operator was sitting in the dark on the third floor of the Tower. "Do you know what extension Engineering is, sir? I don't have any light down here."

"Jesus H. Christ, gimme a break," the VP of *The Nightly News* screamed to a much higher authority.

The phones went dead as Ryan threw the fourth circuit breaker in the basement.

Then Steve Israel uttered the worst phrase imaginable in a network control room:

"We've lost the signal. We're off the air," he said.

In the basement, when Ryan and Lucinda threw the last power circuit, they could hear the airflow starters struggling to get the backup generators going. Both generators turned on for one rotation, then fell silent as the blankets were sucked deep into the intakes.

The basement was dark except for the battery flashlights that threw their beams on the wall. Ryan continued to bang away at the ice-cold power lever handles. Lucinda had been right, the cold had hardened the viscosity of the metal and the first handle snapped off with the third or fourth blow from the sledgehammer. It flew across the room and clattered against the far wall.

Ryan closed his eyes to increase the effort as he swung the heavy sledgehammer, occasionally missing his target in the dim light. Lucinda stood to his right, aiming the nozzle of the fire extinguisher at the base of the steel levers while he swung.

"What's going on down here?" a man's voice called.

They turned around but couldn't see him. "Engineering," Ryan said. "Trying to get these damn levers back on."

"Stay where you are. I'm Security. Drop that."

Ryan and Lucinda were dimly lit by the flashlights and they couldn't see the security man standing in the blackened doorway. "I got a gun. Drop it."

Ryan wasn't about to stop. The guard could reverse everything by just putting the remaining three circuit breakers back up. They'd gone too far. He wasn't convinced the man had a gun, or would use it, so he kept swinging the sledgehammer. The second handle broke off, snapping halfway up the arm, and flew across the room. When the Security man fired, the noise was deafening in the enclosed concrete space. The bullet hit near Ryan's head, chipping out a piece of the wall and blowing concrete dust into his eyes. For a moment, he couldn't see. Then Lucinda turned the nozzle of the fire extinguisher toward the sound of the gunshot and filled the doorway with cold, white carbon dioxide gas.

In the truck, Cole was waiting. The network was off the air, but the local stations didn't know it because they still had ten more seconds of local airtime before the network was scheduled to take the signal back and come out of black. John had already done a cross-check on the polarity to guarantee they were solidly on both the East and West coast transponder.

"Okay," John said. "Uplink . . . in ten we're coming out of black."

Cole started the tape and John hit the Transmit button, shooting the signal up onto the bird. "We're on in five . . . four . . . three . . . two . . . one . . ." he said, as the network news break bulletin music led the tape. John had found the *Special Report* music in the sound caddy in the truck. John opened the "announcer's pot," and Cole leaned in toward the mike:

"This is a UBC Special Report," he said sternly.

The tape they had made at Madison Junior High came onto the screen, but without the Special Report bulletin card which would normally precede a break-in. Then Cole's image filled the screen.

"This is Cole Harris with a late-breaking story," he said into the camera with professional reporter ease. He was sitting at the desk in the small video lab in his tie and paisley suspenders. They had pulled a school bookcase in behind him to create an office set. To both Cole and John, it looked cheesy, but they hoped it would get past the local station directors. John knew that they would become suspicious shortly, so he was going to send them a "network alert." Normally, when a special bulletin hit the airwaves, it was preceded by a network alert, warning the local stations it was coming. For obvious reasons, they had not been able to do that, but in emergencies, the network alert could come a few minutes into the news break. John could type the special-frequency message onto the transmission and it would appear at the bottom of the screen so that only the local program director and his staff could see it. He decided to send it a minute or two into the broadcast, just as the news directors were becoming concerned and reaching for their phones. It would be part of a familiar pattern and should calm them. Meanwhile, Cole was doing his preamble on the line monitor. The story was raining out from Galaxy Four all across the United States:

"Governments are fragile," Cole started, importantly. "They exist by virtue of the whims and passions of their populations. Power is, indeed, a heady perfume, so it is not surprising that in this decade, we have seen governments fall to political insurrection and intrigue."

Naomi had pushed the small Trinitron camera in the Madison Junior High School video lab in slowly, tightening the shot to give Cole's words more impact.

"Normally, these coups d'état take place in third world countries. So it is doubly surprising when one is attempted here, at home in the United States of America." He stood and walked around and sat on the corner of the desk. "We will show proof that the Democratic nominee Haze Richards entered into a contract with Mafia kingpin Michael Alo in New Jersey. The goal of the alliance between these men was to put Haze Richards into the White House. Before this broadcast is complete, we will show you tapes and film connecting these two men with the late underworld financial boss Meyer Lansky. More importantly, we will prove that the New Jersey Alo crime family, working through Meyer Lansky, financed C. Wallace Litman's purchase and control of the United Broadcasting Company. These men used this powerful electronic communications network to influence, control, and script the events of the primary campaign. . . . To influence public opinion for the purpose of hijacking next week's national election for the presidency of the United States."

John started to type his "network alert" into the transmission.

"Attention Stations . . . This Special Report will conclude at 6:14." He signed it: "Air Control, New York."

On the roof of the Lincoln Plaza, the printout flashed on Red Decker's GPS Sony hand unit. He scribbled the latitude and longitude on a piece of paper.

"Get the helicopter going," Mickey yelled.

The pilot, who was already in the Bell Jet Ranger, started to turn the blades.

Red Decker looked at the map in front of him and found the latitude and longitude: 40°47'1" north, 73°48'8" west. He tracked his fingers on the map until he found the exact location. "Gotta be a mistake," Red said.

"Why? What's wrong?" Mickey yelled over the noise of the helicopter.

"This is our own dish. It's right here." He pointed on the map to the block where the UBC parking structure was located. "That's where we have our main C-band uplink. This is our own signal."

Mickey looked at him, trying to understand. "Whatta you talking about?"

"That's our uplink," Red said, trying to get Mickey to understand.

Babbling John Baily had hoped to create confusion by broadcasting right next to the UBC ten-meter C-band dish. He hoped it would buy valuable time. It did. It bought fifty-three seconds.

Red Decker moved away from the helicopter and reactivated his GPS unit, waited for it to get the bounce-back ATIS signal, then shook his head. "This is nuts," he said as he got the same reading.

"What!" Mickey was losing patience.

"Our big dish is a C-band and this GPS receiver is only for K-U band transmission, so it can't be our signal. . . . But it's coming from the same place. How can that be?"

"They're on the fucking roof with that stolen dish, asshole!" Mickey turned and ran to the helicopter and jumped in.

Red watched as some of the men in the helicopter grabbed up automatic weapons and began pulling the slides, chambering rounds. He saw the chopper take off and lean to starboard. Then the rotor changed pitch as they streaked off toward UBC and the final confrontation.

TRUMP

C. WALLACE LITMAN AND HIS WIFE SALLY HAD INVITED KAREN and Max Jergenson over for a game of bridge. Litman always kept the UBC broadcast on low in the living room. He had one eye on the TV as he looked at his hand. Diamonds were trump. C. Wallace pondered his opening lead. Then he saw a picture of Joseph Alo on the TV. He reached for the remote control and turned up the volume. Sally and the Jergensons swung around to look at the screen.

Cole's voice still carried the narrative: ". . . financing that set up the broadcasting empire of C. Wallace Litman came from Meyer Lansky's offshore Bahamian company Mary Carver Paints. This painting supply company, which had been acquired in the sixties, was a corporate shell funneling offshore cash payments from Meyer Lansky to C. Wallace Litman. These cash transfers occurred all throughout the seventies and into the eighties. It was these underworld funds that enabled C. Wallace Litman to purchase his broadcasting empire."

"What . . . ?" C. Wallace Litman got unsteadily to his feet, torn between turning off the set so the Jergensons wouldn't be able to see it, and keeping it on to hear what was being said about him. Then he heard his own tape-recorded voice talking to Meyer Lansky.

"Good to talk to you, Meyer."

Meyer's brittle voice answered.

"Did you get the package, Wally?"

Pictures of Meyer and C. Wallace Litman from old magazines that Naomi Zur had collected from the wire service were side by side on the screen.

"Sure did, but we're gonna hold it in the paint company offshore until we need it."

"That's you, Wallace," Sally said, a look of pure confusion on her face.

"Okay, good," Meyer continued. "I think you should level off on the newspaper and radio. We got four chairs but I'm much more interested in television."

"I agree, Meyer. I got my eye on United Broadcasting. They're a group of independent stations, but I think they can be bought for the right price. We can leverage the buy. And I'd recommend that because I think we're gonna need a lot more cash downriver to acquire additional stations and fund programming."

C. Wallace Litman was frozen, unable to turn off the TV or stop this searing indictment. The Jergensons laid down their cards and looked first at Wallace then at each other, as the conspiracy between their host, Meyer Lansky, and the Mafia came into sharper focus.

"How's Teddy?" Litman said on the tape, referring to Meyer's wife.

"She's fine. And Mrs. Litman . . . ?"

"She's fine. You two are gonna have to meet sometime."

"We can't meet. Joseph wants you in the clear. If he puts a man in the White House, you're the one who's gonna do it. You and that TV network. Once we own the Man, we're gonna put all these fucks in the Justice Department out of business."

The Special Report ended with film footage from FBI hidden cameras, first of Joseph Alo and Meyer Lansky, then one shot of Joseph

Alo with Litman in the Vegas elevator of the Frontier Hotel twenty years ago. Litman still had hair, but the billionaire was plainly recognizable.

Cole wound up the broadcast as the camera came back to the Madison Junior High video lab. He was still sitting on the edge of the desk:

"It is not hard to understand why an organized crime family in this country would attempt to buy a President. In Italy, in 1993, government corruption from the Mafia went all the way to the prime minister. It destroyed the institutions of that government. As Haze Richards stands on the threshold of the White House, you can bet that he has made a pledge of obedience to the men who financed him and controlled his candidacy, men who created his image and popularity through the subtle use and manipulation of network broadcasting." The camera moved in closer.

"This report was prepared by four people, including myself, who are currently being sought by the FBI. We have been accused of planning the assassination of Haze Richards, a charge that was made to discredit us and this report. All of the material we have gathered is available now to the press and law enforcement agencies. Voice prints will validate the accuracy of the audiotapes. The film speaks for itself."

"Naomi Zur, Lucinda Alo, Ryan Bolt, and I will offer ourselves up for arrest. A brave man, retired FBI agent Solomon Kazorowski, gave his life for this story and for his country."

The camera was now in an extreme close-up as Cole concluded: "I have devoted my life to the concept of a free and open press. In a democracy, the press is the watchdog for the evils men commit, but what happens when the press has been captured? What happens if our greatest freedom is sold to society's villains? What if free speech is constrained by media conspiracies? If the pen is to remain mightier than the sword, then it must be defended passionately. . . . Defended by . . ."

And the broadcast was interrupted. The screen turned to snow.

The helicopter hovered low over the parking garage as two of the Italian "cousins" leaned out of the bay and riddled the SNG truck with .223-caliber copper-jacketed devastators. They shot off the "feed flow" and took the pirate transmission off the air. Naomi Zur ran out from behind the truck, her eye glued to her Nikon. She strobed fifteen pictures of the helicopter before she got caught in the hailstorm.

She was hit twice.

One bullet went through the palm of her right hand. The other went through her chest puncturing her heart.

She was dead before she hit the ground.

Cole urged John to take off on foot. His part of the plot was over and Cole didn't want the engineer exposed to more danger. They could hear the gunfire in the distance. The RF engineer carefully shut down his equipment in the MCC and took off into the rainy night.

In the basement next door, Ryan and Lucinda had taken cover behind the generators as the security guard, his eyes watering from Lucinda's blast of carbon dioxide, moved into the dark room with his gun out. Ryan hurled himself at the man as he approached and drove him back against the wall. The security guard was a sixty-seven-year-old ex-cop from Brooklyn. He folded up, wheezing out a lungful of smoker's breath. His gun flew from his hand and landed next to the wall. Lucinda grabbed a flashlight and went to scoop it up as Ryan snatched the handcuffs off the guard's belt and cuffed the old man to one of the pipes in the basement.

"I'm sorry," Ryan said to the security guard, who was unable to answer as he struggled to get his breath.

They climbed the stairs, Ryan's leg quivering from the effort. When they went out into the alley, it was dark and a heavy rain was falling. They could hear automatic gunfire, and as they ran to the mouth of the alley, they could see the gray and red helicopter hovering above the parking structure with four men leaning out, firing. He sensed that Mickey was in the chopper. The moment Ryan had predicted was upon them.

The cold rain drenched them as they took off running, moving as fast as Ryan's leg would allow. They reached the staircase where the mobile control room was parked. The helicopter was now hovering above, but the men had stopped firing momentarily. Ryan banged on the door of the big truck while Lucinda ducked into the building.

"It's me! . . . It's Ryan!"

Cole swung the door open, his face flushed with excitement. "The fucker put six or seven rounds right through the top of this bastard," he said, grinning and pointing to the roof of the mobile control center.

"Get the tapes and get into the garage," Ryan said. "I'm going after Mickey." He didn't wait for an answer but ran to the fire door.

Ryan was forced to pull himself up the fire stairs by the banister rail. His leg had lost almost all of its strength. It felt wobbly under him.

Finally, he stepped out onto the roof and stood staring at the helicopter a hundred yards away, still hovering. He could see Mickey in the seat next to the pilot.

"Come here! Come here, Mickey," he yelled into the wind and rain. He knew Mickey couldn't hear him. "Come down here, you son of a bitch!" he shouted, waving his fist at the chopper.

From the helicopter, Mickey saw Ryan come out of the stairwell. Anger fueled by adrenaline hit him, frying all reason.

"Cocksucker!" he screamed at the windshield. The pilot looked at him in amazement and alarm. Mickey was in a new zone, someplace he'd never been before. His emotions were completely controlling his actions. He banged the pilot on the shoulder and pointed down. The four Italian "cousins" jammed new clips into their AR-15s.

Mickey yelled at them, "You shoot this asshole if he gets me . . . put him under if I go down."

The Italian cousins looked at him blankly, and Mickey repeated the instructions in Italian. They nodded, grave expressions on their faces.

"Gimme," he said to Pulacarpo, pointing at a nine-millimeter Beretta in the Sicilian's belt. Pulacarpo gave the gun to Mickey as the helicopter set down on the side of Hertz Castle farthest away from the big dish. Mickey jumped out onto the rain-soaked roof.

Mickey and Ryan were now only fifty feet apart. The wind from the rotor blades was blowing rainwater everywhere. Mickey waved at the pilot to back off. The gray and red chopper pulled back slightly and the prep school roommates stood facing each other, Naomi Zur's dead body between them. Rain hammered down on the concrete. Ryan moved to Naomi, knelt awkwardly, and checked her pulse. He knew when he touched her. He knew she was dead. Then he stood up and looked at Mickey.

"It was bound to come to this," Mickey shouted over the noise of the rain and the helicopter. Anger and bitterness were in his voice. He raised the gun and pointed it at Ryan.

"I'm not armed," Ryan yelled. But Mickey didn't respond. "You need a gun, 'cause you never could take me one-on-one. You're a pussy, Mickey. A fat, oily little piece of shit with no guts."

Mickey looked across the pavement at the handsome blond man. God had given Ryan the gift of beauty . . . Mickey had always scorned that gift, but Mickey had the devil's gift of power. And now he vowed to take Ryan's beauty from him . . . take it with his bare hands. Anger swelled. Emotion flooded through him. It filled his empty vessel with rage. Mickey dropped the gun and moved forward.

Ryan stood his ground. He put his weak left leg forward so that he would get punching power off his stronger right leg. They met in the center of the roof, drenched from the downpour. Both held up their fists.

"You could a' been my friend," Mickey said, bitterly. "I was trying to help you."

"No, you weren't. You don't have any friends. You liked watching me squirm. . . . I was just like Rex. . . . Running with my head off, going nowhere."

Mickey swung.

The fight didn't last very long. Mickey's first blow hit Ryan square on the jaw. It rocked him back. Ryan pivoted to his right on his good leg and threw a left hand into Mickey's ribs, following it with a low right cross. Mickey stumbled back but didn't go down, then faked with his right and threw a looping overhand left that Ryan ducked. Then Ryan launched a vicious uppercut that caught Mickey square. He staggered backward, dropping to one knee. He let out a roar of anger and charged Ryan, who tried to pivot left, but his bad leg collapsed and he fell. Mickey flung himself on his fallen enemy, screaming with rage and joy. He had lost all control. He grabbed Ryan's neck in both of his chubby hands and tried to strangle him. Ryan struggled to throw Mickey off, but adrenaline powered Mickey's grip, giving him ungodly strength. Finally, as Ryan was about to pass out, with a last surge of energy, he rolled up and over on top of Mickey. As if pushed by an invisible force, the two of them rolled down the slight incline of the ramp to the level below. Ryan encouraged the roll and used it to break Mickey's grasp around his neck. He struggled to his feet, trying to favor the left leg, but Mickey turned and ran.

Ryan realized he was going after the nine-millimeter Beretta and limped futilely after him. Mickey picked up the gun and pointed it at Ryan.

"Fuck you, Bolt," he yelled. "Fuck you. You're going away." And he fired.

Ryan felt a stinging in his right shoulder and then three shots rang out in succession and Mickey stumbled backward.

Stiff-legged.

A man on stilts.

Mickey's stomach opened up. . . . Stomach lining, kidney fluid, and intestines poured out into the rainwater at his feet. He looked down in horror as his life gushed out of the ragged hole in his abdomen.

Standing in the doorway with the security guard's pistol still in her hand was Lucinda. She was staring wide-eyed at her brother.

Mickey looked down. The gun was still in his hand. He dropped it and stumbled backward, trying to get to the helicopter, which was returning for him. He was moving by sheer force of will. His vision was blurred; he lost perspective, stumbling blindly on the rain-slick pavement.

The helicopter was still a few yards from the edge of the building and the Italian cousins let out a nine-millimeter stream of death. The lead chipped the concrete around Ryan but, miraculously, didn't hit him. Mickey moved on unsteady legs toward the chopper and they stopped firing. Mickey lunged for the helicopter skid and fell off the roof, catching the ledge at the last second with both hands.

Ryan looked down at Mickey. They were now only a few feet apart. Mickey had a strange, empty look on his face. With death almost on him, Mickey still held the ledge, his grip firm. Something ungodly came up from the depth of Michael Joseph Alo, a grumbling sound, powerful and angry. Ryan kneeled down to hear. Then Mickey spoke two chilling sentences.

Mickey's eyes were shining, more intense and alive than any eyes Ryan had ever seen. A jack-o'-lantern grin spread his face wide, and then he simply let go.

He fell backward off the roof, tumbling in the air, turning and rolling, the hideous leer still stretching his plump cheeks.

Four stories below, his body exploded on impact.

Sirens sounded in the distance as the helicopter abruptly changed direction and streaked away into the rain-swept night.

Ryan, with his shoulder bleeding, limped over and picked up Naomi's camera, then went back to Lucinda. He put his good arm around her. "Thank you," he whispered.

"What did he say?" she asked, still stunned.

Ryan looked away. "I couldn't understand him."

They moved into the garage to get out of the rain and found Cole on the first level looking out at the street as the cop cars pulled up, a cherry orchard of flashing red lights.

"Naomi's dead. Here's her camera." Ryan handed it to Cole.

Cole bowed his head. She had gone to join her Israeli.

They walked into the street, where the cops took them into custody. They were cuffed and read their rights. The rain slowed as they were put in separate squad cars.

Ryan sat alone in the backseat, listening to the windshield wipers flip-flopping the moisture away. He was in the middle of a city of eight million people, yet he was alone and afraid. He couldn't forget the last words Mickey had said to him.

"I'll come back," his prep school roommate had promised. "I'll come back and get you."

WHY WORRY?

WHEN HAZE RICHARDS ARRIVED HOME FROM EUROPE AND stepped off the plane at Dulles, he was taken into custody by federal marshals and whisked to FBI headquarters. Two days later, Malcolm Rasher made a brief statement to the news media from the steps of the Rhode Island governor's mansion:

"Haze Richards has withdrawn his name from the ballot for President of the United States. This, in no way, indicates wrongdoing on Governor Richards's part, but until this investigation is completed, Governor Richards feels it would be unhealthy for our democracy if he continued to pursue the presidency. Governor Richards wishes to thank all of his supporters and he will make a statement in a few days."

But he didn't come out of hiding to defend himself for over a week. The press swarmed on the story and turned up more and more damning information. There were allegations that Anita Richards had been about to file for divorce and had made an appointment with a divorce attorney in Providence. Wasn't it strange that she died one day later? And wasn't it odd that Haze had received such an astounding amount of campaign funding under the five-hundred-dollar reporting requirement? Questions without answers.

Nobody had seen A. J. Teagarden in a week.

Cole had told Ryan, two days after they'd been released from custody, that Haze was headed for a conspiracy to commit murder indictment. Cole and Ryan had tried to feel close, but the two of them had very little in common. Events had brought them together, not friendship. With Ryan's bandaged shoulder aching from the gunshot wound, they finished a drink in Ryan's hotel room and said good-bye, knowing they would probably never see each other again.

Lucinda had gone home to be with her mother, who was distraught over Mickey's death and the revelations about the Alo family, so Ryan was left alone in his suite at the Sherry Netherland Hotel. News crews prowled the halls, climbed onto fire escapes across the street with long lenses, and tried to get pictures of him. His phone never stopped ringing. He told the hotel switchboard to turn it off. They delivered the phone messages and mail every evening in a canvas mailbag that weighed over two pounds.

Marty Lanier had called five times.

Every night, he talked to Lucinda from the hotel room. She was in the New Jersey house with Penny.

"It's weird," she said the night before he left for L.A. "She's so distant." Lucinda was quiet for a long time. "She doesn't understand why I . . ." And she stopped, unable to finish the sentence.

"You didn't kill him, Lucinda. . . . He killed himself. He forced it."

But she couldn't believe him and the evening conversations between them had become filled with long, empty spaces where neither said anything.

"I'm going to go home," Ryan finally said. "I have to say good-bye to Matt. I can finally do that, I think. But I miss you. I wish I could see you."

When she finally spoke, her words chilled him.

"I told you I loved you . . . and I do . . . but can we carry so many bad memories? Are we strong enough? Is anybody?"

"I don't know," he finally said. And he honestly didn't.

Ryan went back to Los Angeles. The media swarmed the airport at LAX. SNG trucks were parked in the white passenger-loading zones. A forest of microphones bloomed in front of blow-dried hair. Pod people pushed and shoved and cursed each other as Ryan was led through the throng by a platoon of L.A. sheriffs. There was a motorcade at the curb.

He had arrived like the presidential candidate he had just destroyed.

The next morning, he sneaked down the freight elevator of the Century Plaza Hotel and waited in a stairwell while a rental car pulled up with the reservation clerk driving. Ryan hid under a hotel blanket as the clerk drove out of the hotel, past the pod people and blow-dries to a spot two blocks away. Then the man handed Ryan the keys and walked back to the rental desk at the hotel.

Ryan had made arrangements to have Linda's real estate agent meet him at the Bel Air house. He drove down the tree-lined street and pulled up in front of the French Regency where he and Linda had once lived—a house filled with decorator-perfect things that Ryan had no appreciation for. The agent let him in.

"I can wait," the thirty-five-year-old leggy blonde with a fitness instructor's body said, smiling at him.

"No . . . I need to do this alone."

He wandered through the house carrying an old suitcase, packing things much more valuable than the pre-Columbian art that adorned the rooms.

Linda still owned the house but she hadn't been here much since the divorce. She'd been traveling in Europe. She would never miss the things that Ryan took. He went into Matt's closet and stood looking at the clothes. He reached out and gathered some in his hands and smelled them.

He could smell Matt.

His heart ached and tears came to his eyes. He folded Matt's Little League uniform. He took Matt's baseball hats off the shelf and put them carefully in the suitcase. He packed both of their mitts. On the wall there was the legend his son had written. It was in Matt's neat handwriting and framed under glass. They'd laughed when he'd put it up four years ago. He took it down, held it, and read it one last time:

WHY WORRY?

There are only two things to worry about: Either you are sick or you are well. If you're well, then there's nothing to worry about. If you're sick, you only have two things to worry about. . . . Either you live or you die. If you live, you have nothing to worry about. If you die, you have only two things to worry about. Either you go to heaven or you go to hell. If you go to heaven, you'll have nothing to worry about but if you go to hell, you'll be so busy shaking hands with old friends, you won't have time to worry.

Then he heard a laugh, or at least he thought he did. Was it his imagination or was it Kaz laughing at life's inconsistencies?

He packed Matt's football, then went into the hall and looked at the pictures on the wall—pictures he had been unable to look at since his son's death. He looked at Matt and Linda together, smiling in the Hawaiian sun. The people in the shot didn't seem like strangers to him anymore. He could relive those old moments and smile. The first fish . . . the second birthday party where only stuffed animals had been invited. He took a picture off the wall. In the shot, Matt and Linda were laughing because their cat, George, was sitting by Ryan's sleeping head, licking Ryan's hair, grooming it. The photograph spoke to him like no other picture in the hallway. He wasn't sure why. He packed it in the bag with the other treasures.

He continued to move through the rooms, looking at everything, saying good-bye. Two hours later, he walked out of the house and drove away.

He had left his two Emmys in the den.

Ryan went to the beach condo and was relieved that no press were there. He let himself in and went out onto the porch. He sat on the old chaise longue and listened to the Malibu surf roll in.

What do I do now? he thought as his mind buzzed with unanswered questions. He knew he needed Lucinda, knew she had to be part of his life. Had he lost her? Would she come back? What about Elizabeth? Why had she died? Why had *she* become a victim? Elizabeth, who never did anything but take care of him, apologize for him . . . love him.

He got up and went into his bedroom. He lay on the bed, listened to the surf, and tried to figure out what to do with his life.

April turned to May. He called Lucinda and she said she and her mother were trying to work things out between them. It would be better if he didn't come to see her.

Ryan began writing a novel but the words didn't flow. He tried to run on the beach every evening. At least, he reasoned, he was getting his body back in shape. He refused to answer Marty Lanier's calls or to have a meeting with his agent Jerry Upshaw. He decided he had to get someplace where the sun didn't shine every day . . . someplace where there were no personal trainers or tanning salons. He thought about moving to the mountains.

The last day in May, while he was running on the beach, she came back to him. He was jogging in the wet sand, angling up from the surf to his condo when he saw her standing on the deck, her rich, black hair blowing in the wind. He increased his pace, his heart pounding.

"Hi," she said, her voice small as he climbed the steps to meet her.

"Hi," he said back, almost afraid to say anything, afraid he would scare her away. He held her gently, his lips against her temple.

"Ryan, can we . . . can we live with all that's happened? Or will it wreck us?"

"I don't know."

"Mother can't forgive me and I'm not sure I can forgive myself. It seems so strange. I never thought that I would end up shooting Mickey. It haunts me. He haunts me. I know he was trying to hurt us, but I shouldn't have had to kill him. . . . And I dream about it all the time. I want it to be the way it was in Mexico but I don't know if I can get back there."

He reached out and folded her in his arms. She pressed against him.

"Love isn't something you control," he said, giving her own words back to her. "It's something that just happens."

She looked up at him as the Malibu surf rumbled in, white water licking the posts at the bottom edge of the deck.

"Then let's let it happen." She laid her head against him.

Ryan felt whole again—rebuilt and rejuvenated. This time, he was not going to let it come apart.

This time he would catch the pass.

E P I L O G U E

COLE HARRIS WON HIS THIRD PULITZER FOR THE STORY HE TITLED "The Plan." He had put Naomi Zur up posthumously, and her family shared the prize with him. He was offered a contract at NBC and he went to work every day in pleated pants and suspenders and quietly drove all of his coworkers crazy with his compulsive behavior. He sent Ryan and Lucinda a pen and pencil set. TO COLE HARRIS, THE BEST OF THE BEST. C. WALLACE LITMAN, the engraved plaque said. He enclosed a note that said, "Not until I met you guys. Have one on me." The expensive champagne that was supposed to accompany the gift never arrived.

C. Wallace Litman was forced by the FCC to sell his broadcasting interests. He was indicted for election tampering and acquitted two months later by a New York jury.

Haze Richards was indicted for conspiracy to commit the murder of Anita Richards; A. J. Teagarden was indicted as a co-conspirator. Haze pled to manslaughter and was sentenced to seven years; A. J. Teagarden sentenced himself to death. He bought a .45 at a Washington gun shop, rented a hotel room, and ended his life in a chipped, dirty bathroom. Nobody claimed his body.

Babbling John Baily remained at Madison Junior High. But Cole and Ryan gave him the funds to build a state-of-the-art video lab, which the RF engineer maintained and ran for the school.

Pudge Anderson was elected the forty-third President of the United States of America.

Ryan and Lucinda got married in June. Their first child was born in March 1998, a seven-pound, three-ounce girl.
They named her Elizabeth.